PERFECTION

PERFECTION

Walter Satterthwait

Thomas Dunne Books/St. Martin's Minotaur

New York

THOMAS DUNNE BOOKS.
An imprint of St. Martin's Press.

www.minotaurbooks.com

Design by Jane Adele Regina

Library of Congress Cataloging-in-Publication Data

Satterthwait, Walter.
  Perfection/Walter Satterthwait.
    p. cm.
  ISBN 0-312-35244-1
  EAN 978-0-312-35244-8
  1. Police—Florida—Sarasota—Fiction. 2. Overweight women—Crimes against—Fiction. 3. Serial murders—Fiction. 4. Policewomen—Fiction. 5. Sarasota (Fla.)—Fiction. I. Title.

PS3569.A784 P47 2006
813'.54—dc22

                                                      2005044596

First Edition: February 2006

10 9 8 7 6 5 4 3 2 1

For Ruth Cavin

PERFECTION

Prologue

Sprawled along the sofa, a red bandanna cinched across her mouth, her hands tightly tied behind her back, Marcy Fleming stared at the strawberry cupcake.

Standing on the opposite side of the coffee table, he saw the terror in her blue eyes, and he recognized it. He had felt it many times himself—although not, of course, for years. But seeing it in someone else, seeing it in poor Marcy, knowing that he had been the cause of it, *was* the cause of it, right here, right now, prompted a curious and surprisingly pleasant sensation at the base of his stomach.

He had known there would be pleasure. Mixed with business, to be sure. Mixed with very serious business. But he had definitely known there would be pleasure. He simply hadn't expected it to begin so early in the game.

Well, well. Live and learn.

He held the cupcake daintily, with just the tippy-tips of his thumb and his slender first finger, the other fingers stiffly extended so as not to blemish the pristine white of his latex glove.

He shook his head. "Marcy, Marcy," he said reproachfully. "This is a big no-no, honey. This is a catastrophe. Do you know how many calories are crammed into this thing? Hundreds of them, sweetie. Thousands, maybe. And think of all the *carbs*!"

He raised the cupcake to his mouth, flicked away a tiny dollop of icing with his tongue. He licked his lip, his eyes crinkling with pleasure. "Hmm. Cream icing. I love cream icing, don't you?"

He chuckled. "Well, golly. Who am I talking to? Of course you do." He nodded to the opened box lying on Marcy's coffee table, beside his black leather satchel. "You've already scarfed down half a dozen of these little cuties, haven't you, hon?"

Holding the cake firmly, and again using only the tips of the fingers, he gently pulled away the paper that clung, like pleated skin, to its side. A few crumbs tumbled to the blue tarpaulin at his feet. Glancing down, he saw that he'd left some creases in the plastic—silly old Marcy had regained consciousness more quickly than he'd expected.

He could take care of the creases later. At the moment the cupcake demanded all his attention. When the paper hung limply from the bottom of the cake like a miniature skirt, brown and clotted, he looked down at Marcy. Her eyes were narrowed now. The poor dear had no idea at all where this was heading.

"But you've been doing it all wrong," he said. "Now watch closely. Here's the way it's supposed to work." He brought the cake to his mouth and took a delicate little bite, a teensy little nibble. "Hmmm," he said. Talking around the morsel of cake, he said, "You chew on it. You savor it. You *appreciate* it. *Capice?*"

He swallowed. "Fabulous." Once again he licked his lips. He smiled. "But what you don't do, Marcy, is this." Suddenly, brutally, flattening his hand against it, he shoved the entire cake into his mouth. A clump of icing pattered to the tarp.

On the sofa, Marcy flinched.

"Umph," he said. A chunk of cake shrapneled from his mouth.

Have to pick that up later, he told himself. DNA. They can test saliva.

"Ummph," he said. "Orummph, glummph, glumph." Again he swallowed. Again he licked his lips. Again he smiled. "Now honestly, sweetie, isn't that just a tiny bit disgusting?"

Marcy merely stared. Marcy didn't seem to be getting into the spirit of the thing.

Carefully, he placed the piece of paper on the coffee table. He would dispose of it later.

"Okay." He looked down at Marcy and frowned. "What do you top out at, Marcy? About three hundred and twenty pounds? Three forty? And you're, what, about five foot four?" He cocked his head. "Wouldn't you say, honey, honestly now, that your figure falls just a tad short of *perfection?*"

Gracefully, he sank down into a squat and placed his gloved hands

2

on the coffee table, palms flat. His eyes now were even with hers. Hers darted for a moment, left to right, looking for help, but of course there wasn't any help, not for Marcy.

At last her glance met his again, and suddenly he experienced a tremendous fondness for her, a sense of gratitude that was deep and true and thrilling. Dear, dear, sweet Marcy. He smiled at her, engorged with affection.

Her chest rose as she took a deep breath, shuddered as she let it out.

He leaned slightly forward. "Marcy," he said, his voice soothing. "Haven't you ever dreamed about it? About perfection? Haven't you ever looked into the mirror and wondered what it would be like? To be slim and sleek and svelte? To be the belle of the ball? The cat's pajamas? To have men get ravenous for you—the way *you* get ravenous for a Little Debbie snack cake? Or a Double Whopper with cheese? Or a pound of Tesler's barbecued pork rinds?"

Marcy's forehead puckered. Confused, poor thing.

He chuckled. "Oh, sure. I know all about the pork rinds. And the Cheetos, crunchy style. I know all about you, Marcy. *Everything.* The Chubby Hubby from Ben and Jerry's, the bite-sized Snickers."

Above the red bandanna, Marcy's eyes had grown wide again.

"Of course I do. You're my very first, Marcy. And I want to make certain that I do everything"—he smiled—"perfectly."

Unzipping the leather satchel, he said, "Perfection, Marcy. Haven't you ever dreamed about it?"

Marcy's eyes were darting again.

He looked down into the satchel, looked up at Marcy, smiled once more. "Sure you have. Of course you have. And I'm here to tell you, Marcy, that it's possible. It's totally one hundred percent possible. And I'm the person who's going to make it happen. It'll take a while— I won't lie about that. We'll be busy most of the night. But come sunup, come rosy-fingered dawn, we'll be all finished, you and I. And by then—Marcy, I give you my solemn promise, cross my heart, that by then you'll be absolutely perfect."

Marcy's chest was rising and falling more quickly now.

He reached into the satchel. "Naturally, the first thing we'll need is the anesthetic."

3

He slipped out the ball-peen hammer and held it up, smiling proudly.

Marcy made an awful fuss, wallowing and grunting and thumping. But that was all part of it, really. Part of the fun.

TUESDAY

Chapter One

Up there in the pale blue sultry sky, a few pelicans soared like pterodactyls cruising for prey, gliding with no apparent effort high above the broad green glimmer of sea. Closer in, nearer to shore, a small white tern angled its wings and then, suddenly looking more like a miniature jet plane than a bird, shot down and skipped along a ridge of slowly curling wave. Abruptly it wheeled about, wings flickering briefly against the water before it flapped quickly skyward, a flash of twitching silver at its beak.

Sophia took a bite of her grilled tuna sandwich and stared across the scarred wooden picnic table at Fallon. Elbows on the table, his lean brown fingers dimpling the crust of the sesame-sprinkled bun, he held the cheeseburger in both hands, away from his perfectly pressed and perfectly boring short-sleeved white shirt. As he ducked his head to eat, ketchup and mayonnaise and glistening beef juices dribbled onto the small pile of lettuce he'd left untouched on the plate. He hadn't touched the tomato, either, or the onion. He'd eaten the pickle, of course. First thing.

How could he do it?

Apparently sensing her stare, Fallon looked up. "What?"

"Don't you ever worry about your arteries?" She took another bite of tuna, dry and tasteless, nearly as boring as Fallon's shirt. And probably no better tasting.

"Why would I do that?"

She nodded to his burger. "Why didn't you just order a pound of lard?"

"Damn. There was lard on the menu?"

He was sometimes an incredible jerk, true.

But how could he do it? Put away one of those catastrophes in a single sitting—almost pure animal fat, about a million calories, enough cholesterol to kill a grizzly bear? And never gain an ounce?

"How's the tuna?" he asked her.

"Great." She took another bite.

He smiled. "You sure you don't want some tartar sauce? Some mayo?"

She would've given her left arm for some mayo. "I'm fine."

"Uh-huh." He dug into his burger. A trickle of ketchup dribbled onto the lettuce.

Sophia looked beyond him, to the Gulf. Between the restaurant's patio and the water, the sandy white beach was only about half-full. The snowbirds, the winter residents from up North, wouldn't start showing up until next month, flying in with the first big flock of tourists. Most of the people out there, sprawled across the sand like battle casualties, were locals. They could, and they would, lie there for hours, baking their minds into stupors, their skin into alligator handbags.

She gazed out at the water. It was nearly flat today, only those slow, oily waves near shore, quietly toppling forward when they hit the gentle slope of hard-packed sand.

It was different every day. Sometimes the differences were small—in the colors, in the textures of the surface, the density of the light that glittered from it. Sometimes they were huge—when the sky went gray and the wind rose, and the waves grew wilder and foam flecked off their tops and the spray made a mist in the air. She loved it always, but she loved it then the most.

There was a hurricane out in the Gulf right now, Hurricane Gerald. It had torn through the Keys a few days ago, and for a while it had looked as if it were heading up the west coast. But now it was on its way to Mexico, and the weather next weekend should be perfect for sailing.

Maybe, next Saturday, she could persuade Janice to take the catamaran out for the afternoon.

Fallon said, "You going out on the boat next weekend?"

She turned to him. "How do you *do* that?"

He wiped the napkin at his mouth. "You look out at the water that way, you're usually thinking about the boat."

"Yeah, well, it's really annoying. In case no one ever mentioned it to you."

He shrugged. "So don't be so obvious."

An incredible jerk. "Why do you want to know?"

"About the boat? I was thinking—"

There was a sudden chirping sound. Fallon's cell phone.

He wiped his hands, plucked the phone from his pants pocket, flipped it open, put it to his ear. "Fallon."

She looked at his face, the leathery brown skin, the slash of mouth, the small deltas that spread from the corners of his deep-set brown eyes. After three weeks, it was still a face that she couldn't read. She wondered now whether her own face would ever become as guarded, as closed.

And what had he been about to say? What had he been thinking?

"Come again?" he said into the phone. There was no change in his expression. There was no expression at all; there seldom was, beyond an occasional faint ironic smile. With one hand he opened the box of Camel Lights that lay on the table, pulled out a cigarette, stuck it in his mouth. She made a face but, as always, he ignored it.

"Right," he said. "Who's covering it now?" He pulled a Bic lighter from his pants pocket, lit the cigarette. "Okay. We're on our way." He flipped the phone shut, tucked it back into his pocket, sucked on the cigarette, and exhaled. "That was Courtney," he told Sophia. "There's been a homicide. Pelican Way. You know it?"

"About twenty blocks south. Off Beach Road."

He nodded, glanced down at the sandwich she still held in her hand. "You ready?"

She put the sandwich on the plastic plate. No great sacrifice. She stood. "Let's go."

ONE THING ABOUT FALLON. He might be an incredible jerk, but he didn't mind riding shotgun. If fact, he seemed to prefer it.

She was a good driver, but when she'd partnered with Cooper, she'd never gotten behind the wheel. And Cooper, swollen with testosterone, had driven like the bully he was—flooring the pedal when the light went green, tailgating civilians, squealing around corners, slamming the black-and-white to a neck-whumping stop at the very last second. She was delighted when he took a transfer to St. Pete Beach.

Fallon, on the other hand, seemed perfectly content to slouch there and watch St. Anselm float past, the houses and hotels, the condos and restaurants, the sun-splashed sidewalks and the swaying palms.

Maybe it was those twenty-five years up North, before he'd retired from the NYPD and come down here. The pace of the city, the violence, the bleakness. Maybe, after all that, he was happy to let things slide by in the brilliant yellow sunshine, under the brilliant blue sky.

"Who's there?" she asked him. "At Pelican Way?"

"Kinkaid, Denton, Garcia."

"What else did Courtney say?"

Without looking at her, he said, "That it was messy." He leaned forward, popped open the glove compartment.

"A man? A woman?"

From the glove compartment, Fallon took the Polaroid camera. "A woman, they think."

"They think?"

"I'm guessing that's what she means by *messy*."

Sophia felt a tightening along her stomach, a faint constriction around her chest. This would be only her second homicide as a detective. The other had been a domestic, a wife beaten to death by her husband. It had been stupid and senseless and transparent—no real police work involved, just picking through the sad refuse of two doomed lives, one cramped and brutalized, the other cramped and brutal.

It had left her with a feeling of outrage and, for a time, a feeling of hopelessness. And it had given her no sense that she had proven herself, that she had accomplished anything—apart from filling out reports.

This one—Pelican Way, and whatever it held—could be her first real test.

Messy. What the hell did that mean?

Well, in a few minutes she would find out. And whatever it meant, whatever it was, she would handle it.

Dear God, let me handle it.

IN ST. ANSELM, as in many Florida communities, Beach Road runs nowhere near the beach. Like Treasure Island to the north and St. Pete Beach to the south, St. Anselm is a barrier island, long and narrow, nuzzling the mainland like a remora nuzzling a shark. On the island's

8

west side, facing the blue expanse of the Gulf, is the beach, a thin ribbon of white sand running its entire length. The island's east side, most of it, faces the Intercoastal Waterway and the mainland's pricey highrise condos. But its southern tip nudges past the northern tip of St. Pete Beach, and here the two islands are separated by a narrow strip of water called St. Martin's Pass. Beach Road, roughly parallel to the Pass and a block away from it, runs through a depressed, low-income area that the zoning laws had so far kept away from the big developers.

Like most of its neighbors, No. 25 Pelican Way was a small wooden cottage with white paint flaking from its chipped siding. It sat back from the street on a corner lot in the shade of an old live oak, edged on three sides by a tiny, unkempt lawn. The curtain was drawn at its picture window.

Two black-and-whites, city Fords, were parked in the gravel driveway, and a third was angled from the street onto the lawn. A few people—some kids, a pair of elderly women, an elderly couple in matching pale blue Bermuda shorts—stood watching from the streets, from Pelican and from Flamingo Way, the cross street. Beyond a vacant lot on Flamingo lay the narrow strip of Pass, its surface glinting between the green fronds of a few ragged palmettos.

Sophia pulled the Ford behind the streetside cruiser, along a hedge that enclosed the lawn of the cottage next door, and she cut the engine. She lifted her purse from the console, riffled through it, found her notebook. She took it out and flipped it open. She glanced at her watch—twelve-fifteen—and slipped the ballpoint pen from the notebook's binding. It was her favorite pen—a Montblanc her uncle Niko had given to her when she'd become a cop.

She wrote down the time. Beside her, Fallon was busy writing into his own notebook. She flipped hers shut, stuck the pen back into the binding.

They got out of the car and walked around to the back. Fallon opened the trunk and the two of them set down their gear—Polaroid, notebook, cell phones—and picked up the plastic packages containing the disposable white coveralls. They tore them open and took out the garments.

Side by side, they walked up the walkway, and at the front porch they climbed into the coveralls. Sophia was glad she'd decided to wear slacks this morning. Even so, getting into the thing was awkward, the paper material stiff and resistant. She grabbed her notebook, slipped it into the side pocket, slipped the cell phone into the breast pocket. She zipped up the front, tucked her hair up into the hood, pulled the drawstring tight. Immediately, she started to sweat. The temperature outside the coveralls was already over ninety degrees.

Fallon handed her a pair of rubber bootees. Both of them put on the footwear. Then the rubber gloves.

To the people watching from the street, she thought, they must look like a pair of astronauts.

"Ready?" Fallon asked her.

"Ready."

Fallon knocked at the door.

It was opened by Kinkaid, one of the uniforms, a big, burly man with freckled red arms. From behind his dark wraparound glasses, he looked at Fallon, then at Sophia. She couldn't see his eyes behind the lenses, but she knew that his glance was wandering up and down her body. Kinkaid believed, against all the available evidence, that he was a stud. What he was, as they put it in Greek, was a *malakas*. A jerk-off.

Kinkaid nodded to Fallon, then turned to Sophia and said, "You don't wanna come in here, Tregaskis."

Sophia's cheeks flushed with anger. *Who the hell was Kinkaid?*

Fallon had been bending down, studying the front-door lock. Now he turned to Kinkaid. "First officer on the scene?"

"Garcia. In the back." Kinkaid smirked. "He just puked up his meat loaf."

Fallon stood upright. "Where's Denton?"

"Next door. With the old lady found the body. She owns this place."

"That your car on the lawn?"

Kinkaid hesitated, as though wondering whether this was a trick question. At last, warily, he said, "Yeah?"

"You check the lawn for footprints or evidence, anything at all before you turned it into a parking lot?"

Kinkaid took off his glasses, probably so that Fallon could see that Kinkaid was looking directly at him, unintimidated. High school stuff. "There weren't any footprints."

"Uh-huh. Don't move the car until I say so. In the meantime, start putting up some tape. Keep those civilians off the lawn."

Kinkaid stared at Fallon for a moment, obviously pissed off. But at last he shrugged his heavy shoulders. "Sure," he said flatly. "Whatever you say, Sarge."

"And if the press shows up, keep your mouth shut."

Kinkaid smirked again. "Right. Absolutely, Sarge."

Fallon stood aside for Kinkaid to pass, then stepped into the house. Sophia followed him, glancing back at Kinkaid. He was on the walkway, and he was glancing back, too. His face was empty, but she knew that he was busy resenting her for being there while Fallon reamed him out.

Tough. Into each life a little rain must fall.

Inside, there was a buzzing of flies and a dense, heavy smell that reminded Sophia of her uncle's butcher shop, up in Tarpon Springs.

Fallon had stopped moving forward. He stood there, looking down at something on the floor. Sophia stepped around him. He raised his arm, as though about to stop her, but then let the arm fall.

Against the east wall, directly ahead, a cheap white plastic coffee table had been upended, its top angled against the room's pine paneling, its legs jutting horizontally out into the air. On the floor in front of the sofa, where the coffee table had probably once stood, a rectangular blue plastic tarpaulin had been carefully flattened. About eight feet long by eight feet wide, it covered most of the carpet and reached nearly to the base of the large-screen television at the south wall. On top of the plastic sheet lay something that looked at first like a store dummy, a mannequin that had been daubed with clay or mud and then painted a dark, dull red.

It took Sophia a moment to understand what it was she saw, and when she did, her stomach lurched and acid rippled in her throat.

She glanced at Fallon. He was watching her, his mouth set in a thin line. She swallowed bile and she took a step forward.

Flensing.

The word sprang, unbidden and unwanted, into her mind.

Years ago she had seen a television documentary about whaling. It had been produced by one of the environmental groups—Greenpeace, maybe—and it had been filled with appalling images. The skulking pursuit of that big, beautiful animal, brave and ungainly and doomed. The sudden thudding lunge of the harpoon into its barnacled flesh. The hopeless run of the beast as it hurtled through the waves, desperate to escape its wound.

But worse, for Sophia, was what happened afterward, after the exhausted creature had finally been killed. It had been draped in chains and then winched, immense and limp and dripping, aboard the mother ship, and there it had been systematically butchered. Men in stained white coats used what looked like pairs of wooden poles, connected at one end to a scimitar-sharp blade, to slice away the skin and blubber. Thick chunks and slabs were casually flung to the deck, where black rivulets of liquid hissed into gray metal drains.

Flensing, it was called. Stripping the whale of its flesh. Reducing it to a shiny red skeleton and tattered pink shreds of tissue.

She stared at the body on the floor.

Most of its skin was gone. And not just its skin—Sophia could see knife marks where entire chunks of flesh had been sliced away. The exposed meat was crusting over now, like raw steak left out too long. The whittled-down, brownish red legs of the body were pressed together, lying straight out along the plastic tarp. Its brownish red arms were crossed over its chest, where some pink strips of rib were showing. Beneath a helmet of curly brown hair, its stripped face was an obscene red mask, teeth grinning insanely, opened eyes staring up at the ceiling. The eyes were blue.

Sophia's breathing was shallow, her heart was thumping. A droplet of sweat prickled down her side, distant, remote.

It seemed suddenly absurd, unreal, that the two of them would be moving around, carrying their cameras and notebooks, perspiring, would be *alive,* while that terrible thing lay, stiff and still, on its plastic tarp. The room, the house, belonged to It, to the Thing, and she and Fallon were intruders, interlopers.

Party crashers.

She almost giggled. For a moment she felt giddy, light-headed, and she wondered if she was about to lose it. Start laughing wildly and not be able to stop.

No. No way.

Abruptly the tiny room was lit in a blinding flash—the tarp went suddenly bluer, that exposed flesh went suddenly blacker, and for a millisecond Sophia thought that her nerves had exploded, that some swollen capillary had burst in her brain.

The flash, she realized, from Fallon's Polaroid.

As Fallon pulled the photograph from the camera, something moved to Sophia's left. It was Garcia, another uniformed officer, coming out of a small room off a narrow hallway. He held a white handkerchief over his mouth and nose.

He lowered the handkerchief. "The rest of her's in here," he said, pointing across the hall.

Chapter Two

For weeks afterward, whenever Sophia relived the next few hours, it seemed to her that a great many things had happened at once, in a confused blur of activity. But now, as she began to live through them for the first time, everything seemed to be happening slowly, as though it were all taking place underwater, dreamlike.

Tucking the Polaroid photograph into his shirt pocket, Fallon strode toward Garcia. Sophia followed, her breath still reaching only the tops of her lungs.

Garcia stepped aside, so the two detectives could enter the room.

You can't go in there, you know there's something horrible in there, something you don't want to see.

Screw you.

But she knew that when she saw it, she would never be the same again. She was about to be initiated into something dark and dreadful. The thought frightened her, and, God help her, it excited her. Her heart was pounding, and she didn't know whether the fear or the excitement was driving it.

It was a bathroom. The air, hot and motionless, was heavy with the butcher-shop stench. White walls, a checkered white-and-black tile floor, a pink throw rug, a white toilet with a fluffy pink lid cover. Fluffy pink towels hanging in neat folds from a chrome rack. Below the sink, a yellow plastic bucket. Everything neat and spotless.

Almost everything. Opposite the door was an old white bathtub resting on ornate cast-iron claws. When Sophia saw what was inside the tub, her knees turned to jelly and the world stopped moving.

She closed her eyes and then opened them, forcing them to look.

The pink plastic shower curtain, printed with pastel wildflowers, spotted and smeared with brown blood, hung to the right, its hem outside the tub. The top of the tub and its upper walls were immaculate, the porcelain gleaming as though it had just been polished. But the tub's bottom was heaped with impossible things, with lumps of meat, slack strands of tissue, greasy gray ribbons and slumped gray coils of skin, clumps and chunks of red flesh, blackening now, stiffening.

Over everything, flies whirled and whined.

Fallon's camera flashed again, the bright light harsh in the small room. He stepped forward, the camera whirring in his hand. He plucked the print from the camera and glanced down at the yellow plastic bucket. "He used the bucket to carry the pieces." His voice sounded perfectly normal.

With a small lurch, as though hidden gears had clicked into operation, the world began to move again.

Fallon had done all this before. This, or something like it. Whatever it was, he had gotten through it.

She would get through it too.

She took a deep breath and clenched her teeth against the smell. Straightening her back—her shoulders had curled slightly forward, as though yielding to the weight of what she saw—she stepped forward and looked down into the bucket. Its sides were streaked with black, and a black liquid coated the bottom, its surface filming over like a chocolate pudding. In the liquid, against the side, lay a stiff black sponge.

Flies droned.

She remembered how clean the blue tarpaulin had been. The person who did this, who created the Thing out there, who created the horror in the bathtub, had calmly mopped up after himself. Had carried the bucket back and forth from living room to tub. Jack and Jill went up the hill.

How many goddamn trips had he made?

The sonofabitch.

Fallon slipped the Polaroid print into his coveralls pocket, raised the camera again. To Garcia he said, "Touch anything?"

"The doorknob. At the back door. I stepped outside. I had to . . ." Garcia glanced at Sophia, looked back to Fallon. "I was sick."

Sophia's anger melted into sympathy. Paul Garcia was one of the Good Guys, one of the men on the force who'd never bugged her, never hustled or hassled her. Poor Paul. He hadn't been any more ready for this than she had.

And then she realized, with a start, that she hadn't been sick herself. Afraid to be, in front of Fallon. But still . . . *Bravo, koritsi mou.* Bravo, my girl.

In the next flash of the Polaroid, she saw Garcia's pallor, and immediately she felt guilty—Garcia had walked in here on his own, without Fallon, without anyone.

Fallon lowered the camera, pulled the print free. "Nothing else?" he asked Garcia.

"No."

"The light in the living room?"

"It was on when I got here."

Sophia hadn't noticed the light.

Damn. *Focus.*

Fallon nodded, looked down at the print. He stuck it into his pocket and pulled out his ballpoint pen. He poked the pen under the lid of the toilet, then raised the lid until it met the square cistern. The bowl contained only water, clear and empty. When Fallon removed his pen, the lid slapped back onto the toilet seat.

"No man around the house," he said.

Because a man, Sophia realized, wouldn't tolerate a toilet lid that didn't stay upright on its own.

"Who called it in?" Fallon asked Garcia.

"The next-door neighbor," said Garcia. "Mrs. Hartley. Silvia Hartley."

Sophia scribbled the name in her notebook.

"She's the landlady," said Garcia. "She says that the renter here was a woman named, uh—" Garcia plucked his own notebook from his shirt pocket, opened it. "Marcy Fleming."

Fallon nodded. "Let's see the rest of the house," he said, and turned. Garcia stepped aside as Fallon strode out into the hallway. Sophia followed.

"The only other door?" Fallon said, taking a step toward it.

"Yeah," said Garcia.

At the top of the door, a frilly white curtain hid the window. Fallon edged it aside with his pen, peered outside, looked left, looked right.

"Chain-link fence." He nodded, as though he approved. He examined the thin bolt at the edge of the door. "This was bolted before you opened the door?"

"Yeah. I had a hard time getting it open."

Fallon nodded. "Painted shut. You checked the windows?"

"The one in the kitchen's locked," Garcia said. "The one in the bedroom's got an air conditioner in it."

"Kitchen window has a screen?"

"No. The lock is painted shut, like the bolt."

"Okay. It was Hartley found the body?"

"Yeah. According to her, Fleming came over to Hartley's house every morning. They got along, says Hartley. They were more like friends, she says, than landlady and renter. They had coffee and cake."

Nodding, Fallon stepped into the room across the hall. A small bedroom.

"Cookies, whatever," Garcia said. "This is every day, according to Hartley. Every morning. So today, when Fleming doesn't show up, Hartley comes over. She knocks first, she says, and then she tries the door. It's unlocked, so she comes in. She was worried, she says. And when she gets inside, she finds . . . that thing."

Sophia glanced at the sash window on the right. Painted shut. Jutting from the bottom of the window on the left was an old, bulky air conditioner. It hummed faintly, and Sophia realized that the air moving against her face was marginally cooler than the air in the rest of the house.

She looked around. A cheap oak-veneered dresser just inside the door, a few knickknacks precisely ordered on its top—a dark-wood jewelry box, a small, framed, black-and-white photograph of an elderly couple. Propped into a sitting position, back to the wall, was an old and battered teddy bear. The bear had seen some history—its fur was worn down to the weave in spots, and one of its round glass eyes was missing. Sophia knew that later, when she was alone, and probably when she wasn't ready for it, she would remember that worn fur and that melancholy missing eye.

To the right, built into the wall, was the sliding door of a closet. Against the far wall was a queen-size bed covered with a nubby cotton spread, neatly made. To the right of this stood a nightstand. On it, a crookneck lamp. Beside the lamp, a thick, glossy magazine.

Here, too, everything was spotless. But the bed had two pillows at its head, beneath the bedspread, and in the pillow on the right there was a round, clearly defined depression. Below the pillow, along the bedspread, was another depression, long and narrow, as though someone had lain there recently. Fallon was staring down at it.

He turned to Garcia, "You didn't touch the bed."

"No. Her, maybe? The . . . woman?"

"She was heavier than that," Fallon said.

"It was *him*," Sophia said.

Fallon looked at her. "Maybe." Raising the camera, he stepped around the bed. "If it was," he said, "he made a mistake."

Excitement flickered through her. "His height. His dimensions."

Smiling, Fallon nodded. "You ever think of becoming a cop?"

He lowered himself slightly—angling the shot, Sophia knew, so the two depressions would show up under the flash—and looked into the viewfinder. The room lit up.

He straightened as the camera whirred and the print emerged. "When did Hartley find the body?" He tugged the print free.

"Ten to twelve," said Garcia. "Approximately."

Fallon glanced down at the print. "When did she call it in?"

"Two minutes later. She ran straight back home, she says, and made the call."

Fallon nodded, put the print into his pocket. "And you got here when?"

"Twelve. A little before. I talked to her first, next door, and then came over here. And then Robby and Ed showed up. Ed's with the woman now."

Fallon notched the ballpoint pen into the recessed handle on the sliding door, eased the door open. "Did Hartley ID the body as Fleming's?"

"Jesus, Sergeant, how could she?" Garcia winced. "That thing out there, that could be anybody."

Fallon was gazing into the closet. In one corner stood a vacuum cleaner. Beside it, three pairs of ugly black lace-up shoes and a worn pair of white running shoes. The closet shelf was stacked with magazines, probably hundreds of them. Beneath the shelf, hanging on plastic hangers, were sweaters, pastel blouses, some dull and unattractive dresses.

"Hartley see the bathtub?" Fallon asked Garcia.

"No." He frowned, thinking, and then added, "I don't think so."

Fallon walked to the nightstand, examined the cover of the magazine there.

"What is it?" Sophia asked.

"*Glamour*."

Sophia knew, without knowing how she knew it, that all the magazines stacked along the closet shelf would be *Glamour*, too, or something like it.

Fallon glanced around the room. "Right. The kitchen."

In the living room, that awful mannequin was waiting for them on its slick blue tarpaulin. Sophia glanced at it, glanced away. She saw that a shaded reading light, on the end table to the right of the sofa, was in fact still burning.

The small kitchen lay to the left, separated from the living room by a counter about four feet tall, topped with fake butcher block. On this side of the counter stood two black plastic stools. On the counter itself sat an old-fashioned black rotary-dial telephone, a telephone book, a brown leatherette address book.

Garcia said, "You think it's Fleming, Sergeant? The body?"

Fallon stepped into the small kitchen, Garcia and Sophia following. "Only one person living here," Fallon said. "From the clothes, a large woman. Unless what we've got in the bathtub came from somewhere else, the body belonged to a large woman."

Inside the kitchen, another counter ran along the far wall, to the left and right of the double sink and the window above it. On the left side, pink metal canisters painted with floral designs were arranged by size, larger to smaller, their contents identified in ornate black script—flour, sugar, coffee, tea. On the right, a wire-rack bookcase held cookbooks. As Fallon looked in the cupboard under the sink, Sophia read the book titles. They were a strange mix—*Fat-Free Cooking, Just Desserts, The No-Nonsense Diet, Low-Cal Treats for Sneaky Snackers, Pasta Pasta Pasta!*

To her left, standing by the old, white electric range, Fallon said slowly, almost sighing the words, *"Ah, shit."* There was the sound in his voice of exhaustion, maybe even defeat.

"Yeah," said Garcia in grim agreement.

Curious, Sophia crossed the linoleum floor.

On the stovetop's right front burner was a flimsy aluminum frying pan, the metal blade of a spatula resting in the pale grease at its Teflon center. On the stovetop itself was an opaque plastic butter dish, a large plastic squeeze bottle of Heinz ketchup, half-empty. Beside that, a white Corelle dinner plate. A cheap stainless-steel knife and fork had been placed on the plate at exactly the 4:20 position. In the plate, beneath a congealed dribble of ketchup, lay a chunk of seared meat, a rough rectangle about three inches by four, perhaps an inch thick. A portion of the rectangle, missing now, had been sliced away. Some pink juices, streaked with white fat, had gelled at the center of the plate.

No, she thought. "He didn't," she whispered. She looked at Fallon, feeling suddenly, ridiculously like a little girl trapped in a world that was too large and disturbing. *"He couldn't."*

It was about then that things began to happen more quickly.

Someone knocked at the door. Fallon's cell phone chirped.

Chapter Three

hank you for coming," said the mayor of St. Anselm into the cluster of microphones.

Antonia "Call Me Toni" Bronson prided herself on her no-nonsense style. In her midforties, she was short and stocky, with a thickset tubular torso and a round pink face. Normally she wore Izod blouses, pleated khaki skirts, white tennis socks, and a gleaming pair of brown penny loafers. Tonight she was still wearing the trademark loafers, but she had replaced the tennis socks with sleek silk hose, and the blouse and skirt with a subdued gray silk suit, nicely pinstriped. She looked like a high school phys-ed teacher attending a funeral.

"As you all know by now," said the mayor gravely, "St. Anselm was the scene of a tragedy this morning. A young woman was viciously murdered. After consultation, Chief Anderson and I have agreed to hold this public briefing to let everyone know how the investigation is progressing so far."

Fallon hadn't liked the idea of the briefing. In his experience, he told Sophia, it only gave the bad guy the attention he wanted. But Fallon wasn't the mayor or the chief of police.

The municipal auditorium, which seated over two hundred people, was full. From her chair behind the table on the stage, to the right of the podium, sitting by Chief Anderson, Sophia looked out at the audience—concerned citizens of St. Anselm, and, it seemed, almost as many print and broadcast journalists and camera crews.

There were more media people, many more of them, than anyone would reasonably expect to be covering a mere homicide in a small Florida beach town. They were here, all of them, because they knew that something horrific, and therefore newsworthy, had happened at No. 25 Pelican Way.

Someone, somewhere, had talked. Sophia had an idea who that might be.

Among the crowd she recognized Dave Bondwell, the anchorman for WPOP's *Action News*. She was surprised to see him here—she'd thought that anchors never did anything but read from a teleprompter.

He did look good, though—better in person than he did on television, in a pair of faded jeans and a snugly fitting red rugby shirt. Very snugly fitting.

And whenever she glanced at him, he was staring back at her.

Obviously he's got the hots for woman cops. Especially the kind who are ten or twelve pounds overweight. Pleasingly plump.

"Before I bring up Chief Anderson," said the mayor, "I'd like to say one thing." Resting her forearms on the podium, she clasped her hands together and leaned earnestly forward. "I'm sure I speak for everyone in St. Anselm when I say that all of us are personally outraged by this heinous crime."

Beside Sophia, Fallon shifted in his chair and crossed his arms over his chest. His face, as usual, was unreadable.

He had tucked in his shirt, buttoned the collar, attached a laughable black clip-on tie, and thrown on a brown knit sport coat—Western style, with one of those silly yoke shoulders. She wished he'd changed the shirt to one with longer sleeves, so his thick, angular wrists didn't look so bony and . . . naked.

"And all of us," promised the mayor, narrowing her eyes, "will do everything we can to see that the person who committed this unspeakable act is brought to swift and certain justice."

"Ms. Bronson!" called a voice from the audience.

"Toni," she said automatically, then frowned and added impatiently, "What?"

One of the reporters had stood from his seat. Aiming a miniature cassette recorder at the mayor as though it were a *Star Trek* phaser, he asked, "Can you confirm that the victim was mutilated?"

The mayor held up her right hand—*Stop*—looking more like a phys-ed teacher than ever. "You're going to have to hold off on your questions until after Chief Anderson makes his statement." She turned to the table. "Chief?"

The chief rose and stepped to the podium, nodding to the mayor as she passed by him.

He put his hands along the edge of the podium. He was a big man, well over six feet tall, broad-shouldered, barrel-chested, and in his beautifully tailored uniform he looked exactly as a chief of police was supposed to look. His face was ruddy with what might have been health, and his blue eyes gleamed with what might have been intelligence. Like everyone else in the department, Sophia knew that the ruddiness came from single-malt lunches, and the gleam from a combination of animal and political cunning.

"Right," said the chief. "Here's how it's going to work. I'm going to run everyone through the basics, and then you press people will have time to ask your questions. First I want to introduce the two detectives who'll be working the case. Sergeant James Fallon is the detective in charge."

Fallon inclined his head slightly as the glances of the audience shifted toward him. Sophia knew she was next, and suddenly her rib cage was a half size too small for her lungs.

"Detective Fallon," said the chief, "is an experienced investigator, an officer who acquired an excellent record, and many commendations, with the New York Police Department before he joined us. His partner is Sophia Tregaskis, one of our finest young detectives."

The eyes of the audience sought her out, including the dark blue eyes of Dave Bondwell. Bondwell smiled and nodded. Sophia's glance fluttered downward, to the table.

Who the hell had invented blushing? In the complicated, tortuous evolutionary scheme of things, what possible purpose was it supposed to serve?

"Right," said the chief. "At eleven fifty-two this a.m., we received notice of a possible homicide. Officers were dispatched. They arrived at the scene within minutes. Shortly afterward, Detectives Fallon and Tregaskis arrived."

And the two of them had wandered through that dreadful house as though wandering through a nightmare, and then things had started happening more quickly.

FALLON HAD SNATCHED THE CELL PHONE from his pocket, flipped it open, raised it to his ear. "Fallon. . . . No, sorry, I can't. For now, just keep everyone away from the house. . . . Tregaskis and I will handle it. I'll call back when I can."

He flipped the phone shut and stalked to the front door. Sophia followed. (*Tregaskis and I will handle it.* She liked the sound of that.)

Fallon jerked the door open, and Sophia saw two more astronauts standing there. One was Dr. Parker Harrison, a county medical examiner, and the other was tiny Kitty Delgado, the department's Crime Unit technician. Both Dr. Harrison and Kitty carried bags, and Kitty's looked as though it weighed as much as she did.

Fallon stood aside to let them in. Kitty and Dr. Harrison walked past Sophia. Despite his coveralls, the smell of stale cigarette smoke trailed from the doctor. Both the doctor and Kitty stopped suddenly and stared down at the thing on the tarpaulin. Kitty's tanned face turned yellow, and Dr. Harrison said, "Oh my dear God."

Fallon said to him, "You can pronounce her?"

Harrison continued to stare at the body for a moment, then blinked, as though awakening from a daydream, and turned to him. "Oh yes. She's quite dead." A short man, plump and pale, he spoke with a precise, slightly high-pitched voice.

Fallon glanced at his wrist, pulled back the elastic sleeve of his coveralls. "Twelve-forty." He wrote in his notebook.

Sophia raised her notebook and wrote in it, *Vic prncd 12:40.*

Fallon turned to Harrison. "Don't let your people move her until I say so."

Harrison frowned. "I *have* done this before, you know."

"I know," said Fallon. "But this one is going to be rough, Doctor. We all need to be on the same page."

Nodding, Harrison glanced down at the body again. "Where is the, ah, rest of her?"

"The bathroom," said Fallon. "The tub. Tell your people to put it all into one bag, and the body in another. But don't let them move her until I say so."

He turned to Sophia. "You do the sketch of the body and tarp. Standard stuff. Dimensions, distances."

Sophia nodded. She looked down at the blue plastic sheet. Those dead blue eyes were still staring up at the ceiling, those obscene teeth were still grinning in the peeled, red face.

Standard stuff.

Beneath the coveralls, Sophia's blouse was sticking to her back. She took another deep breath and began to sketch.

Fallon turned to Kitty. "There's a piece of fried meat over on the stove, on a plate. Bag the meat and the plate. The pan and the spatula, too. When you get it all to the Crime Lab, have them do an enzyme test on the meat, before they put it in the cooler. I want to know if it's human."

"It could be the vic's dinner, no?" said Kitty. "Maybe she didn't finish it. Maybe she didn't get a chance."

Sophia glanced over, saw that Kitty's color had returned. Thin and fine-boned, she seemed too young and too delicate to be doing the work she did. But she was, Sophia knew, one of the best techs in the county.

Fallon said, "No meat wrapper in the garbage. No plastic wrap. Nothing."

Fallon was good at this.

"They'll bitch at me," Kitty said. "They're usually backlogged a week or two."

"Push them. It's one thing we need to know right now."

"Right," she said. "How about the house? You want a full walk-through?"

"Yeah. Video and stills. And make sure you shoot the bed. Someone was lying on it. Get measurements of the impression."

"Right."

"Get what you can from the body."

"There won't be much," she said.

"Get what you can."

Fallon turned to Garcia. "No one comes in here. No one. Not Dr. Harrison's people, not the mayor, not the chief. Got it?"

"Got it."

"Tregaskis and I will be next door, talking to your witness. Anyone leans on you, send them over."

"Right."

"You've done a good job so far, Paul."

"Thanks, Sarge."

"Don't screw it up now."

"I won't."

"Tregaskis?"

"Ready. Done." She closed the notebook.

She and Fallon stripped off the coveralls—her blouse was soaking wet, blotched with sweat—and then the bootees and gloves, and left everything just inside the front door. Then went back out into the sunshine.

She saw that the crowd had grown still larger. Past the yellow line of crime-scene tape, people were standing in small groups, two or three or four of them clustered together, some of them at stiff attention, some of them leaning toward each other, all of them staring as though hypnotized at No. 25 Pelican Way. Civilian automobiles were parked up and down the street, a few of them poking out into the road. A Channel 13 news van was parked directly opposite, and Sophia wondered how it had gotten here so quickly.

Just beyond the tape, a man holding a large commercial video camera was aiming it at another man and at Kinkaid. The second man held a microphone a few inches from Kinkaid's mouth. Kinkaid was nodding importantly, his fists planted on his hips, his sunglasses flashing in the sun.

Later, at the public briefing, Sophia would remember Kinkaid and the reporter.

At the moment, standing on the porch, it occurred to her that she had been right before, and that things were different now. She had changed. She had been inside No. 25 Pelican Way and she had seen what these people believed they wanted to see. She had crossed a boundary that none of them, no matter what they believed, would ever wish to cross, and she had separated herself from them in a way that was probably final.

Fallon touched her arm, gently steering her to the left, where a path worn in the grass led from the porch to an opening in the hedge. The two of them passed through it and across the next lawn to the porch of the landlady's house. They climbed up the steps and Fallon knocked at the door.

Ed Denton opened it, let them into the living room, which was blessedly cool. Denton introduced them to Silvia Hartley. Sitting at one end of a padded wicker sofa, her legs crossed, her arms locked across her chest, she was a small, birdlike woman in her sixties. Her white hair, loosely curled in a dying permanent, was so wispy that Sophia could see through it to the bright pink scalp that gleamed beneath. She wore black plastic flip-flops, pale green capris, and an oversize Tampa Bay Bucs T-shirt with limp, floppy sleeves that made her thin arms look fragile and brittle. She seemed to be in a daze, the thin white fingers of her right hand plucking absently at the sagging shoulder of her T-shirt.

Fallon told Denton, "Use your car radio. Tactical frequency. Ask for a couple more uniforms. Tell them to report to me here." He swung toward Silvia Hartley. "Is that all right with you, Mrs. Hartley?"

"What? Oh. Yes, of course." She plucked again at the T-shirt. Blue veins and wiry ligaments moved beneath the pale, mottled skin at the back of her hand.

"When you're done," Fallon said to Denton, "take over Kinkaid's spot at the tape. Tell him to start a D to D"—a door-to-door—"around the corner on Flamingo."

"Okay, Sarge," said Denton.

"And nothing to the press. Don't confirm, don't deny. We'll brief them later."

"Okay, right."

"Good, Ed, thanks."

Denton glanced at Sophia, nodded at Fallon, turned, and walked away.

"Mrs. Hartley?" said Fallon. "Okay if we sit down?"

"Of course, yes." She uncrossed her legs, put her hands on her thighs. "Can I get you something? Some iced tea? It's, you know, that sun tea? Lipton's. I made a big jar of it yesterday, so it's no trouble at all."

Fallon smiled. "If you're sure it's no trouble."

"May I help?" Sophia asked.

"Oh, no, no." Hartley put her left hand on the arm of the sofa and rose slowly. "You just sit down and I'll be right back."

And things slowed down for a moment as Sophia and Fallon sat in wicker chairs and Hartley shuffled off, limping slightly, favoring her left leg. The kitchen lay to the right, beyond a small counter identical to the one in the cottage next door.

Sophia glanced around. The basic structure of the two cottages might be identical, but No. 25 had looked like a motel suite, spare and sad, with only a few personal touches. Here there were bookcases with framed photographs running atop them, paintings of seascapes on the wall, magazines on the coffee table.

Mrs. Hartley returned with the tea, and Fallon started asking his questions.

"CHIEF ANDERSON," asked the reporter with the *Star Trek* phaser, "can you confirm that the body was mutilated?"

Behind the podium, the chief set his mouth in a thin grim line. "We won't discuss that now."

Which was, Sophia realized, pretty much the same thing as saying, "Why, yes, by golly, it was."

"We have reports," said the reporter, "that pieces of the victim—"

"I've made my comment." The chief glanced quickly around the conference room, pointed to another journalist. "Yes?"

Sophia recognized Jean Heller, from *The St. Petersburg Times*. She had interviewed Sophia a few months ago for an article about women on the force. "Chief, do you have any leads so far?"

"We've accumulated a substantial body of evidence, and, yes, we're working on several promising leads at the moment."

Bullshit, thought Sophia. Except for that faint impression left on the bedspread in the bedroom, like an afterimage, there was *típota*. *Típota kathólou*.

Nothing. Absolutely nothing.

Chapter Four

Into the glass on the countertop, Fallon poured his second bourbon, the last one he would allow himself tonight. He screwed on the bottle's cap, opened the cabinet door beneath, set the bottle on the shelf. He picked up the glass and carried it through the darkened living room out onto the apartment's small patio. He sat down on the canvas chaise lounge and looked out at the line of palmettos that marked the boundary of the apartment building's backyard.

It wasn't much of a yard. And the apartment wasn't much of an apartment—a first-floor one-bedroom in a four-unit building in Pasadena, on the mainland. Rentals were tight in St. Anselm, and Fallon had been forced to live outside the SAPD's jurisdiction. Chief Anderson had given his okay, but Fallon was still looking for a place on the island, near the beach. Why live in Florida if you can't live near the water?

Abruptly, once again, the image of the dead woman flashed into his mind. He felt the muscles around his mouth tighten.

How the *hell* could anyone do that to another human being?

He took a sip of bourbon.

Over the years he had seen what people did to each other, and he had listened to them explain why they'd done it, and invariably the explanations made sense only if a big chunk of your brain was missing, or your soul. A young girl raped and battered to death because "she dissed me, man." A homeless derelict doused with gasoline and set alight because "it was, like, a joke."

But this. This had taken long, quiet, deliberate hours to accomplish. Slicing, slicing, cutting away. Carrying that damned bucket back and forth. Cleaning up afterward.

Why? Why cut the woman like that?

And why Fleming? Why her? So far, the woman was a cipher.

MRS. HARTLEY HAD CAREFULLY PLACED a red and a green plastic glass, each filled with iced tea, atop cardboard Budweiser coasters on the coffee table, and then, sighing, she had sat back down on the sofa. After he and Tregaskis had each taken a sip of tea, she leaned slightly toward Fallon, concern deepening the lines of her thin face. "Can I ask you a question, Officer Fuller?"

"Fallon, ma'am. Sergeant Fallon. Of course."

"I'm sorry." She turned to Sophia. "My memory's not what it used to be."

Sophia smiled. "Mine never was."

Hartley tittered uneasily.

Tregaskis was handling herself well.

Hartley turned to him. She hesitated, searched around the room as though the words she was seeking might be lying somewhere in sight, then looked back at him and blurted, "Who *was* that at Marcy's house? That . . . horrible *thing* on the floor?"

"We're not certain yet, Mrs. Hartley. But we think it's Marcy Fleming."

"No, no." Hartley sat back and shook her head. "No, that can't be. Really, Sergeant Fallon. Marcy is . . . Marcy is a big woman. I've known her for two years. That isn't Marcy, honestly. It couldn't be."

Fallon found himself wishing that the glass on the table were filled with Jack Daniel's instead of iced tea. "Whoever did it, ma'am, he cut her."

Hartley was staring at him as though he were an idiot. "But Marcy is a *big* woman."

Patiently: "We think it's Marcy, ma'am."

She looked at Tregaskis, as though hoping she would deny what he'd just said.

Tregaskis said, "I'm sorry, Mrs. Hartley."

Hartley's glance darted away. The fingers of her right hand, so pale they had the bluish tinge of skim milk, began to pluck again at the shoulder of her Tampa Bay Buccaneers T-shirt. "My God. Oh my God."

"Mrs. Hartley," he said. "I know this is difficult for you. But in a case like this, the more quickly we move, the more likely we are to find the person responsible. We need to learn whatever we can about Marcy."

"My God." She closed her eyes, and beneath the oversize T-shirt her thin body shivered faintly.

"When did you see her last, Mrs. Hartley?" Fallon asked.

She opened her eyes, looked at Fallon, and blinked, as though she were surprised to find him sitting there. "See Marcy?"

"Yes, ma'am."

"I don't know. I'm not sure. Yesterday?" She nodded. "Yesterday. Yesterday afternoon. She was coming back from the beach. She sometimes goes for a walk on the beach in the afternoon."

"You're sure it was yesterday?"

"Yesterday, yes. About four o'clock."

To Fallon's right, Tregaskis wrote this down in her notebook.

"She was coming back from the beach," Hartley repeated. "I was outside, pulling up some weeds, and I said hello. Called out to her, you know? She waved at me."

She looked down, her face suddenly sad.

Fallon saw that he was about to lose her. "What was she wearing, Mrs. Hartley?"

The woman looked up, blinking again. "Pardon?"

"What was Marcy wearing? Yesterday."

"A dress. Pale blue, with flowers printed on it."

There had been no pale blue dress in Marcy's closet. He glanced at Tregaskis. She looked up at him from her notebook, shook her head slightly. She hadn't seen it either.

"It buttoned up the front," said Mrs. Hartley. "It was loose, like all of her dresses. But it was the pale blue one. I remember that."

She looked down again.

Fallon asked, "Did you see Marcy after four o'clock?"

She looked up. "No. Usually I didn't see her at night. Usually she just stayed in the house and watched TV."

"Did you see anyone approach Marcy's house yesterday?"

"At night?"

"Anytime yesterday."

"No. But at night, you know, I don't really pay attention to what

31

goes on outside. I'm usually reading. And I go to bed early. Ten o'clock."

"Did you hear anything last night?"

"No. It's awful to think, isn't it, that I was lying here last night, and all the time someone was over there . . . doing that to poor Marcy . . ." Once again, she looked down.

"You couldn't have done anything to help her, Mrs. Hartley," Fallon told her. "You say you've known Marcy for two years?"

"Two years." She looked up. "Two years in September. Next month." Her face suddenly twisted with pain. "Who could *do* such a thing?" She looked from Fallon to Tregaskis.

"We don't know yet, ma'am," Fallon told her. "But we'll find out. How old was Marcy?"

"I'm sorry, what?"

"Do you know how old she was?"

"Twenty-seven. She turned twenty-seven in March. March twenty-third. I made her a chocolate cake." She turned to Tregaskis. "She loves my chocolate cake."

Tregaskis nodded.

"Did she have a steady boyfriend?" Fallon asked.

"No. No one. I kept telling her she should get out more. You know? Meet people. But she's . . . she's self-conscious about her size. I told her, I said, some men *like* a big woman. But she just smiled and said she'd had enough of men, thank you very much."

"What did she mean by that?"

"I think she had, well, *you* know, a bad relationship once. She never talked about it, but that was the impression I got."

"When was that, Mrs. Hartley?"

"I don't know. Before she came here. Back in New York, I think."

"New York City?"

"Buffalo, New York. That's where she came from. Where she was raised."

"She have family there?"

"They died. Her father and mother. In an automobile accident, three years ago. She moved here a year later. She had some money, from the insurance."

"Where did she work?"

32

"She didn't. She still had some of the money left. She always said she was going to look for a job. Any day now, she always said. But she never did. I used to tease her about it. It was a shame, I thought. Maybe she would've met someone. If she had a regular job, you know? A place to go to, a place where other people were. But she just sat there in the house all day, watching television. I mean, I'm retired, ten years now, and I'm a widow, but I still get out. I still do things."

"Any brothers or sisters back in Buffalo?"

"No. I don't think so. She never said anything about brothers or sisters." She was looking off again, frowning, and Fallon suspected that she was thinking back over what she'd said, wondering if she'd been too critical.

She turned to him. "Don't get me wrong now. She was a sweet young woman, and she had every right to live her life the way she saw fit."

He nodded. "Any aunts or uncles? Anyone?"

"No. Not that I know of. She never mentioned anyone."

And so it had gone, a big blank, a zero, until finally a new pair of uniforms had arrived, Blakely and Stevens. Fallon told Hartley that he'd like her to go down to the station, where she could make a formal statement. She had agreed, and he'd asked her if he could use her house for the next few hours, assuring her that no one would damage anything. He needed an operational center, close to the crime scene. She had agreed, and Fallon had arranged for Stevens to replace Denton at the tape, and for Denton to take Hartley downtown. He sent Blakely to help Kinkaid with the canvass.

He had called the station on Hartley's phone, filled in Lieutenant Courtney, and then Fallon and Tregaskis had gone back to No. 25 Pelican Way, to see what they could find.

HE TOOK ANOTHER SIP OF BOURBON and looked above the line of palmettos to the stars flickering in the darkness.

Darkness. That was pretty much what he and Tregaskis were wandering around in.

And unless something turned up, they were going to stay there.

Maybe that shrink. That psychologist. The name Tregaskis had found in Fleming's appointment book. Maybe she'd be able to help. They could use any help they could get.

33

Tregaskis.

She had handled herself well today. She'd been shaken by that stripped and brutalized body—but so had he. Anybody would have been shaken. But she'd recovered and acted like a cop, like a professional, cool and deliberate.

Whereas earlier on, James T. Fallon, the supersleuth from the Big Apple, the honcho who was going to show these local yokels how it was done, had nearly acted like a jerk. If that call from Dispatch hadn't come in when it did, out there on the beach, he would've blundered ahead and asked her if she wanted to see a movie this weekend. Go out to dinner. Maybe something even more pathetic. Miniature golf?

Shit.

He lit another cigarette.

She was only a year younger than the dead woman, twenty-six years old—he'd checked her records—which meant she was exactly two years more than half his age. She could be his daughter.

And nothing turns on those young chicks like an older guy. They could lie next to him and count his wrinkles all day long—loves me, loves me not. And later, a few years down the road, they could wheel him down to the supermarket to pick up the Depends and the Fixodent.

What the hell had he been thinking?

He'd been surprised to find himself reacting to her. Reacting like that. He had believed that the part of him that *could* react like that had died, and been buried, with Laura.

It wasn't just her looks—although there was nothing wrong with those. She was a healthy woman, firm and solid and sexy. A mass of tumbling black hair. A pair of big brown eyes. A lush red mouth.

Nope, there was nothing wrong with her looks, eh, Jimmy?

But there was more to it than that.

He liked her earnestness, her seriousness, the way she kept those big brown eyes so open and alert you could see the sharp intelligence moving behind them. He liked the way she listened, the way she paid attention.

To you, you mean? Is that it, Jimmy? You flattered because the young chick cop hangs on your every word?

Don't take it too much to heart, ace. She's ambitious, she wants to get ahead. Remember when you were like that? You listened, too. You paid attention.

He raised his glass to his lips, discovered that it was empty.

Everything was turning up empty today.

He swirled the ice around the bottom of the glass.

Earlier on, he had felt the small shift in perspective that meant the alcohol had kicked in.

But now he was slowly shifting back to normal.

And normal, like everything else, was empty.

Well. Maybe just one more.

Chapter Five

As usual, he had taped the evening newscast. And tonight he was particularly looking forward to watching it—according to the ads that had blared all day from the radio, the newscast would include bits of the police department's public briefing.

But first things first.

Carefully he poured the wine, a '97 Far Niente chardonnay. Lightly he swirled it around the crystal glass, studying its clarity, its color. He raised the glass, held it beneath his nose, inhaled, savored the bouquet.

Promising.

He took a sip, rolled the wine around his mouth, sucked in some air, rolled the wine again, and finally swallowed.

Very good, he decided. Excellent, really. Not too oaky. Dry, but not astringent. A nice smooth finish. Hints of vanilla and butterscotch. Peach, as well. And . . . almond, was it?

California wines were coming along nicely these days. The whites especially. Not so very long ago, they had been undrinkable.

He put down the glass, set a clove of garlic on the cutting board, and covered it with the flat of the chef's knife blade. Sharply, he smacked the heel of his hand against the blade. Squish. He put aside the knife and peeled the papery skin from the crushed clove, then briskly rubbed the clove around the inside of the mahogany salad bowl. He stepped over to the sink, dangled the clove over the disposal, let it fall. We commit his body to the deep.

Back at the table, he peeled and minced the shallots. Chop, chop, chop from one end to the other, rearrange the pieces, and then chop, chop, chop some more. He scraped the translucent shreds into a mixing bowl, then chopped the tarragon, the parsley, the chives. Into the bowl he added a tablespoon of Dijon mustard, a tablespoon of capers, a squeeze of fresh lemon juice. A dash of salt, a quick grind of Malabar black pepper. He poured in the red-wine vinegar, whisked the mixture for a few moments, and then, still whisking steadily, slowly added the dark green olive oil. Italian. Stone-ground virgin.

Lovely phrase, that.

When the dressing was nicely emulsified, he unwrapped the paper towels from around the escarole and romaine. Gently, he tore the leaves into manageable pieces and dropped them into the wooden bowl. He gave the dressing another quick whisk, then dribbled it over the salad. Using a wooden fork and spoon, he tossed the greens until the dressing was evenly distributed and every leaf wore a slick, shiny coat of its own.

With the fork and spoon he scooped out a portion of salad and snuggled the leaves into a china bowl. He placed the bowl on the pewter tray. Delicately, with the tip of his finger, he prodded the cheese, Explorateur, a buttery triple crème. He plucked the bread knife from the rack, cut some slices from the baguette, set them on a small china platter. He put the platter and the cheese on the tray, filled up his wineglass, added that to the tray. From the cabinet above the sink he took out a damask linen napkin and laid it beside the salad. From the drawer he took out a silver knife and fork and set them atop the napkin.

No point in eating a meal, as Marla used to say, unless you can make it a little bit special somehow.

He picked up the tray, carried it into den, set it on the end table. He sat down, slid the napkin from beneath the knife and fork, shook it gently open, arranged it over his thighs. He picked up the remote control, sat back, and clicked the rewind button for the VCR.

As the tape whirred, he took a sip of wine.

Yes, definitely almond.

He tapped the TV button. The screen snapped awake.

Some silly sitcom. Imbeciles disguised as adults, wisecracking midgets disguised as children.

The VCR ready light blinked. He hit the PLAY button.

A flutter, a ghostly image of some long-ago program, and then today's broadcast.

"The *Ten O'clock Action News*," intoned a portentous baritone voice over the stirring theme music. "With Dave Bondwell and Connie Zimmer."

A close shot of the two behind their desk, Connie upbeat as always in a sportif gray blazer over a pale organdy blouse, Dave a tad more sober in his Brooks Brothers suit.

"Good evening," said Dave into the camera.

"Good evening," said Connie.

"A brutal murder in St. Anselm," said Dave. "Allegations of corruption in the state capital . . ."

Fancy that. Corrupt politicians.

"Hurricane Gerald heads for the coast of Mexico. And the Devil Rays continue their losing streak."

"But first," said Connie. "Our lead story."

Hard to believe, when you thought about it, that this job required two people.

"The quiet community of St. Anselm," said Connie, "was rocked today by a brutal murder." A long shot of Pelican Way, neighbors milling mindlessly about, all of them looking appropriately rocked. Long shot of the cottage, sad little place tucked beneath the live oaks. "*Action News* is cooperating with local police and withholding the victim's name until the family has been notified . . ."

That may take a while, Connie. I've done my homework, you see.

". . . but according to them she was a single woman who lived alone in this small Gulf Coast community. The police have also refused to release details as to the manner of her death, but *Action News* has learned from reliable sources that she was savagely mutilated."

Savagely? My goodness, madame, your sources deceive you.

"This evening, at the St. Anselm City Hall, the St. Anselm police held a public briefing. *Action News* was there."

Long shot of Dave himself standing up in the center of the audience. "Chief," he asked, "will you be asking for assistance from the FBI?"

That might be fun. Come and get me, G-man. Top of the world, Ma!

Medium shot of the chief of police, a man who had obviously been snared from central casting. "We've already asked for certain technical assistance. But I have complete confidence in Detectives Fallon and Tregaskis, and in all the fine officers of this department. I feel sure that we'll be able to bring this case to a successful conclusion."

Smiling, he sipped at his wine.

A medium shot of the confidence-inspiring detectives. Fallon, thin and dour. Tregaskis, handsome, thick hair, strong cheekbones, a broad mouth. Big brown eyes. A cutie-pie.

Long shot of Dave. "Have you discovered any motive for the crime?"

Medium shot of the chief. "As I say, we're working on several promising leads."

Permit me to harbor, my chieftain, a tiny doubt in that regard.

Back in the studio. Medium shot of Connie and Dave, Connie turning to Dave. "Did the police reveal what kind of leads they're working on, Dave?"

"No, Connie. They're playing this one close to the vest."

Connie shook her head. "It's a tragedy."

"Yes, it is, Connie."

Back to Connie. "In Tallahassee today, charges were leveled—"

He clicked the remote. The picture fluttered and died.

He cut a portion of cheese.

Wonderful. Simple pleasures were the best pleasures. Good food. Good wine. Cutting up Wibble-Wobbles.

He giggled.

He thought back to the public briefing and decided that he didn't much like the look of that Fallon character. Clint Eastwood on a bad day.

But that Tregaskis, she was just as cute as a button.

Chapter Six

Sitting at the kitchen table, Sophia took a bite of her Deluxe Eat-Rite Chicken Primavera TV dinner. It tasted like glue.

She'd been hungry when she got home, but in no mood to cook a real meal, and the only other TV dinner in the freezer had been a Deluxe Eat-Rite Steak à la Burgundy. After that horrible cold lump of meat lying in the greasy plate on the stove at No. 25 Pelican Way, the idea of eating any kind of steak wasn't right up there at the top of her list.

Her salad wasn't so hot, either. But she'd read somewhere that broccoli sprouts had something like fifty times the amount of anticarcinogens that grown-up broccoli did, and this was obviously a Good Thing. Particularly when you hated grown-up broccoli. Broccoli sprouts were definitely an improvement over grown-up broccoli.

If *Mamá* could see what Sophia was eating, she'd have a fit. "*Agápi mou*"—my love—"it's all plastic! You sit down, right now, and I'll run to the store and I'll pick up some ground meat, and I'll make a nice big plate of *keftéthes*." Meatballs. "And a nice big bowl of *horta*"—greens—"and a nice big loaf of bread and a nice big plate of fried potatoes." Sophia might as well save herself some time with them, just staple them directly to her thighs.

If Sophia wasn't careful, didn't watch what she ate, it wouldn't take her long to turn into . . .

She set down her fork. Oh my God.

Marcy Fleming. That poor woman. That wreckage on the living room floor.

When she and Fallon had gotten back to No. 25 Pelican Way, both Dr. Harrison and Kitty Delgado had something to say.

"IT LOOKS," HARRISON HAD SAID, mopping at his forehead with a damp white handkerchief, "as though she died from a single blow to the head. There's a deep fracture at the top left of her skull. Deep enough to be fatal, and almost instantaneously so. And there's very little external hemorrhaging."

Fallon nodded. "Scalp wounds bleed. Unless the victim is dead."

"Yes," said the doctor. "That's correct." To Sophia he seemed disappointed, as though he'd wanted to make that point himself. More high school stuff. A lot of it going down today.

In the notebook, she wrote, *Dp skll frctr, psbly ftl—no hmrge.*

The four of them—Kitty, Dr. Harrison, Fallon, and Sophia—were standing at the far side of the room, near the short hallway leading to the bathroom, opposite the empty spot on the carpet that had recently held the tarpaulin and the ravaged body. Both Harrison and Kitty had taken off their coveralls.

Fallon had sent Garcia outside, to coordinate with Blakely and Kinkaid on the neighborhood canvass. Two paramedics were in the bathroom, working at the tub.

"Internally," said Harrison, "she would have bled quite a lot—if, as I suspect, she suffered an epidural hematoma. But externally, not much at all."

"Just the one blow to the head?" asked Fallon.

Tucking the handkerchief into his back pocket, Harrison pursed his thick lips. "There was another blow. Earlier. Also to the head—at the back of the skull. It left a welt, but didn't break the skin. It wouldn't have been fatal, but it might've caused unconsciousness."

"He knocked her out, and then he killed her?"

"Possibly. If she *had* been unconscious, she could have recovered before she received the second blow."

"What did he hit her with the first time?"

"I'm not certain. A sap of some sort, perhaps."

Fallon turned to Kitty.

"No," she said. "Nothing like that around." She winced as she slapped away a fly. "I *hate* these bastards."

Fallon asked the doctor, "And the second time?"

41

"A ball-peen hammer, I believe. A ball-peen hammer would match the impact wound very nicely."

Fallon looked at Kitty, who shook her head.

Sophia wrote in her notebook.

"But she was dead," said Fallon, "when he did the cutting?"

"Yes. Thank goodness for that."

"Okay," said Fallon. "Let's work this out. We know the front door wasn't jimmied."

Sophia realized that she hadn't looked at the doorjamb, hadn't even considered it.

First she misses the reading lamp, and then she forgets to check the doorjamb.

"The bolt on the back door," Fallon continued, "had been closed until Garcia opened it. Painted shut. Same with the kitchen window and the bedroom window. Our guy used the front door. She let him in. Front-door lock is a Medeco, factory-restricted. Hartley says there are only two keys, hers and Fleming's."

Factory-restricted Medeco locks were technically pickproof, and the keys were impossible to duplicate.

Kitty said, "A boyfriend?"

"*Aw, Jesus!*" One of the paramedics, in the bathroom. "*Careful!*"

Fallon said, "Hartley says no."

Sophia said, "Maybe a boyfriend Hartley didn't know about. A married man?"

"Maybe." He glanced quickly around the room. "Right. No matter how he gets in, at some point he maneuvers her over to the sofa. He saps her, knocks her out. Later, he kills her with the hammer." He looked at Harrison. "How much later?"

"Fifteen minutes, I'd estimate," said the doctor, "judging by that welt. A half an hour, at the outside. But you've missed something."

"What's that?"

"The skin at the wrists." Harrison seemed pleased with himself. "He left the skin on the hands and part of the wrists. Like gloves."

Fallon nodded. "And?"

"There were abrasions along the skin at the wrist. From a rope, I suspect."

Fallon turned to Kitty.

She nodded. "I got photographs."

He turned back to Harrison. "The guy tied her up."

Harrison nodded. "And did so before she died."

"All right. He knocks her unconscious, and then he ties her up. Which means he expected her to regain consciousness."

"He *wanted* her to regain consciousness," said Sophia.

Kitty said, "He wanted her to know who was in control."

Fallon looked at Kitty for a moment, glanced at Sophia, and then nodded. "Good. So he talks to her, maybe. For ten, twenty minutes. And then he kills her. And maybe that's when he takes off the dress."

"What dress?" Kitty asked.

Sophia said, "According to the landlady, Marcy was wearing a pale blue dress yesterday."

"There's no pale blue dress here," Kitty said.

"He took it with him," Fallon said.

"I don't like that idea," said Kitty.

Fallon nodded. "A memento. A trophy."

"A serial killer?" Kitty said.

Serial killers, Sophia knew, often took items from the victim's body, or the victim's house, and kept them as trophies of the murder.

"I hope not." Fallon turned to the doctor. "If he killed her on the sofa, he'd have to move her to the floor. How much do you figure she weighed?"

"*Christ, Bob, watch it!*" The paramedic again.

The doctor glanced toward the bathroom, frowned, then turned back to Fallon. "At a guess, I'd say a good deal over three hundred pounds. I can give you a more accurate answer after the autopsy. I'll be weighing everything." He frowned again. "You're thinking that he would've needed a certain amount of strength to move the body. Or possibly an accomplice."

"I was," Fallon said, and smiled bleakly. "But I have a feeling you're about to shoot me down."

"Well," said Harrison, "from the location of the bloodstains on the sofa, and the location of the wound, I'd say she was lying down at the time."

Fallon looked at the sofa for a moment, then looked back at the doctor and nodded. "Once she was dead, he could've rolled her onto the tarp."

"Yes."

"He'd still need to be strong."

"But nothing out of the ordinary."

"You think it was just one person."

"I see nothing to suggest that it was more than one."

"Was she sexually assaulted?"

"I don't believe so. There are no obvious indications of it. I'll know more after the autopsy."

"Could a woman have done all this?"

"A woman? It's physically possible, I suppose. A woman could've used the hammer. A woman might've been able to move the body about on the tarpaulin. So, strictly speaking, there's nothing that absolutely rules out a woman."

"But you don't buy the idea."

"Unless other evidence presents itself, I'd be inclined to believe it was a man."

"Why?"

"For one thing, women are seldom serial killers."

"Wournos," Sophia said.

Aileen Wournos, the prostitute who had killed at least six men in south Florida.

"Yes," said Harrison, "but Wournos is essentially the exception that proves the rule."

Fallon said, "We don't know for certain that this was a serial killer."

Harrison frowned again. "I suppose I simply don't want to believe that one woman could've done that to another. Or to anyone." He looked at Kitty and Sophia, smiled. "But I'm from the old school. I hold open the door for women."

Sophia smiled wanly back. *So do I. For men, too.*

"Time of death?" asked Fallon.

"Difficult to estimate," said Harrison. "With the body carved up like that. Most of the skin has been removed, so we'll have no livor. Most of the muscle tissue has been excised, so we'll have no rigor.

And the removal of skin and tissue skews the body temperature results. Do we know when she last ate?"

Fallon shook his head. "According to Hartley, she didn't eat at any set time."

"Then even stomach contents won't tell us much. And, by the time I can perform the autopsy, the potassium in the aqueous humour won't be of any help. Sometime last night. That's the best I can do at the moment. I may be able to tell you more when we run the blood tests."

"How long would it take to do it to her? Everything he did?"

"All of it? Several hours, I should think."

"I figure he mopped up as he went," Fallon said. "Used the bucket in the bathroom."

Harrison nodded. "After a time, there would be less blood, and what was left would flow less readily. The residual under the body, on the tarp, was a mixture of blood and lymphatic fluid. It seeped out afterward. When he stopped working on her."

"Any way to use that, the residual, to figure out when he *did* stop?"

The doctor considered for a moment. "That's an interesting idea," he said finally. "Possibly. I'll give it some thought."

"He show any special skills?"

The doctor frowned. "Medical skills, you mean? You don't think a medical person did that?"

"I don't think anything yet, Doctor."

"No, no. No medical skills. No skills at all. He cut through the mesentery, he punctured the stomach, he severed any number of arteries and ligaments. He clearly has no knowledge of anatomy. He made a mess of things."

"What did he use? To cut her?"

"Several different instruments. A scalpel of some sort, at least on the area around the face. He made delicate cuts there, or at least more delicate than the others. Whatever knife he used, it was very sharp. For the largest and deepest cuts, where he removed sizable segments of muscle and tissue, along the thighs and stomach, along the hips, I suspect he used a long carving knife, the sort with a rounded tip."

"The kind you use to slice up roast beef."

"Correct. After he made those large cuts—"

"*Beep, beep!* Coming through!"

45

It was the paramedics, one of them leading the gurney as his partner pushed it down the hallway. Fallon, Sophia, and Kitty stepped to the left, Dr. Harrison to the right, and the gurney passed between them.

"Nice work you give us, Doc," said the first of the paramedics. There were bloodstains on his blue shirt.

"I don't kill them," said the doctor. "I merely examine them."

"Yeah, well," said the second paramedic, passing by Fallon, "next time, call Roto-Rooter."

Fallon tapped him on the shoulder. The man stopped pushing the gurney and turned to him.

"Next time," Fallon said, "keep your mouth shut."

The man stood upright. He outweighed Fallon by thirty or forty pounds. "Hey."

The first paramedic said, "C'mon, Danny. Let's go."

Danny looked around the room, looked back at Fallon. Fallon hadn't moved.

"Right," Danny said. "Yeah." Looking down, his lower lip between his teeth, he moved the gurney forward.

The first paramedic opened the door and together they wrestled the gurney out onto the porch. Without looking back, Danny pulled the door shut behind him.

Fallon turned back to the doctor. "After he made the large cuts?"

"Excuse me?"

"What happened after he made the large cuts?"

"Oh. Yes. He used another knife, a smaller knife, to do the close-up work. I do apologize for Danny. He's new."

Fallon nodded. "Close-up work?"

Harrison nodded. "To even out the cuts. He seems to have been trying, in effect, to pare her down. As I say, he was inept. The human body simply can't be carved like a bar of soap. But on the evidence, that's essentially what he was trying to do."

"Those knives. They're everyday, right? Household stuff? He'd be able to get them anywhere?"

"No problem at all."

Fallon nodded. "When can you do the autopsy?"

"Unless the chief ME pushes, not until the day after tomorrow, at the earliest."

"We'll get her to push."

"Then tomorrow afternoon."

"You checked her teeth?"

"Yes. A fair number of fillings. Nothing that looks recent. You'll want an X-ray, for identification purposes?"

"Can you get it to us today?"

"I can try." The doctor glanced at his watch. "Well, I'll be off, then. You'll be there tomorrow, for the autopsy?"

"Yeah. Thank you, Doctor. I appreciate your help."

"Yes. Thank you." Harrison picked up his bag and shuffled across the room. He cast a single glance toward the empty carpet, where the body had been lying, before he opened the door and disappeared through it, pulling it shut behind him.

Fallon turned to Kitty. "What else do you have?"

"I tagged her," Kitty said, "scraped under her nails, printed her, and I bagged her hands and feet."

"You vacuum?" Fallon asked.

"Yeah. Separate bags for the living room, bedroom, and bathroom. I picked up some hair in every room, but it's all hers, I think. There's some junk, too. But nothing that looks like it might've come from the bad guy."

"What about the bed?" Fallon asked her. "That depression on the cover?"

"Nothing. No hair, no fibers."

"How can that be?" Sophia asked her.

Transfer and Exchange. Whether they intend to or not, people inevitably pick up traces of the places they go. And, whether they intend to or not, inevitably leave traces of themselves behind.

"For one thing," Kitty said, "someone cleaned up the house before I did. I've got pictures of the carpet—you can see the brush marks in the pile."

"There's a vacuum in the bedroom closet," said Fallon.

"Yeah. With no bag on the inside. And no brush."

"He took the brush?"

"He must have."

"Prints?"

"Nope."

47

"Terrific."

Kitty shrugged. "He probably watches the Discovery Channel. Those *Modern Detective* documentaries."

"Any prints on the plate and silverware from the stove?"

"None." Kitty smiled sourly. "Thank the Discovery Channel."

"What about prints in the rest of the house?" Fallon asked.

"Two sets, it looks like. Like I said, most of them look like they belong to the victim. The other set was on the coffee table. Some old, some recent. The landlady?"

"Maybe. She's at the station. We'll get her printed. In the meantime, send a copy of the vic's prints to the Sheriff's Lab." He glanced back toward the bedroom. "But that bedspread. It wasn't vacuumed."

"No," Kitty said. "There should've been something."

Sophia lowered her notebook. "Unless—" She stopped herself.

"What?" said Fallon.

"What if the impression is a setup? A fake. What if he wants us—"

"To buy those dimensions. When they aren't really his." Fallon grinned. Fallon didn't grin often, and for Sophia there was something almost wolflike, predatory, in his face when he did. He nodded. "A guy cleans up after himself, vacuums the carpet, cleans the goddamn vacuum afterward, he's not going to lie down on a bed."

"So we know he's smart," said Kitty.

"He just thinks he's smart," said Fallon.

"So far," she said, "I agree with him."

AFTER FALLON TOLD KITTY TO CHECK for tire tracks and any other possible evidence on the lawn, he and Sophia had slipped their plastic gloves back on and begun the search, breaking each room into grids. Fallon had been silently methodical, taking a Polaroid of each area before he moved any of the items within it. Afterward, he meticulously replaced each item. Sophia had wondered why he was being so careful to leave the house as it had been. She knew there were cops who'd tear the place apart and then walk away from it without a backward glance. He wasn't doing it for the sake of Marcy Fleming, who was long past caring. Nor for the sake of her living relatives— according to Mrs. Hartley, she had none. Sophia decided that he was doing it that way simply because that was the way he did things, methodically and meticulously, and she decided that she liked him for it, even admired him for it. Fallon wasn't always an incredible jerk.

They searched. The long minutes slid slowly past. The flies kept moving, buzzing and whining, annoyed that their lunch had been ripped away. They seemed especially annoyed with Sophia, bumbling into her forehead, into her eyes, flicking across her lips. She waved them away, trying not to think of what they'd been touching before they touched her.

After a half an hour, Kitty returned to tell Fallon that she'd found nothing in the yard, including tire tracks, except for those left by Kinkaid's cruiser. Fallon thanked her, and she left for the lab with all the evidence.

It was in the leatherette book on the kitchen counter that Sophia found the one piece of information that might potentially be useful. Going through it, she discovered that it was an appointment book, and not an address book, as she'd first thought. Nearly all the pages were blank. But on the page for August 19, one week ago, there was a notation: *Dr. Eva Swanson. 4 o'clock.*

She carried the book into the bedroom. Fallon was squatting on the floor, quickly riffling through a magazine.

He had moved the stacks of magazines from the closet to the carpet. Sophia had been right about them—*Glamour, Vogue, Elle, Marie Claire.*

"No blue dress?" Sophia asked him.

Riffling the pages, he shook his head.

"I know this woman," she said, holding out the appointment book. He looked up. "What woman?"

"Eva Swanson. She's a psychologist. She worked with us last year."

Fallon put a hand to the floor and pushed himself up. He took the book, glanced at the notation, then flipped back through the pages.

He said, "Marcy didn't get out much, did she?"

"I feel sorry for her."

Fallon glanced at her.

"That closet," she said. "Nothing in there. Nothing nice, anyway. Nothing pretty." She nodded to the stacks of *Vogue* and *Glamour*. "Those must've been like travel magazines for her. Taking her away, off to places she'd never be able to see on her own."

49

He nodded. "Tell me about Swanson."

"If this is the same woman, she's the psychologist who consulted with us last year. In the spring, before you came on. We were getting a lot of arsons, random, no obvious motive. Lieutenant Courtney called her in. She came up with some good ideas. She said it was probably a young boy, thirteen or fourteen, probably a computer geek, and she was right."

"And you know her?"

"I met her. For a minute or two. I was only working patrol back then."

He nodded. "We'll give her a call when we get back to Hartley's. Maybe she can tell us something."

After they searched the house—without finding a blue dress—they went briefly out into the backyard. Atop the bare earth just outside the door, to the right, was a small puddle of vomit. Garcia's.

The yard was separated from the neighbors' by a thick hedge and by the chain-link fence that Fallon had noticed before. The grass was thick and overgrown. As Fallon pointed out, no one could have come through it without leaving tracks. There were none.

By the time Sophia and Fallon returned to Mrs. Hartley's house, the assistant state attorney, Peter Collinson, had arrived. He was a short, wiry man in his thirties, looking very dapper in a tropical-weight gray suit as he spoke in terse monosyllables and scratched notes into a small, leather-covered book. While Fallon filled him it, she called Dr. Swanson's number.

It was after five o'clock and the psychologist was no longer in her office. Sophia left a message on her machine, called Lieutenant Courtney, told her about the doctor's name being found in the victim's appointment book.

Fallon had talked to the uniforms doing the canvassing—no one in the neighborhood had seen or heard anything strange last night—and then he and Sophia had gone downtown, to the station.

Courtney had told them that she'd called Dr. Swanson at home and had learned that the doctor had indeed met with Marcy Fleming a week ago. The doctor had volunteered to help with the investigation, and she would be coming to the station tomorrow morning.

SOPHIA CARRIED HER EMPTY SALAD BOWL to the sink, rinsed it off, and slipped it into the dishwasher.

She was still hungry. Another big surprise. She'd been born hungry, and none of the meals she'd eaten since then had changed that for long. She stepped over to the freezer, opened it, took out the package of Häagen-Dazs pistachio. It had been there for three days, like a secret stash of gold, and she'd taken as much pleasure in knowing it was there as she would have taken from eating it. Almost as much.

It had been a hard day. And she'd run the full four miles this morning, before she went to work. She deserved a reward. She had earned it. And she'd lost two pounds since June.

A pound a month. Awesome. Don't let Oprah find out or she'll never leave you alone.

The container held only a pint—with its famous four servings, a mere 240 calories per serving—because Sophia refused to buy anything larger. The ice cream inside was as hard as a rock. She carried it over to the microwave, tucked it inside, and set the timer for one minute. After ten seconds, she opened the door, tested the container, then gave it another ten seconds. Hard, but improving.

Ten seconds later, a bit of give to the sides of the container. Perfect.

Forget computers. The microwave was the most important invention of the twentieth century.

She pried off the cap, peeled away the plastic foil, dabbed her fingertip into the surface of the ice cream. Stuck the fingertip into her mouth.

Wonderful.

And then suddenly, for no reason, she remembered the paramedics cursing in the bathroom as they transferred the pieces of Marcy Fleming from the bathtub to the bag.

She ran to the sink and was sick.

WEDNESDAY

Chapter Seven

Robert never knew, ahead of time, whether the evening would turn into one of the Weird Nights.

He never knew until he heard her start playing the music

Every night, after she watched the eleven-o'clock news, she would pour herself another drink and put a cassette into the stereo.

Every night, curled beneath the thin sheet, beneath the stiff, fuzzy blankets that smelled of her, Robert listened for the music that slithered down the hallway and wormed through the thin, bright crack at the bottom of the bedroom door.

Sometimes it was just music, something unfamiliar. When it was, Robert knew that everything was okay and that he could stop listening and let himself sink back down into the bed and melt away into darkness and sleep.

But on other nights, and more and more often these days, she would put on Our Special Song. The one about the people who need people.

She had explained to Robert how she and Robert's father had shared it between them. How they had listened to it together every night, in the months and weeks and days before his father went away to foreign shores and disappeared forever.

Tonight, as always when the news was over, she turned off the television. For a moment, as always, the house was silent. And then Robert heard the shuffling sound of her slippers as she lumbered across the tiles of the kitchen floor. He heard the cabinet door open and close, heard the refrigerator door open, and then the freezer door.

Sometimes he told himself that he could hear the sound of the Popov vodka as it gurgled into the glass, the sound of the ice crackling. But he knew that this was probably just his imagination.

He listened carefully as her slippers shuffled against the tiles again, moving back toward the living room.

Another few moments of silence as she moved across the thick carpeting. More silence as she decided which cassette to put in the machine.

After a moment, Robert knew that she was sliding the tape into the stereo. He could picture everything in his mind. The little door popping open like a mechanical mouth. Her thick fingers sliding the cassette inside, closing the door, stabbing the button.

And now the stereo started playing. . . .

And tonight—Robert's heart, all at once, came alive in his chest—it was playing Our Special Song.

The air in the bedroom began to grow thicker, heavier. Robert had a harder time breathing it.

He made himself think about the daytime.

He thought about Davie, next door, and Davie's big, hairy yellow dog, Sam. And he thought about Mrs. Hanrahan, Davie's mom, a really nice lady. Every weekday she would make dinner for Davie and Robert, and sometimes she'd make Robert's all-time favorite meal, fried bologna sandwiches with fried tomato and Bac-Os and Hellmann's Real Mayonnaise.

Mr. Hanrahan, Davie's dad, was really nice, too. Sometimes on the weekend he'd take Davie and Robert for walks down by the creek, and Sam would come along, too, prancing happily, his yellow tail waving like a flag. The forest on either side of the path was as deep and as dark as a jungle, and there were probably Florida panthers back in there somewhere, but the Florida panthers were a lot more scared of Davie and Robert, Mr. Hanrahan said, than Davie and Robert were scared of the panthers. Davie said he wasn't scared of the Florida panthers at all, and Robert said that he wasn't either, but as he walked along the path between the crouching shadows, his breath would come a little faster, as it did on the Weird Nights when he was waiting for the music to end.

On nights like this one.

And just now, as he lay there curled like a caterpillar beneath the blanket, the music did end.

Robert felt his body go rigid.

After a moment, he heard the sound of her slippers as they slapped down the hallway, left, right, left, the impact of each slipper distinct and electric and growing louder as she approached the bedroom.

It was strange how he could hear the sound with his entire body, as though the slippers were marching, slap slap slap, left right left, along his stiffening skin.

He heard the door creak open, saw the flash of pink beyond his shuttered eyes, heard her breathing as she entered the room, heard the door close.

And then the mattress dipped toward the door as she moved onto the bed, and without wanting to but without fighting it, surrendering, Robert rolled gently down along the incline, toward the expanse of her and the smells of her, of perfume and vodka and cigarette smoke, and one of her soft, thick arms came around his shoulder, the flesh wobbling and shivering, and the hand found his back, pulling him still closer toward her, and the other hand moved down along his stomach . . .

HE AWOKE WITH A START.

Good Lord.

He'd dreamed about the Cow. He hadn't dreamed about the Cow for years.

What on earth . . . ?

Marcy, he realized.

The thing with Marcy yesterday, their lovely adventure together, had brought back the old memories.

And what dreadful memories they were. Jesus wept! Fried bologna sandwiches indeed.

Thank goodness he'd gotten away from all that. Thank goodness for Marla, and for everything she'd done.

He glanced around. Through the thin sheet of early-morning sunshine that fell into the room from the edge of the curtain, golden motes danced, invisible before they arrived, invisible when they left.

He looked at the bedside clock. Six-thirty. Nearly time to get up.

He yawned, a long, slow yawn, his hands pushing out against the air above him, his body stretching languorously against the mattress, the skin of his feet sliding sweetly along the slick, smooth satin.

He looked up at his hands. An ordinary pair of hands. Well, more handsome, it might be said, than some. More elegant, perhaps, than some. More elegant, certainly, than poor Marcy's stubby little paws.

But still, a simple pair of hands. Who would guess, looking at them, the wonders they could accomplish? Who would guess, who would *dare* guess, the astonishing acts these hands had performed yesterday? Shaping, forming, *creating* . . .

He lowered his arms and slipped them beneath the sheets, and he shivered with pleasure.

It had been wonderful, his time with Marcy. Wonderful. Literally filled with wonders.

This morning would be busy, very busy.

And then later, this afternoon, he would be picking out the next one. That would be fun. That would be great fun.

Right now, though, right now he wanted to savor his time with Marcy.

His hands moved down along his stomach . . .

Chapter Eight

The soles of Sophia's Nikes slapped against the damp, hard-packed sand—left, right, left, right . . .

Six thirty in the morning, the best time to run. The air wasn't yet superheated and the beach was nearly deserted, only a few shell-gatherers here and there, elderly women and men who slowly ambled along, their heads bent, their glances sweeping shrewdly back and forth across the sand.

Once in a while, rarely, there would be another jogger. But the early-morning joggers were different from the sleek, tanned champions who ran later in the day, the athletes who wore tiny strips of spandex and cutoff tops to flaunt their taut pneumatic glutes and their washboard abs. Sophia always thought of the early-morning people as The Overweight Runners Club. Like her, they wore old sweats or baggy shorts and tops, and they tended to ignore, or even avoid, the few bystanders on the beach.

It was a beautiful day, the blue sky pale and cloudless. A few pelicans were soaring overhead. Here on land, near the water, an occasional small flock of gulls stood patiently staring out across the Gulf, as if they were all waiting for the same ship to come looming over the horizon.

Sophia ignored the gulls. Heels slamming down, calf muscles clenching, toes digging in and springing off, she ran. Left, right, left, right . . .

Today she felt that she wasn't so much running toward a goal—the four miles she covered, five days a week—as running away from something. She hadn't slept well last night. Garish visions of that blue tarp and that gruesome bathtub had kept sliding to the front of her mind.

And at some point, early in the morning, an idea had come to her. She had tried to dismiss it, but like many of those ideas that come drifting from the early-morning shadows, it had taken on a life of its own—deepening, thickening, swelling into something dark and inescapable.

"OKAY," SAID COURTNEY. "The piece of meat you found in the kitchen. We got the report from the Crime Lab. It's beef."

The four of them—Courtney, Fallon, Sophia, and Kitty Delgado—were sitting around the table in the station's second-floor conference room. When the building was designed and constructed, the city had been going through a boom time, and no one had stopped the architect from installing an expensive floor-to-ceiling window in here. Through the opened blue curtains, Sophia could see out to the shiny sailboats and the sleek motor cruisers moored at the Flanders Landing marina.

It was still sunny out there, but now a few puffy white cumulus clouds were sailing across the sky. The wind had picked up and the boats were bobbing in the bright blue dazzle of the marina's water. On the slender swaying masts, pennants fluttered.

"He's playing games with us," Fallon said. "What about the victim's prints? Did the sheriff's office find a match?"

"No," said Courtney. "Neither did the FBI."

"What about the second set of prints in the cottage?" Kitty asked.

"The landlady. Mrs.—" Courtney looked down at the yellow legal pad on the table.

"Hartley," said Fallon.

"Hartley, right," said Courtney.

Chief Anderson was big and impressive, but he was primarily a showpiece. It was actually Lieutenant Ellen Courtney who ran the St. Anselm Police Department.

Short and trim, forty years old, today she wore a cream-colored cotton blouse and a taupe cotton-twill skirt. Her blond hair was close-cropped and discreetly frosted. Her nails were short, polished with a neutral lacquer. Her features had seemed hard, almost harsh, when Sophia first joined the department—the sharp nose, the thin mouth, the pointed chin. And she wore just a shade too much foundation, trying to hide those large pores along her cheeks. But over time, Sophia had seen how the features were enlivened and somehow softened by the mobility of her face, by her quick smile and sudden laugh—and there was no hiding the intelligence in her pale green eyes.

"But Harrison," she said now, "came through with the X-ray of the victim's teeth. I talked to the Buffalo PD, sent a copy up there. And we got a break on the phone records. There were two calls to Buffalo, both to the same number, both of them made just after Fleming moved into the place on Pelican Way. I called the number. It's a cousin. She hasn't talked to Fleming for nearly two years, doesn't know about any men in her background. But she thinks she can find the name of Fleming's dentist. The Buffalo cops'll be in touch with her. If she gives them the name, and they can match the dental records, then we'll have our positive ID. But it was the woman's house, and the body is basically a match. Until we learn otherwise, we're working on the assumption that she's the vic."

Kitty said, "So the people who're doing the D to D, they can use the driver's license photo?" More patrolmen would be going over the neighborhood today, trying to find anyone who'd seen Marcy yesterday. Even a driver's license photograph would be helpful.

"Yes," said Courtney. "I want a corroboration on that LSA we got from Hartley." The Last Seen Alive account.

Fallon said, "That photograph's not going to enlarge very well."

"It's all we've got," said Courtney.

She glanced down at the legal pad, then looked up. "Okay. Mortenson had Monday night's patrol in south St. Anselm. He drove through Fleming's neighborhood at eleven-thirty p.m., and then at one-thirty, three-thirty, and six-thirty. He says there was a light on in Fleming's window at three-thirty. He noticed it, he says, because it was the only light on Pelican Way. It was still on at six-thirty."

Fallon said, "It was still on when we got there."

"Was it on at one-thirty?" Sophia asked Courtney.

"Mortenson didn't notice."

"At three o'clock," said Kitty, "the bad guy was in there, working on her."

Courtney nodded. "Too bad we can't call out a SWAT team whenever someone leaves a light burning." She glanced down again at the pad, looked up. "We've got a subpoena from the state attorney's office and we'll be getting Fleming's financial records from the bank this afternoon. We'll see if there's been any big movement in or out of her account. But I'm thinking that's probably a dead end."

She turned to Fallon. "What else've we got?"

"Squat," said Fallon.

"Squat," Courtney said. "Very colorful, Jim."

Fallon had gone back to his white short sleeves, still boring but a definite improvement over that cowboy sport coat. "According to Harrison," he said, "the guy could've gotten the knives anywhere. The tarp, the one he put the body on, we think it probably came from Kmart or Wal-Mart. None of the neighbors saw or heard anything. There were no prints, no foreign hair or fiber."

"Okay," said Courtney. "One thing at a time. The tarp was definitely his?"

Fallon said, "Hartley, the landlady, said she never saw it before."

"Fleming could've bought it."

"Not nearby, and she didn't have a car."

"Buses. Taxis."

"Sure, but what's she need a tarp for?"

Courtney turned to Kitty. "No prints on it?"

"None," said Kitty. "Like it just came out of the wrapper."

Courtney nodded. She turned to Fallon. "Why leave it? He took everything else away with him, right?"

"He knew we couldn't trace it," said Fallon.

"Who's working on it?"

"Kinkaid and Garcia. They're checking the Wal-Marts, Kmarts, camping-supply places, auto-supply places. But he could've gotten it by mail order. The tarp isn't going to get us anywhere."

Courtney turned again to Kitty. "What's happening with the other evidence?"

"The lab is giving us priority," Kitty said, "and they should get back to us within a week. But I don't think they'll find anything. The place was clean."

"And what's that tell you?"

"Like I told Sergeant Fallon. The guy is smart."

Courtney looked around the table once more. "What else do we have?"

"He's probably single," said Kitty. "Or he's got a wife who doesn't care if he stays out all night."

Courtney nodded. "What else?"

"He brought his own knives," said Fallon. "And probably some kind of sap."

"A professional sap?" asked Courtney. "Leather and lead?"

"Maybe Harrison will know, after the autopsy." Fallon shrugged. "But even if it was, that doesn't tell us anything. Anyone who reads *Soldier of Fortune* magazine can pick one up."

"He planned it out," said Kitty. "He brought along the sap, the tarp, the knives. Probably a pair of gloves. The only thing he left behind was the tarp, and that impression on the bed."

"What's the story on the impression?" Courtney asked her.

"Sophia thinks it's bogus," Kitty said.

Courtney glanced at Sophia.

"And I think she's right," said Kitty. "I think the guy faked it. Trying to put one over on the stupid cops. Like he did with the meat."

"Maybe," said Courtney. "But we can't eliminate the possibility that those *are* his dimensions. What do they give us?"

"Approximately five foot seven, a hundred and sixty pounds."

Courtney turned to Fallon. "If that's true, could he have moved her around?"

"Harrison says it's possible. But I think Tregaskis is right. Those dimensions are a setup."

Courtney turned again to Sophia, smiled. "I think she's right, too."

Sophia managed to return the smile without producing another damned blush.

"Like you said, Jim," said Courtney, "he's playing games." She looked around the table. "Okay. How did he get into the house?"

"She let him in," said Fallon. "A Medeco lock. No signs of forced entry."

"She had a boyfriend? Girlfriend?"

"Hartley says no."

"Then how? In the middle of the night?"

60

"He must talk a good story."

She turned to Kitty. "What about outside the house? Tire tracks, anything?"

"No. If he used a car, he parked it in the street."

Courtney looked at Fallon. "What about that dress?"

"According to Hartley," said Fallon, "Fleming was wearing a pale blue dress when she walked by Hartley's house at approximately four in the afternoon. We can't find it. Our guy must've taken it."

Courtney made a face. "A serial?"

"I think he is," said Sophia.

Everyone turned to her.

She suddenly felt uncertain. She had less homicide experience, less experience in general, than anyone else in the room. "I've got an idea, but I could be wrong."

"Go," said Courtney.

Sophia glanced around the table. Fallon and Kitty were waiting, watching her.

Make it reasonable, she told herself. *Let them see it.* "From everything we've learned, Marcy Fleming had no real friends here. No relatives, no connection to anyone who lives in St. Anselm. She didn't know anyone except for Hartley, the landlady. And no one knew her. But if that's true, no one had a reason to kill her."

"That we know of," said Courtney

"I think he selected her," Sophia said. "Picked her out. And if he picked out Marcy Fleming, then he can pick out someone else. For the same reason."

"What reason?" Courtney asked.

Sophia leaned forward. "This is going to sound weird, probably. But what if he picked her because she was overweight? Look at what he did to her, the way he cut her—Dr. Harrison said it was like he was trying to pare her down. What if that's exactly what he was trying to do—cut away the extra flesh?"

She realized that she was talking too quickly, trying to bring them all to her own level of excitement, and belief, with a rush of words. She sat back and forced herself to speak more slowly. "And if he was, maybe he was doing it to Marcy *because* she was overweight."

"But why?" said Courtney

"I don't know," Sophia said. "Something in his background, God knows what. But it makes sense. At least it does to me."

"I like it," said Kitty.

"I do too," said Fallon, surprising Sophia. "But there are two problems. First, we don't know that Hartley was right about Marcy. Maybe Marcy did have a boyfriend, someone Hartley didn't know about. You suggested that yourself yesterday."

Sophia nodded. "I know. But I've been thinking about it, and I don't see how Marcy could have carried on an affair without Hartley knowing about it. She lives right next door. It's her house that Marcy lived in. She'd be paying attention to what happened over there."

"What's the second problem?" Courtney asked Fallon.

"Even if Sophia's right," he said, "it doesn't get us very far. Say he hates fat women—"

"Women of size," said Sophia.

Fallon smiled, a tolerant, patronizing smile. *The Return of the Incredible Jerk.* "Fine. Women of size. Say he hates them. For whatever reason. How does that help us nail him?"

"First," said Courtney, "let's find out whether he's done this before. Jim, you send the details to VICAP, find out if they've got a similar. Sophia, you run your idea past Dr. Swanson." She glanced at her watch. "She'll be here in half an hour."

Courtney looked at Fallon, who was frowning. "What?"

"Nothing."

"Come on, Jim. What is it?"

"Swanson. I'm not comfortable with bringing in a hired hand. You start getting leaks. I've seen it happen."

Courtney shook her head. "I've worked with her. She's good, she's smart, and she's discreet. She's actually met the victim, which is more than any of us can say. And she volunteered her help. We need all the help we can get, Jim. The chief, the mayor, they're both climbing up my back."

Fallon shrugged, his face empty. "Whatever you say."

"When you were in New York," Courtney asked him, "did you ever work a serial?"

"No. But I've got a suggestion."

"Go."

"I hope Sophia's wrong, and this guy isn't a serial. But if he is, we'd be better off with more tech people. Nothing against Larry Schnabel and nothing against Kitty. But if this guy hits again, we should ask the Sheriff's Department for some county techs."

Courtney turned to Kitty. "Any problems with that?"

"No. The county techs are all good."

Courtney nodded. "Anything else, Jim?"

He shook his head.

"Okay. You think of anything, you let me know." She glanced around the room. "That goes for all of you."

She moved her legal pad slightly to the right, looked up. "One more thing. The press. You all saw the papers this morning?"

Sophia had—before the meeting with Courtney, Fallon had shown her *The St. Petersburg Times*. The lead article on the front page had been coverage of Marcy's death. They hadn't mentioned her by name, but they'd described the mutilations accurately, quoting "a source close to the investigation."

"No-comment them," Courtney said. "The press. Refer them to Sergeant Morton. He'll be handling media relations out of City Hall. As for the public—the witnesses, the cranks, whatever—I've got Smith and Jeeter working liaison. They're on a special line, and if they get anything that sounds promising, they'll send it on to you, Jim."

She looked at her watch, looked up again at Fallon. "I talked to Harrison. The autopsy's at twelve. You and Sophia are going?"

"Wouldn't miss it for the world," he said.

Chapter Nine

What've you got against psychologists?" Sophia asked him.

"Nothing," Fallon said.

They were in the interview room, the two of them sitting on one side of the Formica-topped table. The walls here were white, and they were trimmed with dark blue. White and blue were the colors of the Greek national flag, and most of the station was done in the same color scheme. Sophia, who had grown up in a house where the Greek flag was displayed as often as the American, had always seen this as a Good Sign—as an indication that she was supposed to be here.

The interview room had no window. A one-way mirror was on the south wall, and the only people it fooled were the ones who had never seen an episode of *Law and Order*.

"You don't seem very happy about Swanson," Sophia said.

"Some shrinks just don't know when to keep their mouths shut."

Sophia smiled. "That's exactly what their job *is*, Fallon. Keeping their mouths shut."

"Some of them don't do it very well." His hand slapped lightly at the cigarettes in his shirt pocket. He frowned, as though he'd just re-membered that he couldn't smoke here, and let the hand fall to the table. He rearranged the manila envelope he'd brought with him, and then he smiled at her, a smile that was just a shade too quick. "That was a good idea, by the way. The fat-woman thing."

Changing the subject.

"Women of size," she said.

"Right. Let's be PC."

"PC's got nothing to do with it. It's not their fault. For most of them, it's a glandular problem.' "

"Yeah. They eat so much their glands all weigh a hundred pounds."

She shook her head. "I never knew you were a bigot."

He seemed genuinely surprised. "You've got to be kidding."

"You—"

A knock at the dark blue metal door.

Sophia stood up, glad for a chance to disengage before the conversation became a fight. And before Fallon saw how close to home it was hitting.

She walked around the table and pulled open the door.

Out in the hallway, Dr. Eva Swanson smiled a brilliant smile.

Last year, Sophia had met Swanson only briefly. Lieutenant Courtney had introduced her to the doctor while Sophia was hurrying through the hallway at the beginning of her shift. But even in those few minutes, she had found the woman intimidating—the tall, elegant body, the expensive clothes, the effortless grace.

Now, face-to-face with her again, she wished that she'd decided to wear something a bit more stylish than the Liz Claiborne blouse and skirt she'd thrown on this morning.

In her midthirties, Swanson was wearing a blouse and skirt as well, but the blouse was crisp gray silk and the skirt was crisp off-white linen, and each looked as though it had been tailored to her poised frame about fifteen minutes ago. A thin brown leather belt, flat against her flat stomach. A delicate watch with a band that matched the belt. Sheer nylon stockings. Gleaming gray leather pumps that were probably Ferragamos. And a sleek gray leather shoulder bag that was definitely a Prada. Sophia had owned cars that cost less.

The air in the room had suddenly been lightened by the scent of expensive perfume.

Smiling easily, the doctor held out a slender hand. "Eva Swanson. We met last year. Detective Tregaskis, isn't it?"

A good grip. *And* a good memory.

"That's right," said Sophia. "Please come in, Doctor."

But probably she'd dropped in on Courtney first, and probably Courtney had brought her up to speed on Sophia.

Fallon stood. Again Swanson held out her hand. He reached over the table to take it, no expression on his face.

"Detective Fallon," he said. "We appreciate your coming, Doctor. Have a seat."

As Sophia circled the table, Swanson sat down and slipped the strap of the bag from her shoulder with an elegant shrug and let the bag drop to the floor. "God," said Swanson, and smiled. "This *heat*."

But not a hair was out of place, no perspiration glistened on the smooth forehead or the sculpted cheekbones. She was one of those women—how the hell did they do it?—who moved within a private pocket of air conditioning.

Fallon smiled politely. As soon as Sophia was sitting again, he said to Swanson, "We understand you had an appointment with Marcy Fleming a week ago."

"Yes, that's right. It's terrible, what happened to her. Ellen— Lieutenant Courtney—filled me in."

Ellen.

"Could you tell us," said Fallon, "what the two of you talked about? You and Marcy?"

"It was an exploratory session. Our first meeting." She turned to Sophia. "Marcy wanted to know if I could help her do something about her weight."

"Is that what you specialize in, Dr. Swanson? Weight loss?"

Fallon's voice was level, but whether he intended it or not, a hint of something like scorn was in the question. If Sophia could hear it, then probably the doctor could, too.

But Swanson only smiled. "Not really. As a psychologist, I suppose I'm the equivalent of a general practitioner. I do a little bit of everything. But a number of my patients have weight problems, and about a month ago I was part of a seminar on weight control. I hadn't been scheduled to do it, but a friend of mine was ill, and he asked me to substitute for him. Marcy was in the audience, and she called me about a week later and asked if I could set up an appointment. The nineteenth was the first free time I had. Last week."

As she spoke, she moved her glance easily between Fallon and Sophia, talking to both of them, even though it had been Fallon who had asked the question.

Fallon looked up from his notes. "Where was this seminar?"

"At the Don Cesar."

A large, upscale hotel on St. Pete Beach. Pink stucco, palm trees, bougainvillea, strolling musicians at poolside. The doctor's kind of place, probably, but almost certainly not Marcy's. She must've felt totally out of place. She wouldn't have put herself there if she hadn't been desperate.

"Who sponsored the seminar?" Sophia asked.

"The city of St. Pete Beach. It was free, open to anyone who wanted to attend."

Fallon said, "How many people were talking at the seminar, Doctor?"

"There were five of us."

"And afterward, why did Marcy decide to go to you, instead of one of the others?"

"I don't know, really. But I was the only woman on the panel. Some women prefer a male therapist, and some don't. Very possibly Marcy was in the latter category. She never said, and I never asked her."

Fallon nodded, wrote in his notebook, looked up. "So what did you decide? About Marcy's weight problem?"

"It wasn't my decision to make. I spoke with her and explained some of the treatment options." She turned to Sophia. "She agreed to think them over and said she'd get back to me."

"Did she?"

"No."

"Did you follow up on her?" His tone was flat, and yet somehow it managed to sound accusatory. "Call her?"

"Of course not."

"Of course not?"

"Any therapist knows that chasing after patients is counterproductive. You can't coerce someone into getting help."

Sophia spoke. "Did Marcy say why she was looking into therapy now?"

"Yes." She took a breath, let it out. "She said she was tired of being lonely."

Sophia flashed on that teddy bear with the missing eye.

"Yesterday," said Swanson, "when Ellen told me what had happened, that was the first thing I remembered about Marcy. What she'd said about loneliness." She turned back to Sophia. "I think she believed that she hadn't lived much of a life. But I'm sure she didn't want it snatched away from her."

Reluctantly, Sophia found herself warming to the doctor.

67

Fallon apparently didn't. In the same flat tone, he said, "Why do you think she never got back to you?"

"I've no way of knowing. But perhaps she simply decided that therapy was too much effort."

"Why would that be?"

"As I told her, obesity doesn't readily admit to treatment. Even with a total lifestyle change, the weight reduction will almost never approach the patient's expectations."

"Why's that?"

She smiled. "To be honest, we don't know. For reasons we don't understand, obesity is a chronic condition, and probably hereditary. Generally the best that we can do, right now, is get the patients to commit to a long-term management program. With exercise and proper diet, they can improve their quality of life. They can reduce the comorbidities, like hypertension, associated with obesity. And those are, I think, very valuable goals."

"They'll still be fat," said Fallon. "But they'll be healthy."

"They'll be healthier," said Swanson, "yes. And their weight will differ, yes, from current norms. But remember, those norms are determined by cultural factors. There's a difference between someone who's morbidly obese and someone with a large body type." She smiled. "Once upon a time, you know, a size fourteen was considered sexy."

"One upon a time, rape and pillage were considered sexy."

The Incredible Jerk Returns Again, thought Sophia.

But again Swanson only smiled. "In some cultures they still are."

Before Fallon could respond to this, Sophia said, "But that's the best anyone can do? No one can help them lose all the weight?"

"Well," said Swanson, "I'm not a physician, but there are some medical alternatives. There's surgery, of course. Liposuction, for example. And a technique called VBG—vertical banded gastroplasty. A large portion of the stomach is basically stapled off."

"Carnie Wilson," said Sophia.

"Exactly. But it's a fairly drastic procedure, and it really should be done only on people whose obesity is immediately life-threatening."

"What about drugs?" Sophia asked.

"Some of them help with weight reduction, but not very much, and for not very long. When they're discontinued, the weight returns."

"Getting back to Marcy, Dr. Swanson," said Fallon. "Did she tell you anything about her personal life?"

"No. Only what I've said. That she'd been feeling lonely lately."

"She mention any friends, people in the area? Boyfriends?"

"No. I assumed she had none. No one close."

Fallon nodded.

"I'm sorry I can't be more helpful." She looked at Sophia. "But Lieutenant Courtney said you had an idea about her killer?"

Sophia glanced at Fallon. He gave her a small, almost invisible shrug, and she turned back to Swanson. "I think that maybe he chose her as a victim because she was overweight."

Courtney obviously hadn't briefed Swanson on everything. For the first time, the doctor seemed confused. "*Because* she was overweight?"

"You'd have to see what he did to her. He—"

"We've got pictures," said Fallon, and picked up the manila folder from the table, held it out. "Take a look."

Swanson reached for it.

Sophia said, "They're rough, Doctor. Very rough. He was brutal." As Swanson took the envelope, Sophia glared at Fallon. He stared back for a moment, expressionless, before his glance shifted to Swanson.

Swanson opened the envelope, slid out the stack of Polaroids. She placed the empty envelope on the table, looked down at the top photograph, frowned for a moment, then made a small sound that might have been a sigh. She looked up at Fallon, narrowed her eyes slightly, looked at Sophia, and finally looked back down at the photograph.

She slipped the topmost photograph to the rear of the stack. As she stared at the next photo, she sighed again.

Neither Fallon nor Sophia spoke as Swanson went through the pictures. When she was done, she used both hands to tap the stack on the tabletop, arranging it, then carefully she placed it on the envelope. Facedown.

She said to Sophia, "Yes, I'd call that brutal."

"They tell you anything?" Fallon asked. Once again, despite the flatness of his tone, he managed to convey a measure of scorn, the skeptic at the Tarot reading.

For a moment or two, she said nothing. At last she smiled. It was a sad smile. "Who was it, Detective?" she asked him.

"Who was who?" said Fallon.

But it was clear that he knew exactly what she meant. He reached again for the cigarette he couldn't smoke. He stopped himself, put his hands on the arms of the chair, stared at her with transparent defiance.

"The person close to you," said Swanson, "who had a bad time with a psychologist. A relative? A wife?"

Fallon said nothing.

"It had to be someone close. And it had to be something bad."

"I don't know what you're talking about." Fallon cleared his throat, as though it were clogged with the obvious lie he'd just told.

Holy shit, thought Sophia.

Swanson sat back in the chair. "I'm sorry. It's none of my business. But I think we should get a few things straight before we go any further."

She crossed one long elegant leg over the other, crossed her long elegant arms beneath her breasts. "I feel bad about Marcy Fleming's death. There may be, in those feelings, a sort of residual guilt. We all like to believe, no matter how illusory a belief it is, that we have some control over what happens around us. There's possibly a small part of me that thinks that if Marcy had only gone into therapy with me, then perhaps none of this would've happened. But that's nonsense, of course."

She looked down for a moment, looked back up. "The fact remains that I still feel very bad about her death. I met the woman only briefly, but I think I have some sense of who she was, of how sad and lonely she was. So last night, when I spoke to Lieutenant Courtney, I had no difficulty at all in offering my help, for whatever it's worth. If I can do anything about the person who did that"—she nodded toward the photographs—"then I'm happy to do it. But there's really not much point in my being here if I have to keep wading through your hostility."

Fallon said, "Now listen, Doctor—"

"May I finish please?"

Raising his eyebrows slightly, he gestured lightly with his right hand, *Go ahead,* then put the hand back on the arm of the chair.

Dr. Swanson placed her hands along the arms of her own chair, fingers gripping it, and now the two of them, she and Fallon, were sitting in almost exactly the same position. Facing off, from opposite sides of the table.

"If you like," said Swanson, "I can tell Lieutenant Courtney that you and Detective Tregaskis and I got together, and that we'd come to the mutual decision that my involvement here wouldn't be helpful. No reflection on any of us."

Giving him an out. Smart woman.

Fallon stared at Swanson for a moment. He looked down, took a deep breath, looked up at the doctor, expelled the breath slowly between slightly pursed lips. Suddenly his face relaxed into a smile. "Okay," he said. "I'm being an asshole. I apologize. If you have any advice to offer, I'll be glad to hear it."

Sonofabitch.

Chapter Ten

So that was all it took.

A few firm words, a steely glance, and Fallon rolled over like a puppy dog.

Of course, it didn't hurt if the words and the glance came from someone who looked like Dr. Eva Swanson.

Dr. Swanson seemed as surprised as Sophia. "Are you sure, Sergeant? I honestly don't want you doing something under duress."

Fallon smiled again, his faint smile. "I hope, Doctor, that you're not one of those people who can't take *yes* for an answer."

The doctor laughed—a light, easy, musical laugh, elegant and charming.

Well, it would be, of course.

Maybe she's a secret slob. Stacks dishes in the sink. Leaves the bed unmade.

"Fair enough," Swanson said. "But please. It's Eva."

Fallon nodded. "Jim."

Sophia realized that Swanson was looking at her expectantly. She smiled, and she could feel the effort of it along her cheeks. "Sophia," she said.

Why the effort? Why the new resentment of Swanson?

Probably because the doctor, basically a passerby, had seen something in Fallon that Sophia, who worked with him, had never seen.

She's a psychologist. She's supposed to see things.

"What do you think?" Fallon asked Swanson. "About Sophia's idea?"

Swanson glanced down at the stack of Polaroids, looked up at Sophia. "You believe that his attack on her, the mutilation, was in some way a reaction to her weight?"

"Isn't it possible? Maybe, for whatever reason, he hates women of size. Maybe he was *compelled* to do that to her."

"Well, yes," said Swanson. "Why not? I've never heard of behavior like that, but one thing I've learned over the years is that if you can conceive of an activity—any activity, no matter how bizarre—then the odds are good that someone, somewhere, is passionately attached to it." She smiled sadly. "Infinite variability. It's one of the glories, and one of the horrors, of the human race."

"You think this guy will try again?" Fallon asked.

"Was it a sex crime?" She turned to Sophia. "Was semen found on the body?"

"The ME hasn't performed the autopsy yet," Sophia said.

"I'm no expert," said Swanson. "But from what I've read, sexual serial killers *are* compelled to repeat their killings. Sometimes the killing is the only way they can achieve orgasm."

"Sometimes?" said Fallon.

"Some of them are married and seem to live perfectly normal lives. But possession of the victim gives him a sense of power, and in many cases that's the only real power he's ever experienced."

"And if there's no semen?" asked Fallon

"Then perhaps it wasn't a sex crime. But clearly he spent a certain amount of time and energy . . . doing that to her. Whatever his reasons, they were compelling to him. I see no reason why they couldn't be compelling again."

She turned to Sophia. "Was anything missing? Clothing, body parts—oh." She looked down at the Polaroids. "I suppose you wouldn't know about body parts . . ."

"We'll know after the autopsy," said Fallon. "But there's a dress missing from Fleming's house. You're talking about trophies."

"Yes." She nodded. "You've already considered that."

"Yeah," said Fallon. "Let me ask you this, Doctor—"

"Eva."

Pretty name. Pretty clothes. Smart, beautiful, graceful.

Maybe she beats her dog.

"Eva," said Fallon. "Is there anything about what he's done, about the way he's done it, that tells you something about him?"

Swanson pursed her lips for a moment. "Psychology isn't an exact science. Whatever I say would be purely speculative."

"Join the club," he said.

She nodded, then looked over at the stack of Polaroids on the table. After a moment she reached out, picked it up, turned it over, and stared down at the topmost photograph. She slipped that photo to the rear of the stack, looked down at the next. "Removing the breasts." She looked up at Fallon. "In a sense he's neutering her. Taking away her femininity. You've seen the prehistoric images of the Great Mother?"

Fallon shook his head.

"Those little statuettes?" said Sophia. "The women with the large breasts?"

"And hips and buttocks," said Swanson, nodding.

She turned to Fallon. "The feminine characteristics, grossly exaggerated. The images represent the goddess as the life force. And in a sense, a woman like Marcy—large-breasted, large-hipped—she'd be a kind of Great Mother image herself, wouldn't she?"

She turned to Sophia. "By mutilating her that way, cutting away those physical characteristics, he'd be stripping away her femininity, removing the symbolic representations of the female, the mother."

"Which would mean?" said Fallon.

"Which would *suggest*," said Swanson, "that he found the idea of femininity, or motherhood, deeply disturbing."

"He hates his mom," said Fallon.

Swanson laughed again. "It's a cliché, I admit. But clichés are clichés for a reason."

"What turns someone into a serial killer?" Sophia asked.

"We really don't know. Something congenital, perhaps, a basic flaw in the wiring of the brain. Or perhaps it's environmental—sexual abuse, possibly. Most sexual sadists, as children, were sexually abused themselves. Possibly the abuse disassociates them from a sense of self, turns them into sociopaths, people with no sense of the reality of other human beings."

Sophia nodded. "What else should we know about him?"

"Fantasy is probably very important to him. He probably fantasized about doing this for a long time before he actually did it. And then, at some point, something came along and triggered him—the precipitating stressor, they call it—and he converted the fantasy to reality."

"*Something,*" said Sophia. "What, for example?"

"We've no way of knowing. It would be unique to him."

"Will his friends," Sophia said, "his neighbors, anyone, have any idea what he's really like?"

"People like this, they live behind a mask. As I said, the man you're looking for may seem perfectly normal. Very likely no one suspects that he's harboring a monster inside him."

Fallon nodded. "So what else? About serial killers?"

Swanson shrugged her elegant shoulders. "Just what's in the textbooks. As a child, this man was probably a bed wetter. He probably set fires, and he probably tortured animals. Those three behaviors show up in the childhood of nearly all sexual serial killers."

"And now?" said Sophia.

"He's probably between twenty and forty years old. He's probably single and white."

Fallon smiled bleakly. "That narrows it down some."

"His intelligence," said Swanson, "is probably higher than average. And there's a statistical probability that his name is Wayne or Ricky Lee."

"You're kidding," said Sophia.

Swanson smiled, taking an obvious and almost childlike pleasure in Sophia's surprise.

Sophia, almost against her will, found Swanson's pleasure disarming.

"No," said Swanson. "Honestly. A surprising number of them really *are* named Wayne or Ricky Lee."

Sophia turned to Fallon. "We round them all up. All the Waynes and the Ricky Lees. Then we beat them to a pulp until one of them confesses."

Fallon shook his head. "Liberal judges," he said, "they'd toss out the confession. Best thing to do is just shoot 'em all."

"The liberal judges?" said Swanson.

"Them, too," said Fallon.

Swanson laughed.

"Okay, look," said Fallon. "From everything I've read about these people, the serials, they have a cooling-off period between killings."

"Usually they do, yes. They tend to reconstruct the event, relive it in their minds, until the memory of the experience no longer serves to satisfy them."

"You think our guy's like that?"

She hesitated for a moment. "Well, that missing dress. That's suggestive, I think. The killers who take trophies use them in their reconstructions. The trophy is a link to the victim, a link to the crime and the excitement it created."

"Is that a yes?"

She smiled. "A tentative yes. But I'm going out on a limb with it. We just don't know enough. We know that he'll be under quite a lot of *external* pressure not to repeat the crime. Having committed the first one—this *is* the first one?"

"Far as we know," said Fallon.

"Well, having committed it, he's brought himself to your attention. You people know he's out there. And he knows that."

"But he has internal pressures, too," said Fallon.

"Exactly, yes. If the killing did excite him, if it empowered him in some way, then sooner or later he'll want to repeat the experience. Sooner or later, the trophies, the memories, won't be enough. I'm oversimplifying here, but when the internal pressures are more powerful than the external pressures, then it's possible, perhaps even likely, that he'll kill again."

"But you think the odds are good that he won't be doing it for a while."

"They're good, I think, yes. But we have no idea how good. And we have no idea how long 'a while' might be."

"Psychology isn't an exact science."

She smiled again. "So I understand."

Fallon nodded. "Is there anything else you can tell us? About this guy, specifically?"

"What else can you tell *me*? About him?"

"He was careful. No one saw him come or go. He brought everything he'd need. A plastic tarp. A hammer. The knives."

"And he left a piece of meat in a plate on the stove," said Sophia. "Cooked. It could have been a piece of human flesh. We had it tested, and it was beef."

"He wanted you to believe it was human?"

"He wanted us to wonder, I think."

Swanson turned to Fallon. "So he's toying with you."

"Yeah. He also left an impression on the mattress in the bedroom, an outline of a body. We think it's a fake. He wants us to think we have his dimensions."

She nodded. "Arrogant. Manipulative." She pressed her lips together for a moment, shook her head lightly. "He's really an asshole, isn't he?"

Fallon smiled. "That a technical term?"

She shook her head. "I don't like this man. He clearly thinks he's smarter than you are. *You* collectively. The police. Very likely he got a big thrill out of leaving that meat. And very likely he's familiar with police procedure."

"He's a *cop?*" said Sophia.

"No, no. What I meant was, he knows something about the way you people conduct an investigation. He's read books, perhaps, or he watches those crime programs on television."

"Our crime scene technician said the same thing," Fallon told her.

"You photographed the impression in the mattress?"

He shrugged. "We had to. It might not be fake."

"I think he knew that you had to. Just as he knew that you had to test the meat." She looked at Sophia. "Has he contacted anyone? You people? The media?"

"No. You think he will?"

"It's possible."

"I'm looking forward to hearing from him," said Fallon.

"I'm not saying that he will," Swanson said. "Only that it's a possibility."

Fallon nodded. "Anything else?"

She glanced down at the photographs, looked back up at him. "May I think about it?" She turned to Sophia. "I've got some papers at home, some studies, some reports, and I can make a few phone calls."

"Sure," said Fallon. "But about the phone calls. We don't want to go public with any of this yet."

"I understand. I'll stress the need for discretion."

"Fine," said Fallon. "If you do come up with something, I'd be grateful if you could get back to us as soon as possible." He shifted slightly, reached around to his back pocket, slipped out his wallet. He removed a card and scribbled something on the back. "There's my cell-phone number. You can reach me anytime."

"Thank you," said Swanson, taking the card and getting out a leather business-card holder from her shoulder bag. "And here's my own cell number. You're better off using this, rather than the office number."

Fallon took it. "Thanks."

"I'll call as soon as I can." She looked at her watch. "I really should be getting along. Unless there's something else?"

"No," said Fallon. "Thank you. Like I say, we appreciate the help."

Swanson stood, slipping the strap of the bag onto her shoulder. She smiled her brilliant smile and held out her hand. Fallon took the hand, shook it, released it. Swanson turned the smile to Sophia. "Good to meet you both." Her blue eyes were direct and open as she shook Sophia's hand. "I hope I can help."

Sophia's smile now, to her surprise, was effortless. "Hey, Wayne and Ricky Lee. That's already a start."

Swanson squeezed Sophia's hand, released it. "I hope I can do more."

Fallon opened the door and held it. "Thanks again."

Swanson moved gracefully through the doorway and Sophia could hear her heels clicking down the tile floor of the hallway. The expensive perfume lingered in the air.

Fallon looked at Sophia. He smiled. Faintly. "I need a cigarette. Want to join me?"

LEANING BACK AGAINST THE WIRE fence that enclosed the marina, his brown hair snapping in the breeze, Fallon cupped his hand around the Bic lighter. Finally he managed to get the cigarette going. He inhaled deeply and slid the lighter back into his pocket. Exhaling, he turned to look out over the water.

After a moment he said, "It was my wife." He didn't look at Sophia.

She turned to him.

"She was on Prozac. She committed suicide." He sucked on the cigarette, then turned to her. The smoke streaming from his nostrils was whipped away by the wind. "The shrink who prescribed the Prozac never mentioned that possibility."

She studied his profile, the crease curved alongside his mouth, the thin white lines radiating from the corners of his eyes out along his tanned cheeks. Keeping her voice level, she said, "He didn't follow up on her? The shrink?"

"*She.*"

Oh, dear.

"No." He gazed off at the boats, or off at his past. "But I can't put all the blame on her. I should've asked around, gotten a second opinion. I should've watched Laura more carefully. She seemed better. Right up to the end, she seemed better. And that was all I cared about. I was relieved. I was *pleased.* I could go on my merry way, get back to work. Focus on *myself.*"

"Fallon, in a situation like that, there's nothing wrong with being pleased."

He turned to her and smiled his faint smile. "You don't get it. I didn't pay attention. I didn't *want* to pay attention."

"But—"

He shook his head impatiently, waved the hand that held the cigarette. "Okay, look. It doesn't matter. It's history. I only mentioned it because I wanted you to know why I acted like an asshole in there. I was being stupid. Swanson didn't prescribe the damned Prozac."

"She's not a psychiatrist. She can't prescribe drugs."

"The point is, she worked me over pretty good in there, and I deserved it. You were there, you saw it, you've got a right to know what was going on. All right?"

"Sure. All right." A good trick, very male—lob a bomb into the center of the table and then refuse to talk about it.

Fallon nodded, took another drag on the cigarette, then ran it against the wires of the fence and knocked the burning ash from its tip. The ash tumbled to the grass and Fallon stepped on it. Tucking the butt into his shirt pocket, he looked at Sophia. "So what did you think of her? Swanson?"

Sophia still wasn't sure what she thought of Swanson. She had liked the doctor's delight in her little Wayne and Ricky Lee number. And she had liked her direct blue-eyed gaze, and the way it kept including Sophia in the conversation.

On the other hand, it was hard to feel entirely enthusiastic about a woman who wore Ferragamo shoes, and wore them so well.

"She's smart," she said.

Fallon nodded, his face as noncommittal as her answer.

"What did you think?" she asked.

He shrugged. Lightly, dismissively. "She's smart."

As if he hadn't noticed that she was also goddamned gorgeous.

IN THEIR CUBICLE ON THE FIRST FLOOR, while Sophia started work on the reports, Fallon used his computer to log on to LEO, Law Enforcement Online, and upload the details of the Fleming murder to VICAP—the Violent Criminal Apprehension Program, the Department of Justice clearinghouse that kept nationwide records of violent crimes.

There were two long gray metal desks in the detective unit's cubicle. Sophia and Fallon sat at one of them, at opposite sides. The other desk belonged to the two other detectives in the unit, Joe Gall and Sam Durrell, who were working a series of burglaries in the high-rise apartments along the Gulf coast of the island.

As Sophia worked, from time to time she glanced over at Fallon. His head bent slightly forward, his face expressionless, he tapped away at the computer keyboard with two stiff index fingers, his hunt-and-peck nearly as rapid as Sophia's touch-typing.

Laura.

His wife.

What had she been like? Tall? Short? Blonde? Brunette?

And how had her suicide affected Fallon?

What a stupid question.

How had it been for *her,* before she'd done it?

Being married to a cop was no picnic. Being married to Fallon— what had that been like? Had he always been so guarded, so hidden? Had his distance contributed to her depression?

Three weeks ago, when she first partnered with him, she had occasionally caught herself glancing over at him speculatively. At nearly fifty, he was a good ten years older than any man she had ever been involved with. But he was lean and fit—way too lean and fit for someone who ate the kind of junk he ate—and he had the leathery good looks of those silly cowboys in the old Marlboro ads.

She had wondered once or twice what he might be like in bed. Would he be as controlled there as he was on the job? Or would he be one of those men who seem cool and calm at first, but who startle you with the wildness of their passion, the depth and breadth of their abandon?

That kind of speculation went nowhere. It couldn't. She cared too much about the job to put it in jeopardy by fooling around with Fallon, or with any other cop.

Not that Fallon was exactly hot to fool around. With most men, from the way they held themselves, the way they spoke to her, she usually got a feeling that in one way or another they responded to her as a woman. Even the men who never made a pass, who never stepped over the line, or never stepped up to it—she could sense that at some level they recognized her as a woman.

With Fallon, there was nothing. No glint in the eye, no suggestion in the voice, típota.

She had believed that this indifference, this distance, was simply a part of him, just another piece of the package. Now she wondered whether it was scar tissue, left there by the wound of his wife's suicide.

Typing at her own keyboard, she glanced over at him. He was still pecking away. There was something charming about it, a grown man typing like a little boy, all his attention utterly focused on what he was doing.

And in a weathered kind of way, like those cowboys, he wasn't a bad-looking guy, really . . .

Oh, for God's sake. Shut up.

Just then, her telephone rang. Fallon stopped pecking and looked over at her.

She picked up the receiver. "Tregaskis."

"Detective, there's someone here to see you." Joyce Hancock, the receptionist. There was something in her voice—amusement?

"Who?"

"Dave Bondwell. The reporter? From WPOP?"

"If he needs something, he can get it from Morton, across the street."

"He says it's important. He says he'll wait."

81

"Tell him I'll be right there." said Sophia.

Fallon sat back and raised his eyebrows slightly, inquisitively.

"Dave Bondwell," she told him, and stood up.

"And who's Dave Bondwell?"

"News anchor. WPOP."

He nodded. "Right. I've seen him. Great hairspray."

"He says it's important."

"Important to who?"

"Him, probably."

She was expecting Fallon to remind her about following the rules—No Talking to the Press. She was surprised and pleased when he merely nodded and said, "Don't be too long. We've got to get over to the ME's office."

He bent over the keyboard again, index fingers poised.

She glanced over the Plexiglas divider that ran along the top of the cubicle, toward the lobby, where Dave Bondwell would be waiting. Once again she wished that she'd worn something other than Liz Claiborne.

Chapter Eleven

Joyce Hancock was in her fifties, a thin woman who wore her dense blond hair in a sculpted perm that was as rigid as a football helmet. She had a dirty mind and a dirtier mouth, and she always reminded Sophia of *Théa* Eleni, *Mamá*'s sister, and Sophia's favorite aunt.

When Sophia came through the swinging door, Joyce was sitting behind her desk. Sophia glanced around the narrow lobby. Thin sunlight, filtering through the wall of smoked glass that faced the street, glowed along the white tile floor. But no one else was in the room.

Joyce looked up from the paperback book on her desktop and leaned toward Sophia. "He's outside," she said in a stage whisper. "Waiting for you."

"Did he say what he wanted?"

Joyce looked toward the smoked glass. "Whatever he wants, give it to him. He's a studmuffin."

Smiling, Sophia crossed the floor, opened the door, stepped out into the glare of sunshine. There were two benches on the green grass, one of either side of the walkway that led to the steps at the station's entrance. Dave Bondwell sat on the bench to the left, in the shade cast by a tall palmetto. As she approached, he rose smoothly, smiled, and held out his hand. He was still better looking than he looked on TV, and taller. And his hair was different somehow.

"Dave Bondwell," he said as she took the hand. Another good grip.

"Detective Tregaskis."

No hairspray, she realized. The thick black hair was loose and floppy, ruffled by the breeze. Fallon had been right—on television, Bondwell's hair looked as stiff as Joyce's.

"I'm not disturbing you, am I?" he asked her.

"I've got a few minutes."

He gestured toward the bench. "You want to sit down?"

She sat down at one end of the bench. He took the other.

He was wearing leather sandals, neatly pressed white Dockers, and another snugly fitting shirt, a gray T-shirt today. Very casual, very revealing. Maybe Fallon didn't exercise, but Dave Bondwell obviously did. You didn't get biceps and pectorals like his without putting some serious effort into it.

Ridiculously, Sophia found the expanse that separated him from her, the three feet or so of shiny green wooden slats, to be oddly comforting, a zone of protective space. She felt she could use some protective space.

"This is kind of awkward for me." He smiled. Awkwardly.

"What is?"

"Well, yesterday, at the briefing, I was impressed by the way you handled yourself. It's not easy to keep your head in a room filled with reporters."

She smiled. "I didn't really have much to do. Mostly I just sat there."

"Yeah, but I liked the way you sat there." He chuckled, shook his head, ran his hand back through his hair. It all looked very boyish and charming, and Sophia wondered how many times he'd done it before, and how successfully.

Ease up.

"I'm not doing this very well, am I?" he said.

"I don't know what you're trying to do, Mr. Bondwell."

But she was beginning to suspect.

Studmuffin Comes On to Lady Cop!

"Dave," he said.

It was a day for first names.

"This isn't a professional visit," he added.

"Oh?"

"I—all right, look." He glanced away, leaned forward, clasped his hands together. His biceps swelled against the gray cotton—an inadvertent reflex, no doubt. He looked down at the ground for a moment, then looked over at her. Earnestly. "Like I said, I'm not very good at this. But I *was* impressed by you yesterday. I was wondering if . . ."

He shook his head and then grinned, displaying quite a few perfect, perfectly white teeth. "God, I'm being an idiot. What I was wondering, would you like to have dinner with me sometime?"

"When?" she said. Calmly, flatly. Ms. Sophisticate.

Laughing, surprised, he sat back. "That's great. You mean it?"

"Sure."

"Tonight? I'm off tonight. Are you free?"

"Where?"

"The Bistro Chartreuse?"

Famous for its duck, it was the best, or at any rate the most expensive, restaurant on Treasure Island, the next barrier island north.

"What time?" she asked.

"Seven-thirty?"

She nodded. "I'll meet you there. Do you have a phone number, in case something comes up?"

"Sure, sure." He tugged a black eel-skin wallet from his back pocket, flipped it open, pulled out a business card, handed it to her. "That's the cell phone."

"Thank you. If you need to reach me, you can call the station."

"I'll make the reservations." He grinned again. "Great. I look forward to it."

"One thing."

His face clouded slightly. "What?"

"No shop talk. Nothing about the murder."

He showed her the palm of his right hand. "Hey. Absolutely not."

She stood up, held out her hand. "I'll see you there."

He stood, shook the hand. "Question, Detective Tregaskis?"

"What?"

Straight-faced, he said, "Would it be okay, when we're having dinner, if I called you Sophia?"

She smiled. "Of course."

"Great." He grinned. "Great. I'll see you then."

Nodding, he turned and strode down the walkway.

Tucking his card into the pocket of her blouse, Sophia turned back toward the entrance to the station.

You handled that pretty damn well, she told herself. Cool as a cucumber. As cool and calm and collected as Fallon.

Except that Fallon's breathing probably wouldn't be a bit strained, and his palms probably wouldn't be sweating.

It could be that Bondwell was looking to weasel a way into the investigation.

Well, it would cost him an expensive meal to find out that she wasn't it.

Could be, though, that Bondwell *did* have the hots for overweight Greek-American lady cops.

Studmuffin Weds Lady Cop! Bride's Mother Implodes!

Joyce looked up from her book and raised her eyebrows. "Well?"

"Nothing. Some questions about the case. Like I thought. I sent him across the street."

Lies, in the circumstances, were easier than the truth.

When Sophia returned to the cubicle, it was Fallon's turn to look up and ask a question. As she'd expected, it was the same question. "What'd he want?"

With Fallon, the truth was easier. And safer—because almost certainly he'd sniff out a lie.

"He asked me to dinner."

He sat back against the swivel chair and stared at her for a moment. "The guy's got some balls, hasn't he? Showing up here, asking you out."

"How else is he going to find me? My number's unlisted."

He nodded. "You probably don't want to hear my famous lecture about reporters and how they're like cops. How they're never off duty."

"Fallon, he says one single thing, asks one single question about the case, and I walk away from my duck."

"Duck?"

"We're eating at the Bistro Chartreuse."

"Upscale. You know about Caesar's wife, right?"

"Why? Does she eat there?"

He smiled. "What I'm saying is, if there's ever a leak on the case, and you've been seen with what's his name—"

"Bondwell."

"—Bondwell, then you're going to get nailed, whether you talked about it or not."

"Thanks. And I promise to get the car back before midnight, Dad."

He smiled. "Okay. Fine." He looked at his watch. Looked up. "Ready for the autopsy?"

"Sure."

"We've got some time. You want to eat first?"

She was ravenous, but this would be only her second autopsy—the first had been Mrs. Dougherty, the woman who'd been beaten to death by her husband. And that autopsy, as depressing as it was, had been a lot more straightforward than this one promised to be.

"That's okay," she said. "I can wait."

As usual, Sophia drove and Fallon sat slouched in the passenger seat. As they rolled from the station's parking lot, he turned to her. "Kinkaid called."

"About the tarp?"

"Yeah. Both Kmart and Wal-Mart carry it. So does AutoZone, so do all the other auto-supply places. But no one keeps a record of who buys them."

"Not even for inventory?"

"For inventory, yeah. But those records aren't tied into the credit-card receipts. And, even if they were, most likely our guy paid cash."

"Like you said," she reminded him. "He left it because he knew we couldn't connect it to him."

He nodded. "He's beginning to piss me off." He turned to look through the window.

The water of the Intercoastal was a bit choppy, its blue flecked with whitecaps—*aphrós,* the foam that in mythology had given birth to the goddess Aphrodite. Only a few sailboats were out there, and these were heeled over, away from the wind.

Hard to believe, under the sunny sky, that only a few hundred miles away a hurricane was churning through the Gulf of Mexico.

On the mainland, Sophia took Seminole Boulevard north. She could remember passing along here with her parents, on their way to visit *Téo* Alexi, her mother's younger brother. And now *Téo* Alexi lived in Miami, with a new wife and two new children. Two new cousins for Sophia.

So many uncles, aunts, great-uncles, great-aunts, cousins once and twice and three times removed. Relatives scattered all over Florida, as far north as Pensacola, as far south as Naples. When she was a little girl, she had believed that the entire United States was populated with members of her extended family.

When she was little girl, someone like Marcy Fleming would have been incomprehensible.

How could anyone exist without family? Without the huge get-togethers at Easter and Name Days, the clatter, the clamor, the laughter, the teasing?

Even now, knowing that not everyone had a family like hers, a network of cousins and aunts and uncles, she couldn't help but feel sorry for someone like Marcy, someone who seemed to have no one, seemed to be a part of nothing.

Had that made her eating problem worse?

Did people like Marcy eat to fill an unfillable emptiness? To acquire, in the food itself, everything they lacked, everything they felt was missing in their lives? Was food a substitute for closeness, understanding, love?

There's a great theory, *koritsi mou*. Make sure you run that one by Eva Swanson.

She'll probably puke into her Prada bag.

No. Like Swanson said. It was probably all hereditary.

But if that were true, why was it that her cousin Eleni, Miss Goddamn Citrus Groves of 1992, could eat like a horse and stay as thin as a stick? When Sophia gained five pounds just by reading the label on a Snickers bar?

Because, *koritsi mou*, Life Is Basically Unfair.

She glanced at Fallon. Still staring out the window, his face expressionless.

She realized that she had been daydreaming, trying once again to avoid the reality of the moment.

The reality of the moment was the autopsy of Marcy Fleming.

Chapter Twelve

Propelling the shopping cart lightly with the tips of his fingers, humming softly to himself, Robert ambled down the condiments aisle. He saw that his favorite chipotle salsa was on sale—what a nice piece of luck!—and he plucked a bottle from the shelf and set it in the cart.

He had nearly finished with the shopping. Carefully arranged along the bottom of the cart were the Belgian endives, the small packet of Roquefort cheese, the package of unshelled walnuts, the snow peas, the green peppers, the vine-ripened tomatoes, the tuna steak, the plump heads of garlic. And now the chipotle salsa.

But the shopping, this afternoon, was merely incidental; this afternoon he was on a quest. This afternoon he was looking for a new Wibble-Wobble.

According to all the experts, of course, he shouldn't be searching for the next one so soon. He'd read the literature, naturally, and he knew that these things were supposed to proceed with a certain measured, and measurable, escalation. Four weeks (or some other, more or less arbitrary, length of time) should pass, and then another incident should occur, this one more violent than the first. And then three weeks should pass, and then another incident, still more violent, frenzied even; and then two weeks and yet another incident, demonic this one, blood on the chandelier, eyeballs in the vichyssoise, shiny bits of gore oozing off the place mats . . .

Yes, but that really applied only to those poor lost deluded souls, the ones driven by obsessions and compulsions. People like Jeffrey Dahmer and John Wayne Gacy. Like that silly Englishman, Nilson.

They were seriously flawed. Captives, all of them, of their own delusions. Slaves to pleasure, every one. None of them had a Crusade, none of them had a Cause.

Not that there was anything fundamentally wrong with pleasure.

Remembering Marcy, Robert thought: indeed. Nothing wrong with it at all.

But in the end, as Marla used to say, pleasure must always be balanced by duty.

Ah, Marla. She had changed him, changed him for the better in every way. He hated to think what his life might've been like without her.

Looking around now, he realized that he had wandered into the wine department. Fortuitous. He needed a nice white to go with the stir-fried tuna. Something not too terribly dry. Yes, perhaps that Riesling . . .

He was reaching for the bottle when, out of the corner of his eye, he sensed a bulky pink figure go plodding, wibble-wobble, past the opening of the aisle, thirty feet away.

What have we here?

Unhurried—at this point he was merely curious—he put the wine in the cart, turned the cart, veered it toward the opening.

He emerged from the aisle and turned right, moving along the admirable fish department—drifts of crushed ice piled with shiny beached schools of silvery trout, throngs of fat gray shrimp, heaps of muscular pink scallops.

Up ahead he saw the bulky figure go waddling through the produce section, past the carefully arranged pyramids of tomatoes and onions, toward the frozen foods.

Passing the meat department, he glanced to his left. Behind the glass divider, a butcher in a stained white coat hacked at a leg of lamb with an enormous cleaver.

No finesse at all.

He remembered the carving knife sliding into Marcy so smoothly, so effortlessly, that it seemed to be discovering, as it moved, an opening in the flesh that had already been there, eagerly awaiting the caress of the blade. He remembered the chef's knife easing through tissue and tendons, remembered the bright red blood fanning out along the tarpaulin . . .

He felt, once again, the tingle at the base of his belly. He felt the strength begin to leave his knees.

No, no. Back to work.

Where's my Wibble-Wobble?

He glanced around.

Ah. There. Admiring the frozen foods.

He ambled toward her.

The size was right. Not quite as massive as Marcy, but a plenteous Wibble-Wobble indeed. A good three hundred pounds of her, stuffed into a ridiculous pink sweat suit. White ankle socks, a pair of inexpensive white running shoes.

Blond hair, cut short, looking stiff and freeze-dried. Maybe thirty years old. Hard to tell from the rear.

The Wibble-Wobble stopped in front of one of the freezers and opened the door, her flesh shuddering beneath the fabric of the sweat suit. Behind her, Robert adjusted his sunglasses and then slowly cruised by.

A quick glance at her ring finger.

Plump and pale, but empty. Therefore no husband.

A glance into her cart.

No milk cartons, and therefore little likelihood of children. Four cans of cat food, but no dog food at all. No dog. Lovely. Dogs could be nasty.

A sixteen-ounce box of Hamburger Helper—the elegant cheddar-cheese-melt version. Very promising.

A thirty-two-ounce jar of Cheez Whiz. A sixteen-ounce package of sliced Velveeta. Because one can never have enough processed cheese, can one?

A two-pound package of Lykes all-beef bologna. A sixteen-ounce bag of peanut M&M's. A ten-ounce bottle of Maalox. But of course.

A four-ounce tube of Preparation H. Not much of a surprise there, either.

What's that she's taken from the freezer?

Oh, *very* good. Ore-Ida bacon-and-cheese-whipped potatoes. The two-pound package.

You are definitely in the running, my dear.

But just as he slid past her cart, Robert noticed another Wibble-Wobble to his right, heading toward him as she lumbered past the produce counters.

This one was perhaps ten years older than Pinkie, and she wore a pale green dress—Wibble-Wobbles were drawn to the pastels like moths to a flame.

Like that awful old dress of Marcy's, that hideous blue thing he'd stuffed into a garbage bag and dropped into the Dumpster behind Wal-Mart.

He wondered if anyone had found it. Maybe some poor homeless woman. Some poor homeless woman who needed a sail for her yacht.

Or maybe the police.

He hoped not. He rather liked the idea of them thinking he'd taken it from Marcy's house. As a trophy. Isn't that what those nasty serial killers did? A compulsion with them, apparently.

Maybe someone had found that brush from Marcy's vacuum? Probably not. It was probably still resting comfortably in another Dumpster, at the opposite end of the island. Like the vacuum bag, cosied up to the refuse in yet another Dumpster.

There was a great deal, in the long run, to be said for Dumpsters.

He cruised toward Greenie, humming again.

Greenie had a few pounds on Pinkie. Probably totaled out at around 320. A dark blue cotton bandanna over pink hair rollers, a charming note. Perhaps forty years old.

Behind the sunglasses, hidden, invisible, his eyes moved and he took inventory.

No ring. No milk cartons. No dog food.

A large box of Cracker Jacks. A six-pack of Bartles & Jaymes strawberry wine cooler, ghastly stuff. All by itself, my dear, that was enough to put you solidly in the running.

A two-pound package of Marie Callender's extracheese lasagna. (Processed cheese being, of course, a consistent motif within the Wibble-Wobble community.) A stack of Banquet frozen dinners. A sixteen-ounce package of cool ranch Tostitos. An eight-ounce jar of Tostitos bean dip. A box of Entenmann's glazed doughnuts.

Sitting prominently at the front of the cart, atop a mutipack of Brawny paper towels, was a large box of supersized tampons.

Showing off a bit, are we, my dear?

I may be on the plump side, but I can still bleed and breed.

Yes, sweetie, and we all take enormous comfort in your reproductive faculties.

Just then, Greenie surprised him. She stopped beside a row of romaine lettuce. As she began to search through the heads, fondling them with thick spatulate fingers, Robert was forced to swerve his cart around her. He cruised over to the melon display, picked up a cantaloupe, sniffed it thoughtfully, tapped it, glanced back at Greenie.

She set a head of lettuce in her cart, then wobbled over to the tomato section.

Setting down the cantaloupe, Robert sighed. If she'd picked iceberg, a mediocre veggie, Greenie would still have been in the running. With the romaine, she had disqualified herself.

Which was a terrible pity. Because, God knows, something really should be done about those rollers.

Perhaps he could, in this case, make an exception . . .

No. Fair is fair.

He glanced around. Where had Pinkie gone?

For nearly five minutes, he rolled his cart up and down the aisles— condiments, baking, canned vegetables—but he couldn't find her and began to worry that she'd slipped away.

And then, retracing his way through the juice section, he saw her wobbling toward him.

He adjusted his sunglasses.

Wonderful. Still no milk. No romaine. And looky, looky—some splendid new grub in the stash:

A package of six Jell-O tapioca-pudding snacks.

A pack of Orville Redenbacher's cheddar-butter microwave popcorn. The *triple* pack. Thinking ahead, eh, Pinkie? Planning. I admire that.

And the crowning touch, the pièce de résistance: two half-gallon bottles of diet Coke. The miracle elixir that would magically prevent any of the other items from adding even a molecule of fat to Pinkie's lovely form.

Ah, Pinkie. Lucky girl. You are the one.

The one who'll reach perfection.

Chapter Thirteen

I prefer to start with the brain," said Dr. Harrison, using a T-shaped chisel to pry off the cap of the skull. "Quite a few pathologists like the chest cavity." Within the white lab coat, he shrugged. "To each his own."

Still tainting the air, despite the air conditioner, was the smell of scorched bone. It had been there since the electric saw had sliced, whining like a dental drill, into the naked pink skull.

Mixed with it was the stench of old cigarettes, rising off Harrison like gas from a swamp.

So far, Sophia hadn't regretted her decision to pass on lunch.

Behind her, lying on one of the room's two stainless-steel tables, still in the black bag into which they had been packed, were the body parts found in the bathtub at Pelican Way.

Keeping her breathing even, she looked down at the other table.

What had once been Marcy Fleming lay there flat and motionless, a large, limp red flap of scalp drawn down over the forehead, concealing the skeletal face and those dull blue eyes. After a full day's exposure to the air, the raw tissues of the body had grown even darker and more crusted over, giving it the look of a burn victim.

His voice picked up by an overhead microphone, his movements captured on video by a pair of automatic cameras, Dr. Harrison had kept up a running commentary as he worked. He had weighed and measured the flesh-stripped corpse ("One hundred and forty-five pounds, five foot three inches tall"), used a long syringe to extract cerebrospinal fluid from between two of the vertebrae, and swabbed the mouth, vagina, and rectum. There was no bruising in any of them, he'd announced, and little likelihood of sexual assault. No semen was visible, but the tests to determine its presence, or its definite absence, would take twenty-four hours.

Before stripping back the scalp, he had determined that the welt on the back of the skull had not been caused by a professional sap. "It appears to me," he had said, peering at the wound through a large, illuminated magnifying glass, "from the abrasions, that it was probably something improvised. A stocking, for example, filled with bird shot. Bird shot or BBs."

"Something," Fallon said, "that anyone could put together."

"Yes."

"Are there any fibers?" Sophia asked him.

"No. The wound's been cleaned."

She looked at Fallon.

He shook his head. "Like I said. This guy is really beginning to piss me off."

Now, delicately, Harrison set the cap of pink, glistening bone, curved surface down, on the slanted surface of the table. It tipped slightly forward and wobbled there for a moment. Sophia could see that Harrison had sawn along the fracture he'd mentioned yesterday—on one side of the cap, at the edge, was an irregular semicircular indentation. The indentation made the cap look—absurdly, horribly—like an ashtray she had created for her father many years ago, at a pottery class in summer camp. *Papá* still had it, still kept it on the mantel beside a photograph of smiling Sophia, one plump hand raised, waving toward the unseeable future from that distant summer.

Sophia wondered whether she'd ever be able to look at the ashtray again without thinking of Marcy Fleming and what had happened to her here.

Harrison picked up a long-bladed knife, bent forward, slipped it into the skull cavity, and began to move it gently, like a finicky waiter sectioning a large grapefruit.

"Massive hemorrhage," he said. "Epidural hematoma. As I said yesterday."

And so it went, the long, complicated, pitiless process that reduced a human being to clinical questions and clinical answers, to excised organs and extracted fluids, to a carefully ransacked corpse and an orderly collection of packaged specimens. Talking away, Harrison worked smoothly and methodically, his white lab coat and latex gloves growing less white as he continued. He weighed the brain, opened the body from sternum to pubis, took urine samples from the bladder and blood samples from the heart. ("Not the best place—it can be contaminated by blood from the liver—but there's not much of it anywhere else.") He removed and weighed the stomach contents, the liver, the small intestine. The room became crowded with smells.

From time to time, Sophia glanced over at Fallon. His face remained expressionless and his eyes remained hooded, as though he had been through this thousands of times before. Which, of course, he probably had.

At the end, after Harrison had washed up and Fallon and Sophia had countersigned the labels on the sample containers, Sophia asked the doctor, "What about the rest of her?" She nodded toward the plastic bag on the other table.

"I'll be going over the, ah, pieces, of course. They may show bruises or wounds. Or bite marks, possibly. But as you can imagine, that may take a while. It'll all be on my final report."

"And afterward?"

Harrison seemed puzzled. "Afterward?"

"Will you be"—she tried to think of a good way to say it—"reconstituting the body?"

"Oh, no, no. No, that's a job for a mortician. Assuming it's even possible, which I doubt."

"Is there anything missing?" Fallon asked. "Any body part?"

"I don't believe so, no. Hard to tell exactly, of course. Lieutenant Courtney says you have a next of kin?"

"Yeah. In Buffalo. I'll call her later, tell her what you said. What about time of death? Can you give us anything?"

"Aha," said Harrison. "Well. We'll be able to make a rough estimate from the blood serum. Serum leaches from the blood cells, postmortem, at a measurable rate. But I thought you might want some corroboration."

"What kind of corroboration?

Harrison smiled. "It was your idea, actually. Come along."

Fallon and Sophia followed him across the tile floor. Harrison opened the door for them and said, "I have a cousin in the poultry business. He knew someone, as they say, who knew someone else."

Sophia wondered, the poultry business?

Harrison led the way down the corridor. "Once I was able to locate a subject," he said over his shoulder, "I had to persuade the chief to let me perform the experiment. The chief pathologist. Dr. Headley." He chuckled. "She thought I was crazy."

Locate a subject? Perform the experiment?

She glanced at Fallon. He shrugged—*Beats me.*

"But I persuaded her," said Harrison, "that the operation would prove instructive. Here we are."

They had come to another door in the hallway. Harrison turned the knob, stepped in, hit a light switch, and held the door for Sophia and Fallon. She glanced at Fallon. He waved her in.

"I've kept the temperature in here," said Harrison, "the same as it was at the house on Pelican Way. Approximately seventy-five degrees."

It was another operating room, smaller than the room that held Marcy Fleming. The air carried the same smell that had thickened the air at the cottage on Pelican Way, the smell that had reminded Sophia of Uncle Costas's butcher shop in Tarpon. Over the single operating table, someone had arranged a blue plastic tarpaulin identical to the one left at the cottage. On top of that, someone had placed a large dead pig.

The pig wasn't merely dead. Someone—Dr. Harrison?—had done to it what the murderer had done to Marcy Fleming. The ravaged body lay on its side, most of its skin and large chunks of its tissue sliced away. Flesh had been peeled from its face—the ragged pink skull, bracketed by large, tufted ears, was grotesque. Bulbous yellow eyes stared out sightlessly at Sophia.

Harrison pulled a pack of Marlboros from the pocket of his lab coat. "It's all right to smoke." He offered the pack to Fallon.

"No thanks, I've got my own." Fallon plucked the pack of Camel Lights from his shirt pocket. Harrison lit Fallon's cigarette with a gold lighter.

"We couldn't get the animal in here until after eleven last night," Harrison said, exhaling. "It's technically a hog—did you know that?

Any commercially raised swine that weighs more than a hundred and twenty pounds is a hog. Kortchmar explained that. This was a female. A sow."

"Kortchmar?" said Fallon.

"The butcher who helped me with the work."

"The butcher," repeated Fallon.

Sophia was beginning to feel like Alice in Wonderland.

"Mr. Fenneman's idea," said Harrison. "Mr. Fenneman is the farmer who provided the animal. He offered us a discount if we could save parts of it. Kortchmar took them with him when he left."

Fallon nodded. "Waste not, want not."

"Exactly." Harrison smiled. "And the chief, I can tell you, was very pleased about the discount. She keeps a close eye on the budget."

"I'll bet," said Fallon. As Harrison walked toward the pig, Fallon glanced at Sophia, smiled faintly, and briefly raised his eyebrows.

Sophia bit her lip.

"You do know, of course," said Harrison, looking down at the animal with a sort of paternal pride, "that the pig has a metabolism very similar to that of a human being. It's quite possible that one day the hearts of pigs will be routinely transplanted into humans. Genetically modified pigs may very well be farmed for their organs."

"That right?" said Fallon.

Still admiring the pig, Harrison nodded. "Oh, yes." He looked up at Fallon and Sophia. "Well, in any event, as soon as Kortchmar killed the animal, at midnight, we started work. We finished at a little after two."

"How'd he kill it?" Fallon asked. He glanced down at the ash building up on his cigarette and looked around the room, saw an ashtray on a cabinet, picked it up.

"A kind of stun-gun apparatus," said Harrison. "It fires a twenty-two-caliber bullet directly into the brain. It's very humane—death is nearly instantaneous. I felt it was important that we kill the animal here, you see, just before we started. I wanted to duplicate, as nearly as possible, the actions of your killer."

"Sure," said Fallon. He looked at Sophia.

"We had some advantages over him, of course." Harrison took another drag from his cigarette. "There were two of us, for one thing, and both of us had some idea what we were doing. Kortchmar is very good at his work. And having the table was enormously helpful. We kept it tilted, and we simply sluiced away the blood as it appeared."

"Handy," said Fallon.

"Very." Harrison leaned forward to tap his ash into Fallon's ashtray. "Well, as I say, we finished just after two o'clock. Your killer was working on his own, and he would've taken more time than we did. Anyway, we washed up the remaining blood, leveled the table, and I took photographs."

He turned to the sink and doused his cigarette under the faucet. From the counter he took a small stack of Polaroid photographs.

"Here." He showed the first of the photographs to Fallon and Sophia.

"This was taken," said Harrison, "just after we sluiced down the tarpaulin for the final time and leveled out the table. You see? No fluid." He slipped the photo to the back of the stack. "This one was taken an hour later."

"You stayed here all night?" Fallon asked.

"There's a small sleeping cot in the east wing of the building. I set my alarm clock to wake me at every hour. The whole point of the exercise, after all, was to document this. You see the fluid? It's beginning to form small puddles. And here, an hour later, you see? More fluid."

Sophia said, "How accurate is this, Doctor?"

"Relatively accurate, I believe. The victim's total weight was approximately three hundred and forty-five pounds. We calculate that by adding up the body and the body parts, and adding the estimated weight of the lost blood. The sow weighed three hundred and fifty pounds. Close enough. We removed an amount of tissue roughly equivalent to the amount removed by the killer."

Fallon asked, "How long did it take to match the liquid on the victim's tarp?"

"Here." The doctor quickly shuffled through the photographs until he found the one he wanted. "This one was taken at eleven o'clock this morning. And here's the photograph I took of the victim at one o'clock yesterday afternoon. You can see that the amounts of residue are very similar."

"You started taking the photographs at two," Fallon said. "So we're talking nine hours."

"Exactly, yes. And so, counting back from one o'clock, we arrive at a time of four in the morning."

"That's when he stopped working on her," said Fallon.

Harrison nodded, looking pleased. "Exactly, yes. Four o'clock in the morning."

"But suppose," Sophia said, "he stayed around for a while, after he finished. An hour or two. And suppose that before he left, he wiped the tarp down again. Wouldn't that throw off your results?"

Harrison stared at her. "Why on earth would he remain there? He was *finished.*"

"I don't know," she said. "He wanted to admire his work, maybe. This guy isn't exactly normal."

Harrison shook his head impatiently. "He had no reason to remain in the house."

"Yes, but—"

"And he'd have absolutely no reason to wipe down the tarpaulin again. He'd accomplished what he set out to accomplish."

"Sure, Doctor, but—"

"So you'd be willing to testify," Fallon said, with a warning glance at Sophia, "that the killer finished his work at approximately four o'clock?"

"Yes." Harrison looked at Sophia, looked back at Fallon. He raised his head. "Absolutely."

"And how long did it take him to do that to the woman?" Fallon jerked his head toward the pig.

"Four hours, at a minimum. More likely five."

"So he probably killed her sometime between eleven and twelve."

"Yes. All these times are rough estimates, of course. But I'd be willing to wager that the blood serum will verify the approximate time of death."

Harrison looked at Sophia again, as though daring her to contradict him.

She glanced toward Fallon.

"That's great, Doctor," Fallon held out his hand. "You'll send us your report?"

Harrison shook Fallon's hand, released it. "Of course. The toxicology tests will take a while, but tomorrow I'll send you what I have."

He didn't offer his hand to Sophia. She didn't offer hers.

"Great, Doctor," said Fallon. "Thanks."

SHE KEPT HER MOUTH SHUT until the two of them were outside the building. As they stalked down the concrete sidewalk, she turned and said, *"Fallon—"*

He held up a hand. "I know, I know."

"A good defense lawyer—"

"I know. But it gives us a rough estimate to work with."

A gust of wind blew Sophia's hair across her face. She brushed it away with a quick, impatient flick of her fingers. "We already had a rough estimate. Fallon, that autopsy didn't give us anything at all."

They were in the parking lot. She suddenly stopped walking. "Shit." Fallon took another step, then stopped and turned to look back at her.

"What?"

"We're not going to stop him, are we?" She heard the forlorn note in her voice, the hopelessness, the resignation, and she hated herself for it. All at once she felt heavy and clumsy and powerless. "This asshole. He's going to do it again."

"We'll stop him."

"We don't have anything—"

"We'll find something," Fallon said. "You heard Swanson. If he's a serial, we've got some time. These bastards take time out between attacks. Weeks, months, sometimes years. And meanwhile we'll be looking for him. We'll find something."

"Swanson said *maybe* he'd take time out. What if he doesn't?"

He shook his head quickly, stubbornly. "We'll find something."

She took a deep breath, sighed it slowly out. "I hope so, Fallon."

"We'll find something," Fallon said again. "We've got time."

It occurred to Sophia that maybe she wasn't the only person that Fallon was trying to convince.

Chapter Fourteen

From the front seat of his car, Robert watched as Pinkie lumbered alongside the Albertson's bag boy who slowly rolled her shopping cart to a small, white Subaru station wagon. The bag "boy" must have been in his eighties and he looked seriously unwell. The station wagon looked even more unwell. The side panel on the passenger's door was deeply dented, the rear fender was missing. The radio antenna was twisted like a pretzel.

But, as usual, the gods were with Robert, because the car was parked only about fifty yards away, out in the open, away from any others. Through his Zeiss binoculars he had an excellent view of its license plate and he neatly wrote down the number: HC182L.

A passerby, observing him, might wonder what he was up to. But in fact no passerby would ever observe him. Behind the tinted windows of his car he was invisible.

At the rear of the station wagon, Pinkie spent some time rooting through her purse before she finally came up with the keys. She unlocked the back door, raised it, then stood back as the bag boy lugged the bulging plastic bags from the cart and set them, one by one, on the bed of the wagon.

The woman stood there, watchful, wary, as though convinced that if her attention wandered for even a second, the old man would sweep all her goodies into his arms and go scrambling with them down the street.

When he finished shifting the bags, he looked over at her. She nodded. Through the binoculars, Robert could see her lips moving in a curt "Thank you."

No tip, of course—Albertson's discouraged tips. And a good thing, too—why give money away when you can spend it on microwave popcorn and tapioca-pudding snacks?

The bag boy nodded back, not terribly surprised, then slowly swung the cart around and slowly began to push it back to the store.

Pinkie waddled to the driver's door, fumbled with the key at the lock for a bit, then opened the door.

Robert started his engine.

THE NEXT PART WAS RATHER EXCITING. Trailing Pinkie to her lair.

Keeping a reasonable distance behind her car, Robert followed her as she made a right turn onto Williams Avenue from the Albertson's parking lot. Once on Williams, he slowed down, letting two cars pass his and tuck themselves between him and Pinkie. Two cars, he felt, created a properly discreet buffer. James Bond would entirely approve.

At 145th Street, she turned left. So did Robert. He had lost his buffer, but he was perhaps a hundred feet behind her. Safe enough. She was almost certainly not expecting to be followed.

Low self-esteem, Pinkie. You underestimate your many charms.

She was heading west, toward the Gulf side of the island. It would be marvelous if she lived somewhere along the shore—a house on the shore would make his work ever so much easier.

Then he remembered that this stretch of the Gulf shore was the most expensive area of the island, spangled with pricey high-rise condominiums and apartments.

High-rises were completely out of the question, of course. Too much security, too many potential witnesses.

But judging by that battered Subaru, it was unlikely she lived in one of those.

At Horner Street, ten blocks from the beach and the mammoth, irregular wall of high-rises that stretched for a half a mile in either direction, gleaming against the pale blue sky, Pinkie turned right. Still a hundred feet behind her, Robert followed.

This was a mixed, but definitely lower-income, neighborhood. Small cottages, frame or cinder block, were blended with occasional one-story brick apartment buildings where exhausted cars dozed in raggedy parking lots.

If Pinkie lived in one of the apartment buildings, Robert would be forced to disqualify her. It would be a great pity, because she was otherwise ideal. But it simply made no sense to take chances. Not when there were other Wibble-Wobbles waiting out there, virtually thousands of them.

Robert glanced from side to side as he followed the Subaru.

Most of the meager plots of land that surrounded the cottages were bare and bleak, untended, treeless, the yellow lawns balding in the sunlight. Some had children's toys scattered about—a tricycle, a bicycle, a large purple plastic dinosaur. The driveways, for the most part, were graveled rather than paved.

And it was—lovely!—into one such driveway that Pinkie drove the Subaru.

No children's rubbish littering the lawn. No fence that might signal the presence of a large, surly canine.

Children's rubbish did, however, adorn the lawns on either side of Pinkie's cottage.

Splendid. Parents with children went to bed early.

The shuffle of slippers growing closer, left, right, left; squeak of bedroom door; creak and sway of mattress; smells of vodka and cigarette smoke; wobble and shiver of flesh; those stubby fingers reaching for him, warm and moist and greedy . . .

No, not all parents went to bed early.

Robert shook his head. Enough. We have work to do.

Pinkie's cottage had been built of cinder block and painted a jaundiced yellow. Two louvered windows, each curtained with lace, looked out onto the street from either side of the front door.

Cruising by, Robert glanced at the mailbox. No name, only a number: 2441.

You're not making this easy for us, my dear.

But we have ways of making you talk.

FIFTEEN MINUTES LATER, in the St. Anselm Public Library, Robert had opened up a copy of the 1999 J. B. Ballin *Pinellas County Directory*.

Years ago, when he was in high school, he had discovered an earlier version of the big book, and he had marveled at it. It was absolutely jam-packed with useful information; and often he had copied a few names and numbers from the listings and taken them home. Sometimes, when the Cow wasn't around, he would call up the people and pretend to be an irate bill collector. Or the police.

It had been great fun, and it had given him a wonderful sense of power.

These days, of course, he knew much more about power. And these days the research, while still great fun, was also Very Serious Business.

He flipped through the book. The green pages, in the third section, contained the streets directory. He turned them. *F . . . G . . . H . . .* Halloway. Hope. Horner.

Horner Street from 140th to 160th Street.

Street numbers: 2000 . . . 2210 . . . 2333 . . . 2400. And bingo: 2441. Purdenelle Cyndi at 218-7154.

Listing your phone number is often a serious mistake, Cyndi my sweet.

But he was tickled by that cute, diminutive *i* at the end of *Cyndi,* suggesting an owner who was equally cute and equally diminutive. A sea sprite, possibly, or a wood nymph.

He flipped to the white pages, the alphabetical directory, and he riffled through the *P*'s. Payne. Pearce. Pearlman. Peasley. And there it was, the second of two entries:

PURDENELLE.

"Brian and Nora technician Brandon Industries apt35 1001 Bellevedere Lane S. St Petersburg 33700."

"Cyndi nurse Mercy Hospital h2441 Horner St St Anselm 33899."

The first entry meant that Brian Purdenelle, a technician at Brandon Industries, whatever that might be, lived with his wife, Nora, in apartment number 35 at 1001 Bellevedere Lane South in St. Petersburg.

Bellevedere Lane South was in the black section of the city, which meant that good old Brian and his lovely wife were unlikely to be any relation to Cyndi the Sea Sprite.

Cyndi lived alone in that house (h) at number 2441 Horner Street, and the odds were good that she had no close relatives in the area, or at least none that bore her surname.

Perfect.

Well, no. Not exactly perfect. Not yet. But moving toward perfection, certainly. Moving steadily, one might say. Moving inexorably.

And Cyndi, it transpired, was a nurse at Mercy Hospital. A caregiver. How charming. Pass the scalpel, would you, Cyndi?

SITTING IN FRONT OF THE COMPUTER, Robert reached for his wine.

FastSearch, true to its name, delivered its results in 0.0973 seconds: "0 documents found."

Ah, well. He hadn't really expected this to be easy. But he felt that he should know at least as much about Cyndi as he had known about poor Marcy. Fair, after all, is fair.

Robert decided it might be fun to get Cyndi's Social Security number. He was feeling awfully creative today.

Chapter Fifteen

Fallon was tired. Sitting in Courtney's small office, Tregaskis beside him in the other chair, all he wanted to do was go home, pour himself a drink or two, or three, and then pour himself directly into bed.

It was the autopsy. He's seen way too many autopsies over the years. The autopsy and that ridiculous pig.

"Okay," said Courtney, and turned to Tregaskis. "What did Swanson say about your idea?"

"She says it's possible. She's going to look through her papers, call some people, see if she can come up with anything."

Tregaskis was holding up well. If she'd flinched during the autopsy, Fallon hadn't seen it. And even now, at the end of the day, she looked as alert and sharp as she had in the morning. When she'd been watching him get his ass reamed by Dr. Eva Swanson.

"What'd you think of her?" Courtney asked her.

"I liked her."

Courtney turned to Fallon. "Jim? You can work with Swanson?"

"Sure."

"You sent the report to VICAP?"

"Yeah. But as usual, it'll be few days before we hear anything. Even if they do find a match. And I don't think they will. I think that if our guy had done this before, it would've made the news. The national news. We would've heard."

"I agree." Courtney glanced down at a legal pad on the table. "Okay. The Buffalo cops are on the ball. They talked to the cousin, got the name of the dentist, talked to him, got a copy of Marcy's dental records. They've faxed it to Harrison at the ME's office. We should have a positive in an hour or so. As soon as we do, we'll release

Marcy's name to the media, along with the photo from her driver's license. Maybe someone saw her with our guy."

"Harrison didn't say anything about the dental records," said Fallon.

"This just happened. And we took a look at Fleming's bank account. No recent withdrawals. What about the autopsy? Anything useful?"

"Not much we didn't already know. It doesn't look like she was sexually assaulted. Anything from the D to D?"

"We've got confirmation," Courtney said, "on the Last Seen Alive. A neighbor up the street saw Marcy walking down Pelican Way at a little before four o'clock."

"From the beach," said Tregaskis. "According to Hartley. Do you think the beach is where he first spotted her?"

Courtney nodded. "Good question." She turned to Fallon. "Have some uniforms do a D to D along the beach. Half a mile north and south of where Pelican hits Gulf. Maybe our guy talked to her, maybe someone saw him."

"I know we've got to do it," Fallon said, "but I don't think they'll come up with anything. I don't think he'd talk to her, and if he did, I don't think he'd do it where he could be seen."

"Maybe not. We'll see." Courtney turned to Tregaskis. "Where else could he have seen her?"

"She didn't work. Didn't go out much. Shopping? She had to buy groceries. She didn't have a car, so the nearest place would be the Kash N' Karry on Gulf. That's only four or five blocks away from Pelican. There's a 7-Eleven on Gulf, too, a couple more blocks north."

Courtney turned to Fallon. "Did the landlady say where Marcy did her shopping?"

"No. I'll call her."

He should have asked the woman, he knew that. But at the moment he was too tired to kick himself. "And I'll have some uniforms get copies of the register tapes from the stores. Maybe he used a credit card. Maybe we can use that, down the road."

"He probably used cash," said Tregaskis.

He shrugged. "Got to do it." He turned to Courtney. "Anything from the liaison people? Smith, Jeeter?"

"They've logged a couple of hundred calls," said Courtney. "Including five or six confessions. But nothing that looks good."

She glanced down at the legal pad, looked back up. "Okay. Here's where we are. We've got people checking state and local records for all the crazies. We'll have someone talk to all of them." She looked at Fallon, who was frowning. "I agree," she said. "It's probably a waste of time. But it's something else we've got to do."

He nodded.

She said, "The Sheriff's Department will handle the county locals, and the Staties will be questioning everyone else. As for us, we'll have some more uniforms back in the neighborhood tomorrow, catching anyone we've missed so far. And you'll have some people work the beach and the markets with Marcy's picture tomorrow."

"Yeah," he said. "But we're spreading ourselves pretty thin."

She nodded. "I've canceled everyone's leave. I want this guy."

Fallon wanted him, too, but he was beginning to think that they were all just treading water. He had sounded convincing, maybe, when he'd told Tregaskis that they'd catch this guy, but he was beginning to believe that they were in this for the long haul. Which meant that sooner or later, no matter what he'd said to Tregaskis, the bastard would kill another woman.

"Okay," said Courtney. "That's it for now. You guys can take off. Except for you, Jim. The chief wants to talk to you."

"What about?"

"He didn't say." Courtney kept her face expressionless, her voice perfectly level, and Fallon knew she was pissed off.

Chief Anderson was probably trying to do an end run around Courtney, and Courtney probably knew that.

"Male bonding?" Fallon said.

Courtney smiled politely.

"I'll let you know," he told her. He stood and looked down at Tregaskis, expecting her to get up.

Instead she turned to Courtney. "Can we talk for a minute?" She looked up at Fallon. "Personal stuff, Fallon."

He nodded. "Female bonding."

Sophia smiled. "Yeah." She turned to Courtney. "Okay?"

"Sure. See you tomorrow, Jim."

AFTER ASSIGNING SOME UNIFORMS TO THE D TO D, Fallon called Mrs. Hartley. As Tregaskis had guessed, Fleming did her shopping at the Kash N' Karry. He radioed the uniforms and told them to check it out, get copies of the register tapes.

Now he sat in the anteroom outside Chief Anderson's office in City Hall, across the street from the station.

He knew that the chief would keep him waiting. Anderson was a politician, and the first thing a politician did, after he settled into his job, was figure out where he fit in the pecking order. The second thing he did was figure out where everyone below him fit. The third thing was to make sure they all knew it.

Fallon looked at Anderson's secretary. In her early twenties, tall and blond, slender, her round breasts thrusting against a short-sleeved, white blouse, she sat bolt upright at her computer terminal, tapping away at her keyboard. She kept her brow furrowed all the while, her lower lip locked between her perfect white teeth. From that, and from the tapping, hesitant and uneven, Fallon was fairly certain that she hadn't been hired for her typing skills.

Whatever else she might be good at, she gave good telephone. The phone rang every five minutes or so, and when it did, she would pick up the headset, coo a breathy "Chief Anderson's office" into it, listen, coo a breathy greeting, and then tell whoever was calling that Anderson was tied up right now, but that he'd return the call as soon as he was free. She would make a note of the caller's name, coo a breathy "Good-bye," hang up, and start tapping away at the keyboard, her brow furrowed once more, her lower lip nipped again between her teeth.

Now, still tapping, she glanced over at Fallon. He smiled and looked away.

She'd surprised him this morning, Eva Swanson. It had been a long time since anyone had seen through him like that, except Laura. And it had been even longer since anyone—except Laura—had dressed him down like that. *May I finish please?* Staring at him from across the desk, cool and remote in her anger, her blue eyes as empty as gun barrels.

"Sergeant Fallon?" The secretary, cooing.

"Yes?"

"Chief Anderson will see you now."

"Thanks." Fallon stood, walked across the thick gray carpeting, opened the door to Anderson's inner office.

Behind the broad mahogany desk, Anderson stood up. He was dressed in a gray suit today, as sleekly tailored as his uniform, the pin-striping so subtle it might have been imaginary. "Sergeant Fallon," he said, holding out a hand. "Good to see you."

Fallon crossed the floor—the carpet here was a large red-and-black Persian that extended over the parquet floor nearly to the darkly paneled walls—and took the meaty red hand. "Chief."

"Sit, sit," said Anderson, waving him to a padded leather chair. "Take a load off."

Fallon sat down and so, behind the desk, did Anderson. Sighing, the chief ran a hand back over his thick, white hair. "What a mess, eh? I've been on the phone all day. The press, the television people, some folks from Tallahassee."

Tallahassee, Fallon knew, meant the Florida state legislature.

"What did they want?" Fallon asked. "The folks from Tallahassee?"

"Wanted to keep on top of things. This is turning into a big story— the newspapers are all over it, like flies on a shitburger. I told 'em we had a handle on the situation." He smiled, his teeth gleaming white in the broad, ruddy face. "I hope that's true, Jim. I wouldn't want to drag my dick on this one."

"We're doing everything we can, Chief."

"What've we got so far?"

"Lieutenant Courtney is in a better position to say than I am."

Anderson nodded, as though he didn't know bullshit when he heard it. Fallon, the investigating detective, was required to know everything about the case. But according to department protocol, Anderson was obliged to get his briefings from Courtney.

An end run. As Fallon had thought.

Anderson wanted his own man on the case, reporting back to him, and Fallon had just been offered the job. And he had just turned it down.

With his whiskey flush and his capped teeth, his sleek suits and his country-club smile, Anderson would be easy to underestimate. But Fallon had been around enough politicians to know that it was generally not a good idea to underestimate them.

Abruptly, Anderson smiled. "You're off duty now, right, Jim? Care for a snort? Someone gave me a nice bottle of single-malt. Lagavulin. It's an Islay. Sixteen years old."

"Sure."

"Ice? Water?"

"Straight is fine."

Anderson grinned. "A man after my own heart."

He leaned forward, tapped a button on the intercom. "Julie, grab us that bottle of Lagavulin, would you, hon? And a couple of glasses."

He sat back and sighed again. He pursed his lips thoughtfully and then looked up at Fallon. "It's changed a lot, hasn't it? Since we started out?"

"The job? In some ways, sure. But in the end it still comes down to the same thing."

Anderson nodded. "Catching the assholes." He smiled. "Sometimes, you know, sitting up here, I actually envy you guys out on the street."

Fallon nodded. He knew that Anderson, twenty years ago, had spent maybe fifteen minutes on the street before he transferred to administration.

"I'm not complaining," said Anderson. "I love my job. But sometimes I feel like I've wandered too far away from the trenches."

He looked up as the secretary swept in, carrying a silver tray that held a dark bottle and two crystal balloon glasses. She set it on the desk. "Anything else, Chief?"

Anderson glanced at his watch. "No, Julie. Thanks. You go ahead, hon, take off. Make sure you pull the plug on the phone."

"There are some messages."

"Leave 'em on your desk. I'll take a look before I leave."

"Yes, sir." She turned and smiled at Fallon and then swept gracefully back across the room. Fallon glanced at Anderson, who was watching her with eyes that were half-shut, like a big sleepy predator's.

When she disappeared behind the door, Anderson's face lost the predatory expression and he turned to smile at Fallon. "Good girl." He pulled the cork from the bottle, poured two or three fingers of dark amber liquor into each glass, and leaned across the desk to hand a glass to Fallon. As Fallon sat back, the drink in his hand, Anderson raised his. "Confusion to the assholes."

Fallon smiled, raised his glass. The two men drank.

"Ah," said Anderson, smacking his lips happily. "Lovely stuff. Tastes of the sea."

To Fallon, it tasted of medicine, like most Scotch. But the burn, going down, was as familiar and comfortable as the road that led back home.

Anderson was looking thoughtful again. "Just how well do you get along with Lieutenant Courtney, Sergeant?"

"Fine. She's a good cop."

Anderson nodded. "A good cop. I've always said so. But there are people out there who think she might be over her head here. This is a high-profile case, lot of media attention, and Courtney's never handled anything like it before. There are people who think that maybe we should put together a task force, use the sheriff's people and the Staties. Maybe even the Feds."

Fallon's gut feeling was that the "people out there" probably didn't exist. Another thing a politician learned quickly was the absolute importance of Covering Your Ass, and Fallon was certain that Anderson was scrambling right now to cover his own. If he threw as many resources as possible at the case, no one could ever come back later and say he hadn't done his job.

Anderson said, "I know you headed up a couple of task forces, back in New York, and I know you did an impressive job. You got a commendation on that Briarleigh thing, right? The kidnapping?"

"Everyone got a commendation." Fallon didn't like the way this was going.

"Yeah, but it was your show. You were the honcho. And naturally, if we did set up a task force, we'd put our most experienced officer in command." He smiled a man-to-man smile. "Someone who's handled situations like this before. Someone who's demonstrated his ability."

Fallon took a sip of the whiskey.

It was a lose/lose situation, but he had to admire the way Anderson had eased him into it.

If Fallon—an outsider, the new kid on the block—took over a task force, he'd alienate Courtney and most of the other cops in St.

Anselm. And then he, not the chief, would be the one getting the heat from the media, from the public, from the "folks in Tallahassee."

But if Fallon blew away the idea of a task force, and this guy killed again, the chief could claim that he hadn't set one up because Fallon, the Expert from New York, had argued against it.

Maybe if Fallon had ratted on Courtney, had let Anderson finish his end run, Anderson wouldn't have set Fallon up.

Payback. Payback was another thing that politicians understood.

Anderson looked at him earnestly. "So what do you think? We plug away at this ourselves, maybe drag our dicks, or we call in some help?"

"It's too soon."

Anderson frowned slightly.

"We don't know enough yet," said Fallon. "We're still doing the door-to-door. We're still waiting to hear from the lab. We don't know if this is a one-shot or a serial, don't know if the bad guy is an acquaintance or a stalker—"

"This prick could be a serial?"

"We don't know. But if he is, we may have some time. With most serial killers, there's a waiting period between their killings."

Anderson looked skeptical. "How long a waiting period?"

"Could be months, could be weeks. We don't know. The fact is, we don't know anything yet. Maybe he's a boyfriend. Maybe he's a neighbor. Tomorrow morning, some uniform could walk into a house on Pelican Way and find evidence that puts him away."

Anderson sat back. "And just how likely is that, Sergeant?"

"Not very. But we start setting up a task force now, and it happens, we're going to look like idiots."

Anderson narrowed his eyes.

"And a task force," said Fallon, "is an expensive proposition. We'd need to locate and furnish an operations area. We'd need to hook up computers and telephones, and we'd need to find trained people to work them. And find more trained people to coordinate evidence and witness testimony, act as liaison, handle the tips. And we'd need to find funding for it all."

Anderson frowned again. "I can get the funding. If that proves necessary."

"And maybe it will. But right now we're already getting help from the Sheriff's Department and the State Police. And there's no way you could get the Feds involved at this point. There's only been one crime, and it's in our backyard. The Feds have no jurisdiction."

"If this prick's a serial killer . . ."

"The Feds need three identical crimes before they'll call them serial killings."

"I know. But I spoke this morning to a friend at the Bureau. An exploratory talk. I'm concerned about this case, Sergeant. It impacts the locals and it impacts the tourists. Do you know what percentage of city revenue comes, directly or indirectly, from the tourist industry?"

"No." But clearly Anderson did.

"Over seventy percent. People are worried. *I'm* worried. And I wanted to find out what our options were. You're right, of course—the Bureau won't come in until there are three deaths—and I pray to God it doesn't come to that. But if we need a profiler, they'll lend us one. They've got one who's on vacation right now, just north of us, up in Clearwater Beach. We need him, we can have him here tomorrow."

Fallon shrugged. "Obviously, Chief, it's up to you. But from what I've heard, those FBI profilers aren't everything they're cracked up to be. And Courtney's already brought in a psychologist."

"Who?"

"Swanson. Dr. Eva Swanson. Courtney's worked with her before."

Smiling ruefully, Anderson shook his head. "All these women. The mayor, Courtney. Now a shrink. Like I said, times have changed."

"She's supposed to be good. She helped Courtney grab some kid who was setting fires last year."

"Right, right. I remember her. Good-looking woman. You've met her? What'd you think?"

"She's smart. She seems competent."

"Is she billing us?"

"She volunteered. As a favor to Courtney."

Anderson shook his head. "Get the relationship formalized. Have her sign on as a paid consultant. Whatever the standard rates are. I'll okay the payments. Hiring a consultant, that demonstrates our commitment to finding this son of a bitch."

Fallon nodded. And it helps cover the chief's ass.

Anderson said, "I'll tell Media Relations to mention Swanson in the next press release."

"Maybe I should talk to Swanson first. Maybe she wants to stay low profile on this."

Again, Anderson shook his head. "We need to show people that we're doing everything we can. Explain it to her, Jim."

"I'll try."

"Good." Anderson glanced at his watch. "Everything else all right? You settling down here all right?"

"Everything's fine."

"Great." Anderson looked again at his watch, then tossed back the rest of his Scotch. "Gotta run. I appreciate your stopping by, Sergeant. And I appreciate your candor."

"Glad to help." Fallon finished his drink and stood.

Anderson rose from behind the desk, held out his hand. Fallon took it.

"And if this prick's a serial," said Anderson, "I hope you're right. About that waiting period of yours."

"So do I."

Anderson didn't point out that if Fallon was wrong, it would be Fallon's ass in the sling.

He didn't have to.

Chapter Sixteen

Okay, thought Sophia. Not perfect, but not bad, really.

She stood before the full-length mirror in the bedroom.

She was wearing the sleeveless black Armani silk sheath she'd bought on sale in Miami last year. Even heavily discounted, it had cost more than she had ever paid for a dress before. But *Mamá* had bullied her into trying it out, and once Sophia had slipped it on, she had loved it. The drape of the material, and the subtle darts in front and back, helped create the promise of a voluptuous—but not too voluptuous—form beneath, without in fact revealing exactly what that form might be.

Her hair was fine. She had no problems with her hair. If she were smart, true, she'd wear it shorter in the summer. But it was one of her best features, dense and black and shiny, and now, carefully piled atop her head, it looked . . . well, all things considered, it looked pretty damn good. With those tendrils falling artlessly to her shoulders, it looked graceful and elegant.

Artlessly, right. Five minutes per tendril . . .

The black, high-heeled sandals were okay, too. They weren't Ferragamos, naturally—they were Gucci knockoffs she'd bought at T.J.Maxx—but they were okay. With her toenails carefully painted a dark Midnight Merlot, matching her fingernails, the sandals were sleek enough for her to get by without wearing hose. Wearing her hair long in summertime was one thing. Wearing hose was another.

To jacket or not to jacket? That was the question.

Her arms were okay. A tiny bit—well, alright, they were just a tiny bit *thick*. At least in comparison to the arms of the Kate Mosses, and the Cousin Elenies, of the world. But her skin—thank you, *Mamá*—had always been good, clear and dark, and working with the free weights had given the arms a nice tone. Her arms were okay.

She stood sideways, put her right hand beneath her breast and ran it down over her sternum and over the small swell of stomach.

Oh, dear.

And her upper arm, as it lay flat against her side, *did* seem a bit thick.

Maybe she could hold her arms out from her body all night.

Like a chicken. An excellent look to shoot for.

Okay, we go with the jacket.

Her arms were okay—they were fine, really—but too much exposed flesh on the first date was probably a bad idea anyway.

The *first* date?

SOPHIA DROVE THE BEETLE DOWN GULF BOULEVARD. Occasionally, between the motels and the high-rises that slipped by on her right, staccato blurs of glass and brick, of stucco and steel, she could catch a glimpse of the water. The sun had slid down the sky and it was poised out there, just above a feathery pink ribbon of cloud, getting ready for its plunge into the flat glistening Gulf.

Now that she was actually on her way to meet Dave Bondwell, Sophia suddenly felt guilty.

What right did she have to go out and eat expensive food and flirt with a handsome reporter? (A reporter who might, after all, have ulterior motives for inviting her.) What right did she have to worry about her hair, her clothes, her shoes? What right did she have to enjoy herself, what right did she have to *think* about enjoying herself— while Marcy Fleming was lying on a slab at the medical examiner's office, and Marcy's killer was still out there somewhere?

What if Fallon was wrong, and the killer was getting ready to strike again, soon, any moment now? She and Fallon should be out there doing something, doing anything, to find him.

But, as Courtney had said, the two of them had done everything they could.

Sophia was glad she'd talked to Courtney.

"WHAT'S UP?" the Lieutenant had asked her, after Fallon left the office.

"I just wanted you to know," said Sophia. "I'm having dinner with a reporter tonight."

"Which one?" More curious than inquisitory.

"Dave Bondwell. WPOP."

Courtney raised her eyebrows slightly. "The anchorman?"

"Yes."

Courtney smiled. "You don't mess around. Where are you going?"

"The Chartreuse."

She nodded, still smiling. "I hear the duck is good."

"I just wanted you to know. I didn't want you to think—"

"Hey." Courtney held up a hand. "Your personal life is exactly that. Personal. I know you'll be discreet. But I appreciate your telling me." She grinned suddenly. "You tell Fallon?"

"Yeah. He explained that cops and reporters were a lot alike."

"They're always working?"

"Yeah."

"He's watching out for you."

"I know. And I feel a little guilty about going out, about having a date, in the middle of all this."

Courtney smiled at her. "Look. You've had a rough couple of days. You and Fallon have done everything you can. You go out tonight, and you make sure you have a good time."

"Okay, Lieutenant. Thanks."

But even with Courtney's blessing, she still felt guilty.

It wasn't fair. Poor Marcy lying there dead, while Sophia pranced around in an Armani sheath as though she didn't have a care in the world.

While the son of a bitch who'd killed her was probably already back on the streets, looking for the next one.

Stop it, she told herself. You don't know that.

Fallon is probably right. Probably the slimeball is hiding in some sleazy room somewhere, thinking about what he did, savoring the memory. Probably there *would* be time to find him before he killed again.

But find him how? He might be a slimeball, but he'd been smart enough to cover his tracks.

Let it go. Just for tonight, let it go. Take one night for yourself.

The Bistro Chartreuse sat on a man-made promontory at the northern tip of Treasure Island, just south of John's Pass. Surrounded by a jungle of palm trees and bougainvillea, staring out over the beach and the Gulf beyond, the one-story building of stone and darkly tinted glass had always looked, to Sophia, like a small but efficient fort.

She parked the Beetle in the lot, stepped from the crisp air-conditioning out into the sultry early-evening air, and clicked her way down the pavement to the heavy wooden front door. She could feel her hair beginning to wilt.

Inside, the entryway was cool and dark.

To her left, a short, slender man in a tuxedo stroked his mustache while he studied something on a wooden stand. His hair was slicked back and his mouth was pursed. As Sophia approached, he looked up, raised his eyebrows, shot a glance up and down her body, and appraised and priced everything she wore, probably to within the exact penny.

He seemed to approve. "Yes, madame?" French, or faking it.

"I'm supposed to meet someone. Dave Bondwell?"

"Ah." He was pleased. "Monsieur Bondwell. *Bon.* Monsieur has already arrived. If Madame will follow me?"

Sophia did, into the main room, where candles flickered on the tiny tables and people in expensive clothes sat murmuring to each other. She passed through a small fragrant pocket of Chanel No. 5 as the maître d' led her to the far side of the room, where the wall of tinted glass displayed a spectacular view of the sea and the setting sun.

Dave Bondwell rose from a table that sat alongside the glass. He seemed to hesitate for a moment, as though flustered, then smiled and held out his hand. "Sophia. Good to see you."

Sophia shook the hand while the maître d' beamed happily at the two of them, as though their getting together here had been the result of some clever scheme he had personally hatched.

"Is this okay?" In Bondwell's voice was an attractive, almost boyish uncertainty, the same sort of hesitancy she'd noticed outside the station. "If you want, we can sit outside on the patio."

"This is fine." A few more minutes outside and all that artless hair would topple off her head.

He grinned, as though gratified by her approval.

"*Bon,*" said the maître d', and held her chair back for her. Sophia sat, Bondwell sat, and the maître d' said, "Would Madame care for a drink?"

Madame would care for a stiff shot of ouzo, thought Sophia. For a small-town cop, this was all very upscale.

And it was worlds away from Sophia's office, worlds away from autopsy rooms.

Suddenly an image of Marcy Fleming flashed across Sophia's mind, Marcy lying on the stainless-steel table, blackened and ruined.

She thrust it away and told the maître d', "A glass of white wine, please."

"Chardonnay? Sauvignon blanc? Sancerre?"

"The sauvignon, thank you."

Marcy, we'll find him. I promise. But please let me have a few minutes to myself. Please?

"At once, madame," said the maître d'. To Bondwell he said, "Enjoy your meal, monsieur."

Bondwell nodded. "Thank you, Henri."

As the man strutted off, Bondwell turned to Sophia and grinned. "It's a great view, isn't it?"

"It's gorgeous."

Out there, beyond the dark glass, the sun was as plump as a ripe peach. Peeking out from beneath the glowing ribbon of cloud, it sent a golden stain shimmering across the Gulf. A few people—a young couple with arms around each other's waist, an older couple holding hands—walked slowly across the white sweep of sand. Sophia thought of *Papá* and *Mamá,* their bickering loyalty to each other, their shared moments good and bad. She wondered briefly if one day she'd be able to walk hand in hand down a beach, as the sun set, with someone who knew her as well as her parents knew each other.

"This is my favorite time of day," Bondwell said. "The sunset. Usually I don't get to see it. I'm stuck in the office until way past dark." He took a sip of his drink—a bourbon on the rocks, judging by the color—and grinned again. "You look great, by the way."

"Thank you." She managed to smile without blushing, and without telling him that he didn't look half-bad himself. He was wearing a light gray suit, a blue shirt that matched his eyes, a dark blue tie striped with red. A bit conservative, maybe, but sleek. His hair was loose again, no hairspray. In the light that filtered through the tinted glass, his handsome features seemed softer, less chiseled, than they did on television.

He sat back in his chair and looked at her for a moment. Then he smiled. "So tell me. If you don't mind. How did you get to be a cop?"

"It started with my uncle Niko. My father's brother. He was a fine man, and he was a cop in Tarpon Springs."

"A great place. That's where you were raised?"

She nodded. "You've been there?"

"I love it. There's a restaurant down one of the side streets, about a block from the harbor, on a corner . . . I don't remember the name . . ."

"Maria's. It's very good."

"It's terrific." He grinned. "I ate the best calamari there I've ever eaten in my life."

"And they do a terrific taramasalata."

Sophia suddenly heard herself.

No one can say, *koritsi mou*, that you don't dazzle in the conversation department. *And they do a terrific taramasalata.* Brilliant.

With perfect timing, thank goodness, a waiter materialized at Sophia's left, holding a crystal goblet of wine. "Sauvignon blanc, madame?"

"Yes, thank you."

He set the glass on the table and asked Bondwell, "Are you ready to order, monsieur?"

Bondwell smiled. "I'm not sure, Paul." He turned to Sophia. "Can I suggest something?"

"Sure."

"They've got a couple of ways of doing duck here, and they're all good, but my favorite is the duck *à l'orange Lasserre*. They use a special duck—where are those ducks from, Paul?"

"From Nantes, monsieur. They are flown in each morning." He turned to Sophia. "The duck, it is browned in butter and then roasted. It is served in a sauce of Grand Marnier and apricot liqueur. It is very good, madame."

Smiling at Sophia, Bondwell said, "How does it sound?"

"It sounds wonderful." It sounded as if she'd be eating broccoli sprouts, and nothing else, for the next few days.

"Great," he said. "Okay, Paul. The *Lasserre.*"

"Certainly, monsieur. And vegetables? We have asparagus in a dill sauce, very nice. Young potatoes roasted in the oven. Courgettes *à la anglaise,* with a thyme butter. A pilaf with *petits pois.* And of course a green salad. This we serve with a roast garlic vinaigrette."

"Sophia?" said Bondwell.

"Just the salad, I think."

"Me, too."

Both of them decided that they didn't want appetizers, and that they'd have their salads with the meal rather than before it. The waiter offered to send over the sommelier, but Sophia said that at the moment she was happy with her sauvignon blanc.

"We'll see about the wine later, Paul," Bondwell told him.

"Very good, monsieur."

As the waiter left, Sophia asked Bondwell, "Do you cook?"

"No." He grinned. "I'm a manly man. Single and inept. What about you?"

"Once in a while. Usually I don't have the time."

No wife, no live-in girlfriend. Check.

Bondwell nodded. "Okay." He picked up his drink. "Shall we make a toast?"

"To what?"

He smiled. "To crime?"

"Well," she said, smiling, "maybe that's not . . ."

"And crime fighters." He grinned.

"Fine." She raised her glass and clinked it against his.

After each of them took a sip, Bondwell sat back and said, "Now. Getting back to Uncle Niko . . ."

She was pleased, and a bit surprised, that he'd remembered her uncle's name. But then he was a reporter, and reporters were good with names. "My father was working in Clearwater then, night shifts, and he was almost never around. It was mostly Niko who helped bring me up. Niko and my mother. Niko taught me how to sail. And how to play baseball, and how to box. My mother was horrified by all of it, of course."

Bondwell raised his eyebrows. "Has the boxing come in handy?"

She smiled. "Now and then."

"You have brothers? Sisters?"

"Neither. You?"

"Nope. An only child. And how was Niko a fine man?"

"He was just . . . honest. Completely honest and honorable. And dependable. I liked him a lot."

"Liked?"

"He died last year. Cancer."

"I'm sorry. That must have been difficult for you." He seemed sincere, but reporters, especially anchormen, were good at sincerity.

"It was. But I think he was very happy that I became a cop."

"What about your parents? How'd they feel about it?"

"My father was supportive, he usually is, but my mother didn't like the idea. She came around, though."

Except for the hysterical phone calls whenever a policeman, anywhere in the world, was injured on the job.

"Good for her," he said. "Did you do anything else before you joined the force?"

Sophia told him the whole story, or most of it—college in Tallahassee, liberal arts, a degree that was pretty much useless by the time she received it. A few years working front office for her uncle Mike in his Tampa insurance office, where she'd felt purposeless and unnecessary. Remembering, every so often, how much she'd admired Niko and the work he'd done. Coming to the realization, finally, that she wanted to be a cop. Talking it over with Niko, talking it over with her parents. Moving back to Tarpon. Doing her training at the Police Academy run by the Pinellas County Sheriff's Department . . .

Bondwell was easy to talk to. The boyishness, the hesitancy, disappeared. He asked good questions and he listened well, nodding to encourage her, the blue eyes peering into hers as though he were fascinated by what he was hearing, or possibly by the person telling it to him.

But then he was a reporter, and reporters . . .

While they talked, a busboy brought water and bread and a small, white china tub filled with butter. Restraining herself, Sophia ignored the bread and butter. Or tried to. She also tried to ignore the smells that drifted past her—garlic and thyme and something simmering in wine.

"And why the move to St. Anselm?" Bondwell asked, picking up a slice of bread, his third, but who was counting?

"It's a small town. There weren't many opportunities there for a woman cop."

"Why not Tampa?" He spread a thick pat of butter on the bread.

"I lived there before, when I worked for my uncle, and I didn't really like it. Too big, too hectic. And I wanted to be near the water. The Gulf."

"You said you sailed?" He took a bite of bread.

"A friend of mine has a Hobie Cat. We go out together on weekends. When I can. Why?"

He swallowed. "I've got a small sloop. Not much bigger than a Hobie, really. A day sailer. But a lot of fun." He took another bite of bread.

No wife, no live-in girlfriend, *and* a sloop. And all this in a guy who didn't chew with his mouth open. "You have it moored in Tampa?"

He shook his head. "In Treasure Island. I'm with you—I like being on the Gulf. I live a couple miles south of here, and there's a slip outside my condo."

A boat slip. And Treasure Island was ten minutes away, tops, from her own apartment.

He smiled the self-effacing smile again. "*Condo.* That makes it sound luxurious. It's okay, but it's just a tiny little place. It's got the slip, though, and I like that." He ate the last fragment of bread.

Sophia remembered asking herself why he'd been in St. Anselm on Tuesday. "That's why you were at the briefing on Tuesday? You live nearby?"

He nodded. "I got a call from the station. They needed someone to cover it. They had a crew, sound and video, but no reporter who could get there in time. I was happy to do it. I don't usually get a chance to do any real reporting. Most of the time they've got me stuck behind that desk."

"You don't like the job?"

"It's—*ah.*"

The waiter had arrived, serenely wheeling a cart of wood and brass to the side of their table. Sophia and Bondwell watched as he set out the salad bowls and then, with a flourish, removed the silver dome from the center of the cart. The duck lay there on a platter, dark breast and darker leg meat, all of it carefully sliced, swimming in a shimmering brown sauce.

The waiter set the dome on the shelf beneath the duck. Using a folded napkin to protect his hand, he lifted one of the plates. "These are very hot," he said. "Please be careful." With silver tongs he lifted some slices of duck meat from the platter and set them gently on the plate. "For Madame," he said, and put the plate in front of Sophia.

He lifted a silver sauceboat from the cart. "More sauce." He placed the boat beside Sophia's plate.

A fruity fragrance of orange and apricots wafted up to Sophia.

The waiter prepared another portion of duck for Bondwell and laid the plate before him. He returned the dome to the platter and then set platter and dome on their table. "Bon appétit," he said to them both. To Bondwell he said, "If you need anything else, monsieur, please let me know."

"Thank you, Paul."

As the waiter pushed away the cart, Bondwell picked up his knife and fork, looked at Sophia, and smiled happily. "Go ahead. Give it a try."

She cut a small piece of meat, bit into it, chewed.

"What do you think?"

The meat was rich and tender and moist, the sauce sweet and densely flavored. It was possibly the best food Sophia had ever eaten.

Koritsi mou, you say that about a Burger King Whopper.

But this was truly something special.

"It's very good." She smiled. "It's wonderful."

He grinned. "Good. Good, I'm glad you like it."

But the sauce—anything that delicious, anything that intense, had to pack a least a million calories into each teaspoon.

"Here." Bondwell set down his knife and fork and reached forward to lift the sauceboat. "Have a bit more sauce." He poured some of the translucent liquid, thick with segments of oranges, onto Sophia's portion of duck.

A whole week of broccoli sprouts. Broccoli sprouts and mineral water.

"You were saying," she said, "that you weren't happy with your job?"

Looking up at her, Bondwell chewed for a moment, then swallowed. "Not really, no. It's an ego boost, naturally. And it comes with a lot of perks. But I didn't get in the business to be a talking head. Like I said, I want to do more real reporting. Investigative stuff." He smiled again. "But being a talking head at least pays for the duck. It's great, isn't it?"

"Yes. It's amazing. All of it."

Bondwell cut a piece of duck. "You know, this case you're working on, the Marcy Fleming thing, if I were an investigative reporter, that's exactly the kind of thing I'd like to cover."

She looked at him. "We had a deal. No talking about the case."

"No, no, no." He set down his knife and held up his hand. "I'm only using it as an example. Have I asked you anything? Anything at all?"

"No." But he'd used Marcy Fleming's name, which had never been officially released, as though baiting Sophia to correct him.

"Sophia," he said earnestly. "No talking about the case. Honest. Scout's honor." He held up his hand again, two fingers raised now.

At this point, probably everyone in the media knew who lived in the house on Pelican Way. The information wouldn't be hard to come by—anyone with a crisscross directory could find it.

"Okay?" he said.

"Okay." She smiled.

"Great."

But although Bondwell never mentioned Marcy again, never alluded to the case, Sophia's doubts cast a shadow over the meal. Bondwell talked about his background—majoring in journalism at Michigan State, working at an NBC affiliate in Lansing, getting his first anchor job in Cincinnati, moving to Tampa when he'd received the offer from WPOP—and Sophia listened and nodded. He told some funny behind-the-scenes stories of life at a television station, and she laughed.

But inside she was on guard, watching him. She hated herself for doing it—she was ruining a perfectly good evening—but she couldn't stop.

When she ordered coffee, she was tempted, out of sheer self-contempt, to order a staggeringly heavy dessert to go with it, maybe the crème brûlée. But she didn't.

Bondwell ordered a blueberry crepe with his coffee.

The man *had* to work out regularly. No one could put away that many calories unless he had a way to burn them off.

Except for Fallon, maybe.

Over the coffee, Bondwell said, "Will you be working this weekend?"

"I don't know yet. We'll be doing a lot of overtime. Why?"

"Well . . ." Uncertain again. "Look. If you *are* free, why don't come out on the boat with me? We could pack a lunch, some sandwiches, some wine, and go up to Honeymoon Island for a picnic. You've been there?"

"Not since I was a kid."

A small island north of Dunedin, sand and palmetto and scrub pine, pretty, mostly unspoiled.

Bondwell smiled. "It'd be good for you to get away for a while, no?"

She was surprised. She had assumed that the evening had become as tainted for him as it had for her. Maybe it hadn't.

Or maybe he was still determined to find himself a source.

Come on, *koritsi mou*. You haven't really given the guy a chance. And an afternoon on a boat, a sail across the Gulf . . .

Wonderful. So now I'm a sloop whore.

"Same promise," he assured her. "No talking about the case."

Finally, she nodded. "Okay."

"Sunday?"

"If I'm free. No guarantees."

He smiled. "Fair enough."

Bondwell paid the bill with his credit card and then walked Sophia to her car.

The awkward part was coming up.

The evening air was still sultry. The dark night sky was clear and a half-moon was shining. From beyond the palms and the bougainvillea she could hear the muffled whoosh of traffic on Gulf Boulevard.

At the Beetle, Sophia turned to him. In the yellow light from the parking-lot streetlamp, his blue eyes looked gray.

But blue-eyed or gray, he was still a damned good-looking guy. And now there was no table between them.

She could feel her heart—traitorous organ—thumping in her chest.

"Thank you," she told him. "I had a really good time. And the duck was fantastic."

"I'm really glad you liked it."

The moment lengthened. Sophia hoped that neither of them would make a mess of this.

Everything went, as it happened, very well. Suddenly his hand was on her cheek, softly, lightly, and her own hand rose up, of its own accord, and settled easily on his upper arm, as though that were the most natural thing in the world for it to do. She could feel his biceps beneath the material of his suit, as round and firm as a stone. As she looked up into those eyes, something moved within her, a small creature gently changing position.

The body feels what it feels, does what it does.

He kissed her, his lips parted slightly, his eyes opened, and then his hand fell slowly—reluctantly?—away and he stood back and smiled, the skin around his eyes crinkling with pleasure. "It was great," he said. "Thank you. Can I call you tomorrow?"

"I won't know yet if I'll be free. For the weekend, I mean." She was, ridiculously, a bit out of breath. "I probably won't know until later in the week."

"Then I'll call to say hello."

He bent forward, lightly kissed her forehead, smiled at her again, and stepped back.

Sophia opened her purse, found her key, put it in the lock, turned it, opened the door. Stepping into the car, she looked over at him. "Good night. Thanks again."

"My pleasure."

She eased herself down onto the seat, pulled the door shut behind her, put the key in the ignition, turned it, tapped the gas. She put the car into reverse, backed slowly out. She glanced at him and waved. He waved back, smiling once more.

A good smile.

And she liked the way he'd waited until she was in the car.

Protective. She was a cop, and maybe she didn't need protecting. But getting it was . . . getting it was very nice.

And he wore no cologne. He had no perfume smell about him. Just a faint scent of soap.

Fallon didn't wear cologne either. Like Bondwell, he smelled of soap. Soap and cigarettes.

Damn. Why did she keep thinking about Fallon?

Chapter Seventeen

Fallon swallowed some more Jim Beam. It was his third or fourth drink, maybe his fifth—who was counting?—but it still tasted better than that damned single-malt of Anderson's.

Stubbing his cigarette into the ashtray, he glanced around the rectangular bar. In the corner to his left, the two truck drivers were still hunched over their Budweisers, still analyzing the lineup of the Tampa Bay Devil Rays. To his right, the young blond couple in T-shirts—his shirt baggy, hers skintight against her small, pert breasts—still huddled against each other as though they had powerful magnets implanted in their shoulders. And directly opposite him, the middle-aged blond woman still stared morosely into her Seven and Seven.

She had come in about twenty minutes ago, a regular. She and the bartender knew each other's name, and the bartender knew what she drank. He had poured it for her and she had taken her first taste, a big one, as soon as he'd set it down on the bar.

She was a type that Fallon had seen fairly often since he'd moved to Florida. A bleached blonde, her skin darkly tanned, a woman still handsome but no longer as beautiful as she'd been a decade or two before, the once elegant face beginning to thicken slightly now, and blur. From the years, the mileage, sometimes from the booze.

But it was still an attractive face, with wide Slavic cheekbones, slightly feline-looking green eyes, a broad red mouth.

She had looked over at him when she sat down, then looked quickly away. From time to time, when he glanced toward her, he had caught her looking at him, then looking away again.

She's probably available, Jimmy. Buy her a drink. Start shooting the shit.

It would be easy. A few more drinks, a laugh or two, a couple of hours spent learning all the fascinating personal things they had in common—*Really? You like Julia Roberts, too?*—and then the move to someplace more comfortable.

Like a mattress.

All of it as casual and inevitable as if it had been preordained.

Why not? Tregaskis was off with her reporter. Eva Swanson was off with—whoever it was that women shrinks went off with.

She certainly didn't know him from the bar. Fallon had never been here before. He had been driving home on Pasadena when he'd decided that he didn't want to face the blank, empty rooms of his apartment, and he had stopped at the first bar he'd come to.

What was the name of that bar in Brooklyn? The one he and Laura used to go to, back in the beginning?

O'Reilly's. Irish, a wild place, filled with laughter.

He remembered Laura sitting across the table, listening to his stories, leaning forward to hear him above the crowd. Her big brown eyes always grew round and excited as he told her some new and preposterous thing that Haggarty, his crazy partner, had done. . . .

Taking a sip of bourbon, he glanced over at the blonde, who was staring at him again. She turned away, her hair shifting along her shoulders.

In his pants pocket, the cell phone rang.

Fallon went cold and he stopped breathing.

The station. Courtney.

There had been another one. Another Marcy.

He pulled the phone from his pocket, flipped it open, took a deep breath. "Fallon."

"Hello, Jim. This is Eva Swanson."

He felt the air leave his lungs.

"Yes, Doctor?" He picked up the pack of Camel Lights, plucked one out, put it between his lips.

"I thought we were past that." He could hear the smile in her voice.

He picked up the Bic, flicked the wheel, lit the cigarette. "Sorry," he said, exhaling. "Eva."

"I just wanted you to know that I've done some research. Nothing much, at this point. But I made a few phone calls."

The jukebox kicked in. Frank Sinatra's "One for My Baby." The alcoholic's national anthem.

He glanced across the bar, saw that the blonde was standing by the machine, putting in another quarter.

Swanson must have heard the music, because she asked him, "Am I calling at a bad time?"

"No, no." He swiveled on the stool, away from the sound, and tucked the phone more closely to his face. "It's fine. I'm just finishing up with dinner."

Not entirely a lie—he had downed a bowl of pretzels thirty minutes ago.

"I can call you back," she offered.

"No, it's fine." He took a drag from the Camel. "What've you got?"

"Well, not very much, I'm afraid. One problem is that the crime has no obvious sexual component. Unless something turned up at the autopsy?"

"Far as the ME can tell, she wasn't sexually assaulted."

"Right. Well, among the people I spoke with, the consensus seems to be that the man is somehow striking out at the parental figure—"

"He hates his mother."

"Yes." Once again, he could hear the smile in her voice. "As you pointed out. His early family life was almost certainly dysfunctional, the father probably absent, the mother probably an inconsistent disciplinarian—indifferent one day, strict the next. One of my colleagues also suggested that our subject, as a child, was probably overweight."

"He have any idea what the guy would look like now?"

"She."

"Whoops."

"She thinks that probably he's slender now, but that he still probably carries a body image of himself as overweight. We see that in anorexics. He may, in fact, be an anorexic himself. But that doesn't really help you much, does it?"

"Not now. Later, maybe, when we have a suspect."

"You're certain that this is the first time he's killed someone?"

"Like I said, as far as we know. But personally, yeah, I think it is. If he'd done this before, we'd have heard about it."

"A couple of people have suggested that if this *is* his first killing, he may live near the victim. For their first strike, serial killers often work within an area that's familiar to them. Not always, but often."

"Makes sense."

"And I mentioned the meat he left at Marcy's house, and the false impression he made on the mattress. One of my colleagues agrees that the man is arrogant and manipulative. And he believes that someone like that would probably have shown up at the public briefing yesterday."

Fallon felt the muscles of his cheeks tighten. "He was there?"

"Possibly, yes. And I saw the briefing, Jim, on television. There were quite a few cameras there. Which means that—"

"That our guy is probably on tape somewhere."

"And won't there be a memorial service for Marcy? A funeral?"

He sucked on the cigarette. "You're thinking he'll go there, too. If we could tape the service—"

"You could compare it to the tapes of the briefing and see who showed up at both events. Can you get copies of the briefing tapes?"

"Probably not. Not unless the TV stations in St. Anselm are a lot different from the stations I've dealt with before. They won't give up their footage. First Amendment rights."

"There isn't any way you can get them to cooperate?"

"I don't know. Maybe."

"I realize that all this won't be easy. Probably a lot of the people who attended the briefing will be attending the service as well."

"Yeah, but it's less people than the population of Florida, which is what we're looking at now. Thanks, Eva."

"I'll keep asking around. There are a few more people I can call."

"I appreciate it. Listen. You still think we've got some time before this guy moves again?"

"If he works to the pattern. But, as I said, Jim, there are no guarantees."

"Psychology isn't an exact science."

She laughed. "No."

"One more thing?"

"Yes?"

"Do you have any objection to a press release that mentioned your help? It's mostly political, something to show people we're doing the best we can."

Once again, she hesitated.

"Chief Anderson," he said, "wants to put you on the payroll. I don't know what the standard consultancy rates are, but whatever they are, we'll pay them."

The smile was back in her voice. "Am I being bribed?"

"Yes, ma'am."

She laughed. "I can't remember the last time anyone called me *ma'am*."

"Call it another bribe. Is the press release okay with you?"

"What do you think, Jim? Is it absolutely necessary?"

"I don't think so, no. But I'm not the one making the decisions."

She sighed. "All right. I'm not crazy about the idea, but go ahead."

"Thanks."

"I'll keep digging around, see if I can come up with anything else."

"I appreciate it, Eva."

"Is there anything else?"

Last chance, Jimmy. "Not about the case. But I was wondering . . ."

"What, Jim?"

"Well, if you're not doing anything right now, I was wondering if you'd like to get together for a drink."

"Oh, Jim—thanks for asking me. I truly mean it. And if you'd asked a couple of hours ago, I'd have been out of the house in five minutes. But I'm beat right now. Totally exhausted. I'll just about be able to drag myself off to bed."

"Yeah, timing is something I've always been good at."

She laughed. "Can I have a rain check?"

"Sure. We'll do it some other time."

"Anytime at all. Call me and we'll arrange it."

"Fine, Eva. Look forward to it."

"Me, too."

"Okay. Good night, then."

"Night, Jim."

He flipped the phone shut.

Shot down.

But not completely shot down.

A rain check . . .

But she could have set another time—"How about tomorrow?"—and she hadn't.

She's busy. She has her own practice, and now she's helping the cops.

Forget about her, Jimmy. You're the last thing in the world she needs. The last thing any woman needs.

Forget Dr. Eva Swanson.

Remember the case. Remember the scumbag.

He had been at the public briefing.

The bastard had just wandered in, grabbed a seat, and sat there for an hour, watching Fallon and Tregaskis and the others make idiots of themselves. Laughing to himself.

Or maybe not. Like Swanson said, there were no guarantees.

He stared at the far wall, cheap dark paneling strewn with baseball pennants.

Across the bar, the blonde smiled sympathetically. "Bad news?" she asked him. He could just make her out over the Sinatra.

"Yeah."

"Sorry to hear it."

You like Julia Roberts, too?

He stood up. "Gotta go."

She nodded. "Take care."

He took a final drag from the cigarette, stubbed it out. "You, too."

He picked up the bill. Five drinks. Twenty dollars. He tugged his wallet from his back pocket, opened it, slipped out a twenty and a five, put them on the bar. He smiled at the blonde again, then turned and walked away.

There was still half a bottle of bourbon left at home.

Chapter Eighteen

Robert sipped at his coffee, Blue Mountain, still warm and tasty in the brushed-platinum, insulated mug that Marla had given him on his birthday. Such a lovely gift. She knew how much he enjoyed his coffee.

He had been sitting in the car for over an hour, since midnight.

He knew that the tinting on the car's windows would keep him invisible to anyone in any of the nearby houses. And enough old cars were parked along the curb, most of them as nondescript as his own, that one more shouldn't draw any neighborhood attention.

Not that attention was likely. Most of the houses along Horner Street were dark, their occupants fast asleep, dreaming dreams of interest-free mortgage loans and vacations in fabulous Orlando.

But Cyndi, it transpired, was something of a night owl. Beyond the lace curtains, beyond the louvered living-room windows, a blue light continued to flicker. She was still watching television.

Probably mesmerized by one of those heartwarming made-for-television movies. Lindsay Wagner battling some terrible disease that strained her belief in God and smeared her makeup. Victoria Principal patiently teaching her beautiful deaf-mute daughter that Life Was Worth Living.

A valuable lesson, Cyndi, to be sure; but one that you, personally, needn't linger over.

He glanced at his watch. One-fifteen.

The woman is supposed to be at the hospital at nine in the morning. Insomnia, dear? Stress? Anxiety? Environmental Sleep Disorder?

Well, on second thought, maybe she wasn't watching anything after all. Maybe she wasn't awake. Maybe she had drifted off and she was lying there, sprawled across the sofa, mouth agape, big head slumped toward her Wibble-Wobble breasts. Sleeping Beauty.

Maybe it's time for a visit from Prince Charming.

The satchel was in the trunk, heavy with his tools.

Maybe it was time for Cyndi to start moving toward—

Suddenly a pair of headlights appeared in his rearview mirror, two hundred feet behind him.

For a moment, Robert assumed it was a neighbor returning home. But the car kept coming, its headlights growing steadily larger, steadily brighter, and then it passed by a house with its front light glaring. And Robert saw the bubble-gum machine on the car's roof.

He threw himself down onto the seat. The hot coffee hurtled across his front.

The glow of the headlights grew brighter. Robert could feel the coffee hot and damp along his thighs.

If the cop *had* seen him, if he stopped and asked Robert to leave the car, Robert would have two options.

He could try to bluff his way through. At the moment—as always when he reconnoitered—he was fairly well disguised. None of his papers, the driver's license, the insurance cards, were in his real name, but they were all in order. The car was registered under the same name, and it couldn't be traced to him.

Robert could explain that he'd been driving around. *Insomnia,* yes! Couldn't sleep, went for a drive, pulled over to rest his eyes.

And if the cop asked him why he'd ducked below the dashboard?

A sheepish smile. "Well, Officer, I guess you startled me. And I thought it must look a bit weird, my sitting out here like this."

But the disguise that fooled the Wibble-Wobbles in a busy supermarket might not fool a trained and suspicious policeman.

And what if the cop found the satchel in the trunk?

Second option. Kill the cop. Strike before suspicion hardened into certainty.

The cop would be on guard—he would have to be, if he'd seen Robert dart away from the headlights. But with smiling, with laying on the charm, very likely Robert could get close enough. A quick slash at the cop's larynx, then a straight-arm slam at the bridge of his nose, driving bone fragments into the brain. Robert had done well in his karate classes. He'd been the star, really, for nearly four years, and he had the black belt to prove it.

If he got close enough to the cop, he could manage it.

But in either case, too much attention would be drawn to 2441 Horner Street. If the cop had seen Robert, he had already reported it. The car's description would be on record. With a dead cop flung across the road where the car had last been seen, every other cop in town would try to track it down.

And even if Robert was lucky, and the cop never saw through the disguise and he let Robert drive off, he would remember the disguise and the car later. After poor perfected Cyndi turned up. And Robert would be forced to abandon both.

So, either way, if that police car stopped tonight, Cyndi would have to be disqualified.

A great pity, because Robert had definitely set his heart on the little sea sprite.

The car will not stop.

The light inside the car grew brighter. Robert heard the low murmur of the cruiser's engine.

The car will not stop.

He could hear his heart beating, louder than the sound of the engine. Extraordinary.

And then the light disappeared, the murmur began to fade away.

Robert smiled in the darkness.

The Triumph of the Will.

But for a few moments he remained where he was, listening for the telltale growl of a reversing engine.

Nothing.

He waited a bit longer.

Still nothing.

Cautiously, his hand against the vinyl, he levered himself up and peered over the top, through the windshield.

A few hundred feet away, a pair of red taillights swung to the right and disappeared. The cruiser, turning onto 145th Street.

Robert turned, sat upright, reached for the ignition, flicked the key. The engine started.

Even when the gods were with you, you took precautions. The cruiser might come back.

Slowly, quietly, Robert pulled away from the curb.

The spilled coffee was still warm and damp in his lap.

He discovered that he was really quite annoyed.

He glanced at the louvered window as he drove away from Cyndi's cottage.

You bitch. You fat, vile, stinking sack of shit. If you'd gone to sleep at a reasonable hour, none of this would have happened.

He felt the familiar delicious tingle at the base of his stomach.

Oh, Cyndi. We'll have to discuss this, you and I.

We'll have to discuss this very soon.

Tomorrow, I think.

THURSDAY

Chapter Nineteen

Panting, slick with sweat from her run, Sophia sat on the sea wall and looked out at the Gulf.

It was the beginning of another beautiful day, but she was pissed off. At herself.

She shouldn't have gone out with Bondwell. It hadn't been right to take time away from the case. It didn't matter, finally, that there hadn't been anything important, anything productive, for her to do. It didn't matter, finally, that Courtney had given Sophia her blessing.

She needed to stayed focused. If she did, if she made the case a part of her, attacked it from every side, concentrated on nothing else, then maybe, just maybe, she'd see something that would break it wide-open.

Everything else was a distraction. She couldn't afford distractions.

Dave Bondwell was a distraction.

A handsome distraction, true. A good kisser, yes. One who genuinely seemed to enjoy her company.

Yes, but he's a reporter, and reporters . . .

On one level, she wanted to believe he was genuine, but, on another, she was annoyed at herself for caring.

It was ridiculous. She was twenty-six years old, and a cop, maybe even a good cop, and her emotional level was still frozen at about the age of thirteen.

Does he really like me, will he really call?

Pathetic.

She looked up and saw a small sandpiper mincing toward her across the sand. He seemed very serious, very intent. With his tiny head tucked down between his narrow shoulders, he reminded her of photographs of President Richard Nixon, the beleaguered Nixon, just before the impeachment, hunching himself away from the questions and the accusations.

The bird strutted to within a yard of her running shoes and then suddenly he looked up, as though noticing, for the first time, the giant who loomed over him. He gave a small squeak, pivoted in the sand, tucked his head back between his shoulders, and scampered toward the water.

Sophia laughed.

All at once, unaccountably, she felt light and free.

The air was soft and clear, the sky was a cloudless pale blue, almost opalescent. The tide was low, the shoreline crisp and absolutely still, the gray water as flat as a sheet of aluminum all the way out to the distant blur of horizon. Overhead, a pair of pelicans slowly soared. Up and down the beach, isolated shell-gatherers slowly searched the sand.

Once again, it was hard to believe that such a thing as a hurricane existed.

And yet Gerald was still out in the Gulf, two hundred miles away, stalled on its way to Mexico. This morning, while she got into her sweats, she'd watched the Weather Channel, seen last week's videos of the storm as it rampaged through the Keys—huge, ragged waves surging against the coast, sheets of spray whipping across flooded streets, tattered palm trees thrashing against a bloated black sky.

Hard to believe, too, that somewhere—somewhere much closer than two hundred miles—sat the man who had killed and brutalized Marcy Fleming. Who had stripped away her dignity, her humanity, as he stripped away her flesh.

Sophia looked up. The sandpiper was gone. And so, too, she realized, was the fine, lovely moment she had wandered into—one of those moments, all too rare, in which time stops moving and everything in the world stands poised on the brink of some crystalline perfection.

The water she looked at now was the same water, the sky was the same sky. But the perfection had bled away from the scene, sucked from it by the horror of Marcy's death.

She shook her head.

What had you done, Marcy, that brought you up against him? How had you come into his orbit?

Victimology. Theoretically, when investigators learned everything about the victim—her family, her friends, her business associates, the tiniest and seemingly least significant details of her daily life—when they learned the entire pattern, and all the deviations from that pattern, then they would also learn who had killed her.

But you, Marcy—you had no family, you had no friends. You did nothing, you went nowhere. You walked along the beach, and that was it.

For a moment she pictured Marcy in her pale blue dress—where *was* that dress?—slowly padding down along the sand, alone, lost in thought.

What had you done to attract his attention?

Let's say I'm right, and he went after you because of your size. Why you? Fallon had a point—there were thousands of women of size in Florida, probably hundreds of them right here in St. Anselm. From all of them, why did he pick *you*? What made you so special?

"RIGHT," SAID LIEUTENANT COURTNEY. "We've got reports from the uniforms who checked along the beach last night. A few people remember seeing Fleming, but no one remembers seeing her with anyone else. Same thing at the Kash N' Karry and the 7-Eleven. We're checking the day shifts now." She looked across the desk at Fallon and Sophia. "Any ideas, people?"

"What about the seminar?" said Sophia. It had come to her on her way to work.

"Which seminar?" said Courtney.

"Eva—Dr. Swanson—said that Marcy attended a seminar at the Don Cesar. On weight loss. That's how Marcy learned about Swanson."

"You think our guy attended it, too?" Courtney asked.

"If he's obsessed with women of size, isn't that possible?"

Courtney turned to Fallon. "Are you in contact with Swanson, Jim?"

Fallon looked tired today. The color in his face seemed washed-out, as though he had gone pale beneath the tan. The lines around his mouth seemed deeper and darker.

He nodded. "I talked to her last night."

Sophia was surprised. Had they talked over the phone, or in person?

Is that why he looked so tired? He'd been jumping Swanson's bones all night?

None of your business, koritsi mou. You were out with your studmuffin.

"Ask her," said Courtney, "if there's any way to trace the people who came to the seminar."

"I will. She came up with another interesting idea, by the way."

"What's that?" asked Courtney.

"She thinks that maybe our guy was at the public briefing on Tuesday."

Courtney raised her eyebrows. "Based on what?"

"On the kind of guy he is. The way he's playing us."

Courtney said, "There were a lot of people at the briefing."

He nodded again. "But she thinks he might have been one of them. And she thinks he might be coming to Marcy's funeral. If we tape the funeral, and we can get the briefing tapes, we could compare the two and see who showed up at both."

"And the seminar," said Sophia, feeling a small stir of excitement. "Maybe someone took photographs of the people who attended."

"And maybe," said Kitty, "they've got a list of the people who paid for tickets. Credit cards, checks."

"It was free," Sophia told her.

Courtney said, "The seminar is good. We can ask Swanson if there was a photographer at the seminar. But the tapes from the briefing—Jim, you know that none of the TV stations are going to release their tapes."

"Can't we get a subpoena?" Sophia asked her.

"Sure we can," said Courtney. "And it would take the stations about five minutes to have their lawyers quash it. They'd find some judge and convince him that this is a fishing expedition—which is exactly what it is. Because there's nothing that says our guy was anywhere near the briefing on Tuesday. And nothing that says he'll be at the funeral."

"But shouldn't we tape the funeral anyway?" Kitty asked her.

Courtney nodded. "I can call the cousin in Buffalo, see if she'd go for a service this weekend. From what she said, I think she'd be tickled pink if we took the problem off her hands. And if she goes along, we'll have people there with cameras."

"But if Swanson's right," said Sophia, "then the whole point is comparing the people at the funeral with the people at the briefing."

"Can't be done," said Courtney.

"Tregaskis," said Fallon. "Could you ask Dave Bondwell for a favor?"

She looked at him, and she realized she was flushing. Both Courtney and Fallon knew that she'd gone out with the anchorman, but bringing it up during an official meeting made the relationship—if that's what it was—seem like public property.

Still . . .

She turned to Courtney. "I could do that."

Courtney sat back in her chair. "You're sure you want to?"

Sophia hesitated. She had climbed all over Bondwell last night when she merely *suspected* he was trying to talk about the case. And here she was, offering to bring him directly into the damn thing. And ask for his help.

This isn't about you, *koritsi mou*. This is about Marcy.

"Yes," she said. "I'm sure."

Courtney nodded. "Okay. Do it. Jim, you call Swanson, ask her about photographs of the seminar."

Chapter Twenty

hanks for making my social life public," said Sophia.

They were back at their desk. Once again, Gall and Durrel's desk was empty.

Sitting back in his swivel chair, Fallon had his hand at his forehead, rubbing at the corners of his eyes with finger and thumb. "I didn't know Bondwell was a secret."

"He's not a secret. But you could've asked me in private."

He looked over at her. "When? You're the one who brought up the seminar. I should have waited, maybe, until after the meeting? We're in kind of a hurry here, remember?"

He was right. She took in a deep breath, let it slowly out. "I remember."

"If you don't want to ask Bondwell—"

"I said I would. Don't head-game me, Fallon."

He made his face go innocent. "I? Head-game?"

"Screw you." Despite herself, she smiled. "Do you have a cold?"

"What?"

"You look terrible."

"Thanks."

"Well, you do."

He nodded. "I think I'm coming down with something."

"Are you going to call Swanson? And when did you talk to her, by the way? Were you planning to tell me about that?"

"She called me on the cell phone last night. There wasn't time before the meeting to tell you about it."

Over the telephone. No bone-jumping.

Who cares whose bones Fallon jumped?

"You're going to call her?" she asked again.

"Yes, ma'am." He reached into his coat pocket, plucked out a card, lifted the landline receiver, tucked it against his neck, and dialed a number.

Sophia looked at her own telephone for a moment. Then she opened her purse, searched through it, found Dave Bondwell's card.

At the other end of the desk, Fallon said into his phone, "Eva, this is Jim Fallon. Can you give me a call?"

He hung up, turned to Sophia. "Voice messaging. She's using her cell phone." He stood, reached into his shirt pocket, pulled out the pack of Camel Lights, held them up for her to see. "Back in a minute."

He strode off, toward the back door of the station.

She took a deep breath, lifted the telephone receiver, put it to her ear, punched the 9 button, got the external dial tone, punched out Bondwell's number.

It rang three times.

Then: "Dave Bondwell." Sounding deep and professionally anchormanish.

"Hi. It's Sophia."

"Hey! How are you?" The obvious pleasure in his voice made her uncomfortable.

That, *koritsi mou*, is what we call guilt

"I'm fine, thanks," she said. "But this isn't really a personal call."

A pause. "No?"

"Can we talk off the record?" She'd never used the phrase before, and it sounded like something from a bad movie.

"Of course."

"It's about the case. Marcy Fleming."

Another pause. "Okay." The word pronounced slowly, warily.

"One of our psychological consultants thinks that the man who killed her might've been at the public briefing on Tuesday."

One of our psychological consultants. Like they're crawling out of the woodwork.

"How does he know that?" Bondwell asked.

"It's a she. She's basing—"

"Sorry."

"That's okay. She's basing it on what we know about the man. I'm sorry, Dave, but I really can't tell you anything more right now."

"She's a profiler?"

"In a sense, yes."

"Okay. Go ahead."

"If he *was* there, then he's probably on videotape. Your cameraman took pictures of the crowd, didn't he?"

It seemed that a couple of minutes passed, uncomfortable minutes, but it was probably only a few seconds before he said, "It's impossible, Sophia. I'm sorry."

"No, I understand." In a way, she was relieved—at least it was over. "I'm sorry, too. I didn't really want to ask you, but—"

"Listen," he said, his voice quickening. "The stuff we broadcast? The stuff that went over the air? I can get you a dupe of that. There were a few reaction shots in there. Shots of the crowd. Parts of it, anyway."

"Only parts of it?"

Another pause. "Yeah." Subdued now. "Right. You'd need all of it. The whole crowd. Damn."

Another pause.

"Dave, I understand. Really. I didn't expect—"

"Okay, look. Let's say I go to my producer and I ask him to let you people take a look at the tapes. I'm willing to do that. But I need to offer him something in return."

"Like what?"

"An exclusive. If you arrest a suspect, we'll want his identity—and before you release it to anyone else. And we'd want first access to you and—what's his name, the other detective?"

"Fallon."

"Fallon, right. Can you swing that?"

"I can talk to the lieutenant."

"Okay. In the meantime, I'll talk to my producer. If I can swing him, he'll still have to get an okay from the station manager. I'll call you back in fifteen, twenty minutes."

"Okay." She felt the stir of excitement once again. Maybe this thing would actually happen.

"Oh, and Sophia?"

"Yes?"

"What about the weekend? The picnic? Are we on?"

"I honestly don't know yet, Dave."

"Okay. Fair enough. I'll get right back to you on the other thing."

"Thanks, Dave. For the help."

"Hey, this is a business thing. You scratch my back, I scratch yours. But it's got nothing to do with you and me, right?"

She flashed on an image of scratching his muscular, naked back. "Right."

"I'll call you back," he said. "Bye."

"Good-bye."

She depressed the phone's plunger, dialed the lieutenant's extension. "Courtney."

Quickly, Sophia ran through Bondwell's offer.

"I'll talk to the chief," Courtney said. "But I think we can do it. I just talked to the cousin and she's faxing me a release. I'll get the ME to sign off on the body, and we'll arrange a service for Saturday. Good work, Sophia."

Sophia was still congratulating herself when Fallon strolled back into the office. He pulled a cigarette butt from his shirt pocket and tossed it in arch toward the wastebasket. It sailed neatly in, without touching the rim. He turned to Sophia. "What's happening with Bondwell?"

"It might work out." She repeated what she'd just told Courtney.

Sitting back down at the desk, he said, "See? It's good to know important people."

"If I'd listened to you, I'd never have gone out with him."

"Good thing you"—his cell phone chirped—"didn't listen to me." He slipped the phone from his pants pocket. "Fallon. . . . Hi, Eva."

Just then Sophia's desk telephone rang.

Dueling telephones.

She snatched up the receiver. "Hello?"

"Sophia," said Courtney. "The chief says go. Tell Bondwell."

"He's supposed to be calling me."

"Okay. Let me know."

As Sophia put the receiver back on the cradle, she glanced across the desk and saw that Fallon was dialing on the cell phone. She'd missed his conversation with Swanson.

So what?

"Hello," Fallon said into the phone. "Dr. Madison, please. . . .

Sergeant James Fallon, St. Anselm Police Department. . . . No, I'm sorry, I can't. I need to discuss it with Dr. Madison himself. . . . Sure."

He cupped the mouthpiece with his hand. "Swanson says there was a photographer there. I'm calling the guy who—" He held up a finger, spoke again into the mouthpiece. "Hello, Dr. Madison. . . . Yes, Sergeant James Fallon. . . . Yes, that's right. . . . In regard to an ongoing investigation. I was just talking to Dr. Eva Swanson, who appeared with you at a seminar at the Don Cesar on"—he glanced down at his notebook—"August seventh."

Fallon waited, finally said, "That's right."

Sophia's telephone rang. She grabbed the receiver. "Detective Tregaskis."

"Okay." Dave Bondwell. "I talked to my producer. He just got a go-ahead from the station manager. When do you want to do this?"

"Right now. Today."

"Sophia, that's not possible. The legal people need to clear it with Network."

Shit.

"When?" she asked him.

"Monday. You could do it on Monday."

Shit.

"And Sophia?"

"Yes?"

"This'll be a one-shot. You come down here, to the station, and you watch the videos here. No dupes, no stills. I'm sorry, but that's the best deal I could get."

By Monday they'd have the videos from Marcy's funeral. They could bring stills to Bondwell's station, use them for comparison. And bring the seminar photographs, if Fallon ever tracked them down.

"No, that's fine, Dave. Thank you."

"Glad I could help. One o'clock on Monday?"

"Fine."

"You'll be there?"

"Yes."

"I'm hoping to see you before then."

"I hope so, too. I'll let you know, as soon as I get the schedule."

"Okay. Bye now."

"Good-bye."

She depressed the plunger again and dialed Courtney's extension.

"Courtney."

Sophia filled her in.

"Monday's the earliest?" Courtney asked.

"That's what he said."

"We'll live with it. What about the seminar? Anything on the pictures?"

"Hold on." She covered the mouthpiece. "Fallon?"

Fallon said, "Excuse me," into the telephone, covered the mouthpiece. "Yeah?"

"The seminar pictures?"

"Working on them now."

Sophia told Courtney, "Fallon's arranging it now."

"Let me know what happens."

"Right."

She and Fallon hung up at exactly the same moment.

He stood up. "Let's go."

Chapter Twenty-one

A guy named Captain Fogarty," Fallon said. "He puts out a thing called *The Beachcomber*."

They were in the unmarked Ford, Sophia aiming the car north on Gulf Boulevard, toward Treasure Island.

"The giveaway newspaper?" She'd seen it on the stands.

"Yeah. Madison—he's the doctor who organized the seminar—he says that Fogarty was all over the place, shooting pictures for the paper."

"And Fogarty's not giving us a hard time about seeing the pictures?"

He shrugged. "Maybe he doesn't know he's supposed to."

"What's he captain of?"

"I don't know. The HMS *Pinafore*, maybe."

She smiled. " 'And a right good captain, too.' "

He turned to her. "You know Gilbert and Sullivan?"

"I know *Pinafore*. My father played it all the time, when I was a kid."

Fallon nodded. "A right good man, your father." He turned to look out the window at the passing storefronts.

No. 1555 GULF BOULEVARD WAS ON THE EASTERN SIDE of the busy street, a squat strip mall of glass and gray-stuccoed cement block. A tourist gift shop (She Sells Sea Shells), a unisex hairstylist, a secondhand clothing store (Re-Gear!), and, at the far end, the office of *The Beachcomber*. The name of the newspaper, sprawled in an arc across the plate glass, was written in the florid style of an Old West newspaper.

Sophia parked the car in one of the empty slots before the office, and she and Fallon stepped out into the heat.

A small bell was attached to the top of the glass door, and it rang when Fallon pushed the door open. He nodded for Sophia to enter.

Inside, the air conditioner was set to Stun. The chilly air reeked of cigar smoke.

A wooden counter was at the rear, a wire basket sitting at the left end of it beneath a sign that said CLASSIFIEDS. Beside it was a neat stack of paper, probably forms for the advertisements. Inexpensive carpeting on the floor, the color of an orange Popsicle. Overhead, a textured, white drop ceiling. On the pine-paneled wall there were tourist posters, mostly beach scenes, and framed front pages from the newspaper. *Inferno at Mini Golf Palace. Shark Spotted off St. Pete Beach.*

Stories of the Century, thought Sophia.

Set into the wall behind the counter, to the right, was an open door that led into a second room.

Fallon called out, "Hello?"

A gruff voice called out, "Coming."

A man walked through the door, holding a thick brown cigar. "You the cops?"

"That's right," said Fallon. "Captain Fogarty?"

"In the flesh."

The captain was maybe an inch or two shy of six feet tall. A black T-shirt was stretched taut against his proud round belly, and his sun-burned meaty arms were furred with white hair. His white-bearded face was as red as his arms, and on top of it perched a navy blue Greek fisherman's cap.

"Detective Sergeant James Fallon," said Fallon. "Detective Sophia Tregaskis."

Sticking the cigar between his teeth, Fogarty leaned into the counter and offered his big red hand to Fallon and then to Sophia.

Releasing her hand, Fogarty leered at her. "Hey there, little lady. Are you really a cop?"

"That's right."

Eisteh aleithia ena malakas?

Are you really a jerk-off?

Fogarty sucked on the cigar, puffed some smoke, took the cigar from his mouth. He turned to Fallon. "This about the fat girl got herself killed on Pelican Way?"

Big men with beards, Sophia had noticed, especially the ones who smoked cigars, almost always thought of themselves as colorful characters, larger-than-life. They were almost always wrong.

"Indirectly," said Fallon. "You say you've got photographs of the seminar at the Don Cesar?"

Fogarty nodded, raised the cigar, took a puff. "Got 'em on the hard disk. I was just taking a look. Come on back." He flipped open a section of the counter and stepped to the side. Once again, Fallon nodded for Sophia to go ahead. She followed Fogarty into the back room. Through the stink of cigar smoke, Sophia caught a whiff of Brut cologne. It was going to be a long day.

Despite the air-conditioning, the room was foggy with smoke. There were computer terminals everywhere.

Fogarty waved a hand toward a monitor displaying a brightly colored weather map of Florida. "Tracking Gerald. That baby's gonna swing north any minute now and head right for us. Just like Harvey did, back in '99."

"Weather Service said it was heading for Mexico," Fallon said.

"They changed their minds. Got a low pressure area forming right here." On the monitor screen, he tapped a thick pink finger at the Florida panhandle. "Thing'll work like a vacuum. Suck old Gerald right out of the Gulf. Right up our ass." He turned to Sophia. "I know my winds."

Windbags usually do, she thought.

"Mind if I smoke?" Fallon asked him.

Fogarty pointed at a sign thumbtacked to the wall: THANK YOU FOR NOT BREATHING WHILE I SMOKE. "Be my guest. Grab a pew." He pointed to two folding, wooden chairs and sat down in the leather executive chair in front of the LCD monitor.

Fallon, his cigarette lit now, swung the wooden chairs around, to Fogarty's right. Sophia sat down to Fallon's right, so she wouldn't be stuck between him and Fogarty and their respective clouds.

Fogarty picked up a glass ashtray from the left side of the desk and set it down in front of Fallon. "Okay. Here's the Don." He stuck the cigar in his mouth.

A panoramic shot of the Don Cesar Hotel, looking stately and elaborate and very pink against the pale blue Florida sky.

He clicked his mouse. "Here's the ballroom. That's where they held the seminar."

In the photograph, the large room was empty, row after row of metal chairs facing the small, faraway stage.

"What kind of camera?" Fallon asked him, exhaling smoke.

Fogarty took the cigar from his mouth, blew a cone of foul blue smoke toward the screen. "Nikon 990. Digital. Over three megapixels. Overkill for what I need. Whole system is digital." He clicked the mouse. "That's the panel at the seminar. All the shrinks."

Sophia recognized Eva Swanson. She sat at the end of the table, to the left of four men in business suits. She was wearing a suit herself, an elegant pale gray linen number, and a black silk blouse, open at the neck. Her blond hair, of course, was perfect.

"Okay," said Fogarty, "here's a shot of the crowd. That's what you wanted, right? Crowd shots? Here's another. And another."

"Wait," said Sophia. "Go back."

Fogarty clicked his mouse.

"Fallon," she said. The photo showed several rows of people sitting on folding metal chairs. Sophia leaned forward. Beneath her fingertip, as she touched the screen, the image blurred and a purplish halo suddenly appeared. She jerked away her hand.

"Careful, little lady," said Fogarty. "Don't poke the LCD."

Fallon had leaned forward. "Marcy?"

"She's wearing the blue dress," she said.

"It's a blue dress." Fallon inhaled on the cigarette. "But is it Marcy?"

She leaned around him and looked at Fogarty. "Can you enlarge it?"

"No problem." He clicked the mouse.

The image jumped, enlarging. Marcy's arms were folded beneath her breasts—protectively, Sophia thought—and her head was cocked slightly to the side. Her mouth was pursed, her blue eyes hooded, and she looked skeptical, dubious, as though someone on the stage had just said something she didn't much believe.

Fogarty puffed at the cigar. "That the fat girl?"

"That's the victim," said Sophia.

"Like I said." Fogarty took a puff from the cigar. "How 'bout that."

Fallon said, "Can you blow it up again?"

Fogarty clicked the mouse.

The image jumped again.

The same permed blond hair as the body at Pelican Way. The same blue eyes.

Enlarged by the computer, the photograph was clearer than the enlargements of Marcy's driver's license, but the two women were one and the same.

For a moment, Sophia was very still. On the brightly lit screen, Marcy sat there in her missing blue dress. Surrounded by strangers, but alive and well. Only a few short weeks ago.

"Is it true what they say?" said Fogarty. "That the guy sliced her up like a piece of brisket?"

Sophia said, "Look—"

"Sorry, Captain," said Fallon. "We can't comment on that. How many crowd shots you have here?"

"Like I told you on the phone, I probably got the whole crowd covered. Not much else to do at a thing like that."

"Can we get copies?"

"Whatta you want 'em for?"

"To help us with an ongoing investigation."

Fogarty's eyes went shrewd. Clark Kent, sniffing a scoop. "You think the guy who sliced her, he was at the seminar?"

"I can't comment on that. Do we get the pictures?"

Fogarty took another puff from the cigar, sat back, and grinned. "What do I get out of the deal?"

"We catch the guy," said Fallon, "we give you an interview. We thank you publicly for your help."

Fogarty puffed again at the cigar. Finally he nodded. "You want hard copies or disks?"

"We don't use Macintoshes," Sophia told him. "We've got Windows machines."

"Got a Zip drive?"

"Yes."

"Then no problem. I can save the shots as JPEGs on Zip disks. Gotta charge you for the disks, though."

"Fine," said Fallon. "We'll want the hard copies, too."

"How come?"

"Easier to handle. You've got a printer here?"

"An Oki Data. Superfast."

"Faster than ours."

BACK AT THE STATION, sitting at their desk in the detectives' cubicle, they pored over the hard-copy photographs. It had taken Fogarty an hour and a half to print all fifty of them—even on his superfast printer—but he'd printed them on glossy photographic paper, and they were all clear and finely detailed.

Sophia looked across the table to Fallon. "There were an awful lot of people there."

"Most of them are women. And most of the men are fat. Eva—"

"Big," she corrected.

He smiled faintly. "I'll say."

Jerk.

"According to Eva," he said, "one of her shrink friends thinks our guy is thin."

"He can't know that for sure."

Another smile. "You did it, too."

"Did what?"

"You assumed that the shrink's a guy. It's a woman."

Sophia could feel her cheeks flushing. "Okay, *she* can't know that for sure."

"No. So we circle all the men. When we check the videos, we look for matches."

Among the photographs, others included Marcy. In most of them her face was without expression. Sophia had set aside the first picture, the one she'd seen on Fogarty's monitor, and from time to time, as she searched through the others, she picked it up and studied it.

Marcy stared up at the stage, her head still cocked, her lips still pursed in suspicion.

Not knowing that only a few weeks later a police detective would be staring down at her picture.

Marcy was sitting between two women, all three of them sitting stiffly upright in the uncomfortable position that metal chairs force people to assume.

Both the other women were big women, one of them even more so than Marcy.

Why you, Marcy?

Why did he pick *you*?

"Hey," said Fallon.

Sophia looked up from the photograph. "What?"

"Here, look." Leaning toward her, he slid a photograph along the desktop, spun it around so that it was right side up to Sophia. He tapped at a face, one of the few male faces in the picture. "This guy look familiar?"

Sophia looked more closely. The man was sitting back in the chair with his arms crossed, wearing a pale blue sport coat and a snug gray shirt open at the neck.

Dave Bondwell.

Chapter Twenty-two

Robert glanced at his watch. Eleven twenty-five. Thirty-five minutes to midnight.

He had spent nearly an hour sharpening the knives, the long thin carving knife and the graceful, beautifully balanced chef's knife. Solingen steel, both of them, the best that money could buy. He had drawn the blades slowly, lovingly, over the dense Washita sharpening stone until they were, each of them, as sharp as razors.

Now, once again, he had set out his gear on the bed. He was using the checklist software on his Palm Tungsten to make certain he hadn't forgotten anything. He had enormous confidence in his memory, of course. But it never hurt to take precautions.

Ball-peen hammer.

He picked up the hammer, hefted it for a minute, enjoying its weight, its solidity, the homey, unpretentious marriage of metal and wood. Almost reluctantly, he slipped it into the leather satchel. He picked up the Tungsten and the stylus, tapped at the little box to the left of the word *hammer*.

The little box and the word itself disappeared.

Tarpaulin. He lifted the tarpaulin, still in its plastic wrapping. THE TUFF ONE! screamed the bright scarlet letters on the label.

He slid it into the satchel. He picked up the Tungsten and the stylus, tapped the box next to *tarpaulin*.

Tarpaulin. Check.

One by one, he went through the remaining items.

Rubber gloves.

Weighted sock.

Carving knife.

Chef's knife.

Scalpel.

Two backup scalpels. (The little devils were fragile, and sometimes, after a lot of detail work, the blades lost their edge.)

Nylon rope.

His Magic Suit.

Red cotton bandanna.

Sponge. (In case Cyndi didn't have one. You really can't rely on these Wibble-Wobbles.)

Plastic garbage bags.

Portable police scanner.

When he was finished, the bed was empty and the satchel was stuffed. Filled with the tools of the trade.

Filled with promise.

There was only one thing more he needed, and that was in the refrigerator. He'd get it out just before he left.

He sat down on the bed, slipped the Tungsten into the satchel, and zipped up the bag. He patted its plump leather side, smooth and reassuring.

He realized that he was humming to himself, and then, abruptly, he recognized the song. It was wonderfully appropriate. It was an old song, one the Cow had liked, a song that was played with clockwork regularity on her golden-oldies radio station.

He sang the words aloud:

"Cindy, oh Cindy, Cindy don't let me down."

He smiled.

The spelling was wrong, but what's a little spelling, eh, Cyndi? Between friends, I mean.

An image flashed across his mind, Cyndi lying there on the tarpaulin, all that white Wibble-Wobble flesh open and exposed, his hand reaching for the carving knife . . .

A shiver of pleasure went through him, so thrilling, so intense, that it left him feeling weak.

He took a deep breath.

Cyndi, oh Cyndi, Cyndi don't let me down . . .

He looked at his watch.

Midnight.

Showtime.

Chapter Twenty-three

Besides these reasons, travel seems to me a profitable exercise. The mind is continually exercised observing new and unknown things; and I know no better school, as I have often said, for forming one's life, than to set before it constantly the diversity of so many other lives, ideas, and customs, and to make it taste such a perpetual variety of forms of our nature.

Coming back to Montaigne, opening up her old copy of the *Essays,* was always like returning to an old friend.

Cyndi had discovered him in high school, in eighth grade, an especially lonely stretch—hormones bubbling, body swelling, the world around her suddenly crowded and confused—and she had at once been taken by him. By his intelligence and his kindness, the scrupulous honesty of his self-analysis, the universal sweep of his observation. She knew she had found a companion, and a guide. And, ever since, she had taken solace in the knowledge that he was there. And that, unlike so many other things in life, he would always be there.

Her feeling for him had sometimes amounted to a kind of crush. Occasionally she would daydream that she was Marie de Gournay, the young woman who so admired him, and whom he so admired, and who became his "covenant daughter" and later his literary executor.

Montaigne had inspired her to learn French, to fill her clumsy American mouth with those awkward, impossible sounds; to fumble her way through those intractable verbs. She had never spoken the language as fluently as she would've liked, but she had gotten good enough, as a reader, to follow Montaigne in the original.

Usually, though, after a hard day at the hospital, it was her old American edition of Montaigne that she would pull out, the dog-eared and underlined Classics Club edition. Sometimes she would read through an entire essay—"Of Vanity," say, or "Of Cannibals." Sometimes she would flip through the book, smiling at the passages, sometimes entire pages, she had underlined so many years ago. The sentences about travel had been underlined by a fourteen-year-old Cyndi, who had never traveled farther from her home in New Rochelle than Manhattan, a forty-minute train trip, and then only with her parents. And yet, in the margin, the young girl had scrawled *How true!*

Smiling, she reached down to the floor, found the bag of Fritos, snaked her hand into it, grabbed a handful of chips. She dropped all but one of them onto her stomach, behind the book, and put that one in her mouth.

Today, in fact, *had* been a hard day at the hospital. Poor Mrs. Sorel had finally passed away, after all those weeks of suffering. She had gone in her sleep, and that had been a blessing. She had been so incredibly brave through all of it, never complaining, almost embarrassed by those horrible bolts of pain that rattled through her. The woman had been a saint.

Unlike poor Mrs. Neiderman, who never *stopped* complaining. The bed was too low or too high, the bedpan was too cold or too hot. The food was horrible. The television was on the blink.

But that was death, the fear of it. The mind skittering away from its own final bow. The complaints were a way to focus on the trivial, the day-to-day. To avoid confronting the inevitable . . .

Cyndi hoped that when her own time came, she would face the end bravely, honestly, the way Mrs. Sorel had. The way Montaigne no doubt had. But she could certainly understand Ms. Neiderman and her fears.

Do not go gentle, Dylan Thomas had said. And maybe he was right.

She popped another Frito into her mouth.

The doorbell rang.

She looked over at the clock on the credenza. Twelve fifteen.

Now who on earth could *that* be?

She plucked the Fritos from her stomach, swung her legs off the couch, reached down and picked up the plastic bag, dropped the chips inside. She set the bag on the arm of the sofa. Standing up, she brushed her hands together, then delicately brushed the crumbs from her blouse.

She walked over to the door, leaned forward, peered into the eyehole. "My goodness," she said.

FRIDAY

Chapter Twenty-four

When the telephone rang, Sophia was already half-awake, coming out of a nightmare.

She'd had a bad night, and it had followed a bad day.

She and Fallon had spent most of the afternoon looking over the pictures they'd gotten from Fogarty, using their computers to enlarge every image of each of the men who'd attended the seminar. At the end of the day, they had printed out hard-copy photographs of thirty-seven men. Seven of them, including Dave Bondwell, were obviously not overweight. Except for Bondwell, neither she nor Fallon had any idea who any of the men were.

Fallon wouldn't shut up about Bondwell. "What's he doing at a weight-loss seminar?"

"He's a reporter," Sophia said.

"He's an anchorman."

"He trained as a reporter. And he lives on Treasure Island, ten minutes away from the Don Cesar. No big deal for him to check it out."

"A seminar on weight loss? That's newsworthy?"

"Come on, Fallon. You don't really think he's our guy?"

"He was there. I'd like to know why."

"I'll ask him. I can call him right now, if you want."

"No. We'll ask him when we can see his reaction. He'll be coming to the funeral on Saturday?"

"I don't know. Maybe. Probably. Fallon, he's not the guy."

Fallon nodded. "He was at the public briefing, too."

She'd already thought of that. "With a couple of hundred other people. And he was there doing his job."

"I'm not saying he's the guy. I'm saying it's a bit strange he was at the seminar."

"Strange, maybe. But not necessarily significant."

"We'll ask him at the funeral."

"Fine."

She didn't believe for a second that Dave Bondwell was the asshole who'd killed Marcy.

But Fallon was right—it was strange that he'd gone to that seminar. And the strangeness was unsettling. It bored, like a worm, through her initial enthusiasm, her sense that she and Fallon were finally *doing* something.

By the time she reached her apartment, the enthusiasm had collapsed and she was more exhausted than she had any right to be. She had climbed up the stairs to her apartment, nuked a TV dinner in the microwave, and eaten it in the living room.

She was able to catch the last few minutes of Dave Bondwell's broadcast. His hair blow-dried and carefully sprayed, he was wearing an expensive suit coat, an expensive blue shirt, an expensive tie, and a sincere, amiable smile at the end of the broadcast.

Why on earth did they all have to end the news, filled with suffering and catastrophe, with those ridiculous smiles?

She wondered just how well he got along, offscreen, with Connie Zimmer, his coanchor. She was as beautiful, and as skinny, as Sophia's cousin Eleni.

She wondered what he'd been doing at that goddamn seminar.

He lived within ten miles of the Don Cesar. It was the kind of hotel, with the kind of hotel bar, that he'd probably like.

After nuking the pistachio ice cream and digging out one small scoop, she carried the bowl to the living room and flipped to the Weather Channel.

Captain Fogarty had been right. The Weather Service was now saying that Hurricane Gerald had shifted its direction and was heading northeast at about fifteen miles an hour. They projected a landfall for sometime early next week, somewhere between Pensacola in the panhandle, and Sanibel Island, about a hundred miles south of St. Anselm. St. Anselm itself was almost exactly in the center of the predicted landfall.

My new boyfriend is a serial killer. But that's okay, because we're both going to get swept away by a hurricane.

Look. On the plus side, you've got pictures of all the people who attended the seminar.

One of the whom, unfortunately, was your date.

Which maybe does fall a bit onto the minus side.

Stop it. Go to bed.

But for a long time as she lay there, sleep hadn't come. She kept seeing those photographs, row after row of staring spectators, line after line of human heads. Overweight women and overweight men. Marcy, looking doubtful and wary. Dave Bondwell. Looking unmistakably like Dave Bondwell.

And when finally she had fallen asleep, even in her dreams she kept seeing those rows of spectators, those lines of heads.

And then a siren rang, but it wasn't a siren, it was the telephone, and the telephone shouldn't be ringing right now, not so early in the morning, not when it was still dark out. This was going to be something bad.

She reached out, fumbled with the receiver, got a grip on it, lifted it, shoved it up against her ear. "Tregaskis."

"Horner Street," said Fallon. "Twenty-four forty-one. You know where it is?"

"Oh, shit," she said.

"You know where it is?"

"I know."

"See you there."

Chapter Twenty-five

Fallon pulled his Chevy up to the curb, behind the two marked units. He put the car in park, stubbed his cigarette out in the ashtray, and sat back.

At the rear of his skull, just below his right ear, a small bright pinpoint of pain was throbbing, as though someone had eased the tip of a knife blade down through a crack in the bone and slipped it neatly into his brain.

He had finished off half a quart of bourbon last night.

He hadn't signed on for anything like this. The St. Anselm PD was supposed to be easy duty. He had figured, back when he joined, that at worst he might get an occasional B&E, maybe a grand theft auto. Amateur hour in the Sunshine State.

But not this. Not some crazy scumbag running around the island, slicing and dicing.

Fallon was too old for this shit.

Maybe he should just cash in his chips and walk away from table.

He looked up, through the windshield.

The sun had come up and a pale gray light was washing across the scraggly grass of 2441 Horner Street. A uniform—Fallon recognized Bob Farrell—was hammering thin wooden posts along the lawn's border, getting ready to put up the crime-scene tape.

The neighborhood was run-down and shabby, a neighborhood for people who were trapped in a holding pattern, or people who were on their way down. Some of those people were already out this morning, gathering on their porches, their front steps, their lawns. A couple of houses down, some fat moron in striped pajamas was sitting back in a lawn chair, left ankle comfortably plumped on right knee, watching the show.

Fallon looked at his watch. Seven o'clock. He sighed.

He leaned forward, popped open the glove-compartment door, and took out the spare Polaroid camera and notebook. He got out of the car and opened the trunk, took out the crime-coveralls, and slammed it shut.

Farrell had stopped hammering and was crossing the lawn, toward Fallon, the hammer swinging at his side.

Fallon nodded. "Farrell."

"Sergeant."

"Who found her?"

"Some kid. A jogger. He's in the car. Santiago's taking his statement."

"Hold on to him. I'll want to talk to him."

"We called his father. He should be here any minute now."

"Okay. Who was first on scene?"

"Garcia. He's inside."

Garcia again. Poor bastard.

"You've been inside?" Fallon asked.

"Yeah. I've seen the pictures of the Fleming scene. It's the same guy."

"Okay. Tregaskis, the ME, and the crime techs will be here any minute. And the state attorney. Don't let anyone else cross the tape."

"Right."

"There are some more uniforms coming. Tell them to start the D to D. Every house within ten blocks."

Just then, Tregaskis pulled up in her silver Beetle. The door opened and she stepped out wearing black slacks and a white blouse, carrying her purse and the protective coveralls.

"Anything else, Sergeant?" Farrell asked.

"No. Thanks, Bob. Just keep those people away from the tape."

Farrell moved off as Tregaskis approached, her face screwed up with worry.

"The same thing?" she asked. "The same guy?"

"Sounds like it."

Together they walked across the small lawn to the front steps. On either side of the door were louvered windows, the lace curtains drawn. A small, ordinary house, in a small, ordinary community.

Tregaskis said, "No jimmy marks on the door here, either."

Same as at Pelican Way.

The two of them clambered into the coveralls and zipped them shut. Immediately, it seemed to Fallon, his body temperature climbed thirty degrees.

He turned and rapped at the door. A moment later it was opened by Paul Garcia. He stepped aside for them to enter, then shut the door behind them.

Bookcases against all the walls, crammed with books, hardcovers and paperbacks. Fallon looked across the living room and saw the blue tarp. He took a deep breath.

Like Marcy Fleming, the thing on the tarp had been flayed, its flesh pared away. Its eyes stared up from the tortured face. Its arms were neatly folded atop the peeled chest, its legs were neatly crossed at the ankles. The arms and legs were merely thin wrappers of raw meat sheathing the bones, the surfaces just beginning to crust over. On the left knee, a white spur of bone knuckled up through the mottled red membrane. Once again, the hands and feet hadn't been cut, making the creature look as though it were wearing unearthly gloves and bootees of its own.

At least it wasn't as hot here as it had been at Pelican Way. The air conditioner was on, full blast.

Fallon glanced at the light on the end table. Off. The overhead light, in the center of the ceiling, was on. He jerked his thumb at it. "Light on when you got here?" he asked Garcia.

"Yeah."

Tregaskis anticipated his next question. She asked Garcia, "The rest of her?"

"Same thing." Garcia jerked his head toward the rear of the cottage. "The tub again. But this time the bastard got artistic."

"Artistic?" said Fallon.

"Take a look," said Garcia.

Fallon and Tregaskis followed him to the rear of the house. Small bedroom on one side, more bookcases in there, small bathroom on the other. They entered the bathroom.

Inside the tub, the same jumbled heap of cast-aside flesh, the same ropes and lumps and limp chunks of human tissue slopped insanely together, dark and glistening against the bright white porcelain.

No, Fallon realized. Not the same.

At the very top of the heap, obviously placed there with intent, lay a large, flattened female breast, pale white, faintly mottled with blue. Attached to it, probably with drying blood, and arranged in a deranged leer, were a pair of bright red human lips.

"Mother*fucker*," growled Tregaskis.

Fallon raised the camera and snapped a picture. "We know her name?"

"Purdenelle," said Garcia. "Cyndi Purdenelle. A nurse. Works over at Mercy Hospital."

"Any impression on the bed?"

"No. But there's another plate of meat in the kitchen. Like at Fleming's."

They followed him back through the living room, into the tiny kitchen. On the stovetop lay an inexpensive dinner plate. In its center sat another chunk of seared meat.

"It doesn't look like the last one," Tregaskis said.

Fallon's sour stomach twisted. "I think this one's for real."

Someone knocked at the front door.

THE INVESTIGATION WENT DOWN, at first, almost like a replay of the Fleming investigation.

It had been Dr. Harrison, the ME, at the door in his coveralls. Kitty Delgado appeared a few minutes later, but this time she was joined by Ray Eckhardt, a tech from the sheriff's office.

More uniforms would be arriving soon, and Fallon sent Garcia outside, to tell them how to work the D to D.

As Kitty started work, Harrison officially pronounced the victim dead. He pointed out that the victim, like Marcy Fleming, had been tied up before she'd been killed. On the back of the victim's skull were wounds identical to those on the back of Marcy Fleming's—a bruise and a separate, probably lethal, fracture.

"Can you give us a time of death?" Fallon asked him.

"As I said before, in these circumstances that will be difficult to determine. But from the seepage—"

Seepage, right. That damn pig on the stainless steel.

"—I'd estimate that he finished . . . um . . . working on her approximately three hours ago."

Fallon glanced at his watch. Nearly eight o'clock. So sometime around five.

"Extrapolating back," said the doctor, "I'd say that she died sometime after one, but probably before two in the morning."

He turned to Tregaskis. "Incidentally, Detective, you might be interested in this. The blood tests on the earlier victim have come in, and they've confirmed the time of death I estimated. You recall that you were somewhat dubious?"

Smug bastard hadn't forgotten that Tregaskis had doubted him, back at the ME's office.

Tregaskis smiled wanly. "I recall. I'm very happy for you, Doctor."

"Yes. Well. It's all a matter of scientific principles, isn't it? My experiment—"

"Excuse me, Doctor," said Fallon. "Is there anything you can tell us? It's the same guy, right?"

"What? Oh, yes. Almost certainly. But his . . . um . . . technique has improved."

"His technique?" said Fallon.

Harrison squatted beside the body, his coveralls whispering, and pointed to the flayed torso. "No internal organs were punctured. You see? The stomach sac is intact. With the first victim, as you may remember, the mesentery was ruptured. And these cuts along the limbs—here, you see, and here—they're much smoother in this case."

"He's gotten better at cutting them?" Tregaskis said.

"Yes." The doctor stood up. "So it seems."

"He's still using the same knives?" Fallon asked.

"The same kind, at any rate. A carving knife for the larger sections. A smaller knife for the close-up work. A scalpel for the details. On the face, primarily."

"Anything else?" said Fallon. "Anything we can use?"

The doctor frowned. "Well. Perhaps. I don't know how significant it is."

"What?"

"It's only an estimate, mind you, but judging by the remains in the bathtub, this woman was somewhat less overweight than the first."

"How much less?" Tregaskis asked.

"Thirty or forty pounds."

"So still overweight," said Fallon.

"Oh, yes. Morbidly overweight. But not as much so as the first victim. Of course, to be certain, I'll have to weigh all the tissue."

"When can you do the autopsy?"

"Not until Monday."

"All right. You'll stick around until your people get here?"

"Of course. I—"

Someone knocked at the door.

Fallon opened it. Farrell.

"The kid's father just showed up," he said. "He wants to take the kid home."

"Excuse me, Doctor," Fallon told him. "Tregaskis?"

Outside, Fallon and Tregaskis stripped off their rubber gloves, loosened their hoods, and zipped open the front of their coveralls. Beside him, Tregaskis shook free her black mane of hair. With the palm of her hand, she wiped at the back of her neck.

Father and son stood at the bottom of the front steps. The father's name was Tom Lister and the boy's name was Robbie. He was fourteen years old and a little over five feet tall. He looked frail and lost inside a pair of baggy sweatpants, a baggy sweatshirt, and a pair of enormous high-tech running shoes. He kept his arms crossed over his chest as though he were cold, despite the sweatshirt and an early-morning temperature that was already in the eighties.

More neighbors were out on their lawns now. The yellow tape was up. Farrell moved to the edge of the lawn, and some of the neighbors advanced on him, asking questions. Farrell shook his head.

Fallon said to the boy, "I know this is hard, Robbie, but we need to get information."

The boy swallowed, looked up at his father, who nodded. The father looked as though he'd just rolled out of bed.

"Sure," said the boy. "Okay."

"What time did you find her, Robbie?"

"About a quarter after six." He looked at his watch. "Almost two hours ago. I already told the other policeman."

"I know," said Fallon. "This is for me."

The father said, "If he already told the other cop, why's he gotta go through it all over again? I wanna get him home."

"Standard procedure, sir," said Fallon. And the standard bullshit answer. But Fallon had been careful to add the *sir*.

He turned back to Robbie. "What happened when you got here?"

The boy rubbed at his upper arms. "I was jogging, and I see the door is wide-open—I could see because of the streetlight, you know? So at first I think it's, like, none of my business, and I run another twenty yards. And then I'm thinking, like maybe it's a burglar or something, so I come back and I walk up the driveway and I go, 'Hello?' But no one answers, so I go in. I mean, I sort of stick my head in the door. And I turn on the light and I see her on the floor. At first I couldn't tell what it was, I thought it was like some kind of weird big doll. Then I knew it was a human being. I heard about that other woman, on Pelican Way, you know? And this was, like, exactly the same thing." He shivered, rubbed his upper arms again.

Out across the lawn, at the crime-scene tape, Farrell was shooing away the neighbors.

"The light was off when you got here?" Fallon asked the boy.

"Uh-huh."

"How'd you know where the switch was? To turn it on?"

The boy blinked at him. "Huh?" Robbie looked at his father, as though Lister might know the answer.

"You said you turned on the light," Fallon said. "How'd you know where the switch was? You ever been inside the house before?"

"Uh-uh. No. I mean, it was right inside the door, you know? On the right. Where the switch always is."

"You didn't go any farther into the house?"

"No. You could see her from right there. It was fuck—" The boy glanced at his father, swallowed. "It was horrible. I mean, who could do that? Who could do something so crazy?"

"We're trying to find out," Fallon told him. "So what happened then?"

"So right away I called you guys on my cell phone. I'm like, hey, there's someone really hurt here, I think she's dead. The guy I'm talking to, he goes, where are you at? So I tell him, I give him the address, and he tells me to wait here. So I did."

"You did good, Robbie," Fallon told him. "But why were you out running at six o'clock?"

173

"I'm on the track team. I practice whenever I can."

"Did you know Ms. Purdenelle?"

"Uh-uh. No."

"Robbie," said Tregaskis, "did you see anyone in the neighborhood when you came through this morning? Anyone on the street?"

"Uh-uh."

"No pedestrians? No cars?"

He shook his head. "There's, like, never anyone around in the morning when I'm running." He looked at his watch again. "Jeez. I'm way late." He looked at Fallon. "I've gotta get ready for summer school."

Lister put his arm around Robbie's shoulder, and the boy looked up at him. "Hey, soldier," the father said. "I'll take you. Don't sweat it."

The boy nodded, bit his lip, looked away.

The father looked at Fallon. "Is that it? We done here?"

"Yeah. Okay, Robbie, thanks. Mr. Lister, could you bring Robbie down to the police station sometime today? He'll have to sign his statement. And we'll need to take his fingerprints."

Lister frowned. "Fingerprints? What for?"

"He left his prints on the light switch. We need to compare those to his."

"How come?"

The knifepoint in Fallon's brain dug a little deeper. "To verify that the prints we find don't belong to the guy who did this."

"And you said a statement? He's already made a statement. He's already made *two* statements, for chrissake."

Fallon took a deep breath. He reminded himself that the guy was only being protective.

Beside him, Tregaskis said, "Yes, sir. He'll be signing the statement he made earlier, to the officer. It's a formality, but it has to be done."

Fallon glanced at her. Doing well again. A smart cop.

Lister was shaking his head in exasperation. "Hasn't he done enough already?"

"He's done a great job," said Tregaskis. "And we're grateful. But we'll need him at the station this afternoon." Firmly.

Sighing, Lister ran his hand through his tousled hair. Finally he nodded. "Okay. Around five. That okay?"

Fallon said, "That'll be—"

A car, a shiny black Mercedes, had driven up to the house. Now it pulled over to the right side of the street and stopped. Another vehicle, a white Ford van with a satellite dish on top and KRRP emblazoned across its side, pulled ahead of the Mercedes and parked.

Fallon recognized the car. Chief Anderson's.

The knife blade dug deeper.

"That'll be fine," Fallon told Lister.

Anderson was stepping out of the Mercedes. He was wearing civvies, another sleekly tailored suit, dark gray this morning. A man carrying a video camera came around the back of the van.

Fallon turned to Tregaskis. "Be right back," he said, and set off across the lawn.

Farrell was saluting Anderson. Anderson returned the salute and then stepped over the crime-scene tape.

Fallon stopped directly in front of the chief, blocking his way. He looked across the street at the cameraman, who'd been joined there by a man in a suit, probably a reporter. Fallon pointed his finger at them, as though it were a gun. "You there," he called out. "No closer."

The two stopped moving and turned toward each other.

Fallon turned to Anderson. "Chief."

Beneath the thick white hair, Anderson's red face was grim. "Looks like you were wrong, Sergeant. About that 'waiting period' of yours."

To Fallon's left, Farrell moved away.

Didn't want to get involved. Another smart cop.

"Yeah," said Fallon. "Can I help you, Chief?"

"I'm here to take a look at the scene." He moved to step around Fallon.

Without thinking, Fallon reached out and took hold of Anderson's left arm. "Not a good idea, Chief," he said evenly.

Anderson looked down hard at Fallon's hand, as though expecting the heat of his glare to make it explode.

Fallon left the hand where it was. He kept his voice even when he said, "Contaminating the crime scene. You'll spend the rest of the day giving hair and clothing samples to the techs. They'll need fibers from your suit."

Anderson frowned.

Fallon released him. "But it's good you're here, Chief. You can talk to the press." He nodded to the men on far side of the street. The cameraman had his camera up, shooting.

"You can reassure them," Fallon said. "Tell them we're doing everything we can."

Anderson glanced over at the two men. He looked back at Fallon. His eyes hardened. "In my office. Two o'clock."

Fallon nodded. "I'll be there."

Chapter Twenty-six

"What was that all about?" Sophia asked Fallon, then walked in step beside him as he continued toward the front door.

"The chief wanted to help. He decided to hand out some sound bites instead."

"Are you in trouble, Fallon?"

"Me? What for?"

Fallon opened the door, and he and Sophia stepped back into the cottage.

Less time had passed here than at Marcy's cottage before the body had been discovered. The flies hadn't started gathering yet. The butcher-shop smell wasn't as heavy as it had been at Marcy's house. But it was beginning to coalesce, a hint of darkness forming in the air.

Sophia looked at the savaged body on the blue tarp. Like Marcy's body, it resembled a grotesque mannequin, the sticklike arms and legs carefully manipulated into position.

The woman's eyes were brown, and her eyelashes had been sliced away. Like Marcy's blue eyes, back in the cottage on Pelican Way, these eyes stared sightlessly up at the ceiling. The teeth were spread in a ghastly lipless grin, bright white against the pink gums and the streaked red flesh that remained on her peeled skull.

Sophia looked away.

In her coveralls, Kitty Delgado moved her vacuum brush methodically across the living room carpet. Sophia could hear another vacuum moving in the bedroom. Eckhardt, the county crime tech.

Dr. Harrison walked over to Fallon. "My people will be here soon. Can they remove the body?"

"Delgado?" Fallon called out.

Within the coveralls, her vacuum humming, Kitty didn't hear him.

He stepped over, tapped her on the shoulder. "You finished with the victim?" he asked.

"Yeah."

"Anything?"

"Not that I can see. She's as clean as the other one."

"Yeah. Make sure you get the lab to run an enzyme test on that meat."

"Right."

Fallon turned to Harrison. "They can take her."

PETER COLLINSON, the assistant state attorney, arrived at a little after eight thirty, looking less dapper than he had at Silvia Hartley's cottage. The knot of his tie was slightly skewed and his eyes were rimmed with red. Like the rest of them, he was probably fresh from bed.

"Shit," he said when he saw the body. "A goddamn serial."

Sighing, he took out his leather notebook and his pen. He said to Fallon, "Okay, what do you have?"

While Fallon told him, Sophia went through the small wooden desk in Cyndi Purdenelle's bedroom. In the large lower drawer on the left side, Sophia found all of Purdenelle's financial records—payroll-check stubs, invoices for credit card bills, checking and saving statements from the Huntington bank, IRS returns going back to 1993. From the records, Cyndi had worked at Mercy Hospital since then, as a nurse's aide at first, and then as a nurse.

Sophia looked through all the drawers for something personal—letters, notes, a diary—but found nothing.

She looked around the room. It was different from Marcy's. It was more lived-in, somehow more *grown-up*. The television was in here, rather than in the living room, as it had been at Marcy's. The furniture was inexpensive, as Marcy's had been, but there was more of it. The desk, a reading chair, the white-veneered fiberboard bookcases lining each wall. There was a small cassette player on the night table, next to the lamp, and a hardcover book had been placed beside it. *The Sybil in Her Grave,* by someone named Caudwell. Sophia turned it over, read the blurbs on the back. A mystery novel.

She walked over to the nearest bookcase. More mysteries, hardcover and paperbacks. Some of the names she recognized, Grisham, Mosley, Sanders, but most she didn't.

She walked to the next bookcase. Big coffee-table books on art, on architecture, on antiques.

Books all over the house. She and Fallon would have to go through them all, looking for things tucked between the pages—slips of paper, notes to herself.

But she knew it would be a waste of time. Cyndi Purdenelle had probably never met the man who killed her, not until sometime last night.

"Find anything?" Fallon, in the doorway.

"No."

"Okay. Let's go over to Mercy Hospital. See what they've got."

Chapter Twenty-seven

Outside, the crowd beyond the yellow tape had grown larger. There were two more news vans now, and reporters were clustered at the tape itself, shoving microphones at Farrell and Garcia, neither of whom was responding.

When Sophia and Fallon appeared on the front porch, one of the newspeople called out, "Sergeant!"

Fallon ignored him and unzipped the front of his coveralls.

As she unzipped, Sophia asked him, "Why are we going to the hospital?"

"As opposed to going where?"

"As opposed to finishing up the search."

Stepping out of the pants legs of his coveralls, he said, "We'll finish up later. The place'll be sealed. But I think Delgado's right. I don't think we're going to find anything there. I don't think our guy left anything. And I don't think Purdenelle knew him."

He took his cell phone from the coveralls, rolled the coveralls into a bundle, and tucked them under his arm. "But she had a job. Maybe someone at the hospital knows something." He flipped open the cell phone, tapped in some numbers, put the phone to his ear. "Fallon. . . . Yeah. Same MO. . . . Pretty much everything. The plastic tarp, the meat on the stove. . . . No. . . . We're on our way to Mercy Hospital. She worked there as a nurse. . . . Right."

He flipped the phone shut, slipped it into his pocket. "Courtney. She wants another meeting, soon as we finish up at the hospital. You know the way?"

"Yes."

"I'll follow you in my car."

MERCY HOSPITAL WAS THE LARGEST HOSPITAL ON THE ISLAND, a ten-story, uninspired building of brick and glass. As Sophia parked in the visitors' lot, Fallon's car pulled in beside her.

The two of them walked across the asphalt into the front entrance. In the center of the lobby was a crescent-shaped, polished wooden desk, and behind it sat a pert woman in her midthirties with closely cropped, hennaed hair. She wore a lime-green rayon blouse and a bright smile that seemed out of place at nine-thirty in the morning. The nameplate on the desk said that she was Ms. Ruth Oakley.

Fallon flashed his shield and asked if he could talk to the head nurse.

"And what would this be pertaining to?" she asked pertly, her smile unruffled.

"This would be pertaining," said Fallon, "to an ongoing police investigation."

The smile didn't waver as she said, "I'm sorry, sir, but hospital policy is that any outside interviews with Ms. Ramirez would need to be conducted in the presence of the hospital administrator."

Sophia watched as the lines at the corners of Fallon's face deepened. Beneath his cheekbone, a muscle twitched. "And who," he said quietly, "would that be?"

"That would be Mr. Wilburforce, sir, but he's not in the building at present."

Fallon leaned toward her, and her smile faltered.

"Ms. Oakley," said Sophia. Fallon glanced at her. "We understand that you've got rules to follow, but this is extremely important. Would you please tell Ms. Ramirez that we're here, and that we need to talk to her about a member of the staff?"

The woman blinked. "Which member?"

"I'm sorry," Sophia told her, "but we can't discuss that. Would you call Ms. Ramirez, please?"

The woman looked from Sophia to Fallon, back again to Sophia, frowned, and then picked up the phone.

Sophia looked at Fallon. Staring up at the ceiling, he was slowly blowing air from between his pursed lips. He turned to her, held her glance for a moment, and then nodded once.

"Yes," said the woman into her telephone. "The police. . . . Yes. A member of the staff, they said. They won't tell me anything else." She shot a resentful glance at Sophia. "All right. Yes. Yes, I will."

She hung up and said to Sophia, "Office number seventy-six. Down that hallway." Her smile was gone and her voice was clipped. She didn't approve.

SOPHIA HATED HOSPITALS, the cramped smell of disinfectant, the endless green corridors, the hushed, bleak quality in the air. The last time she'd been in one was to visit her uncle Niko, just before he died.

As she and Fallon walked down the hallway, they passed a doctor wearing an opened white medical coat over a plaid flannel shirt and a pair of white pants. She noticed a dark brown stain, shaped like an irregular teardrop, on the coat's lapel.

It didn't have to be blood. It could be ketchup. Tomato soup.

She hated hospitals.

Fallon knocked on the door of office number seventy-six. A woman's voice called out, "Come in," and he opened the door.

Behind a wooden desk, a woman hung up her telephone and rose from her chair. In a battleship-gray linen suit, she was short and heavyset. Her marcelled hair was the same color as her suit, and the lines of her broad Hispanic face were deep and determined, as though they'd been chiseled there.

"Norma Ramirez," she said.

"Detective Sergeant James Fallon. And this is Detective Sophia Tregaskis."

"Please have a seat." She indicated the chairs in front of her desk.

After the three of them sat, Ramirez leaned forward and clasped her hands together on the desktop. "I've just gotten off the phone with Leonard Wilburforce, the hospital administrator. Within certain limits, I should be able to answer your questions. Ruth said something about a member of our staff?"

"That's right," said Fallon. "Cyndi Purdenelle. There's no easy way to tell you this, Ms. Ramirez. Ms. Purdenelle is dead. She was murdered."

Ramirez at first narrowed her eyes, as though puzzled. And then the narrowed eyes became a wince of pain, and the lines of her face deepened. "Cyndi? Murdered?"

"Late last night or early this morning. I know that this is a shock for you, but in a situation like—"

"But *how*? *Who*?" Her mouth awry, she looked back and forth between Fallon and Sophia.

Sophia heard herself say, "I'm very sorry," and they seemed to her the most inadequate words in the world.

"We don't know who," Fallon said. "Not yet."

Ramirez was shaking her head. "Everybody loves her. The patients, the rest of the staff, everyone. She's one of the best nurses I have. Who on earth would do such a thing?"

Sophia said, "We think that—"

Ramirez suddenly closed her eyes and rocked slightly back in her chair. "Oh, no. *Oh, no*. It's not . . ." She opened her eyes and stared at Fallon. "It's not the same as that other woman?" She turned to Sophia. "Earlier in the week? That terrible story in the newspaper? The woman who was . . . mutilated?"

Caught off guard, surprised that Ramirez had made the connection so quickly, Sophia felt her throat tighten. "I . . ."

Fallon said, "Yes. We believe that the same individual was responsible. I'm sorry, Ms. Ramirez."

Sophia looked over at him, grateful.

Ramirez closed her eyes again. "Oh my God." For a moment she sat there, her eyes shut, her body still.

"I know it's difficult for you. I'm sorry about this, but we have to ask you some questions." Fallon's voice was gentle.

Sometimes, for an incredible jerk, he could be surprising.

After another moment, the woman opened her eyes. "Yes. Yes, of course." She reached forward, plucked a tissue from a chromium cube on her desktop. She blew her nose, took a deep, snuffling breath. "I apologize." She looked at Sophia. "I'm . . . I was very fond of Cyndi. I've known her since she was a nurse's aide. Almost ten years now." She dabbed at her nose, looked down, shook her head emphatically. "I just can't *believe* this."

She leaned to the side, put the tissue into some kind of wastebasket, then sat upright. Once again she clasped her hands together on the desktop.

Trying to reestablish her poise, Sophia thought. Trying to return, somehow, to normalcy.

"All right," Ramirez said to Fallon. "How can I help you?"

"Have you spoken to Ms. Purdenelle recently?" he asked.

"I see her—saw her—nearly every day. We didn't talk much, just to say hello, how are you. We weren't great friends, we didn't socialize. But as I said, I was very fond of her. Everyone was."

"Had she seemed any different lately?"

"No." She shook her head. "Cyndi was always the same. Cheerful. Optimistic. She's been like that as long as I've known her."

"Did she have any enemies?"

Smiling sadly, Ramirez shook her head. "No. None. If you'd known Cyndi, you'd understand. Everyone loved her. She was kind, she was helpful. I'm making her sound like a Pollyanna, I know that, and she wasn't. She was . . . she was *cheerful*. She was the same with everyone. Patients and staff alike. The doctors, the other nurses."

"Did she have any close friends among the staff?"

"You mean a boyfriend?"

"Yes."

"No. Officially, it's against hospital policy for the staff to fraternize with one another. Some of them do, of course, but not Cyndi. Not that I know of, at any rate. And I think I'd know."

"Did she have any male friends outside of the hospital?"

"I wouldn't know. But to tell you the truth, I doubt she did. She always struck me as indifferent to men."

"What about women?"

Ramirez raised her jaw. "She wasn't a lesbian, if that's what you're implying."

"I'm not implying anything, Ms. Ramirez. These are questions I have to ask."

She sat back, moved her hands to the arm of her swivel chair. "Yes. Yes, of course. I'm sorry." She nodded. "All right. Let me see if I can say this properly. Cyndi always struck me as someone who lived for her work, as someone who didn't have time for relationships. Personal relationships, I mean."

"Did she have any close women friends?"

"Not really, not here on the staff. She got along well with everyone, but as far as I know, she wasn't actually close to anyone in particular."

"Could you give me a list of the people who worked with her?"

"Of course. But it'll take me a little while. I'll have to check the records."

"Fine. Did Cyndi have any close relatives?"

"There's a sister, I think. Somewhere in the Midwest. But no one who lives nearby. Should I get that list ready?"

"Yes, thank you. In the meantime, would it be possible for us to talk to your personnel officer?"

"Janet? Why?"

"Just some routine questions."

Ramirez nodded. "I'll give her a call."

"IT'S JUST AWFUL," said Janet Fisher, the human resources officer. "When Norma—Ms. Ramirez—when she told me just now, I couldn't believe it. What a terrible thing! Cyndi was such a wonderful person."

Fallon and Sophia were, once again, sitting in chairs set before a wooden desk. Fisher sat behind it. She was a short plump woman in a dark blue rayon-crepe blouse. Her black hair was pulled back into a ponytail, a style that for Sophia seemed a bit too young for someone of her forty years. Behind her tortoiseshell glasses, her brown eyes were excited.

Cyndi might have been a wonderful person, thought Sophia, and her death might be a terrible thing, but this was a real live police investigation. Just like on TV.

"Ms. Fisher," said Fallon. "Has anyone contacted you recently regarding Ms. Purdenelle?"

Sophia looked at him. In the hallways, coming here from Ramirez's office, he'd been guarded about his reason for wanting to talk to Fisher.

"Why, yes." Fisher adjusted her glasses. "Just the other day, as a matter of fact."

"And who was that?"

"A finance company. Hold on. I keep a record of all personnel inquiries." She opened a drawer, pulled out a leather notebook. She set it on the desk, flipped it open, leafed through it, ran her index finger down a page. "Two days ago. Wednesday. A Mr. Adley. D. E. Adley. Knight Finance." She looked up. "Cyndi had applied for a loan, and he needed to confirm some information."

"What kind of information?"

She shrugged. "The usual. Length of employment. Current work schedule."

"D. E. Adley?" said Fallon.

"That's right."

Fallon looked at Sophia.

Suddenly she saw it.

Fallon turned back to Fisher. "Did you call Knight Finance to confirm that this man worked there?"

She frowned. "No. It was a legitimate request. He had her SS number and—" She looked from Fallon to Sophia and then back. "What are you saying?"

"Do you have a phone book?" Fallon asked her.

"Yes, but—"

"May I see it?"

She frowned again, and for a moment she simply stared at him. Then she opened another drawer, pulled out the big St. Petersburg phone book, and, using both hands, passed it across the desk.

Fallon stood up to take it, sat back in the chair, put it on his lap, opened it to the yellow pages, and began to flip through them.

Sophia glanced at Fisher, who was leaning forward against her desk, watching Fallon. Sophia almost felt sorry for her.

Fallon looked up at Fisher. "There *is* no Knight Finance," he told her.

She shook her head. "It was a legitimate inquiry. He had her Social Security number. Maybe it's a new company, one that's not in the book yet."

Fallon nodded. "When you talked to him, did you notice anything unusual about his voice? Anything distinctive?"

"No, it was a totally normal voice."

"No accent?"

"It was a regular voice, no accent, nothing. What's going on here?"

"He didn't give a full name? Just the initials?"

"Just the initials, right." Her face tightening with confusion, she looked again at Sophia.

"Knight Finance," Sophia said. "D. E. Adley. Deadly. Deadly at Night."

Fisher turned to Fallon.

"He likes to play games," Fallon said.

Fisher went white.

"I REALLY DON'T LIKE THIS GUY," Fallon said as they walked back down the corridor, toward Ramirez's office.

"How'd he get the Social Security number?" Sophia asked.

He shrugged. "A private eye. The Internet."

"Not a private eye. He wouldn't want anyone around who could tie him to Purdenelle."

"So all we've got to do is arrest everyone who uses the Internet."

She stopped walking. "Fallon."

He stopped walking, turned back to her. "What?"

"He's not leaving any evidence. No fibers, no hair, nothing."

"He's vacuuming the scene. Taking the bag and the brush with him."

"Yes, but he's not leaving *anything*. If you vacuum a floor, you're going to be leaving evidence *while* you vacuum. Hair, fiber, something."

He frowned.

"Coveralls," she said. "What if he's using the same coveralls that we are?"

He looked at her for a moment, and then reached for his cell phone.

Chapter Twenty-eight

He lay there, the satin sheets deliciously cool against his naked skin. Across the room, the air conditioner purred softly.

Last night had been lovely. Everything had gone wonderfully. Everything had been sheer . . . perfection.

One thing was rather curious, though. Unlike Marcy, Cyndi had seemed more puzzled than terrified by the entire procedure. During Robert's witty little dissertation on the perils of microwave popcorn and tapioca pudding snacks, he'd sometimes had the feeling that if he were to remove the bandanna from Cyndi's mouth, she would merely ask him why he was acting this way.

In similar circumstances, given the opportunity to make an intelligent contribution to the conversation, Marcy would have squealed like a stuck pig.

Which in the end, of course, she had been.

To be fair to Cyndi, he had to admit that over the course of the evening she had demonstrated an almost unsettling sangfroid. No grunting, no groaning, no pathetic little whimpers behind the bandanna.

It had been, to tell the truth, a bit of a disappointment.

To tell the truth, for a while there, before the anesthetic, it had almost sullied the perfection of the evening.

Possibly her sangfroid came from reading Montaigne. Montaigne had practically invented the damn stuff.

Robert had been astonished to see the battered old book at Cyndi's house. Who'd have thought a Wibble-Wobble would pass time with Montaigne when there was so much intellectually stimulating fare on television?

Cyndi being a reader, now that didn't surprise him. But she should've been the kind of reader who cuddles up with a big juicy romance novel, all heaving bosoms and thrusting manhood. Or a dark mystery thriller, plucky young female sleuth matching wits with the wicked criminal mastermind.

And, indeed, there were many such books in Cyndi's humble little abode. After he'd perfected Cyndi—and she had looked absolutely gorgeous, all that Wibble-Wobble excess cut away and slopped into the tub—Robert had ambled through the cottage. He felt, curiously, that after what he and Cyndi had just been through, he had *acquired* the cottage. Like Cyndi herself, it belonged to him now.

There had been books everywhere. And hundreds of mystery novels. But hundreds of other books as well, quite a few of them in French, no less. Including a French edition of Montaigne.

Montaigne had been one of Marla's favorites. He remembered her reading the *Essays* in Puerto Escondido as she lay on the lounge chair beneath the *palapa* of thatch, her long legs outstretched, her long brown hair shining in the bright light that glinted off the surrounding white sand. From time to time, as he lay beside her, under a *palapa* of his own, Robert would look up from some textbook—sociology, criminology, whatever—and admire her poise, her stillness, her absolute completeness.

Ah, well. Marla was gone now.

And so was Cyndi's battered copy of Montaigne. Tossed into a Dumpster on the south end of the island, along with the dismal pastel pink dress he'd stripped from her limp, wobbly body. Naturally, he'd used another Dumpster to dispose of the brush from her vacuum, and a third Dumpster for the bag.

He stretched again against the satin. Slowly. Luxuriously.

It was a wonderful day. Maybe he'd just stay in bed for the rest of it. Cancel everything else and lie there and remember Cyndi.

Remember the way the big blade had eased so smoothly into her plump white flesh, slice, slice, slice . . .

That beautiful dark excitement came trembling over him again, rushing through his head, his chest, his stomach, leaving him nearly breathless.

Yes, cancel everything and just stay here, remembering . . .

Chapter Twenty-nine

We get our crime-scene coveralls," said Fallon, "from Dall's Uniform Supply in St. Pete. So does nearly every police department in Pinellas County."

Courtney nodded.

They were all back in her office—Courtney, Sophia, Fallon, and Kitty Delgado. It was just past one o'clock.

From Mercy Hospital, Fallon had called Kitty. She'd given him the name of the supply company, but she didn't have the phone number with her. He'd used Information to find it, and then he'd telephoned Dall's and explained what he wanted—sales of the coveralls to anyone who wasn't in law enforcement.

"I talked to Dall, the owner, but he was busy," Fallon said. "I gave him the cell phone number. He said he'd get back to me. So far, he hasn't."

"There are hundreds of uniform companies in Florida," said Courtney. "Thousands of them all across the country."

"And if we don't get lucky with Dall's," said Fallon, "we'll check them all out. But those coveralls aren't the kind of thing that most people, most civilians, would buy. And if I were selling them in Chicago, let's say, and I got an order from somewhere in Florida, I'd be a little suspicious. It's something that stands out. And I don't think our guy wants to stand out."

"He doesn't have to be using coveralls," Courtney said. "He could be using something else. Painter's overalls."

"The coveralls are specifically designed to not leave fibers behind. Painter's overalls aren't. I think he'd know that, too. And if he's using the coveralls, I think he's the kind of scumbag who'd get a big kick out of getting them from the same place we get ours."

"And how would he know where that is? How would he know about Dall's?"

"After I called Dall's, I called the Pinellas Sheriff's Department, said I was a writer researching a book. I asked the guy who answered if he could tell me where the department got its crime-scene coveralls. He told me Dall's. He said that all the police departments in the area use Dall's."

Courtney raised her eyebrows. "He flat out told you?"

"Yeah."

Kitty said, "But we don't know that our guy called him, or any of the other PDs."

"It's exactly the kind of thing he'd do. It's what he did with Fisher, the personnel woman at the hospital."

"Does the sheriff's office keep a record of the calls?" asked Kitty. "Get the numbers on caller ID?"

"Yeah, and I asked him to track them for us. But if our guy did call, he probably used a pay phone."

Courtney said, "Good work, Jim."

"Tregaskis's idea," he said.

Courtney turned to Sophia and nodded. "I hope it pans out. But even if it doesn't, it was good thinking, Sophia."

Sophia blushed.

Damn.

Courtney turned back to Fallon. "Okay. What about the people at the hospital? Purdenelle's coworkers?"

"We talked to most of them. Nurses and doctors. According to everyone, she was a saint."

"Close friends?"

"Saints don't have close friends, it looks like. She stayed pretty much to herself."

"Boyfriends? Girlfriends?"

"Not that anyone knew about."

"The same as Fleming," Sophia said. "He picks big women who've got no family, no close friends."

Kitty said, "He doesn't want to be disturbed when he's working on them."

"He has to check them out somehow," said Sophia. "Watch them. First he has to locate them, however he does that, and then—"

A muffled chirping sound interrupted her.

Fallon's cell phone.

Sophia stopped talking, stopped moving.

No one moved, except for Fallon. He slipped the telephone from his pocket, flipped it open, put it to his ear. "Fallon."

Sophia realized that she was holding her breath. She let it out.

"Yes, Mr. Dall." Fallon looked at Courtney. "I appreciate it," he said into the phone. He took out his pen, took the notebook from his shirt pocket.

"Right." He wrote down something, looked at Sophia, grinned again.

Oh my God.

We've got him, Marcy.

"And the credit card number?" Fallon wrote that down. "Visa, right? . . . And the address?" He wrote.

We've actually got the evil son of a bitch.

Please God make it be the right guy.

She looked at Courtney. She was sitting slightly forward, arms on the arms of the chair.

"Right," said Fallon. "When?" He wrote. "How were they delivered? . . . Did he sign for them? . . . And what size? . . . How many?"

He listened, blew air from his mouth, wrote on the yellow sheet. "Right. Thank you, Mr. Dall."

He hung up, looked at Sophia, looked across the desk at Courtney. "Only one citizen over the past year has ordered any of the coveralls." He looked down at the sheet. "Robert Ambrose. One thirty-four Paradise Road, Elfers." He turned to Sophia. "Where's Elfers?"

"North of Tarpon Springs," she said. "Just past Holiday. Pasco County."

"When did he order them?" Courtney asked.

"Last week. Four days before Fleming was killed. He paid extra for overnight delivery. And he wanted them left at the address. Without a signature from him." He shook his head. "Overnight goddamn delivery." He held up the notebook. "This is our guy."

"Maybe," said Courtney.

"How many did he order?" Sophia asked.

"The coveralls come in boxes of twelve. He ordered two boxes of mediums. Twenty-four pairs."

"Shit," said Courtney.

No one else spoke.

"Okay," Courtney said to Fallon. "Kitty and Eckhardt can finish the search at Purdenelle's house. You and Sophia take off for Elfers. I'll call the Pasco Sheriff's Department, have them get a warrant. I'll call you on the road, let you know where to meet them. I'll need that credit card number."

He tore the sheet from his notebook, handed it to her.

She nodded. "I'll get a court order," she said, sitting back. "Track the card, see what else our friend has been buying lately."

Fallon glanced at his watch. "I'm supposed to see the chief at two."

Courtney lowered the sheet. "What about?"

"Remaining on the force."

After a moment, she smiled. "Him or you?"

"Me."

"I'll call him, tell him what's happening. You take off."

"WHAT DID YOU MEAN?" Sophia asked him. "About remaining on the force?"

Once again they were heading north, toward Treasure Island.

"The chief got a little upset this morning," Fallon said. "When I stopped him from going into the crime scene."

"Damn it, Fallon. You said you weren't in trouble."

He smiled the faint smile. "If this guy is our scumbag, then I won't be."

She looked at him. "Then I guess he'd better be our scumbag."

He nodded. "I guess he'd better." He turned to look out the window.

She took Gulf Boulevard through Treasure Island until they reached the Causeway, then she turned right and they drove over the Intercoastal. Today the water was still, the air was calm. Above, the sky was bright blue, not a cloud anywhere. It still seemed impossible that a hurricane could be ripping across the Gulf of Mexico, heading directly for them.

The traffic on U.S. 19 was as heavy as usual. This was the main north and south route through western Pinellas County, and it was crowded not only with locals but with the tourists who were silly enough to come down here in August. She stayed in the far left lane, passing cars whenever she could, and drove up through Largo, Clearwater, Dunedin, Palm Harbor. None of these were actually visible as distinct cities and towns—this stretch of road had become one long swath of malls and record stores and chain bookstores and chain restaurants. Even Tarpon Springs, or the part of it they drove through, was indistinguishable from the rest. And yet only a few miles west lay the neighborhood in which Sophia had grown up—the sponge docks, the Bayou, Costas's Butcher Shop, the house that had been her parents' before they moved to Miami.

"Fallon," she said.

He turned to her. "Yeah?"

"The credit card. He's been so careful about everything else."

"People make mistakes."

"Our guy hasn't. Not so far."

"All we need is one."

His cell phone chirped.

He slipped it out, flipped it open. "Fallon. . . . Okay. . . . Okay. . . . Right. . . . As soon as I can. Bye."

He flipped the phone shut and turned to Sophia. "Courtney. There's a strip mall in Elfers on State Road 54, south side of the street. A store called Beauford's. You know it?"

"I'll find it. Elfers isn't very big."

"We're meeting the sheriff's people there. A Deputy Morrison will have the warrant."

She nodded. "Okay."

Please God make it be the right guy.

Chapter Thirty

Robert lightly whisked the free-range eggs until they were a lemony yellow—the color, as Marla used to say, of Tuscany sunlight. One day he'd have to go to Florence and see that sunlight for himself.

Setting the bowl on the countertop, he went to check on the electric broiler.

The red indicator light had blinked out. The broiler was ready. Splendid.

He turned on the gas beneath the Calphalon sauté pan, sliced a thick pat of butter from the stick, tapped the pat into the center of the pan. After a moment it began to creep across the nonstick surface.

He had canceled everything and spent most of the morning lying in bed, recollecting in tranquillity his lovely encounter with Cyndi. But the hours had passed quickly, time flies when you're having fun, and now it was well past noon. Lunch was definitely in order.

He had decided upon a frittata. He hadn't done a frittata in ages.

Fortunately, he had all the ingredients he needed—the Monterey Jack, the avocado, the black American olives, the sour cream. He had grated the cheese, sliced the avocado, chopped the olives. He had thrown together a quick salad of endive and sprouts, whipped up a simple dressing of walnut oil and sherry vinegar, with a dollop of Dijon and the tiniest pinch of cayenne. He had opened up the bottle of Sterling sauvignon blanc and poured himself a glass. Tasted it. Not bad.

The pan hissed. Robert lifted it slightly, letting the foaming butter trickle down the surface. He changed the pan's angle, swirled the butter to the far side, sizzling and sputtering. He set down the pan, grabbed the bowl of eggs, whisked them a bit more, and then, just as the butter began to brown, eased the eggs into the pan.

Bubble, bubble, toil and trouble.

He put aside the bowl, picked up a fork, gently stirred the eggs. As the edge of the frittata began to crisp, he used the fork to pry it slightly from the pan, letting the yellow custard flow underneath. When there was no liquid left, but before the custard had completely set, he quickly tossed the grated cheese on top, distributing it evenly, left, right, up, down, around and around, and then shuttled the pan over to the oven. He opened the door and slid the pan under the broiler. He closed the door and thumbed the button that turned on the oven light. He slipped on the pot-holder glove.

After only a few seconds the cheese began to melt. He waited until it was bubbly, just starting to glaze with brown, and then he opened the oven door, grabbed the pan's handle, tugged out the pan, slipped the frittata onto the plate that waited on the serving tray. He plucked off the glove, rapidly arranged the avocado slices, the olives. A shake of sea salt, a grinding of black pepper. He dribbled some salsa over the top, then capped everything with a plump spoonful of sour cream.

Yummy.

He looked over the tray to make sure that everything else was there. Wine, salad, napkin, knife, fork.

Check.

And now, back to the bedroom. Put something thoughtful on the stereo. Enjoy some more recollections. He had the whole afternoon to himself.

Chapter Thirty-one

The house was set back from the narrow country road in the dark shade beneath towering live oaks trees draped with Spanish moss. The road itself dead-ended another fifty feet beyond the house, stopped abruptly amid the pines and cypresses, a road that had simply given up.

If nowhere actually had a middle, thought Sophia, this would be it.

It was a small one-story house, one that probably held no more than two tiny bedrooms. It had been white once, but the paint was dingy now, as though the shadows of the live oaks had seeped into the wooden siding over the years, slowly and irreparably staining it. There was a pitched-roof porch with a low, white wooden balustrade that ran around its perimeter except for an opening in the center, at three rickety-looking front steps. On the porch, to the left of the door, was a wooden swing seat. There were three curtained casement windows to the left of the front door, and two more to the right. Jutting out the window farthest from the door was a bulky air conditioner.

There was no real yard. Raggedy palmetto and shag pine grew in the sandy soil in front of the house. To the right, at the end of the driveway, and separated from the main building by more palmetto, stood a pitched-roof, white wooden garage, as dingy and stained as the house.

Deputy Morrison drove his Chevrolet cruiser into the rutted dirt driveway. In the Ford, Fallon sitting beside her, Sophia followed and parked behind him.

THEY HAD MET THE DEPUTIES at the parking lot of Beauford's, on State Road 54. Morrison was a tall, big-boned, big-bellied man in his forties with a patient manner and a surprisingly soft voice. Conners was in his twenties, nearly as tall as Morrison but gangly. He was red-haired, his white skin spattered with freckles. He kept casting quick, shy glances at Sophia, his pale eyelashes fluttering, his mouth moving in a small, nervous smile, as though he'd never seen a woman cop before. Maybe he never had.

Morrison had brought along the warrant, a survey map of the area, and some information. The four of them stood out in the sun-baked parking lot beside the Sheriff's Department cruiser while Morrison gave Sophia and Fallon what he had.

"House belongs to a Millicent Ambrose," he said in that gentle voice, reading from his notebook. "Been in her name since 1961, belonged to her parents before that. I ran her through DMV. Florida license, renewed in 1998, still good. Date of birth, March twenty-third, 1940. Height, five foot three. Hair, brown. Eyes, brown. There was a license on a Robert Ambrose, issued in '81, expired in '86. Date of birth, April twenty-eight, 1965. Height, five foot eight. Hair, brown. Eyes, blue. We've got nothing on either of them. No arrests."

"So Robert's the son," said Fallon.

"Looks like."

"Registered vehicles?"

"Nothing in his name. An '82 Chevy in hers."

"And where's this house?"

Morrison shut his notebook, slipped it into his back pocket. He unfolded the map, spread it along the hood of the Chevy. "Here's where we are." He tapped his thick forefinger at the map. "And here's Paradise Road. It's not really in the township—Elfers is just the mailing address. This is number 134, at the end. The road stops right after the house. We got good cover all around, stands of slash pine and cypress. What I'm thinking, you and me and Tregaskis here, we approach from the front."

Sophia shot him a look.

Tregaskis here. As though she were an afterthought.

He didn't notice the look. "Billy, now," he said, nodding to Conners, "he goes around back, on foot. In case our boy takes off into the woods. We stop here, this bend in the road, 'bout a hundred yards from the house, and Billy springs into action. Right, Billy?"

"Right, Bob." Conners smiled at Sophia, fluttered his lashes, smiled his nervous smile. Despite his height, he looked about twelve.

Sorry, Red. You're just not my type.

Morrison took off his cap, ran his left hand back over his balding scalp. He asked Fallon, "That work for you?"

Fallon looked at Sophia, raised his eyebrows.

She turned to Morrison. "It works for me," she said.

Fallon said, "We want him alive."

Morrison nodded. "That'd be my first choice."

"I just want to be sure we're all in the same movie."

"And you two folks," said Morrison, "you're the stars. I know that. But this here is gonna be my one big scene. So if it's okay with you, I'll do the talking. To start out with, anyway."

"Your jurisdiction, Deputy," said Fallon.

"Kay, then," said Morrison. "Let's do it."

ALL THREE OF THEM WERE OUT OF THE CARS in the shade beneath the live oaks. The shade was deceptive—from inside the car, the area around the trees had looked cool and inviting. But the air was hot and heavy and still, and Sophia was sweating before she walked three feet along the dusty driveway. Above them, the gray Spanish moss hung limp and unmoving.

She had clipped her holster to the small of her back. Except for practice on the range, she had never fired the Smith .41 it held.

Up ahead, Morrison stood at the base of the front steps and stared at the building. He adjusted his holster. He turned to Fallon.

"My scene, remember," he told Fallon.

"Right. Air conditioner's running."

"I hear it."

The three of them climbed up the steps. There was no doorbell. Morrison drew his Glock, held it down by his right thigh, tugged at the screen door with his left hand, swung it open, caught it on his thick right shoulder. He knocked on the wooden door.

"I can hear music," said Sophia. She felt her heart thumping against her chest.

Morrison nodded. He rapped his knuckles at the door again.

Nothing.

Morrison called out, "Mr. Ambrose?"

Nothing but the music, faint and muffled.

Pianos and strings. Something classical.

"Mr. Ambrose?"

Still nothing.

Morrison tried the doorknob. Locked.

He stepped away from the door, turned back to Fallon. "We're going in."

Fallon nodded.

Morrison looked at Sophia. "You ready, Detective?"

Sophia felt her heartbeat quicken. "Yes."

She and Fallon eased back. Fallon reached behind him, under his shirt, and pulled out his Smith. Sophia pulled out hers. The grip was damp against her fingers. Flicking the safety with her thumb, she raised the pistol and snugged her finger along the trigger guard.

Her heart was slamming against her rib cage now. Her scalp itched and sweat was stinging the corners of her eyes.

Morrison looked at them, nodded, and turned to the door. Holding the pistol up, his elbow cocked, he stepped back, braced himself on his left foot, raised his right leg, then lashed it out like a piston. The door snapped open with a sharp *pop* and swung wildly out of sight. Before it crashed against the interior wall, Morrison had already shifted to the left, out of the doorway, his shoulder against the siding. He moved quickly for a big man.

"Billy!" Morrison hollered into the doorway. "You stay put! We're going in!"

The door swung slowly back toward the shattered jamb, creaking.

Morrison looked at Fallon. "I go in first, and I go left. You two go right."

Fallon nodded. "Your big scene, Deputy."

"Right."

Morrison tapped lightly at the door with the barrel of his pistol. It creaked open again, and stayed open. The Glock held upright with both hands, he stepped quickly into the house, Fallon grabbing the screen door before it closed behind him. Inside, Morrison swung left, swung right, then turned back to Fallon and nodded.

Fallon stepped in. Sophia followed.

This had once been a living room. There were two more windows on the far wall. In the murky light that filtered through the heavy curtains, Sophia could see that the room was empty. No furniture, no pictures on the dark paneled wall, nothing.

Nothing but the music. Louder now but still muffled, it was coming from the hallway to the right.

She looked to the left. The kitchen was empty—no chairs, no table, no appliances except for the old, white round-shouldered refrigerator. But a cutting board lay on the Formica countertop, and a large black cast-iron frying pan on the left front burner of the stove.

At the far end of the house, beyond the kitchen, was a door with another curtained window. As Morrison walked toward the door, Sophia looked at Fallon.

He nodded toward the hallway, then moved toward it. She followed.

The air inside here was stifling. A bead of sweat trickled down her forehead. She wiped it away with the back of her left wrist.

Above the hollow sound of their footsteps on the wooden floor, Fallon's brogues, her pumps, she could hear her own breathing.

Two doors on the right. When they came to the first of them, Fallon signaled her to move ahead. She did, and then, just past the door, she stopped and put her back to the wall. Holding the Smith with the barrel at ninety degrees from the floor, she glanced to her right, at the final door. The music was coming from there.

On the opposite side of the first door, keeping his own back to the wall, Fallon reached for the doorknob, turned it, shoved the door open. He waited a moment, then wheeled into the room.

Sophia stayed where she was, ready to swing left or right.

A rasping noise from the living room startled her. She turned, bringing her Smith down.

Morrison, using the barrel of his Glock to slide open a curtain. Behind him, peering at her around his shoulder, stood Conners.

Sophia let out breath.

Fallon came out of the room, saw the two deputies, held up a hand, made a pushing motion. Stay back.

He looked at Sophia, jerked his head toward the final door.

The music grew louder as they approached, the strings racing toward a climax.

They went through the same procedure, Sophia taking position on the far side of the door, Fallon on the near side. He reached out, turned the doorknob, threw open the door. The music swelled, the violins furiously chasing after the pianos. Fallon swung into the room.

Sophia was holding her breath.

She saw Fallon's shoulder move, and then a light came on inside the room.

He leaned back, looked at her. "Hold on a minute." He went into the room.

She waited for a moment or two, then thought, screw this. She stepped into the room.

Except for Fallon, no one was there. But the room wasn't empty.

To the left, against the wall, was a neatly made single bed covered with a red-and-yellow-striped bedspread, a pillow plump beneath it. At the base of the bed was a pinewood footlocker, a folded Mexican blanket smoothed out along its top and hanging down its sides. At the head of the bed, just to its left, was a small pinewood nightstand that held a bright yellow gooseneck reading lamp. Beside the lamp was a perfectly ordered stack of magazines. The topmost magazine was something called *Famous Monsters of Filmland*. On the shelf underneath the magazines was a boxy, old-looking radio and cassette player. The music was coming from the radio, reaching a crescendo now.

Fallon stood at the opened door of a small closet. He holstered his pistol, pulled a pair of gloves from his pocket, slipped them on. He crossed the small room, stabbed his index finger at the radio's OFF button. Silence. Suddenly the room seemed larger.

Sophia looked around. Thumbtacked to the walls were movie posters—*Frankenstein*, *Dracula*, *The Wolf Man*. To her right, just before the closet, was a pinewood dresser. Along the dresser's top was a small fleet of plastic model airplanes, jets and propeller craft, each held aloft on a gray plastic pedestal.

"A kid's room," said Morrison, behind her. Sophia spun around.

Morrison and Conners stood in the doorway.

"A boy's room," Fallon said.

He went back to the closet door and moved down into a squat.

Sophia came closer.

Hanging neatly inside the small closet were small jackets and coats, a red nylon windbreaker, a yellow plastic raincoat. On the floor were shoes and sneakers, a pair of rubber galoshes, everything carefully paired off, everything child-sized. To the left of them, up against the wall of the closet, was some kind of box hidden beneath a fitted piece of gray canvas. Fallon reached into the closet, pulled off the canvas. It was an animal cage. He put a hand on either side of it and stood up, lifting it from the floor.

Morrison said, "What the hell . . ."

On the floor of the cage, lying atop a pile of yellowed strips of newspaper, beside the wire running wheel, was a stiff bundle of white fur. It looked like a handful of toilet paper, crumpled and tossed aside.

"A rat," said Fallon. "Maybe a hamster. Hard to tell. Most of it's rotted away."

"Been dead awhile, looks like," said Morrison.

Fallon nodded. "Years."

"Maybe," said Morrison, "we should take a look inside that garage."

IT WAS SEALED FROM THE OUTSIDE, at the bottom of the one-piece door, with a padlock and chain. As Morrison retrieved a pair of bolt cutters from the Chevy, Fallon, Sophia, and Conners stood out there in that deceptive, sweltering shade.

"He's using the house as a mail drop," Fallon said.

"You still think he's our guy?" she asked him.

"The house was a setup. He wanted us think he was still here. That's why he left the radio on, put that stuff around the kitchen. The cutting board, the pan on the stove."

She nodded.

She felt drained.

Adrenaline overload.

And that little bedroom was just too *weird*. The neatly organized clothes, the horror-movie posters, the brittle little carcass in the cage. Except for the dead animal, the room could have come out of some 1950s sitcom. But inside that silent, empty, sterile house, the stiff little scrap of skin and fur had seemed ominous and . . . nasty.

"You been a cop for long?" Conners asked her. His accent was Southern.

"A couple of years," she said.

"You like it?"

"Love it."

He grinned, and she understood why his standard smile was nervous. His teeth were misshapen and gray. "Me, too," he said.

Morrison lugged the bolt cutters to the garage door, bent down, slipped the blades around a link in the chain. Beneath his shirt, the heavy shoulder muscles bunched together, and then the link snapped apart. He dropped the cutters to the dirt, pulled the chain through its hasp, flipped it to one side. He took hold of the door handle at the bottom of the door and pulled. The door swung out and up.

The inside walls and roof were unfinished, the studs visible. Here and there, between the studs, Sophia saw elaborate spiderwebs.

The front part of the garage was empty, except for two stacks of flattened cardboard boxes against the left wall, each about four feet high. Whoever had stacked them had been neat. The boxes were all the same size, the corners all scrupulously aligned. The topmost box was thick with dust, maybe years of dust, but beneath it, against a faint red background, Sophia could read the words POPOV VODKA.

Halfway into the garage, about seven feet from the door, a pleated, folding metal wall ran across the entire width of the building. Its top and bottom were held in place by stainless steel runners on the ceiling and the cement floor. On the right side of the wall, in a small circular opening in a metal faceplate, next to the framing, there was a Yale lock.

There was a short cylindrical electric switch on the left wall, above the boxes and between the studs. Morrison flicked it on.

Nothing happened. Sophia saw that one of the wires from the switch ran back along the framing and disappeared behind the metal wall. If there was a light, it was back there.

Morrison and Fallon walked up to the right side of the wall.

Morrison tapped a knuckle at the metal. It gave off a hollow ring. "Pretty solid piece of hardware," he said.

"Your warrant," said Fallon. "Will it cover breaking that open? If there's any evidence in there, I don't want some judge tossing it out."

"Judge Needham, he writes a good warrant. Billy? Go get me the crowbar, sport."

As Conners passed Sophia, he gave her another quick, fluttery glance.

Morrison looked over at the cardboard boxes. "Those things, they've been there a long time. That dust there?"

"Yeah," said Fallon. "But none on the cement floor. He swept it, and not long ago."

"The house, too."

Conners returned, swinging the crowbar. "Here you go, Bob."

Morrison took the crowbar, angled it between the lock and the framing. Facing the framing, he leaned his weight against the bar. A small squeak. He reversed his hands on the bar, and this time he pulled outward. Once again, the muscles bunched up along his shoulders.

Another squeak, a bit louder this time.

His hands resting on the bar, Morrison took a deep breath, let it out. "He's got the damn thing screwed to a two-by-four that runs along the frame. Nice piece of work. The prick."

"Want some help?" Fallon asked.

Morrison slid his hands along the bar and stepped lightly to his right, leaving Fallon room between Morrison and the metal wall. "Be my guest."

Fallon grasped the bar. "Pull or push?"

"Pull. Ready?"

"Go."

The two men pulled. Fallon's face tightened.

The bar moved, the lock made another squeaking sound.

"She's coming," said Morrison.

The door tore loose with an explosive, splintering crack. Holding the crowbar in his left hand, Morrison pushed the door along with his right, snagged it on something, and pushed again, forcing it. The door folded against itself with a clatter.

"*Holy Jesus*," Conners said. Fallon and Morrison stepped back.

For a second Sophia didn't quite understand what she was seeing.

Raised on a wooden platform two feet above the floor was a huge glass tank, a giant aquarium filled nearly to the top with clear liquid.

It was perhaps six feet tall and six feet deep by eight feet wide, its widest side facing them. The light on the garage ceiling shone down on the glass cover of the tank, down through the liquid; and inside it, floating there, suspended, was the thing she didn't understand.

And then she did.

It was the bloated body, immense and gray and naked, of a woman. She lay in the liquid at an angle, facing them, the dark soles of her feet toward the front of the tank, her big head and her softly bobbing gray hair toward the rear, as though she had begun to topple backward and had then magically stopped in midfall. Her thick arms were outspread, the hands and fingers limp, and her massive, mottled thighs were parted. Her jaw was sagging, her mouth awry, and her dark eyes stared out through the liquid, out through the glass.

But why floating there? Why hadn't she risen to the surface?

She looked more closely at the woman's feet.

They were chained to the floor of the tank.

Morrison said, "Now who—"

Suddenly, at the bottom of the tank, in the center, there was a blur of movement and something clanged against the glass, loudly. A crack appeared in the front of the tank and shot upward, jagged, like a lightning bolt.

Sophia stared. What the hell . . . ?

"Back back back!"

It was Fallon, and he was grabbing her arm and wrenching her around, toward the front of the garage, and she was moving into a run when she heard a monstrous shattering sound behind her, and then a monstrous roar, and then something cold and wet slammed hard against her legs and she was flung, spinning, arms flailing, onto her back, into the rush of foul-smelling current, the liquid sweeping over her, over her legs, her stomach, her face, filling her nose and throat, burning like acid against her eyes, blinding her. She coughed, choked, thrashed her arms. Her shoulder smacked against the concrete floor and then something huge and rubbery and dark embraced her, and she was gone.

Chapter Thirty-two

"She's okay," Fallon said into the cell phone. As he leaned against the Ford, he glanced up at Tregaskis. She sat huddled on the swing seat on the porch, wrapped in a blanket that Morrison had pulled from the trunk of his cruiser. She had rinsed her hair in the outside faucet, and it hung darkly wet and curly against her shoulders.

For at least twenty minutes the house and the porch had been swarming with crime-unit techs and deputies from the Pasco County Sheriff's Department, everyone in white coveralls. After speaking to Morrison, they had all studiously ignored her. Fallon suspected that at the moment she preferred to be ignored.

"She swallowed some of the alcohol," he said, "but—"

"*Swallowed* it?" said Courtney.

"She threw it up when she came to. She's okay."

"How the hell did it happen?"

"He booby-trapped the tank. It was made out of plate glass, maybe an inch thick. There was a spring mechanism under the support, attached to a length of steel. Rigged to go off after a delay. When Morrison opened the folding door, he pulled loose a cotter pin that set it going."

"Is Morrison all right?"

"Yeah, but his partner isn't. When the tank went, a big piece of glass caught him in the throat. He's dead."

Tregaskis and Conners had been standing closest to the tank when it ruptured. Fallon had thought he could get Sophia clear, but the tank had blown too quickly and the flood had torn her from his hands. He'd been staggered, nearly knocked off his feet himself, but the flood had quickly washed away, flushed itself out onto the driveway, and he'd rushed to Tregaskis and pulled away that huge rubbery body. The gray flesh, reeking of alcohol, was slippery and spongy beneath his fingers. His eyes were stinging from the fumes as he checked Sophia's pulse. She was all right.

It was then that he glanced over at Conners. Morrison was saying, "*Shit, shit, shit,*" and he was kneeling in a puddle of alcohol on the cement floor beside the younger deputy, using both hands as he tried to stop the bright red arterial blood that spurted from Conner's neck and fanned out across the shiny wet floor. Conners' hands had been beneath Morrison's, holding on to his own throat, and his eyes had been staring at his partner's face, looking up at Morrison as though he wanted to ask him some important question.

There had been no way to stop the bleeding.

"Jesus," said Courtney. "Tell him I'm sorry."

"Yeah."

Courtney was silent for a moment. "What about this delay? On the booby trap?"

"The scumbag wanted us to see the woman. Inside the tank, before it went."

"He knew you were coming."

"He knew someone was coming."

"What kind of alcohol?"

"There's a bunch of old vodka cases piled up in the garage, but the ME says that vodka wouldn't be a strong enough solution to preserve a body. From the smell, he thinks the tank was mostly filled with high-proof grain alcohol."

"This is the Pasco County ME?"

"Yeah. Stillwell. He sounds like he knows what he's doing."

"Does he have any idea how long the body's been in there?"

"Could be years, he says. I think it was. She was attached to the floor with chains and bolts. The bolts had corroded. That why the body broke free when the tank went."

"Chains? She was *alive* when he put her in there?"

"Stillwell won't know for sure until he takes a look at her lungs and stomach. We'll have a copy of the report by tomorrow afternoon. But why else would he use the chains?"

"How did he get her in there? She was a woman of size, you said."

"One of the side walls of the tank is dovetailed into the others. We figure he put her in there first, dead or drunk or drugged, then slid that final wall into place and used some kind of epoxy to seal it. Then he filled it."

"But you said the platform is raised. He'd have to be fairly strong to get her up there by himself."

"Maybe he used some kind of hoist. There's nothing like that around, but he could've gotten rid of it. Or maybe he drugged her, and then helped her climb up there."

"He's a real Boy Scout."

"Yeah."

"Any idea who she is?"

"I'm guessing Millicent Ambrose."

"Mother? Wife?"

"Mother."

"Lovely." She paused for a moment. "All right, look. You're sure Sophia is okay?"

"As okay as anyone could be, considering."

"She can travel?"

"After we pick up some clothes, get her cleaned up."

"She doesn't want a doctor?"

"She says no."

"All right. I've been in touch with the company that issued Ambrose's credit card. They'll be faxing me a list of his charges."

"Good."

"How soon can you get back here?"

"We've both got to get some clean clothes."

"Can you make it by eight? Chief Anderson is holding a press conference tonight, at nine, and he wants a debriefing at eight."

"Debriefing?"

"He's called in a FBI profiler."

"For Christ's sake."

"It's *his* call, Jim. He wants all of us to meet this guy before the conference."

Fallon glanced at his watch. It was only five-thirty.

How could all of this have happened in only a few short hours?

"Where?" he said.

"City Hall. Conference room number three."

"We'll be there. But what about tracking down Robert Ambrose?"

"Let Pasco County handle it for now. The woman's body is in their jurisdiction. Maybe they'll turn up a picture of him. You can head back up there tomorrow."

"First thing in the morning."

"The memorial service for Fleming is tomorrow morning. At eleven. Press releases have already gone out."

"Then tomorrow afternoon. You've got video cameras arranged for the service?"

"Yeah. And we'll get some set up for tonight, for the press conference."

"Listen. Can you get Eva Swanson into that debriefing?"

"Good idea. Anderson will probably want her at the press conference, too. I'll call her."

"Thanks. We'll see you at seven."

"Tregaskis?"

She stared up at him, her hair still damp. What little makeup she usually wore had been wiped away. She looked about fifteen years old.

Except for her eyes. Her eyes looked ageless and empty, and Fallon wondered if she was looking at him or through him.

"How you feeling?"

"I stink," she said, her voice small. Shivering, she looked away.

He sat down beside her, and the swing seat swayed. A small squeak came from the chains that supported it.

She looked so lost and frail that he wanted to reach out and take her in his arms. But he was afraid he might startle her, and afraid that if he made her frailty explicit, if he let her know that he'd seen it, she'd never stop resenting him.

"We've got to head back," he told her. "Anderson wants a meeting. He's bringing in a profiler."

Still looking away, frowning as though she didn't understand the word, she pulled the blanket more tightly about her shoulders. "Profiler?"

"FBI."

Another frown as she turned to him. "What about Swanson?"

"She'll be there, too. Courtney's calling her. And after the debriefing, we'll all be having a little press conference."

"Fallon, I *stink*."

"We'll stop in Holiday, get some clothes, find a motel where you can take a shower. Or I can take you home. No sweat. No one's going to think you faded. You've been through a lot today."

"No. We'll find a motel."

He heard a vehicle pull into the driveway. He stood up.

Beyond the yellow crime-scene tape, beyond Fallon and Tregaskis's Ford and the five or six Pasco County black-and-whites, an ambulance pulled off the driveway, onto the sandy earth along the county road. The paramedics. Come to take away the bodies.

Two of them, both in blue shirts, stepped from the ambulance and started walking toward the garage, where Stillwell, the ME, stood waiting for them.

Fallon looked down at Tregaskis. She was still staring forward.

"Hold on," he said. "I need to talk to Morrison for a minute."

He stepped over to the screen door, called out the deputy's name. After a moment, Morrison appeared behind the mesh, looking bulky and bulbous in his coveralls. His eyes were as empty as Tregaskis's. He didn't open the door.

"Yeah?" he said.

"Find anything yet?"

Morrison just looked at him, as though trying to decide whether to answer. Finally he said, "Like you said. No prints, no fiber, no hair. Everything's been washed and wiped. Even the bedroom. All that kid stuff is clean."

Fallon nodded. "I hate to say it, but this scumbag is good."

"This scumbag is dead," Morrison said. "The minute I find him."

"He won't be anywhere nearby. And he probably won't be calling himself Robert Ambrose."

"Doesn't matter. Wherever he is, whatever he is, I'll find him."

Fallon could hear the anger in the deputy's soft voice, and he knew that there was guilt behind it. And he knew that the anger was directed as much at Morrison himself as it was at Robert Ambrose.

A simple little cotter pin.

Fallon nodded. "We're taking off for St. Anselm. We'll be up here again tomorrow."

Morrison glanced over at Tregaskis. "How's she doing?"

"She'll be okay." Fallon took a breath. "Look. I'm sorry about Conners. My lieutenant, she told me to tell you that she's sorry, too."

Morrison didn't speak for a moment. Then he said, "Yeah. Thanks. Thank her for me."

"I'll call you in the morning."

"Right."

Fallon turned, stepped over to the swing seat. "You ready?"

Tregaskis looked up at him. "Okay."

She stood up, a bit unsteady on her feet.

"Fallon?" Morrison called out.

Fallon turned.

"I'll find out what I can," said Morrison. "About Ambrose. I'll let you know."

"Thanks. Same here."

Morrison looked again at Tregaskis, turned, and then moved away, a hulking white form sinking back into the shadows of the house.

Fallon walked across the porch beside Tregaskis. As they reached the steps, she stumbled, and he reached for her, wrapping his arm around her shoulder. For a moment she swayed against him. Her hand slipped out from beneath the blanket, rose to her shoulder, and found his.

Fallon glanced to his left and saw that one of the paramedics, over by the garage, was aiming a camera at them. He knew that some paramedics took photographs of catastrophes and sold them to the wire services.

He wanted to run down the driveway, rip the camera from the man's hand, and shove it down his throat.

The medical examiner moved between Fallon and the paramedic, said something under his breath, and the man lowered the camera.

Tregaskis swayed away from Fallon, let her hand fall from his. "I'm okay."

He released her shoulder. "I'll drive."

She looked at him. "You never drive."

"I'll drive."

Chapter Thirty-three

Her head bowed, her eyes shut, her arms hanging at her sides, Sophia stood in the shower and let the hot water sting her scalp and shoulders and back.

She was unspeakably tired. She felt as though every particle of energy in her body had been drained away, the way the water at her feet was draining away now, swirling and gurgling, at the bottom of the cheap fiberglass tub.

And no matter how tightly she shut her eyes, no matter how tightly she tried to shut her mind, images kept flooding across it. Those cruel chains shackling the thick gray ankles. That enormous body floating silently in the tank, the fat, gray, dimpled arms and legs extended, the huge, black-nippled breasts sprawled above the bloated, pendulous gray stomach.

That sudden blur at the base of the tank, the clang of metal, the zigzag fracture bolting up the glass as she stood there, stupidly marveling.

The sweep of the stinking fluid as it enveloped her, inescapable, blinding her, gagging her. The sudden, awful impact of that horrible bloated thing against her own body. Blackness.

And then coming to, slowly and painfully rolling onto her hands and knees, gasping at first, sucking in that piercing chemical stench, and then puking her guts out onto the floor of the garage, her shoulders heaving, Fallon's hand at her damp back.

And then raising her head and turning to see Conners lying there on the floor in a broad puddle of alcohol that had inexplicably turned a bright scarlet . . .

She slumped against the tile wall.

The tiles were cold against her skin, but she didn't care.

She put her hands to her eyes, pressed her fingers against them, as though the pressure would somehow blot away the images. Stars and pinwheels danced in the blackness. The scalding water drummed against her neck.

Abruptly she dropped her arms.

Fallon was waiting. Courtney was waiting.

Marcy was waiting.

Let's go, *koritsi mou.*

SHE OPENED THE DOOR OF THE FORD, climbed into the passenger seat, pulled the door shut. Her hair was still damp, and the cool air inside the car seemed almost arctic.

Fallon turned to her. "Better?"

"Yes." She looked away, out the window, across the parking lot of the Motel 6.

"The clothes are okay?"

"They're fine. Thank you."

They weren't bad, really. Not anything she'd buy for herself, but not completely horrible. A simple white cotton blouse, a black skirt, a pair of black leather flats. Underneath, a plain white cotton bra and cotton panties. There was a Target in Holiday, close to the motel, and Fallon had stopped outside the store and she'd given him her sizes. Normally she'd have been embarrassed about doing that, particularly with someone like Fallon, but just then she couldn't bring herself to care.

When he came back to the car, he was wearing a new white shirt, a new pair of khaki slacks, a new pair of shoes. Somehow he'd managed to buy everything, his and hers, then clean himself up in there and change his clothes, all in less than half an hour.

Leaning back against the headrest, Sophia watched the town of Holiday slide by.

"What'd you do with the old clothes?" Fallon asked her.

"I left them there." In the wastebasket, still stinking of alcohol.

He nodded. "I stripped your Smith. And wiped it down. It's on the backseat."

The pistol had gotten drenched when she'd been swept away.

"Thank you," she said.

What sort of a gun had Conners used? A Glock, of course, like Morrison's.

Who would be stripping it down for him, who would be wiping it clean?

Someone would have to, of course. The pistol would be carefully dismantled, the clip removed and unloaded, the slide stripped away, and everything would carefully be cleaned and oiled, and the weapon would carefully be put back into stock, and then, sometime in the future, it would be reissued.

To some new young cop. Maybe even one with ridiculous red hair and freckles and a gangly body and a gawky smile that showed off his mismatched teeth.

"How long you been a cop?"

"Couple of years."

"You like it?"

"Love it."

"Me, too."

She didn't really know she was crying until she felt, in the cool air, the chill of drying tears along her cheeks. She lowered her head and raised her right hand and tented it over her forehead, as though she were trying to rest. She bit her lower lip.

Fallon slowed the car, made a right, pulled to a stop.

She looked out the window, blinking.

An Albertson's parking lot. They were parked maybe fifty yards from the nearest car.

She didn't look at Fallon. She couldn't. Staring out the window, she took a deep, ratchety breath and said, "I'm okay."

"Sure."

"Really." She sucked in another breath. "Let's go."

She tried to get it all back together. But the tears just kept oozing out, slowly but steadily, coming from some part of her that was independent of her will. She lowered her head, hid her eyes again.

"Look," said Fallon. She heard him take a deep breath and sigh.

"I'm not much good at this," he said quietly. "So you're going to have to bear with me. I know you've had a bad day—"

She snorted, something that was half a laugh, half a sob. *"Bad day?* Jesus, Fallon." Still not looking up, she shook her head. A teardrop pattered onto her skirt.

"I know you feel like shit about Conners—"

"I hardly knew him." She swallowed, then raised her head to look at Fallon. "He was flirting with me, grinning like a goon, and I thought he was just . . . just some dumb redneck. And if I'd been standing a foot more to the right—"

"You'd be the one who's dead, maybe, and he'd be the one who feels like shit." He took another deep breath, sighed it out again. "We have the kind of job where bad things happen. People get hurt. They die."

She looked down again.

"And we're left to deal with it," he said. "We're alive and they aren't, so there's relief on top of the grief, and there's guilt. But we've got to remember that other people with the same job have gone through the same shit, thousands of times before. We've got to remember that we can get through it. And that maybe it'll even make us better cops."

She sniffled, and she hated the sound it made. "Right. Sure."

"How do you think Morrison feels? Conners was his partner. If Morrison had been a little more careful, maybe Conners would still be alive." Fallon's voice changed, got lighter. "And you wouldn't be sitting there in a cheap blouse from Target."

She tried for a smile, felt it falter.

"How long you been a cop?"

Sorry, Red. You're just not my type.

And then she was sobbing full out, both hands against her face, tears burning her eyes, spasms wracking her shoulders.

She knew, at some deep level, far beneath the grief and tears, that this was somehow ridiculous, somehow pathetic. Because she wasn't really crying for Conners, for his death, or for Morrison and his guilt, but for herself. People always cried for themselves. But she couldn't stop it, and she didn't really want to.

Beside her, Fallon said nothing, did nothing.

After a few moments—three minutes? five?—it stopped on its own, a storm spending itself. She felt even more drained than before. But the fog that had surrounded her was gone.

She wiped at her eyes with the backs of her index fingers. Raising her head, she turned to the window and looked out at the parking lot. She wiped her hand on her skirt and held it toward Fallon. He took it, squeezed it. She squeezed back.

She turned to him, sniffled again.

"It's not true," she said. "That you're not good at this."

He squeezed her hand again, let it go, smiled faintly. "Dr. Phil."

"Thank you."

He shook his head. "Forget it. Listen. No one's going to be surprised if you pass on this debriefing deal. I can drop you off at your apartment, you can—"

"I'm okay. What I want is some coffee. And some time to fix my makeup. Again."

He studied her. "You're sure?"

"I'm sure."

ON THE WAY BACK, neither of them spoke much. Fallon drove, and drove well, while Sophia stared out the window at the strip malls and chain restaurants. Even after the two cups of coffee she'd grabbed in Holiday, she was still exhausted.

As they were passing Countryside Mall, Fallon sailing the car through a long, slow curve in U.S. 19, Sophia heard the cell phone ringing inside her purse. She leaned forward, reached down, opened the purse, took out the phone, flipped it open, sat back. "Tregaskis."

"Jesus. Sophia? Thank God!"

"Dave?"

"I just heard what happened. Are you okay?"

"I'm fine."

"They said you were hurt. They said some kind of big tank exploded up there in Pasco."

"I can't talk about it, Dave. I'm sorry. But I'm fine." She glanced at Fallon. His eyes on the road, his face blank, he was doing a fine job of pretending he was out for an afternoon spin all by himself.

"Thank God," said Bondwell. "That's really all I wanted to know. When I heard about it, I didn't know what to think."

"Listen, Dave, I can't really—"

"Yeah, sure, of course. I understand. I was just worried, is all."

"Thanks. I appreciate it. Honestly."

"Okay, this is a bad time to call, so I'll be quick. I know that we're off for tomorrow. The picnic thing—I know that's shot. No problem. But you'll be at the press conference tonight, right?"

"I'll be there."

"Could we get a few minutes together? Before or after, either's fine. I'd just like to say hello, spend a little time. If that's possible."

"I don't know yet, Dave." She glanced again at Fallon. Concentrating on his driving. Ignoring her. "Maybe. Probably. A few minutes."

"That'd be great. Okay. See you there. And, listen, I'm really pleased that you're okay."

"Thank you."

"Bye now."

"Good-bye."

She flipped the phone shut, leaned forward, slipped it back into her purse, sat back. She looked out the window again. "That was Dave Bondwell."

Fallon turned to her. "Oh yeah? You had a phone call?"

"He's going to be at the press conference tonight."

Watching the road, Fallon nodded. "Good. We can ask him what he was doing at the Fattie's Seminar."

"*Fallon.*"

He smiled the faint smile. "Right. The Big Person's Seminar. The important thing is, we can ask him."

She wished she could share Fallon's satisfaction.

But she was remembering, for the first time since last night, Bondwell's deep blue eyes, and the hard muscle beneath her fingers. His lips against hers.

Chapter Thirty-four

Fallon knocked on the door to conference room number three. From behind it a male voice—Chief Anderson—called out, "Come in." Sophia was still tired, and she took a deep breath, sucking in air as though it were pure oxygen, hoping it would give her the jolt she needed.

Anderson sat at the head of the table, a leather binder lying in front of him. His dense white hair was freshly brushed, his pink skin glowed as though it had just been buffed. Sitting next to him, on the right, was a man in his thirties wearing a tropical-weight gray suit lovingly tailored to his wide, square shoulders. The man's face was tanned and it was almost impossibly handsome.

This would be our profiler.

Eva Swanson sat to the man's right. On Chief Anderson's left was Lieutenant Courtney, and to Courtney's left was Kitty Delgado.

Eva Swanson was wearing a suit, a simple white linen number that had probably cost a month's salary—a month of Sophia's salary.

Sophia and Fallon had been running late, but she was glad she'd taken the time to change into the spare clothes she kept in her locker—an old Donna Karan outfit, a pale blue blouse and silver-gray slacks. It didn't quite come up to Swanson's suit, but it was a bit more presentable than the clothes Fallon had bought at Target.

Chief Anderson rose from the table, big and pink and imposing, and marched past the blond man to Sophia and Fallon. "Detective Tregaskis," he said, and held out his right hand to take Sophia's. He covered it with his left hand, like someone protecting a wounded bird. He leaned toward her, his pink face solicitous. "Lieutenant Courtney told us what you've been through. Are you all right?"

Sophia could smell Anderson's cologne, something heavy and piercing.

Then she realized that it wasn't cologne. It was Scotch.

She remembered the river of alcohol at the house in Elfers, and her stomach twisted.

"Yes, sir," she said. "I'm fine. Thank you."

He still held her hand in both of his. "And she tells me it was your idea to track down those crime-scene coveralls. That was excellent work, Detective."

Sophia would have been more flattered, just then, if Anderson hadn't started patting her hand gingerly, tap tap tap, a patronizing uncle patting the hand of his clever little niece. A horny patronizing uncle.

"Excellent work," he repeated, and beamed at her. He patted her hand once more.

But when Anderson dropped her hand and turned to Fallon, Sophia had the feeling that she'd completely vanished from his mind.

"And you did a fine job, too, Sergeant." He said it with a bluff heartiness, but he didn't offer his hand.

"Thanks, Chief," said Fallon. "We got lucky."

"Well," said Anderson cheerfully, "nothing wrong with luck, is there? As long as it's *good* luck." Grinning, he looked around the room. Everyone smiled politely, including the profiler.

Anderson turned to Sophia. "This is Special Agent Brent Messing from the FBI's Investigation Support Unit. Agent Messing is one of their best profilers. He's been staying over in Clearwater Beach, and he's been kind enough to cut short his vacation and lend us a hand. And as I've already told him, I'm extremely grateful to him."

Messing was tapping the eraser end of a pencil softly against the table. He nodded his big handsome head. "Detective." His voice was low and silky. A movie star's voice, too.

Sophia nodded a greeting,

"And this is Sergeant Fallon," said Anderson.

"Sergeant," said Messing.

"Agent Messing."

"Right," said Anderson. "Let's get started, people."

He marched back to his seat at the head of the table. Fallon and Sophia took chairs, Sophia beside Kitty.

"Lieutenant," said Anderson, "maybe you should bring Fallon and Tregaskis up to speed on the enzyme test."

Courtney leaned around Kitty to look across to Fallon and Sophia. "The tissue you found at Purdenelle's house this morning. The county lab says it's human."

Fallon nodded.

"But it wasn't Purdenelle's," she said. "We think it was Marcy Fleming's."

Shit, thought Sophia.

"We won't know for sure," said Courtney, "until we get a DNA matchup, but the blood type is Fleming's."

Fallon said, "When we talked to Harrison, he said he didn't think that any body parts were missing."

"I called him this morning. He says there's no way to know for sure. He can't put everything back together—he can only check all the intact skin surfaces for bite marks or injections, which he did."

"He find any?"

"No."

"Has it been frozen?" Fallon asked. "The tissue?"

"The lab didn't say," said Courtney. "Why?"

"If it's been frozen, that means he planned to keep it around for a while. Maybe a long time. But if it hasn't been, then—"

"Then he planned to use it soon," said Kitty Delgado. She grinned at Fallon. "Hey. Good one, Sarge."

She turned to Courtney. "Which'd mean he planned to do the second woman soon. Maybe he even had her set up before he did Fleming."

Courtney nodded. "I'll call the lab and ask them to check."

"All right," said Anderson. "Sergeant, why don't you tell us what happened up in Pasco."

When Fallon finished, Anderson nodded. "Thank you, Sergeant. Agent Messing? Any comments or questions?"

Messing was sitting back, his arms along the arms of his chair. "Sergeant," he said in that silky baritone, "I gather, from what you say, that you believe Robert Ambrose to be your UNSUB."

Unsub? thought Sophia, then remembered the word from her class in victimology. *Un*known *sub*ject.

"You believe he isn't?" said Fallon, his face expressionless.

"I believe that you definitely have linkage between the Fleming kill and the Purdenelle kill. You have exactly the same MO, exactly the same signature."

Messing looked toward Sophia. "I understand that you're fairly new to homicide investigations, Detective. You're aware of the distinction?"

She suddenly felt as though she were back in class. "The MO is the way he commits the crime. The signature is something he does because it turns him on."

"Correct."

So where's my gold star?

"In this case," Messing explained, "the signature would be the mutilations."

He turned to Fallon. "There's no question, in my mind, that the two kills in St. Anselm were perpetrated by the same offender. But the kill in Elfers bothers me. From what you say, the woman wasn't mutilated. She wasn't damaged or cut in any way."

"She was dead," Fallon said. "I'd call that damaged. And it was Robert Ambrose, her son, who killed her. She's exactly the same body type as both our victims. It was Robert Ambrose, or someone using his name, who ordered those crime-scene coveralls four days before Fleming was killed. It was Robert Ambrose who was careful not to leave any evidence at the Elfers house—just like our guy, at both crime scenes."

Messing nodded. "Perhaps. But, A"—he tapped his right index finger against his left thumb—"we don't know for a fact, at this point in time, that the woman in Elfers was Millicent Ambrose."

Sophia noticed that his fingernails were manicured.

"B," said Messing, and tapped his left index finger, "we don't know, for a fact, that Robert Ambrose killed her."

Courtney said, "Hold on. We've got his credit card records. The account was opened in July of 1991, and since then all the bills have been sent to the Elfers address. He spent time there. If he didn't kill her, didn't he ever wonder what she was doing in that tank?"

"You're assuming," said Messing, "that Robert Ambrose is alive and well and using the card. For all we know, as Sergeant Fallon himself admits, someone else could be using it. For all we know, Robert Ambrose is dead, buried somewhere in the swamps."

He turned back to Fallon and tapped his middle finger. "C. You don't know that your UNSUB is actually using crime-scene coveralls."

Pretty soon, thought Sophia, he'll be running out of fingers.

"D," he said, tapping his ring finger. "As I'm sure you know, many offenders are careful to leave no evidence. Logically speaking, therefore, we can't conclude that any two suspects *not* leaving evidence are one and the same."

Logically speaking, Sophia had to admit, he was right. Logically speaking, he was right about all of it.

But logically speaking he was also a dork.

Messing tapped his pinkie finger. "And finally, the MO in the Elfers kill is altogether different from that used in the others. And so is the signature—I'd suggest that the alcohol in the tank is almost certainly a signature. Now I'm not saying you're wrong about all this, of course"—he smiled politely at Fallon—"I'm simply saying that I prefer to withhold my judgment until all the facts are in."

"Fine," said Fallon. "But the woman in the tank was killed years ago. Ambrose could've changed his MO since then."

"If in fact it was Ambrose who killed her," said Messing. "In our experience, serial offenders may indeed change their MO—they become more experienced, they get better at their work, in a sense—but they seldom change their signature. Confronted with the precipitating stressor that triggers them, they invariably revert to the behavior that, in the past, helped relieve their stress."

Eva Swanson leaned slightly forward, turning toward Anderson. "May I say something?"

"Of course, Doctor," said the chief.

"I respect Agent Messing's expertise in these matters," she said. "But I'm inclined to agree with Sergeant Fallon. I think that whoever killed the woman up in Elfers is likely the same person who killed your two victims."

Agent Messing frowned.

"What makes you think so?" asked Anderson.

"Whoever booby-trapped the tank expected it to be found. That's the whole point to a booby trap. And he arranged a delay on the trap, before the tank blew apart—he wanted the people who found it, whoever they were, to see exactly what he'd done to the woman. He was setting up a tableau, a scene. He set up another in the kitchen of the house. And one in the bedroom. The man here in St. Anselm has been doing exactly the same thing. Creating tableaus. That impression on the mattress. That meat on the counter. I believe we're dealing with the same mentality."

"The same *kind* of mentality, perhaps," said Messing. He smiled blandly. "But you can't know for a fact that they belong to the same offender."

"I find the similarities extremely suggestive. And I find the body type even more so. She was a woman of size, like the two victims here in St. Anselm. I doubt that's a coincidence. Until I hear evidence to the contrary, I have to agree with Sergeant Fallon."

"Even assuming," said Messing, "that the woman in Elfers is Millicent Ambrose, you don't know that Robert Ambrose killed her. As I said, he may himself be dead. The fact that the offender didn't worry overmuch about the Ambrose name being traced—I find *that* suggestive."

"I expect we'll learn, down the road, that there's some other explanation. But at the moment—"

"Plastic surgery," said Sophia. It came tumbling out her mouth before she had time to think it through.

She felt the pressure of their stares along the surface of her face.

"Shit," said Kitty.

Swanson nodded. "That's certainly a possibility."

Fallon was frowning; Chief Anderson was looking over to Agent Messing.

"If he's had plastic surgery," said Courtney, "Robert Ambrose could be any of the men at the press conference, any of the men at the seminar."

"Or any of the women," said Swanson.

"Oh, come *on*, Doctor," said Messing. "A transsexual?"

"Why not?"

"Every serial killer in history, with the exception of Aileen Wuornos, and she's obviously a special case, has been a male."

"And so has every female transsexual."

"It's *never* happened, Doctor."

"How do you know that? Aren't there a fair number of unsolved serial killings out there?"

Messing smiled. "And you believe they were all committed by transsexuals?"

"I believe that when it comes to the human personality, there's very little that isn't possible."

"I read somewhere," said Kitty, "that after the operation, after the hormones, they lose a lot of their male characteristics. Not just the physical stuff, like facial hair, but the psychological stuff, like aggression."

"Yes," said Swanson. "Generally. But it takes only one exception." She turned to Messing. "One special case."

"But this isn't it." Messing shook his head. "It's impossible."

"There was no semen found on Marcy Fleming's body," Swanson said.

"He didn't violate her," said Messing. "Or he used a condom."

"Perhaps, but you can't *know* that. As you said—"

Fallon said, "Dr. Swanson?"

"One second, Jim." Back to Messing: "You said it yourself—we can't conclude anything from an *absence* of evidence."

"Eva," said Fallon.

"What?" A bit curt.

"In order to hide out by pretending to be a woman, he'd have to be totally convincing."

"*She,*" said Courtney.

"Whatever. But that just doesn't happen, Eva. You can always spot a transsexual. The Adam's apple, the voice, the walk—they're all dead giveaways."

Her face had clouded. "How can you be so *naive,* Jim?"

Fallon blinked.

"Yes," she said, "you can always spot the *obvious* transsexual. But that's a truism. Many of them aren't obvious at all. They have their Adam's apple reversed. They practice walking, they practice talking. They learn how to behave and how to sound exactly like a woman. You've probably passed one on the sidewalk or sat down next to one in a bar, and you've never noticed."

"Not in a bar, I hope," said Fallon.

Kitty laughed. Chief Anderson chuckled.

Swanson took a long, deep breath, let it out, finally smiled at Fallon. She turned to Anderson. "I apologize. We've gone fairly far afield here. Up to a point, I agree with Agent Messing. I think it's unlikely—even extremely unlikely—that the person we're looking for is a transsexual. I just think that we should be open to all the possibilities."

"I didn't say *unlikely*," said Messing. "I said *impossible*. In all my years as a profiler—"

She turned to him. "Let me ask you this, Agent Messing. Could you tell me whether there's ever been a single investigation, anywhere in the world, in which profiling on its own has led directly to an arrest?"

"There have been hundreds of cases, perhaps thousands of them, in which profiling has confirmed the guilt of a particular offender."

Swanson nodded. "Once he's been taken into custody. So the short answer to the question would be . . . ?"

"Not directly to an arrest, no. But—"

"Thank you."

"But—"

"All right, Agent Messing," said Chief Anderson. "Dr. Swanson." He glanced at his Rolex. "I thank you both. I genuinely appreciate your input. But the press conference is in half an hour. We've got to get some wheels under a strategy here." He looked around the table. "What do we let out of the bag, and what do we keep?"

Chapter Thirty-five

We keep as much as possible," said Fallon. "There's no point in scaring the whole town."

"I disagree," said Messing.

Big surprise, thought Sophia.

"For one thing," he said, "the more information we put before the public, the greater their ability to assist us. Someone out there knows this offender, whoever he is."

"Either the guy is Robert Ambrose," said Fallon, "and he doesn't care who knows it, because he's in hiding somewhere or"—he nodded to Sophia—"he's had plastic surgery."

Agent Messing's face was unreadable.

Fallon continued, "Or he isn't Robert Ambrose. Either way, he's pretty sure that no one's going to identify him. There are a lot of overweight women in this town. They hear that this guy is seeking them out, they're going to panic."

"I think you underestimate the public, Sergeant," said Messing. "And besides, those women have a right to know. They have a right to understand the danger, and to take precautions against it."

"I don't think—"

Anderson held up his hand and turned to Messing. "You said *for one thing*. What's the other?"

"We need to go proactive. We need to establish a dialogue with the offender, provoke him into communicating with us. The more he reveals of himself, the more we learn, the better our chance to run him down. And the best way to provoke him is by disclosing what we know. Let's use the Robert Ambrose name. Let's put it out that he's the suspect."

"I thought he was dead," said Fallon.

With elaborate patience Messing said, "What I said was, we don't know for a fact, at this point in time, that he's alive. Maybe you're right, Sergeant, maybe he is, and maybe he is, in fact, our offender. But if our offender *isn't* Robert Ambrose, then he'll have duped us, as he sees it. And he may very well decide to let us know that."

"And suppose," said Fallon, "he decides to let us know by killing another woman."

Messing raised his handsome eyebrows. "Who's to say he won't kill another woman anyway, no matter what we do?"

Chief Anderson frowned.

Sophia said, "What if he *is* Robert Ambrose?"

"Then Sergeant Fallon is right. For whatever reason, he doesn't care whether we have his name. And he may very well decide to let us know *that*."

"He's already let us know that," said Fallon, "by giving us the name."

"All right, Sergeant," said Anderson.

He turned to Messing and nodded. "Right. We go with the name. What else?" He glanced around the table, as though he'd just realized that he was ignoring everyone else, and he added, "In your opinion, Agent Messing."

"In my opinion—"

There was a sudden, hurried knock at the door. Brusquely Anderson called out, "Come in."

The door opened and a head poked tentatively into the room. Officer Jeeter, one of the uniforms working liaison. He looked around, saw Anderson. "Sorry, Chief. Some faxes just came in for Lieutenant Courtney. From Deputy Morrison up in Pasco."

Anderson glanced at his watch, flicked his hand. "Go ahead, go ahead."

Jeeter scurried into the room, quickly handed some sheets of fax paper to Courtney, then scurried back out again, pulling the heavy wooden door shut behind him.

Courtney studied the topmost sheet.

"Well?" said Anderson. "What'd Pasco get for us?"

"A high school yearbook picture of Robert Ambrose." She handed the sheet to Anderson, looked down at the second sheet, looked up.

"And a positive ID on the body. It's Millicent Ambrose." She handed the second sheet to Anderson and looked over at Messing.

Messing nodded. "I'm pleased to hear it. Sincerely. I'm not trying to be adversarial here." He smiled. "How did Deputy Morrison determine the ID?"

"He used this." Courtney held up the final sheet. It was a photograph, darkened by photocopying or faxing or both. "It's a copy of the Polaroid he took of the dead woman. A man who owns a minimarket in Elfers recognized her. Said he hadn't seen her for over ten years."

Courtney handed the sheet to Anderson, who took it and then handed over the first two sheets to Messing. After a quick frown at the photograph, Anderson passed that, too, on to the FBI agent.

Messing flipped through the sheets. "Morrison obtained all this very quickly."

"He's in a hurry," said Fallon. "His partner's dead."

Messing nodded. Leaning across the table toward Sophia, he held out the sheets. "Detective." He smiled.

Sophia took them.

The photograph on the top sheet, badly centered, was part of a page from the yearbook, three rows of black-and-white portrait photographs, three photos to a row. Robert Ambrose was the second student from the left in the top row.

The picture didn't reveal much. It was a typical yearbook photo—the boy wore a black suit and a black tie and a small, uncertain smile, and he seemed perfectly nondescript, perfectly normal, with slightly pudgy cheeks and dark, floppy hair. His eyes, too, were dark, and they told Sophia absolutely nothing.

He didn't look like someone who would kill his mother. He didn't look like someone who would kill and mutilate Marcy Fleming and Cyndi Purdenelle.

What did you expect, *koritsi mou*? 666 tattooed across his forehead?

Under the picture was a list of Robert Ambrose's extracurricular activities. The Karate Club. The Home Economics Club. The Glee Club.

In the background she heard the others talking—Messing asking how the woman had managed to renew her driver's license while she was floating in the tank, Courtney explaining that Florida law allowed drivers to renew by mail. Fallon added that Robert had probably forged his mother's signature. Messing pointed out that they still didn't know, for a fact, that it was Robert who'd killed her.

She heard Messing say, "We definitely need to give the Robert Ambrose picture to the press. Someone may recognize him."

"I agree," said Anderson.

With a last look into those young eyes, so impenetrable, so unhelpful, Sophia passed the sheet to Fallon. She read Morrison's handwritten note. Morrison promised to send more information as soon as he had it.

She hesitated before looking at the photograph of the dead woman. She'd already seen the woman once, and once had been enough. More than enough.

But she lifted the second sheet, handed it to Fallon, and looked down at the image of the dead woman's face.

She felt a sudden chill along the back of her neck. "Oh my God."

"It's a rough picture," said Courtney.

Sophia looked up, shook her head. "It's not that."

She looked back down again, to make sure.

In the murky photo, the woman's face was slack, the heavy flesh tugged by gravity toward the ground on which she lay. Her hair, which had looked gray when she was inside that horrible tank, looked black now as it hung limply back from the round, gray forehead, like seaweed from a rock.

So the hair was wrong, maybe. And the eyes were too dark—brown, probably. But that could be because the photo itself was so dark. Or because the body had been in alcohol for so long.

But the rest of the face—the forehead, the nose, the mouth . . .

Why hadn't Courtney realized?

Because Courtney had never seen the photographs of the Don Cesar seminar.

Sophia looked back up, at Courtney. "This woman looks . . . this woman could *be* Marcy Fleming."

Courtney stared at her for a moment, then turned to Eva Swanson.

As Sophia handed the sheet to Fallon, she saw that both Courtney and Swanson were turning to Messing.

Of course. If Marcy looked like the dead woman, looked *exactly* like the dead woman, then obviously the same person had killed them both.

That was the *why*.

That was why Robert Ambrose had chosen Marcy.

Because she looked like his mother.

Beside her, Fallon glanced up from the picture and said to Courtney, "Tregaskis is right."

Messing asked Fallon, "You didn't see the resemblance when you were up there? You didn't take pictures?"

Fallon shrugged. "It wasn't my jurisdiction. Deputy Morrison was exercising his authority, as he had every right to do. He said he'd send pictures, and he did."

Fallon leaned behind Sophia and passed the sheet to Kitty.

Messing turned to Sophia, his eyebrows raised again. "Detective Tregaskis?"

"I never got a close look at the woman," she said. "To be honest, I didn't want to."

Messing's face softened. "Of course." His voice resonated with sympathy.

"I think," said Eva Swanson, "that this changes things a bit."

Messing looked at her. "Yes, of course it does." He turned to Anderson. "Clearly Dr. Swanson was right. And so, it seems, was Sergeant Fallon. If it's true that Millicent Ambrose resembled Marcy Fleming, I'd say it's very nearly certain that the same offender killed all three women."

"It *is* true," said Sophia. "They could be twins."

Messing nodded graciously. "I accept that."

"Fine," said Anderson, and glanced again at his watch. "But what do we give to the press?"

"I'd suggest," said Messing, "that we mention everything but the human tissue on the kitchen counter."

Anderson nodded. "No tissue. Right."

"I think," said Fallon, "we should—"

"Yes, Sergeant," said Anderson, turning his big, pink face toward him, "I believe we know what you think."

Jerk.

Anderson turned to Courtney. "What's your opinion, Lieutenant?"

"I think," she said, "that Sergeant Fallon may be right. Putting it out that a serial killer is targeting women of size may not be a good idea."

Way to go.

"Officer Delgado?" said Anderson.

"I'm with Sergeant Fallon."

Anderson looked at Sophia.

"So am I," she said.

Anderson turned toward Eva Swanson. "Doctor?"

"Once again, I'm inclined to go along with Sergeant Fallon. There's really no telling how the public might respond."

Anderson nodded. "Objections duly noted. But as a public official, I believe the public has a right to know. If Agent Messing is correct, and this helps us find the lunatic, then I'm all for it."

He looked around the table once more. "Right." He rubbed his hands together. "Let's go." He stood.

So did everyone else, including Messing. Sophia was startled to see that at his full height, Special Agent Messing was a good four inches shorter than she was. Despite his broad dreamboat shoulders, his big handsome head, the man was no more than five foot, three inches tall.

Chapter Thirty-six

Robert sipped at his pinot noir, a Sterling Vineyards '96. Normally he quite enjoyed the '96. It had a lovely body, a good nose, hints of chocolate and cinnamon and blackberry, a subtle and satisfying finish. But tonight he might as well be drinking Gatorade.

He set down the glass, lifted the remote from his lap, pushed the BACK button. The picture on the screen stuttered, began to whirl backward. He pushed the PAUSE button and the picture froze on Connie Zimmer and Dave Bondwell.

Robert put the remote back on his lap, listlessly speared a chunk of lamb, listlessly put it into his mouth. He chewed. The lamb was tender, the basmati rice was, once again, a triumph. But the food lay at the bottom of his stomach like a large round lump of lead.

He set down the fork, picked up the remote, pushed the START button.

"—startling new developments in St. Anselm," said Connie. "Another savage murder in this small seaside community. At a press conference this evening, Police Chief Darryl Anderson said that both crimes appear to be the work of the same individual."

Medium shot of Deadly Dull Darryl and his brass buttons and his ridiculous crew cut. "Both victims were young," said Darryl, "in their twenties or thirties, both lived alone, and both were women of size."

And what size might that be, exactly, Darryl? Might it not be *huge*, you pompous blue twit? Might it not be *fucking enormous*?

Robert took another sip of wine. This was all so terribly annoying.

He'd been at the press conference himself—secretly, of course, with absolutely no one the wiser—and he'd had an opportunity to become annoyed in person. Now he found it perversely fascinating to watch the thing on tape—five or six times already—and become annoyed all over again.

"I emphasize," said Darryl, "to you people in the media, and to the citizens of St. Anselm, the fact that there is absolutely no cause for alarm."

Think again, Chiefie.

"We've increased our patrols, day and night. And, more important, we've identified a suspect. His name is Robert Ambrose, an Elfers resident. I have here a photograph of the individual in question." He held up a flimsy sheet of paper. "This was taken some time ago—"

Try twenty years, you lummox.

"—but our computer experts will use it to create a projection, one that will show us approximately what Robert Ambrose looks like today."

Robert smiled. This was really the only entertaining sequence in the entire production.

"In the meantime, we'll release this photograph to all the media. I urge anyone out there who recognizes the individual to contact us immediately."

Cut to a long shot of Dave Bondwell—taken out of sequence, because Dave didn't actually ask his questions until some ten minutes later.

"Chief Anderson," said Dave, "can you tell us exactly how you located the suspect?"

Anderson nodded ponderously. "It was the result of first-rate work by our team of detectives, and in particular by Detective Sophia Tregaskis. It was Detective Tregaskis who traced a financial transaction that led us to the suspect."

The credit card Robert had used to buy the coveralls, his Magic Suits.

He had expected the police to get to the credit card—how else would they stumble upon the Cow? And he had definitely wanted them to stumble upon the Cow—if they hadn't gotten to the card on their own, he'd have found a way to hand it to them

But he hadn't expected them to get to it so quickly. He had underestimated them. Underestimated Tregaskis, at any rate.

A shot of Detective Tregaskis, glancing demurely down.

Robert frowned. Bitch.

He hit the FORWARD button, then quickly hit PLAY.

"—have a copy of that picture, Dave?" said Connie.

"Yes, we do, Connie," said Dave.

The yearbook picture flashed onto the screen.

Robert clicked the PAUSE button and studied the image of his earlier self.

Utterly hopeless. Look at those ears.

He hit the PLAY button.

"WPOP has confirmed," said Connie, "that Robert Ambrose is also a suspect in the murder of his mother, Millicent Ambrose of Elfers, Florida. Pasco County Sheriff's Department deputies discovered her body earlier today, working on leads provided by the St. Anselm police. One deputy, William Conners of Holiday, lost his life during that investigation when a water tank exploded. Police believe the tank was booby-trapped."

A brilliant deduction.

"In Tampa today," said Dave—

Robert hit the PAUSE button.

Dave sat there, frozen in midsentence.

At least the police were beginning to get the point. Beginning to understand the nature of Robert's little project.

He hit the BACK button.

Connie chattered silently, the yearbook photo flashed, Connie and Dave looked earnest, Dave stood there with his mike, Darryl babbled, Tregaskis looked down . . .

He hit PLAY.

Tregaskis looked demurely down.

Yes, indeed, he had seriously underestimated the bitch.

And not only underestimated her; he'd misjudged her. When he'd first seen her, he'd thought she was as cute as a button. Why hadn't he noticed before how . . . big she was?

She was wearing an off-the-rack, short-sleeved, blue blouse—rayon? a blend?—that could barely contain her heavy breasts. When she lowered her head, she had moved her arm slightly and—

Robert hit the BACK button, then PLAY.

Yes. There. When she moved her arm, you could see it. A definite wobble in the upper arm.

Chapter Thirty-seven

Sophia and Fallon and the others arrived on the stage at five minutes after nine that night. Mayor Bronson was already there, sitting behind the table in a black pants suit. Before each seat at the table stood a small microphone.

When she saw Chief Anderson, the mayor frowned and looked pointedly at her watch.

The auditorium was less crowded than it had been on Tuesday night, at the public briefing—tonight only the press were allowed. But the room was busy with journalists, sound and camera technicians, media people from St. Petersburg and Tampa and even Miami, most of them milling around, individually and in groups. As the chief's small contingent crossed to the table, flashbulbs popped and cameras whirred and people started shouting out questions and names. *"Chief! Mayor Bronson! Toni! Chief Anderson!"*

Mayor Bronson cast a sour glance at Anderson, stood, and raised her hands to grip the microphone. "When you people settle down," she said, "we'll begin. Everyone take a seat, please."

Sitting between Fallon and Eva Swanson, Sophia peered out into the audience and found Dave Bondwell. He was already seated, three or four rows back on the right side, wearing his anchorman uniform—a dark gray suit, a light blue shirt with a button-down collar. He grinned and raised a hand in greeting. She nodded, and felt her treacherous face flame again.

Fallon leaned forward, around Sophia, put his hand over the microphone on the table in front of her, and said to Eva Swanson, under his breath, "You think he's here?"

She glanced out at the crowd, looked back to Fallon. "If he's had plastic surgery, he'll certainly feel secure enough to show up. Jim, listen, I truly do apologize for snapping at you, back in the conference room. I suppose I was feeling a bit beleaguered."

He smiled. "You *were* a bit beleaguered."

"But I shouldn't have taken it out on you. I'm sorry. And I'm sorry about the other night."

"No problem." He sat back.

The other night? thought Sophia. What other night?

Ask Fallon later. Right now, concentrate.

Swanson turned to her. "Are you all right, Sophia?"

"I'm fine. Thank you."

Swanson patted her lightly on the forearm. Sophia smiled.

What other night?

She looked out at the crowd. On either side of the auditorium, flanking the stage, officers in civilian clothes took videos of the audience. She glanced quickly around, trying to find in any of the faces out there a resemblance to the young boy in the yearbook photo.

No one looked remotely like him.

But that didn't necessarily mean a thing. With plastic surgery, he could be any of the men in the room. And, if Eva Swanson was right, any of the women.

Christ. They had no specific physical information about Robert Ambrose at all. No current height or weight or body type. Nothing. Despite the Ambrose photograph, they were no nearer to knowing what he looked like than they had been at the very beginning. He could be anyone in a fifty-mile radius. He could be anyone in the auditorium.

Basically, the only person here who *couldn't* be Robert Ambrose was Special Agent Messing, who had been up in Quantico, the FBI headquarters in Virginia when—

No. Wait.

Anderson said that Messing had been on vacation in Clearwater Beach. Only half an hour away.

How long had he been in Clearwater Beach? Since before the first killing, before Marcy?

Come on, *koritsi mou*. An FBI profiler as a serial killer? In a movie, maybe, but not in real life.

"*Everyone please take a seat,*" said the mayor, clearly losing what was left of her patience.

Slowly, reluctantly, they did. Clothes rustled, papers rattled, someone coughed.

Mayor Bronson looked out over the room. "As you know," she said, "we've had a second horrible murder here in St. Anselm. Once again I want to take a moment to say that all of us in the community are appalled and saddened by the death of this young woman . . ."

For a while, the press conference proceeded much like the public briefing of three nights before. Mayor Branson introduced Chief Anderson, Anderson introduced Fallon and Sophia and Dr. Eva Swanson, referring to her as "a noted local psychologist who's assisted the police in the past." Messing he described as "one of the top FBI profilers in the country."

After the introductions, Anderson gave a clipped, curt recital of the day's events—the discovery of Cyndi Purdenelle's body, the discovery of another victim in Elfers, the rupture of the booby-trapped tank . . .

As a result of the investigation, he said, it was now clear that both recent murders in St. Anselm had been committed by the same individual. Both the victims were young, single women, unconnected to each other, and both were women of size.

There was a small stir among the audience. Anderson raised his hand. "I emphasize to you people in the media, and to the citizens of St. Anselm, the fact that there is absolutely no cause for alarm. We've increased our patrols, day and night. And, more important, we've identified a suspect. His name is Robert Ambrose, a former resident of Elfers."

Anderson opened the binder, took out the yearbook picture, held it up. "I have here a photograph of the individual in question. This was taken some time ago, but our computer experts will use it to create a projection that will show us approximately what Robert Ambrose looks like today. In the meantime, we'll release this photograph to all the media. I urge anyone out there who recognizes the individual to contact us immediately."

He looked around the auditorium. "Now, are there any questions?"

There were, quite a few of them. The reporters waved their hands, shouted, jumped up, waved their hands and shouted some more. They were like schoolkids—hyperactive, obnoxious schoolkids. Sophia glanced at Dave Bondwell, saw that he was still sitting back in his chair. His hand was raised, but he wasn't flailing it around like some brat with a bad bladder.

"Yes," said Anderson, and pointed to a reporter for the local NBC affiliate. "Chuck?"

Trust Anderson to know the man's first name.

"Chief Anderson," said Chuck, "are you saying that this killer is deliberately selecting women of size as his victims?"

"Based upon the victims here in St. Anselm," said Anderson, "that's correct."

"What about the body up in Elfers? Was that victim a woman of size, too?"

"The investigation in Elfers is being conducted by the Pasco County sheriff's people. But I can tell you in brief that, yes, she was."

"Have there been any other victims?"

"None." Anderson turned to his left, pointed again. "Terry?"

An older man, one Sophia didn't recognize. "The first victim was mutilated. Was that true of the two other victims?"

"It was true of one of them," said Anderson. "The victim here in St. Anselm."

"Can you discuss the nature of those mutilations, Chief?"

Anderson frowned. "Not at this point. Fred?"

Another TV guy. "How is he selecting the victims, Chief Anderson?"

"We're working on that. Monica?"

A woman Sophia didn't recognize. "May I direct a question to Agent Messing and Dr. Swanson?"

Anderson nodded graciously. "Of course."

"Agent Messing, do you have any idea why this individual would pick the kind of victims he's picking?"

Messing inclined his big handsome head toward the microphone. "I'm afraid I can't answer that," he said in that silky baritone. "As Chief Anderson said, I've only just arrived here. It will take me a day or two to familiarize myself with all the particulars of both cases."

Weasel.

He hadn't bothered to familiarize himself with anything before he'd tried to shoot down Fallon.

"Dr. Swanson," said the woman, "would you care to speculate?"

"No," she said, "I wouldn't. Beyond noting the obvious fact that he bears a deep hostility toward women, and particularly toward women of size, I really can't say much about him."

"Would you say that this killer is symptomatic of our times, of the persecution so often suffered by women of size? That in a sense he represents the dark side of the American obsession with slimness?"

Swanson frowned. "It's true that women of size in this country are often the target of persecution. But we can't say, at this point, whether this individual is symptomatic, or representative, of anything."

"Thank you, Monica," said Chief Anderson. "Dave?"

Bondwell stood up, looking fit and professional.

"Chief Anderson," said Bondwell, "can you tell us exactly how you located the suspect?"

"It was the result of first-rate work by our team of detectives, and in particular by Detective Tregaskis. She traced a financial transaction that led us directly to the suspect."

Sophia shot a glance at Anderson.

He knew damn well that Fallon had done as much work as she had.

Shifting in her seat again, she lowered her head, hoping that no one would see how angry she was.

"Bill?" said Anderson.

A lanky man in jeans and a white shirt was standing up, holding his recorder to his mouth. "Is it true, Chief, that the police are calling this suspect the Diet Doctor?"

Sophia looked up, startled.

"What?" Anderson sputtered. "The what?" He glanced down at the yearbook photo, as though he'd just remembered it was there. He stabbed his stiff pink thumb at it. "We're calling him Robert Ambrose. That's his name." He put his hands on the podium and leaned forward, his face redder than usual. "Where'd you get that?"

The reporter seemed unfazed. "It's common knowledge."

"Common? *Common?* It's a load of—I want to go on record as saying it's absolutely false." Anderson looked around the room, jaw clenched. "No one involved in this investigation has ever used that term." He looked at the reporter. "Is that clear?"

"Yes, sir."

More reporters asked their questions, of Chief Anderson, of Swanson, of Messing, of Fallon. Even of Sophia—had she been seriously injured in Elfers? No, she'd just had the wind knocked out of her, she was fine now.

As soon as Anderson announced that the conference was over, she saw that Dave was standing up, waving to her. She put her hand over her microphone and leaned toward Fallon. "You wanted to talk to Dave Bondwell? About the seminar?"

"Yeah." Fallon looked into the auditorium. Dave was moving toward the aisle now. "Okay. Let's go."

As they passed along the aisle, some of the remaining journalists leaned into their space, poking the air with their microphones and recorders, asking more questions, and Fallon kept calmly intoning, like a mantra, "That's it, we're done."

Dave was talking to his cameraman. He turned and saw them and smiled at Sophia. He put out his hand to Fallon. "Sergeant."

Fallon said, "Got a minute?"

"Of course." Dave looked at the cameraman. "You take the stuff to the station, Larry. I'll meet you there." He looked back at Fallon. "What's up?"

"Let's go outside."

"Sure."

As they walked down the aisle, heading for the entrance, Bondwell leaned toward Sophia. "You did a great job up there tonight."

Yet another blush. Maybe she could have metal valves installed along the veins in her neck, so the blood couldn't rush to her head. "Thank you."

Outside, the air was still hot and muggy.

"This way," said Fallon, and led them off to the left, along the broad top step of the building.

When they were ten or eleven paces away from the door, out of earshot of the people leaving the auditorium, Fallon stopped. He turned to Dave and said, "Mr. Bondwell, a few weeks ago you attended a seminar at the Don Cesar. Why?"

Bondwell frowned, confused, looked a question at Sophia, than turned back to Fallon. "Why are you asking, Sergeant?"

Fallon smiled his faint smile. "We're the cops, Mr. Bondwell. That's what we do."

Dave glanced at Sophia again.

"We just need to know, Dave," she said.

He turned to Fallon. "No real reason. Boredom. Curiosity. I was there, at the bar, having a drink, and I saw all those people wandering off into the conference room. I just followed them, to see what was going on, more or less."

"Followed them into a seminar on obesity?"

Bondwell grinned. "Yeah, it's not usually the way I spend my evening." He shrugged his square shoulders. "But as I said, I was bored. And it actually turned out to be a fairly—"

He frowned, looked back and forth between the two of them. "Wait a minute," he said to Fallon. "*Damn it.* One of them was there, wasn't she? One of the victims."

"I didn't say that."

"Which means she was."

"Dave," said Sophia, "we can't comment on that. I'm sorry."

He glanced at her, turned back to Fallon. "You've got pictures. Of the seminar. That's how you knew about me. And you think the killer was there. I know you think he was at the press conference. That's why you want the tapes. You're going to compare the two sets."

"Sorry, Mr. Bondwell," said Fallon. "But—"

"Jesus, you think *I* could've done that?" He turned to Sophia, his eyebrows raised.

Fallon said, "Where were you last night, Mr. Bondwell? From midnight on?"

"You're *serious?*"

"Very."

Dave looked at Sophia again.

"Dave," she said, "these are questions we have to ask. We'll be asking everybody who attended the seminar."

His face went blank. "Right," he said flatly.

He turned back to Fallon. "At midnight I was leaving the station. By one, I was home. And, no, I can't prove that. I was alone."

Fallon said, "Where were you last Monday night?"

"Home again. Same thing."

"Alone."

"That's right."

"Have you ever met Marcy Fleming?"

"No."

"Cyndi Purdenelle?"

"No."

"All right, Mr. Bondwell. Thank you." Fallon looked at Sophia. "See you inside."

He turned and walked toward the building's entrance.

Dave turned to Sophia, his lips pursed. In the half-light, his eyes were gray, the same color they had been in the parking lot outside the Bistro Chartreuse.

"Dave, I'm just doing my job. So is Fallon."

"Sophia. Do you honestly think that I killed those women?"

"No. I don't."

His face relaxed. After a moment, he smiled with a kind of wry sadness. "Well, that's something, anyway."

"We need to talk to everyone who showed up at that seminar. You were there."

"Yeah. Well. I know one thing."

"What?"

Another wry smile. "I'm never going to the Don Cesar again."

"You're not a suspect, Dave. But we had to ask the questions."

"I know. I understand." He ran his hand behind his neck, raised his face skyward, rolled his head. He dropped the hand and looked at her, smiling again. "It's just a little bit weird. Being interrogated by someone you had dinner with."

She smiled. "It's a little bit weird to interrogate someone you had dinner with."

He looked at her for a moment. "It was a very good dinner. All of it."

"Yes, it was. All of it."

"So. Are we okay? You and I?"

She nodded. "Yes."

"Good. Good."

He glanced at his watch. "Damn it. I've got to run over to the station. I'll be working all night. But you're going to be at the funeral for Marcy Fleming tomorrow, right?"

"Yes."

"I'll see you there. If you've got some time, we'll talk. Okay?"

"I can't promise anything, Dave. I'll be working."

"I know. We'll see what happens."

He put out his hand, lightly touched her shoulder, then he bent his face toward her. She lifted her face, moving toward his lips, and then, at the last moment, she turned slightly to the side.

As she kissed his cheek, she felt his soft peck against her skin.

He stood back. He smiled, but a sadness pinched at the corners of his eyes.

"Okay," he said. "Tomorrow."

Why had she done that?

Turned aside like that?

She was lying in bed, under the covers, a copy of *People* magazine lying open and facedown on her stomach.

Are we okay? he had asked.

And she had said, *Yes,* and she had believed it.

But without actually intending to, she had turned away from the kiss.

Maybe the simple act of questioning him—being there while Fallon questioned him—maybe that had altered everything. Maybe, no matter what she believed, or wanted to believe, it had thrown a thin spiderweb of doubt between the two of them.

You're not a suspect, she had said.

But in fact, right now, everyone at that seminar was a suspect.

And, whatever else she was, she was a cop. And any cop was inevitably wary of any suspect.

And what, after all, did she know about Dave Bondwell?

He was charming and handsome and persuasive. But he was a reporter, and reporters, especially anchormen, were all those things.

She knew nothing, really, of what went on behind that handsome face, beyond those big blues eyes . . .

Suddenly his hand was on her cheek, softly, lightly, and her own hand rose up on its own and settled easily on his upper arm, as though that were the most natural thing in the world for it to do. She could feel his biceps beneath the material of his suit, as round and firm as a stone. As she looked up into those eyes, something moved within her, a small creature subtly shifting position.

He kissed her, his lips slightly parted, his eyes open, and then his hand fell slowly—reluctantly?—away and he stood back and smiled, the skin around his eyes crinkling with pleasure.

Wednesday night, that had been. Only two nights ago.

She had liked him then, responded to him.

She still liked him.

But who was he, really?

Did it make sense for him to go into a seminar about obesity out of simple boredom. Simple curiosity?

Well, yes, maybe it did. He was a reporter, and, theoretically, reporters were curious.

But she wished he hadn't gone.

Chapter Thirty-eight

Mallon was standing with Courtney at the far end of the auditorium lobby when he saw Tregaskis come back into the building. He held up a hand. She nodded and went toward them. Some more reporters were leaving, heading back to their jobs at the newspapers and the television stations, and one or two of them tried to stop her. She ignored them. Good girl.

He wondered what had happened between her and Bondwell.

None of his business.

But when she came up to Courtney and him, he asked her, "Everything okay?"

"Fine." Giving away nothing.

None of his business.

He told her, "The lieutenant's got some information. About the Ambrose credit card."

Courtney said, "The card was issued when Ambrose was twenty-six. It's a starter, a card you use to build credit. He put down a deposit of five hundred dollars, made all his payments on time. After a while they returned the deposit and gave him a credit line. The bills were all sent to Elfers."

"What was he buying?" asked Tregaskis.

"Except for those coveralls, the only thing he bought was gasoline. He bought it at gas stations between here and Holiday. Shell stations, Quickstops. They all take credit cards at the pump—no way for anyone at the station to know who's using which card. Jim's got a copy of all the charges."

He handed Tregaskis the folded sheet of paper.

She opened it, glanced down the columns. "Wait a minute. Didn't

Deputy Morrison tell us that Ambrose's driver's license had expired in 1986?"

Fallon nodded. "So either he's driving without one, or he's got one under another name. I'm betting on the other name."

Tregaskis tapped the list and asked Courtney, "Is there some kind of pattern here?"

"Weekends. He always got the gas on weekends. He never went to the same station twice. And the stations are evenly distributed between here and Elfers. But he didn't use any stations south of here, or any stations east."

Tregaskis nodded. "So he probably lives nearby. Maybe right on the island."

"Right."

Tregaskis looked down at the charges again. "But sometimes he went up there twice a month. Sometimes three times a month. What was he doing?"

"We don't know," said Courtney.

Just then, Fallon saw Eva Swanson come out of the auditorium and head along the hallway toward the front doors. "Eva!" he called out.

She turned, saw them, smiled, changed directions, and moved gracefully toward them, her heels clicking on the tile floor.

Fallon admired the straight back, the long lean legs striding smoothly beneath the hem of her white skirt.

Forget it, Jimmy. You already had your shot.

She nodded to them all, then turned to Courtney. "What time is the service for Marcy tomorrow?"

"Eleven. You'll be there?"

"It's the least I can do. Say good-bye to her."

"Doctor," said Tregaskis.

"Please. Eva."

"Eva. Could you look at this?" She showed her the credit card charges, then recapped what the three of them had been discussing. "He kept going back to Elfers. There was nothing up there but that creepy little room and the body of his mother. Why did he keep going back?"

"Very likely" said Swanson, "to see the body of his mother."

"The body was a kind of trophy?"

"I suspect so," said Swanson. "Seeing what he'd done to her, remembering the event itself, reliving it, was probably empowering for him."

"What about the room?" Fallon asked her. "Why was he keeping all that kid stuff up there?"

"Well, from the way you described it, the room sounds almost like a shrine."

"A shrine to what?" Courtney asked.

"To his childhood? To an identity he's left behind? But we have to remember that he knew you'd be seeing the room."

"He *wanted* us to see it," said Tregaskis.

Eva nodded. "And by letting you see it, he's communicating something to you. Or he believes that the room will communicate something."

"Communicate what?" said Courtney.

"I don't know. Possibly *he* doesn't know."

"I think he does," said Fallon. "I think he knows exactly what he's doing."

"I'm not saying he's not smart, Jim. He's obviously capable of planning and preparation. What I'm saying is that very possibly he has no insight into what actually motivates him."

"Yes," said Courtney, "but neither do we."

"No. And I don't think we will get that until we find him." Eva looked at her watch, looked at Courtney. "I'm sorry, Ellen, but I need to run. If I'm going to that service tomorrow, I'll have to do some rearranging."

She turned to Tregaskis, reached out and lightly touched her arm. "Get some rest, all right? You'll be at the service?"

"Yes."

"Then I'll see you there. Bye, Ellen. Bye, Jim."

She strode away, her heels clicking, the long muscles of her calves clenching and unclenching.

Courtney said, "Time for me to take off, too. I'll see you in the morning."

As Courtney moved away, Fallon turned to Tregaskis. "You sure you're okay?"

Wearily, she smiled. "If anyone asks me that again, I'm going to shoot him."

"Come on. I'll walk you to your car."

And he had walked her to the car, neither of them speaking, and he had watched her climb into the silver-gray Beetle. Before she closed the door, she looked up at him, and in the yellow light of the parking-lot streetlamp her eyes were shiny. "Thanks, Fallon. For today. Up in Elfers, in the parking lot. You were a help. Really."

"Like I said. Dr. Phil. You get home, get some rest."

She nodded, started to pull the door shut, then stopped herself. "Oh. Fallon?"

"Yeah?"

"What did Eva mean about the other night?"

"What?"

"Inside. Before the press conference started. She apologized for the other night."

He shook his head. "We got into a little argument. On the phone. Nothing serious. She didn't really need to apologize."

Tregaskis nodded. "Okay. I'll see you tomorrow."

"G'night."

She pulled the door shut. Through the window, she smiled again, another tired smile, and waved a hand.

She was a tough one. Smart and resilient and strong.

As he watched her drive from the lot, it occurred to him that he had spent most of his life watching people leave him. Drive away, walk away. Die.

And when they weren't busy leaving him, he was busy leaving them.

IT WAS A GOOD DAY FOR A FUNERAL, Fallon thought:

He sat on the toilet seat in his boxer shorts, his forearms on his knees, his head hung low. His eyes were lined with grit. His mouth, even after two desperate glasses of cold water, felt as though it had been blasted with a flamethrower. Running his tongue along the roof of it, he could feel little bits of something stuck to the parched, dry skin.

This is bad, Jimmy. Tregaskis has been picking up on the way you look.

Maybe you should forget about this. The job, Florida, everything.

Maybe you should just sit here on the crapper and wait for a heart attack, so you can keel over like Elvis.

Keep dealing with this case, pretty soon you'll be hitting the booze first thing in the morning again. You start showing up smashed at the station, Anderson won't be asking you into his office for a friendly shot of sixteen-year-old Scotch. He'll be kicking your ass out the door.

SATURDAY

Chapter Thirty-nine

The next morning, when Sophia got to the detectives' cubicle, it was empty. As usual, neither Gall nor Durrell was there. But Fallon wasn't there either, and that had never happened before.

Unbuttoning her raincoat, she noticed a newspaper lying on her desk. A yellow Post-it note was stuck to the front page.

Have you seen this? read the note. It was signed *Courtney*.

The headline was *Horror House in Elfers*. She glanced down the page.

Oh, shit.

Just above the fold was a large black-and-white picture of her and Fallon, tottering down the steps of the Ambrose house in Elfers. Both their names were given in the caption beneath.

She had no idea who had taken the picture—she couldn't remember seeing any photographers around.

In the photo, she was wrapped in Deputy Morrison's old blanket, her hair hanging in limp, greasy strands, her face white, her expression stricken. She was holding on to Fallon—desperately, it looked like—and he had his left arm curled protectively around her shoulder. They looked like lovers fleeing a burning house.

Except that no one in the world could possibly love the pathetic, bedraggled woman in that blanket.

She had tripped, hadn't she? Coming down the steps? She remembered tripping. The picture must have been taken then.

What kind of a *malakas* takes a picture of someone tripping?

Just then, Fallon's telephone rang.

She walked around the desk, picked up the phone. "Tregaskis."

"Morning, Detective. This is Deputy Morrison, Pasco County sheriff's office."

"Good morning, Deputy. How are you?"

"As well as can be expected, thank you. How 'bout you?"

"I'm okay, thanks. Listen, I didn't get a chance to say it yesterday, but I wanted to tell you that I'm very sorry about your partner."

"Thank you, Detective. And I'm glad to hear that you're feeling better. I mean that."

"I appreciate it. And we all appreciate those photos you faxed last night. They were a big help."

She told him about the resemblance between Marcy Fleming and the Ambrose woman.

"So it's definitely the same guy," he said.

"Yes."

There was an small pause, and she knew that he was going to ask for Fallon.

"Look, Detective Fallon isn't around, is he?"

"Not at the moment. What do you have, Deputy?"

"Right." She thought she could hear him sigh. "Okay. You got a pen?"

"Hold on." She reached across the desk, grabbed her purse, slipped out her notebook and the pen. "Go ahead."

"I talked to Etta Marlowe. Used to be the principal over at Elfers High School. Goin' on ninety now, but still sharp as a tack. She remembers Bobby Ambrose, remembers his mother, met her a couple times. Didn't like her. A boozer, she said. And she remembers an English teacher at the school, woman named Marla Weston. Seems like Ambrose was the teacher's pet. Weston's favorite student. What Miss Marlowe says is that after Ambrose graduated, he got kind of adopted by the Weston woman."

"Adopted?" Sitting down in Fallon's chair, Sophia wrote the word in her notebook, followed by a question mark.

"The kid moved in with her. This was in '83. Ambrose was eighteen. Even if the mother objected, she couldn't stop him."

"Did Miss Marlowe know if the mother objected?"

"No."

"When was it you talked to her?"

"This morning."

"Early work."

"I want this guy."

"Of course. I understand."

"Anyway, that summer, summer of '83, Weston and Ambrose, they left Elfers."

"For where?"

"Sarasota. Weston took a job at a private school down there, place called Morgan Prep. Miss Marlowe got a letter asking for references. She showed it to me. Kept all her correspondence, from when she was principal. But so far, I can't reach anyone at the school."

"The weekend."

"Yeah, but I know some folks down in Sarasota, and one of them knows the principal. He gave me his home number. Fella name of Hatfield. Ray Hatfield. Tried to call him, but no answer. You want the number?"

"Please."

She wrote it down as he gave it.

"I checked with the DMV," he said, "got Weston's license and registration. Driver's license expired in May of '92. Never renewed. Height, five foot eight. Hair and eyes brown. Date of birth, August first, 1939. In 1983 she would've been forty-four."

Just then, Fallon stepped into the cubicle, looking terrible. Eyes bloodshot, features haggard.

"Vehicle registration?" Sophia asked Morrison.

"Volvo station wagon, '81. White. But the registration expired in '91. She never renewed it."

Fallon sat on the edge of the desk, noticed the newspaper, picked it up, frowned.

"She sold the car?" Sophia asked.

"No record of it."

"Her address?"

"Eight fifty Datura Street. Rental. But she hasn't lived there since 1991. No current phone number for her, listed or unlisted."

"She could've moved out of state, sold the car somewhere else."

"Maybe," agreed Morrison. "But the women around this Ambrose fella, seems like they tend to get dead."

"You talk to the Sarasota PD?"

"Yeah. Nothing on a Marla Weston. No missing person report, no matching Jane Does. She just disappeared in 1991, looks like, along with the car. I talked to Stillwell this morning, too. Our ME. He says that '91 could be about the time the mother went into that tank. Hard to tell, though, the body preserved like that."

"When's the autopsy?"

"Later this morning."

"You'll let us know what he gets?"

"Yeah." Morrison paused again. "Okay, look. Someone's got to go down to Sarasota, poke around. Sheriff says it's your case. Those two killings down there in St. Anselm, you've got priority. But you find anything, I'd be real grateful you let me know."

"Absolutely, Deputy. You have anything else? Anyone on Paradise Road see anything?"

"You saw Paradise Road. Not a whole lot of folks hanging around. I get anything, I'll pass it on."

"Thank you. And I promise, we'll keep you up-to-date."

"Good to hear it. Hello to Fallon. You both watch out for that storm. S'posed to be a doozy, and it's heading right your way."

"We will. Thanks again. Good-bye."

She hung up the phone, stood up from Fallon's chair, stepped away from his side of the desk. "Morrison," she said.

"I figured." He nodded to the newspaper. "They didn't get my best side."

She sat down in her own seat. "At least you had one. I look like shit."

He flipped the paper to the desk. "If it bleeds, it leads." He eased himself off the desktop and then sat down in the chair, carefully, as though his bones were made of glass. He sighed.

"Morrison says hello. Come to think of it, right now you look like shit, too."

"I feel like shit. How are you?"

"I'm all right. Except for that." She nodded to the newspaper.

"Forget it. It'll be old news by tomorrow. What else did Morrison say?"

"Are you taking anything for that cold?"

"Yeah. What'd Morrison say?"

Sophia filled him in.

"Thirteen years ago," he said. "Long time."

"I know. But we've got to go down there."

"You know there's a hurricane coming in?"

She nodded. "We can run down there, after the service for Marcy Fleming, and ask around Weston's neighborhood, talk to the principal, and still get back here before dark."

"A little wind and rain never hurt anyone, right?"

"They never hurt me."

"Let's see what Courtney says." He stood up, sighing again. "What was that address?"

"Eight fifty Datura."

"Be right back."

She slipped a report form into the printer.

Marla Weston. She could be the key.

If she was still in Sarasota. If she was still alive.

She typed away until Fallon returned.

He shuffled into the cubicle and sat down on the edge of the desk. He *did* look like shit.

"Here's the deal," he said. "In a few hours, the county's going to issue a mandatory evacuation order. Courtney says that you and I can go down to Sarasota, after the service for Marcy, but we've got to get back here by eight. She's arranging things with the Sarasota PD, and she'll tell Anderson and Special Agent Messing what we're doing." He put a soft, ironic spin on *Special Agent*. "We'll take two cars, in case we need to split up, talk to different people."

"Great."

IT WAS RAINING WHEN SOPHIA REACHED THE CHURCH, a soft gray drizzle. Appropriate for a funeral, she thought.

She knew that it was only the mildest of hints at what would be coming later: the downpour, the slamming winds.

She parked in a space reserved for the police, and Fallon pulled in behind her.

As they walked, under their umbrellas, toward the entrance, Dave Bondwell approached them, wearing a belted trench coat under an umbrella of his own.

"Sophia." He smiled.

"Hi, Dave."

255

She felt a flicker of pleasure that was immediately blunted by the same wariness she had felt last night. She let out a small sigh of regret, at the loss, and she hoped that Dave hadn't heard it.

"Sergeant." Dave didn't hold out his hand.

Neither did Fallon. "Mr. Bondwell."

"Could I have a minute with Sophia?"

"Not up to me."

Sophia told Fallon, "I'll see you inside."

He nodded and then trod up the broad walkway, his black brogues slapping at the wet concrete.

"So." Dave smiled, but the smile seemed uncertain. "Will you have some time afterward?"

"I'm sorry, Dave. We've got to go out of town."

"Where to?"

She hesitated.

His smile turned wry as he held up a hand. "Never mind."

Did she really believe that Dave Bondwell had killed Marcy Fleming and Cyndi Purdenelle?

Out of guilt, and with a kind of salute to the vanished pleasure, she added, "Just down to Sarasota. We'll be back later today. But we'll be busy working the storm after that."

"I understand. But could you promise me one thing?"

"If I can."

"You'll call when you get clear?"

"I promise."

"You know that my producer and your lieutenant have canceled the visit to the station Monday?"

"Yes." Courtney had told her before everyone had left for the funeral.

"Okay. Call me."

"I will."

BESIDE SOPHIA, Fallon shifted on the hard wooden pew. She glanced at him. That cold of his must really be a monster. He looked awful, his face somehow longer than usual, as though the flesh were melting down away from the bone.

The service for Marcy had just begun, and she and Fallon were sitting toward the rear of the building. It was a nice church—not huge but very pretty, with a high, vaulted ceiling and brightly colored stained-glass windows.

"Very few of us here in St. Anselm knew Marcy Fleming well," said the minister, a distant figure up there at the podium. "She was, in a sense, a stranger here among us . . ."

He was right. The building was filled with people, but the only person here who had really known Marcy was Mrs. Hartley. She sat up toward the front, along the aisle, a tiny, white-haired figure wearing a plain black dress she probably hadn't worn in years.

Sophia tuned the minister back in. "But in a larger sense, of course, all of us are strangers, one to another . . ."

She looked around. Off to the left, up ahead, Eva Swanson sat beside Lieutenant Courtney. Sophia had spoken to both of them earlier, too. Like Mrs. Hartley, both were wearing black, but Swanson's silk suit, with its fitted jacket and tapered lines, clearly outclassed the lieutenant's simple frock.

Agent Messing was here, too, off to the right, his head large and imposing beside the white crew cut of Chief Anderson.

"For no human being," said the minister, "is a stranger to God. He sees into our hearts, into our very souls . . ."

It was a skill, seeing into hearts and souls, that Sophia wished she had.

She glanced around the church again.

Someone sitting inside this very building could be their asshole. Could be the sonofabitch who'd killed Marcy Fleming and Cyndi Purdenelle.

But maybe the trip to Sarasota would help them find him.

Please let us find what we need. Please let us get this guy.

"And no matter what we've done," said the minister, "God is capable of forgiving us all . . ."

Sophia thought of Marcy, and of Cyndi Purdenelle.

God was capable of forgiveness, maybe. But God was in a different line of work.

Chapter Forty

Robert left the St. Pete *Times* lying on the kitchen table while he prepared his lunch. That way, he could glance over at the newspaper's front page from time to time, and savor the look on Tregaskis's face.

Have a nice meeting with the Cow, did you, Sophie? One cow to another?

He tossed some salt onto the gleaming red flesh of the porterhouse steak, then ground some fresh pepper over it.

Cyndi's flesh had been gleaming as well. Red and shiny and warm, warmer than the porterhouse. Fresher and slicker. It had opened up beneath his fingers, beneath the knife, like a Christmas present . . .

Lightly, he patted the seasoning into the meat, flipped the steak over, salted and peppered the other side, then lightly patted that.

Wiping his hands on a paper towel, he padded over to the range. He turned on the gas beneath the thick black cast-iron pan, made certain that it was set to medium-high, and poured two tablespoons of corn oil into the pan.

He walked back to the table, lifted his glass of pinot noir, took a sip, and stared down at the picture.

Fallon and Tregaskis. Hanging on to each other like dogs in heat.

He'd seen them both, of course, at that ridiculous memorial service for dear departed Marcy—Marcy getting more attention as a corpse than she'd ever received in her entire wretched life—and they'd been careful to conceal what they felt for each other. Naturally they weren't as accomplished at concealment as Robert. (But then who was?) Their involvement was immediately obvious—from the way they stood together, the way they sat together.

And the very notion of concealment was absurd. Anyone who

glanced at that photograph could see immediately that they were humping away, like rutting pigs, whenever they had a spare minute.

And now the two of them were on their way down to Sarasota. Probably they'd check into the first Motel 6 they found and start slobbering all over each other.

He drank some more wine.

It didn't bother him at all, the idea of their going down to Sarasota and snooping around. Obviously, someone in Elfers had mentioned Marla, and obviously the police, in their plodding way, had managed to track her to the house on Datura. Fallon and Sophia would be all over Datura Street today, ringing doorbells and pestering the neighbors.

Well, let them. There was absolutely nothing they could find that would be even *remotely* useful to them. They certainly wouldn't find poor Marla.

He realized that he could smell the hot corn oil. It was starting to smoke.

Damn it!

He glanced at the photograph of Tregaskis.

See what you made me do, bitch?

Back at the stove, he grabbed the pan's handle and tipped it left and right, swirling the streaky oil around the bottom, dissipating some of the heat. He walked back to the table and picked up the steak, carried it over to the range. Gingerly, he lay it in the pan, whipping back his fingers as the oil sputtered. He let the meat sear on one side for a minute, lots of savory smoke curling up from the pan, then he used the spatula to turn it over. After another minute, he turned it back onto the first side, lowered the gas to medium, and returned to the table and the photograph of Tregaskis and Fallon.

They could prowl around Sarasota for years and never find a single solitary thing that represented even the slightest threat to him. He wasn't worried about *that* at all.

But this fraternization, this sordid little affair—that did disturb him.

It was an obvious dereliction of duty, wasn't it? The two of them were supposed to be working. Not playing hide-the-Slim-Jim in the backseat of an unmarked car.

Now what could we do about that?

He began to put together the salad, tearing the leaves gently. Radicchio, chicory, Belgian endive.

Well, one thing we could do, of course, was give them a bit more work. If they could find the time to grab a quickie in the middle of a crucial investigation, then clearly the investigation wasn't really all that crucial, was it? At least not for *them*.

He swallowed the rest of his wine, set down the glass, lifted the bottle, poured himself some more.

What we *could* do is make another excursion to Safeway tonight, or to the Kash N' Karry, and pick out a brand-new Wibble-Wobble. Three perfect Wibble-Wobbles in a little over a week—that might put a damper on their ardor.

He went back to the stove, turned the steak over, and took the sherry vinegar and the olive oil from the cupboard. Back at the table, he shook a squirt of vinegar over the greens, then drizzled some oil. He opened the package of Roquefort, carefully crumbled a few chunks into the bowl.

Lifting the wineglass, he looked down at the photograph.

We *could* do that. Perfect another one.

But that would be so *obvious,* wouldn't it?

I'm sure we can think of something much more inventive than that. Some really *wonderful* surprise for Tregaskis. That bitch. That cow.

Chapter Forty-one

Datura Street crossed Route 41, the Tamiami Trail, about a mile south of Fruitville Road in Sarasota. The rain was still lighter, only a drizzle, but the traffic on the Trail was heavy, tourists heading north and south, locals heading for the strip malls. Or maybe all of them were actually heading away from the upcoming hurricane. Sarasota wouldn't suffer the full brunt of the storm, but even the outer edges of a hurricane could be messy.

Datura was a narrow, tree-lined street that ran through an older neighborhood, quiet and sedate. No. 850 was a trim, one-story, yellow frame house set back on a small, rectangular lot. On its left side was a Florida room, louvered windows running all around. On its right was a carport, and in the carport was a late-model, beige Honda Civic. Overhead, the limbs of a large live oak tree were dripping with rain, the Spanish moss swaying sluggishly in the breeze.

On the way down from St. Anselm, Sophia had spoken over her cell phone to an Officer Hummel of the Sarasota PD, who had given her directions and promised to meet her at the house. His black-and-white was parked against the curb in front. She pulled in behind it. In the rearview mirror, she saw Fallon pull in behind her.

Fallon had let her handle the trip. She'd dealt with Hummel, she'd led their little caravan of two down the Interstate.

She grabbed her umbrella, opened the door of the car, got out, opened the umbrella, waited for Fallon to get out of the other Ford.

Hummel was a short, heavyset man, his black, regulation raincoat taut against his belly. After Sophia introduced herself and Fallon, Hummel said to Fallon, "I guess you folks won't mind if I ask to see your ID."

She and Fallon showed him their badges. Rain pattered at the umbrellas.

Hummel nodded and looked back at Fallon. Another male cop who preferred to deal only with other male cops "So, what? You're gonna to talk to all the neighbors, is that right?"

"Yeah," said Fallon, holding his umbrella upright with his left hand, keeping the wallet in his right. "See if we can find someone who knew the Weston woman."

"Okay," said Hummel. "Chief says that's fine. Says to welcome you to Sarasota, wish you luck. Anyone calls the station, asks about you, we'll verify your ID. You need any help, warrants, like that, you let us know."

Fallon nodded. "Thanks, Officer."

"This is about the guy who's cutting up the women, right? Up in St. Anselm?"

"Yeah."

Hummel shook his head. "Weird shit."

"Yeah," said Fallon.

"We don't get much weird shit down here."

"You're lucky," Sophia told him.

He looked at her as though he'd forgotten she was there. He probably had.

"I guess. Well, good to meet you," he said, and returned to his car.

Still holding his wallet in his right hand, Fallon thumbed the buzzer. A moment later the door was opened by a slender, dark-haired woman in her thirties. She held on to the edge of the door and kept it open by only a foot or so, trying to keep out the bad weather. Or the strangers on her doorstep.

She glanced from Sophia to Fallon, raised her eyebrows. "Yes?"

Fallon showed her his badge. "Good afternoon, ma'am. We're police officers. Sergeant Fallon, Detective Tregaskis. We'd like to ask you a few questions."

She glanced back and forth again, warily. "Police? Questions about what?"

"An ongoing investigation. You're Ms. . . . ?"

"Shearer. Sally Shearer. What investigation?"

Fallon said, "It's a homicide investigation, ma'am. How long have—"

"*Homicide?*"

"How long have you resided here, Ms. Shearer?"

"We only just moved in last year. My husband and me. Someone got killed? Here in the neighborhood?"

"You weren't living here in 1991?" Fallon asked her.

"No, no. We were in Fort Myers then." She opened the door another inch or two. "This happened way back then? The murder?" Her questions had changed from wary to curious.

"Do you know any of your neighbors, Ms. Shearer?"

"No, not really. Well. Ms. Durning, two doors down. I see her sometimes at the supermarket. The Food Lion, up on the Trail. But I don't really know her."

"Has Ms. Durning been living here since 1991?"

"I think so. But I couldn't swear to it."

"All right, Ms. Shearer. Thanks for your time. Sorry to trouble you."

"No one's been hurt? I mean, recently? Here on Datura Street?"

"No, ma'am. Thank you."

Raising their umbrellas, Fallon and Sophia walked back down the cement steps.

"All right," Fallon said, "we split it up. You take this side of the street. I'll take that one." He glanced at his watch. "Two fifteen. Give it an hour. Meet back here at three fifteen. If you raise anything, call me on the cell phone. I'll do the same. Okay?"

"Fine."

NO ONE WAS HOME AT NO. 852, next door to the Shearer woman. And the Durning woman, it turned out, hadn't moved onto Datura Street until 1992. She knew nothing about Marla Weston. But she said that her next-door neighbor, Ms. Norton, had been living on the street for years.

Ms. Norton had in fact lived on Datura since 1980, but she'd never met Marla Weston. She'd seen her many times, she said, driving into the driveway of 850, and she'd seen the son, Robert, once or twice, but Robert must've moved away in the eighties, long before Marla Weston left. How did she know the son's name? Mrs. Leroy, next door, had told her. Did Mrs. Leroy know Marla Weston well? Ms. Norton thought she did.

Sophia got a description of Marla Weston—thin, maybe five foot seven, brown hair.

Eye color?

Brown, Ms. Norton thought.

Basically the same description that Morrison had given Sophia, off the driver's license.

Sophia thanked her, went next door, and pushed the doorbell button.

Mrs. Leroy opened the door. She was a thin woman, as tall as Sophia, in her late sixties or early seventies. She wore a neatly pressed blue cotton blouse with long sleeves, a tan cotton skirt, gray support hose, and a pair of black flats. Her hair was permed and blued. Holding a book in her right hand, her index finger curled into it to keep her place, she peered at Sophia from over a pair of half-lenses in a gold frame. "Yes?"

"Mrs. Leroy?" said Sophia.

"That's right."

Sophia showed the woman her badge. "Detective Sophia Tregaskis, Mrs. Leroy. I understand that you were living here in 1991."

"Since 1970. Why?"

"Do you remember a woman named Marla Weston? She lived—"

"Oh my God." Mrs. Leroy took off her glasses. "Is she alive?"

Sophia's heart punched against her chest. "Why do you say that, Mrs. Leroy?"

"I was sure when it happened, the way she disappeared, that something dreadful had happened. I told my husband—" She shook her head. "I'm sorry. I've forgotten my manners. Please come in."

"Thank you."

Mrs. Leroy stood to one side, so Sophia could enter, then shut the door. "Shall I take your coat? Oh, please, that's all right, just leave the umbrella there."

She hung Sophia's coat on a rack behind the door. "The house is a bit of a mess, but I wasn't really expecting company. This way."

She led Sophia into the small living room. The room was, in fact, as well maintained as Mrs. Leroy herself. Heavily padded, brown leather furniture—a long sofa and two plump club chairs. Dark wood coffee table and end tables. Dark wood bookcases neatly packed with hard-cover books, covered along their tops with upright, framed photographs. The only suggestion of disarray was a copy of *The New York Times* that lay folded halfheartedly on the coffee table. A smell of citrus and cloves was in the air.

"Can I get you something?" said Mrs. Leroy. "Some coffee? Some tea?"

"No, thank you."

"Please, have a seat." She gestured to the club chairs, and she sat down at the end of the sofa. Sophia sat in the nearest of the two chairs, taking her notebook from her purse. She set the purse on the floor.

Mrs. Leroy put her book on the end table. Her knees together, her hands clasped on her lap, she leaned slightly forward. "*Is* she alive?"

"We honestly don't know, Mrs. Leroy. We know that she lived at No. 850 until 1991. After that, it looks like she disappeared."

"That's exactly what she did. In the summer of 1991. One day she was there, and the next day she wasn't. I told my husband, I said, something's happened to Marla. I thought it was our Christian duty to talk to someone, you see, and let them know. The police. Someone. But Norman said we shouldn't get involved. He said people were leaving their homes all the time. Well, that's true, of course, isn't it?"

She seemed to be seeking validation of, or maybe absolution for, her husband. And maybe for herself. Sophia nodded. "Were you and Marla Weston friends?"

"In a way—although I can't say I really knew her. Knew her well, I mean. She was a very private person. Not secretive, I don't mean that. Just very private."

"How did you meet her?"

"We met at the hairdresser's, Leon's, on the Trail—" She frowned. "May I ask you something?"

"Of course."

"Why is it you're investigating this now? It's been so many years since Marla disappeared."

"We think she may be connected to another case we're looking into. Up in St. Anselm."

Mrs. Leroy didn't react to the name of the city. Sophia found that puzzling. "It's been in the news lately," she said.

"We never bought a television, Norman and I, and I haven't read a local newspaper in years. It's all the same, isn't it? Alligators in the swimming pool, hurricanes, developers ruining everything they can get their greedy hands on. One little catastrophe after the other."

Mrs. Leroy nodded toward *The New York Times* on the coffee table. "That's the only news I get." She smiled. "Maybe I just prefer bigger catastrophes. Wars and revolutions and things."

Sophia smiled back. "You said you met Ms. Weston at Leon's?"

She nodded. "At Leon's, yes. And we got to talking. This was back in, oh, '83, I think. She'd been here a few months by then, I'd seen her on the street, going in or out, but we'd never met. We talked, and I suppose you could say we got along. At the time, we were the only people our age in the neighborhood. We were both in our forties, and everyone else was either much older or much younger."

She sat back, her hands still in her lap. "Well, we started to get together for coffee once a week, on Saturday afternoons, at a little place on St. Armand's Circle. Dominick's Café. I suppose it was my idea at first. Norman and I never had any children, and he was usually working on the weekends. He was an air traffic controller. He died in 1995."

"I'm sorry."

Mrs. Leroy nodded her thanks. "Well, as I say, I had no children, and then, about a year after we met, Marla and I, her son went away to college. Robert. So on the weekends she was on her own, too."

"Did she ever talk to you about Robert?"

"No. She was a very private person, in a lot of ways."

"Do you know where Robert went to college?"

"No, I don't. I'm sorry. She may've told me, but I just don't recall." Sophia nodded.

"Anyway," said Mrs. Leroy, "it was nice to spend time with someone. We'd meet and we'd talk and we'd have our coffee. It was all very pleasant. We did that for nearly seven years. Not every Saturday, of course. And she usually went off on a vacation in July, and sometimes we were gone, Norman and I. But when Marla and I were both in town, we met nearly every Saturday. And then one Saturday she just didn't show up. I stopped by her house, to see if she was all right, but no one answered the door."

"You'd seen her the Saturday before?"

"Yes."

"Do you remember when that was? The approximate date?"

"In June. Um. June the, uh . . . Wait. I can tell you exactly. June the fifteenth. Yes, because Norman's birthday was the sixteenth, the very next day. I remember I was shopping for a present, over there on the Circle, before I went to meet Marla."

"So she disappeared sometime between that June the fifteenth and June the twenty-second?"

"That's right."

"And you never saw her again?"

"No. When I tried to call her, the phone had been disconnected."

"And your husband didn't think you should notify the police?"

"He said it wasn't any of our business. He said Marla probably had a good reason for leaving the way she did, and if we brought the police into it, maybe we'd be getting her into trouble. Well, I certainly didn't want to do that. But I knew a woman who worked for the management company that Marla rented from, and I called her. She said that Marla had terminated her lease, forfeited her deposit *and* her last month's rent, and then left town. Don't you think that's a little strange, just giving up all that money?"

"Yes. Did she terminate the lease in person or by mail?"

"By mail."

"They'd already received the letter when you called?"

"Yes. I called Monday, after the Saturday she didn't show up."

"Did she give them a forwarding address?"

"No, she didn't. And the other strange thing. The woman told me that Marla left everything in the house. All her furniture, all her kitchen appliances, all her clothes. She had beautiful clothes."

"What happened to her things?"

"The management company called in movers to take them all away. That was about a week later. I saw them on the street. The truck. But I ask you, does that make any sense at all? To leave all your things like that?"

267

"What did the company do with them?"

"I don't really know. Sold them, I suppose."

"What was the name of the company?"

"Compton. Compton Management. They're still here in town. They're on Lloyd."

"And the name of the woman you spoke to?"

"Betty. Betty Johannson. She owns the company now."

"And you never heard from Ms. Weston again?"

"No. But, you know, there was never any fuss about it, nothing on the radio, nothing in the newspaper—in those days I used to read the local paper. And Marla didn't have any enemies, not so far as I knew. And so I suppose I tried to tell myself that Norman was right, that she'd left on her own. Some kind of personal thing. A problem of some kind."

Mrs. Leroy frowned. "But you know how it is? When you get a bad feeling about a thing and it won't go away? For the longest time I kept expecting to hear that something terrible had happened. That her body had been discovered in the swamp somewhere, or they'd found her buried in the backyard of the house." She looked to her right, in the direction of No. 850, and she shivered.

She turned back to Sophia. "By the time Norman died, of course, it was too late for me to do anything. I'd almost forgotten about her, to be honest. That's a terrible thing to say. I know that. But you *do* forget after a while, don't you?"

"Of course. Was Robert living with Ms. Weston when she disappeared?"

"Robert? Oh, no. He was off at school. I don't think I saw him more than once or twice, in all the years I knew Marla. And that was at the beginning, before he went away."

"He didn't come back during the summer?"

"No. Marla used to go away in the summer. Mexico. Somewhere along the Pacific Coast. Puerto something." She brightened. "Escondido. Puerto Escondido."

"Did Robert join her there?"

"I don't know. She never said."

"And you never asked her?"

She smiled. "You don't understand about Marla. She wasn't the sort of person you asked personal questions. I asked her once why she didn't have a boyfriend. She was a beautiful woman—a wonderful figure, a wonderful face, like a model. But she just smiled at me and said she was perfectly happy the way she was."

"Did she have any other women friends?"

"Yes." Mrs. Leroy pursed her lips. "Let me think. She mentioned a woman named Charlotte. Another teacher at the school. Morgan Prep. It's over on Murphy Key."

Sophia wrote down the name. "What about Robert? What sort of a person was he?"

"He seemed nice enough. He was very polite, and very quiet. I never really got to know him."

"Did he have any girlfriends? Boyfriends?"

"None that I ever saw. But neither of them did, not Marla and not Robert. It was like they didn't really need anyone else."

"Because they had each other?"

Once again, Mrs. Leroy frowned. "Do you mean a . . . neurotic sort of attachment to each other?"

"Is that what *you* mean, Mrs. Leroy?"

"No, no, I think they were perfectly normal. I don't think they were any different, really, from any other mother and son. It's just that they were both very . . . self-contained. If you know what I mean."

No different from any other mother and son. Except that they weren't mother and son.

Sophia reached down, lifted her purse, opened it, slid out a copy of the yearbook photograph of Robert Ambrose. She put back her purse, unfolded the photograph, stood up, and walked across the room to Mrs. Leroy. She handed her the photograph. "Is that Robert, Mrs. Leroy?"

Mrs. Leroy lifted her glasses from the end table and put them on. She peered down at the photograph. "Why, yes. He's heavier in the face here, though." Frowning, she looked up at Sophia. "And this says Robert *Ambrose*."

Suddenly, from within the purse behind her, Sophia's cell phone rang. "Excuse me." She walked back to the chair, leaned over, opened the purse, took out the phone, flipped it open. "Tregaskis."

"You okay?" Fallon.

She looked at her watch and realized she was due back at the car. "Look, I think you'd better get over here."

Chapter Forty-two

After Fallon heard what Mrs. Leroy had to say, he called Betty Johannson, the woman who owned the Compton Land Management Company, and arranged to meet her at the company's office. Sophia called Ray Hatfield, the principal of Morgan Prep. Hatfield had already spoken with Deputy Morrison, but he had no objection to being interviewed by Sophia, so long as she could get there within the next hour. He and his wife were getting ready to leave, to avoid the storm.

AS SHE DROVE ACROSS THE CAUSEWAY that led to Murphy Key, the rain was slowing. But beyond the key, black clouds were still grinding in from the southwest, swollen and blotched. The water in the bay was leaden, dull, oppressive. Everywhere on its surface, ragged wavelets shuddered and shifted.

Like all Florida keys, Murphy Key was essentially a large, exposed sandbank on which a few bits of scraggly vegetation—scrub pine, palmetto, mangrove—had managed to grab a handhold at some distant point in the past. But as the city of Sarasota grew, the island had been developed, groomed, and expensively landscaped. Tall palm trees, sabal and royal, grew along the side of the road, swaying now in the gathering breeze. Huge stately houses, their windows brightly lit, were set back behind dark shivering thickets of cedar and live oak.

Morgan Preparatory School was on Sandy Lane, halfway down the length of the key. A driveway of crushed oyster shell swooped across the wet expanse of lawn to an imposing two-story building with white stucco walls and a steeply angled Mediterranean tile roof.

Hatfield's house was behind the school. Like the school, it was stuccoed in white and roofed in tile. Sophia parked in the driveway beside a red Jeep Cherokee and grabbed her umbrella. She dashed up the flagstones to the front door, rang the doorbell, and waited.

After a moment the door was opened by a woman wearing a white, long-sleeved linen blouse, a pair of neatly pressed khaki slacks, and loafers of ivory-colored patent leather. In her midforties, she was as slender and elegant and blond as Eva Swanson.

Sophia knew that her own hair was frizzing into Brillo as she stood there. Why did she have to keep running into women like this?

The woman smiled. "Detective Tregaskis? Please come in."

Sophia stepped in and the woman shut the door behind her. "I'm Deborah Hatfield. My husband's in his study. May I take your things?"

"Yes, thanks." Sophia handed her the umbrella. Unbuttoning her raincoat, she glanced around the living room. "You have a lovely home."

The living room was long and open, floored with bleached-oak parquetry. The oversize furniture—chairs, sofa, a recliner—was upholstered in a white, nubby fabric. There were bookcases of smoked glass, all of them filled with books. On the off-white walls, a few brightly colored paintings.

"Thank you," said the woman, hanging up Sophia's coat. Smiling, she turned back to her. "We're hoping it'll still be here when we get back. We're staying at my parents' house in Bradenton until the hurricane is over. This way, please."

Sophia followed her down a corridor to a closed door at the opposite end of the house. Mrs. Hatfield knocked on it. "Ray? It's Detective Tregaskis."

A few second passed before the door opened.

Maybe fifty years old, Hatfield was bald, but he was one of those bald men who had the grace to *be* bald and not hide his scalp under a comb-over and a coating of shellac. He wore old running shoes, faded designer jeans, and a light blue dress shirt, its cuffs rolled back along muscular forearms. He moved lightly on the balls of his feet, like someone who played tennis or squash.

He held out his hand. "Ray Hatfield."

"Detective Sophia Tregaskis."

"Good to meet you." He turned to his wife. "You all packed, Deb?"

The woman smiled. "Yes, dear. For an hour now."

Grinning, he turned to Sophia. "My wife thinks I'm a little anal about packing. I probably am."

Mrs. Hatfield turned to Sophia. "Can I get you something? Coffee?"

"Thank you, no. I'll try to get this over with as soon as I can."

"No, please, take your time. We're not in all that big a hurry." The woman smiled. "No matter what my husband thinks. Just let me know when you're finished, and I'll get you your coat."

"Thank you," Sophia said.

"Come on in," said Hatfield.

"DEPUTY MORRISON," said Sophia, "explained that Robert Ambrose is the person we're interested in?"

From behind his desk, Hatfield said, "Yes. And I'd heard about him on the news. I didn't know, obviously, that he was the Robert who was supposed to be Marla's son. I told Deputy Morrison that I'm happy to help in any way I can, and I meant it. This is a terrible thing. These murders. But I'm not sure, really, how much I *can* help. I never met Robert."

Except for a window to the left that looked out onto the palm trees, Hatfield's study was lined with floor-to-ceiling bookcases. Sophia sat in a comfortable club chair opposite the desk.

"You did know Marla Weston," she said.

Hatfield nodded. "As I told the deputy, we both worked in the English department. I started here the year before she did. She arrived in 1983. Morrison mentioned that you might be coming, so I went over to the school and grabbed some things for you."

On his desk was a manila folder and what looked like a yearbook, bound in white leather. He opened the book, reversed it, and eased the book across the desk. He tapped a finger at the opened page. "That's Marla."

Sophia examined the picture. A faculty photograph, in color, it showed the teachers and administrators of the school standing on the front steps of the building. The woman Hatfield had indicated stood at the end of the first row.

"It's not a great picture," said Hatfield.

It wasn't. Sophia could see that the woman was slender, and that she wore her clothes well—a calf-length black skirt, a gray blouse. Her hair was light brown or blonde, but the image was too small for Sophia to make out her facial features clearly.

From the way she held herself, she was yet another of those elegant women. Eva Swanson, Deborah Hatfield, and now Marla Weston.

"And this," said Hatfield, "is her employment folder."

Sophia riffled through it.

An employment application. A letter of recommendation from Ms. Marlowe in Elfers: . . . *intelligent . . . reliable . . . extremely competent . . .*

Sophia leafed through the rest of the papers. Yearly reports on Marla's work, from 1983 to 1990, compiled by someone named Schuman. It hadn't occurred to Sophia that teachers got report cards, just as students did.

All the reports said essentially the same thing—that Marla Weston did a fine job.

All the reports, that is, but the last one, dated 1991–92. The form was empty, but someone had scrawled TERMINATED across the front of it. Sophia took out the report and showed it to Hatfield. "Terminated?"

Hatfield nodded. "That was Jack, venting. Jack Schuman, the principal at the time—back in '91, I was only the vice principal. Jack was furious at Marla. She never showed up for the faculty orientation, at the beginning of August. Never called, never wrote. Nothing. When Jack tried to reach her, he found she'd had her phone disconnected. She'd left town."

"He didn't think that was strange? That she'd leave without giving notice?"

"He thought it was thoughtless and selfish. He had to scramble to find someone else to cover her classes."

Some rain rattled against the window.

"And what did you think, Mr. Hatfield?"

"Me? Well, yes, I suppose that I thought it was strange. Marla never struck me as the sort of woman who'd act irresponsibly. She was smart. And beautiful. And remote." He thought for a moment and then shook his head. "No. That's not really fair. Not remote so much, I suppose, as self-contained."

Mrs. Leroy had used exactly the same phrase.

"Some of us socialized with each other back then," he went on. "Nothing fancy. Dinner parties, barbecues. Marla never came to any of them. We'd ask her, but she'd always refuse. She was always very gracious about it, but she'd refuse."

"Did she have any men friends among the faculty?"

"No." He smiled. "And believe me, a few of us tried."

More rain clattered against the window.

"*Us?* You mean you?"

"Among others. She was older than I was, by maybe ten years, but we were both single. And as I said, she was beautiful. I asked her out a couple of times." He smiled. "She turned me down. Both times."

He shrugged. "Again, she was gracious about it. But after two strikes, I stopped asking."

"Did she ever talk about Robert?"

"Never." He frowned. "If you do find Marla, do you think she'll help you locate him?"

"I think that if we find Marla," she said, "we'll be finding a body."

"A body?" He blinked. "You think Robert killed her?"

"She disappeared. For no good reason. Her car disappeared. No one's seen her since. No one's heard from her."

Slowly, Hatfield blew some air out from between his lips. "Dead? All this time?"

There was sadness in his voice, and loss, and Sophia realized that his feelings for Marla Weston had probably been a lot stronger than he'd been willing to admit—perhaps even to himself.

"I think so," she said.

"Jesus." He looked away for a moment, toward the main part of the house—where his wife was. A woman who resembled Weston.

More rain clattered against the window.

"She had a friend here," said Sophia. "A woman named Charlotte."

"Pardon? Oh. Yes, Charlotte Lorimar. She taught French. She died a few years ago."

Damn.

"How did she die?"

"Cancer. She quite teaching the year before."

Sophia remembered Niko, wasting away in his hospital bed.

Even Robert Ambrose couldn't engineer a case of cancer.

She asked Hatfield, "How close was she to Marla Weston?"

"As you say, they were friends."

But something flickered across Hatfield's eyes, and then he blinked again.

"What is it?" she asked him.

He compressed his lips. "I didn't mention this to Deputy Morrison. And I'm not sure I should mention it to you."

"Mr. Hatfield, this man has killed at least three women. He probably killed Marla Weston. And he'll probably kill again, unless we find him and stop him. If you know anything that might be helpful—"

"I don't know that it *will* be helpful. It was just gossip. Malicious, like all gossip."

"About Weston and Lorimar?"

He nodded. "It was ridiculous. Well. I thought so at the time. Both of them had children—none of us knew, back then, that Robert wasn't actually Marla's son. But Charlotte was a widow, and she *did* have a daughter. Michelle, a student here. And neither of them, Charlotte or Marla, were even remotely masculine."

He held up a hand. "I know. That's a cliché. The masculine lesbian. Anyway, my feeling then was that the talk began out of simple resentment. Resentment of Marla and her aloofness toward the men who worked here. Maybe there was some envy of their friendship as well. They were both attractive, intelligent women."

"But that was all it was? Gossip?"

Hatfield frowned. "There was one thing. When Marla didn't show up for the orientation meeting, I think Charlotte was as surprised as the rest of us. I remember thinking that she seemed a bit lost."

"This was at the beginning of August?"

"Yes. Marla usually went to Mexico in July. I think we all assumed, at the meeting, that for some reason she'd been late getting back. But then later, Jack—Jack Schuman—found out that she'd canceled her lease in June and had her phone disconnected. He called Charlotte and asked her if she knew what was going on. Jack was sometimes less than diplomatic—but, remember, he was furious at Marla for leaving him stranded. Anyway, he told me that Charlotte broke down on the phone and just hung up on him. This was about a week before the semester began. Charlotte missed her first few days of class. A stomach flu, she said."

He took a deep breath. "Well. At the time, I told myself that she didn't have to be Marla's lover—to be acting that way, I mean. Even if she were only a friend, she'd be upset if Marla just disappeared. But now. This thing with Robert. Marla pretending he was her son." He shrugged. "I honestly don't know what to think."

"You said that Charlotte had a daughter."

"Michelle. She was, ah, class of '93."

"Is there any way to find out where she is now?"

Another scatter of rain lashed the window.

He looked at her for a moment. "You know," he said, "there may be, at that."

Chapter Forty-three

Robert drove along Bank Street. The rain was letting up, thank goodness. He could see *much* better now.

He was at No. 180. Close.

He knew that Fallon lived in an apartment building, apartment 1-B, 250 Bank Street, South Pasadena.

It had taken only a teensy-weensy bit of research. And a good credit card, naturally, to pay for the unlisted phone number and address.

Things were working out quite well.

It was astounding, really, when you thought about it, how often things seemed to work out well for him. Work out perfectly.

Marcy, for example. And then Cyndi.

And coming soon to a theater near you—Sergeant James Fallon.

Ah, there it was.

250 Bank Street. Palmetto Court.

Normally, of course, an apartment building would be a serious no-no. Even for a little reconnaissance like this one.

But with the storm, the rain, the darkness, all the citizens glued to their television sets, he felt sure that he was reasonably safe.

He pulled into the parking lot.

It was two-story building, extremely drab, shingled with that ridiculous gray, weathered cedar. There were four apartments, two above and two below, and 1-B was the one to the right on the first floor.

An excellent piece of luck. The first floor was so very convenient.

It was another nice piece of luck that Fallon lived in Pasadena, on the mainland, and not on St. Anselm itself. St. Anselm and the other barrier islands were being evacuated, but Pasadena was out of the evacuation zone.

Things were working out—there it was again—perfectly.

He leaned to the right, pushed the button on the glove-compartment door. It popped open and he reached inside for his flask. He unscrewed the cap, took of sip of the lovely old Calvados.

He screwed the cap back on.

Shall we reconnoiter? Leave the car, tiptoe round back, take a peek at the accommodations?

Best not. There was still too much light.

We'll be back later.

Chapter Forty-four

By the time Sophia got to Denny's, Fallon was already sitting in a booth, eating a hamburger. He was still wearing his raincoat. A man who knew how to dress for dinner.

"How'd it go?" he asked her.

She propped her umbrella against the end of the bench seat. "I got something," she said, unbuttoning her coat. She set down the Morgan Prep yearbook, opened it to the faculty picture, turned the book around, and set it beside Fallon's plate. She pointed. "Marla Weston."

Fallon nodded, chewing on the burger.

She moved her finger. "Charlotte Lorimar. She's dead. Ambrose didn't kill her. Natural causes, cancer. But listen—she might've been having an affair with Weston."

"Might've been?" He set down the burger, picked up his beer.

"That was the gossip at the school." She sat back. "But she had a daughter, Michelle. She has to know something."

He sipped at his beer. "*If* it happened."

"Fallon, Marla Weston may be the key."

"To what?"

"To Robert Ambrose. Okay. Look. We've got Ambrose. He grows up out in the boonies, in that horrible little house. With that horrible, big, bloated woman—"

"Of size," he said, and smiled.

She ignored him. "An alcoholic, according to Morrison. And if Eva's right about serial killers, an abuser, too. By the time he's in his teens, he's already hopelessly warped."

Fallon nodded, took a bite of the hamburger.

"And then he meets Marla Weston. Doesn't just meet her—he moves in with her. She's older, more sophisticated. But if that's true, then why is she involved with him? Why Robert Ambrose? Maybe in her own way, she's as warped as he is."

"Maybe she's trying to help him."

"I don't think so. I think there was something deeply weird about Marla Weston. I think there had to be."

He sipped at the beer. "You can't have it both ways. You can't have her involved in a weird relationship with Ambrose, and also be involved in a lesbian relationship with Charlotte Lorimar."

"Why not? We don't know *how* weird she was. She could've been a complete bucket of worms. But if we find the daughter, maybe she can tell us. Her married name is Spurgeon. Hatfield, the principal, got her address and phone number from the woman who keeps the Alumni Association records. She lives here in town."

"You call her?" He took another sip of beer.

"Yeah, no answer, but we can find her, Fallon—"

"No. We can't. I just talked to Courtney. The State Police are closing down the Skyway Bridge at eight tonight. They've already closed all the westbound lanes from Tampa—all the bridges, all the causeways. All the cops in St. Anselm—except us—are already working emergency duty. You get something to eat and we'll take off."

"Fallon, the girl was *there*. Back in '91, when Weston disappeared."

A waitress appeared at Sophia's right and Sophia ordered a tuna-fish-salad sandwich. She turned to Fallon. "Look. How about this? You go ahead. Get back to St. Anselm. I'll keep trying to locate Michelle. All I need is a couple of hours."

"You don't have a couple of hours. The bridge will be shut"—he looked at his watch—"in an hour and a half."

"Then give me an hour and a half."

"It takes an hour just to get to the bridge from here."

She remembered something. "Wait, wait, wait. I don't need the bridge. I can take I-75 north through Tampa, then cut west to Pinellas. It's the long way around, but I can do it."

Shaking his head, he smiled. "Let me rephrase it. Courtney wants us to head back."

"But she wants Ambrose, too. Come on, Fallon. You know that if you talk to her, if you pitch it right, she'll say okay."

"What's to pitch? According to Mrs. Leroy, Ambrose wasn't even in Sarasota when Weston disappeared. This Charlotte woman probably didn't know anything about him. And neither did her daughter."

He drank some more beer.

Sophia said, "Weston went to Mexico every summer."

"That's what she told Mrs. Leroy." He picked up his burger, took a bite. "She could've been going anywhere."

"It doesn't matter where she was going. Wherever it was, she might've been seeing Ambrose. And if she was, then maybe Charlotte knew."

He swallowed. "Charlotte's dead."

"But the girl was there."

"How old was the girl?"

"Fifteen. How's your cold, by the way?"

"Better." He took a sip of beer.

He did, in fact, look better now. Some of the color had returned to his face.

"Look," she said. "I promise I'll only stay for a couple more hours. If I can't find Michelle by nine o'clock, I'll head back to St. Anselm."

He set down the beer. "Why are you so hot on this?"

"Hatfield, the principal—"

"Tuna fish salad," said the waitress, suddenly at Sophia's shoulder once again.

"Thank you," Sophia told her. She turned back to Fallon. "Hatfield said that when Weston disappeared, Charlotte was as surprised as the rest of them. She was upset—she actually missed the first few days of school. Her daughter was *there*, Fallon. She had to see *something*."

"So, basically, what we're talking about is a hunch."

"All right, yes, a hunch. Don't you ever get hunches? It'll only cost me a couple of hours. Ambrose is still out there. He could be working on his next woman right now. Fallon, I promise—when I get back to St. Anselm, I'll work all night. I'll knock on doors, I'll patrol the streets, I'll do whatever Courtney wants. But please, just get me a couple of hours."

He looked at her for a moment, then wiped his hands on his napkin, reached into his pants pocket, and pulled out his cell phone. He flipped it open, speed-dialed a number, and put the phone to his ear. Lowering his head but keeping his eye on Sophia, he said, "Hi, it's Fallon. . . . Yeah. . . . I'll be taking off in a minute or two, but Tregaskis wants to check out a lead. . . . She knows that. She says she can come up I–75 through Tampa. . . . I don't know."

He raised his head. "Through Oldsmar?" he asked Sophia.

She nodded.

"Yeah," he said into the phone. "By nine, she says. . . . Yeah. . . . I know. . . . She thinks it's worth a couple of hours . . . and I think she's right. . . . Yeah. . . . Yeah. . . . Okay. . . . Okay, I'll be there. . . . Right. Bye."

He flipped the phone shut, slid it back into his pocket. "No later than nine, she says. She says to call her once you're on the road."

"*Great*. Thank you. You're terrific."

"Yeah." He nodded to her sandwich. "Eat."

"Really. I appreciate it."

"Eat."

She picked up the sandwich, took a bite. She hadn't eaten for hours, she realized. She'd actually forgotten about food.

The Tregaskis diet. Chase a serial killer—burn up calories.

She swallowed. "Did you get anything from the management company?"

He nodded. "I made copies." He reached into the inner pocket of his coat, pulled out two folded sheets of paper. He opened the first, turned it around, put it on the table. "Weston's original lease." He opened the second, put it next to the lease. "The letter canceling the lease."

She took another bite of her sandwich and leaned forward. The letter was typewritten and brief, with no salutation.

Due to circumstances beyond my control, I am reluctantly forced to cancel my lease. I hereby forfeit any moneys on deposit with your company.

Sophia checked the signatures on each document, looked up at Fallon. "The signatures are close. But that's the whole idea with a forgery, isn't it?"

He nodded. "And we know that Ambrose was forging his mother's signature, his real mother, on her driver's license renewal forms."

"So Ambrose could have signed this."

"Or the signature could be genuine."

"A handwriting expert could probably tell. But I think she's dead, Fallon."

"Maybe."

She took another bite of the sandwich.

"I talked to Morrison," he said. "Their ME finished the autopsy on the Ambrose woman."

She swallowed. "And?"

"There was alcohol in her lungs. Ambrose put her into the tank alive, chained her down, filled it up, drowned her in the stuff."

"The son of a bitch. The *bastard*!"

AN HOUR LATER, sitting in the car, the cell phone on her lap, Sophia looked out through the driver's window, past the rivulets of rain that shimmied down the glass. The big apartment building was part of a large complex off Fruitville Road—five three-story buildings separated by parking lots and thin strips of grass. Despite the rain and the heavy clouds, the sky wasn't entirely dark yet, and Sophia could see, tucked here and there around the property, a few tattered palmettos, a few threadbare citrus trees, all of them flapping and snapping in the wind.

It was possible that on a sunny day, the building would look comfortable. At the moment, with its stucco blackened by rain, its parking lot awash, it looked ominous and sullen. In the light cast by the tall lamps that dotted the perimeter of the lot, she saw bits of debris racing by. Leaves, bits of newspaper, a plastic bag.

Most of the apartment windows were lit from within. Many had been crisscrossed with tape, to prevent the glass flying if the window shattered. A few of them were completely dark, and one of those—she didn't know which one—belonged to Mr. and Mrs. Neil Spurgeon.

She had called the Sarasota PD and picked up some information about the husband. No police record. Employed at Mark's Auto Shop. She'd called the shop and gotten only a recorded message.

Now she was wondering if maybe she shouldn't just take off.

Fallon was probably right. If Weston had been involved in some kind of weird sexual relationship with Robert Ambrose, a young boy, then probably she wouldn't have been involved in a sexual relationship with Charlotte Lorimar, a woman. And if she hadn't been intimate with Lorimar, then probably she'd never talked to her about Robert. She'd never talked about him to Mrs. Leroy, her neighbor.

Or maybe the relationship with Robert had been altogether innocent, surrogate mother to surrogate son. Maybe she *had* been trying to help him.

Sophia tried to picture the woman described by Mrs. Leroy and by Ray Hatfield. Blond. Beautiful. Smart. Self-contained.

Could a woman like that have been sexually involved with a budding young sociopath?

Yes, if she'd been some kind of sociopath herself. If she'd been wearing a mask, as Robert must have been. Must still be doing.

But again—if she was involved with Robert that way, how could she be sexually involved, later, with Charlotte Lorimar?

She sighed. None of it made any sense.

And, let's face it, probably the Spurgeons wouldn't be back for hours, if they were coming back at all.

And she felt guilty—she was just sitting there in the car, twiddling her thumbs, while everyone on the St. Anselm force was busy helping the town get through tonight's storm and brace for the hurricane tomorrow.

It was seven-thirty. Maybe it was time to get on I-75 and start heading for Tampa.

The beam of a headlight cut through the darkness, illuminating the inside of Sophia's car. A Dodge truck came across the parking lot and pulled into a slot near the front of the building. A man got out and ran toward the entrance, his head lowered against the rain. He knifed a key into the door's lock, opened the door, and disappeared inside.

Sophia waited.

After a few minutes, the lights in one of the darkened apartments on the second floor went on. She lifted the cell phone from her lap, flipped it open, dialed the Spurgeons' number again.

Someone picked up. "H'lo?" A man's voice.

"Neil Spurgeon?"

"Yeah?"

"This is Detective Sophia Tregaskis of the St. Anselm police. I'd like to talk to your wife."

A silence, and then the man said, "Fuck you." He hung up.

She snapped the cell phone shut, grabbed her purse, rammed the phone inside, opened the door of the Ford.

The wind tugged at her umbrella as she splashed across the lot. Her raincoat billowed and fluttered, cold rain smacked against her legs. At the entrance, along the row of buzzers, she found one for the Spurgeons' apartment. 2-B. She thumbed it.

The same voice came through the small speaker. "Yeah?"

"Police. Open the door, please."

"Huh?"

"Police. Open up."

When the door made a rasping, metallic buzz, she pushed it open.

She took the elevator up to the second floor, walked down the corridor to apartment 2-B. The brown carpet beneath her feet was worn and faded. She could see the water spots left by Spurgeon's passage.

By the time she reached the door to the apartment, she had her wallet out, the badge showing. She wiped her shoes on the doormat and pressed the doorbell.

The door opened and a man stood there in blue coveralls splotched with motor oil. *Neil* was written in script on a white oval over the left chest pocket. Lanky, loose-limbed, he was maybe six feet tall and looked about twenty-five. From the way his thick black hair had been styled in a pompadour, he'd obviously seen *Grease* one too many times.

And he'd obviously combed the hair since he ran across the parking lot. An impressive spit curl dangled down the center of his pale forehead.

She could smell the beer on his breath.

"Detective Sophia Tregaskis. St. Anselm Police Department."

"That was you on the phone?"

"That was me."

He winced. "Shit." He shook his head, then raised his thick eyebrows and held up his hands. "Hey, I thought it was someone tryna screw with me. One of Michelle's fucked-up friends. Excuse my French."

"May I come in?"

"Yeah, sure, come on in. House is a bit sloppy, I guess."

Unlike Mrs. Leroy, Neil Spurgeon wasn't exaggerating. The small couch was littered with dirty clothing, the top of the table in the tiny dining area was draped with old TV dinner trays and empty Budweiser cans.

Spurgeon said, "You wanna sit down or something? I could get you a beer, you want it."

Sophia slipped her wallet back into her purse. "No, thanks. This won't take long. Where's Michelle?"

"I don't know. She run out on me, six months ago now."

"Ran out on you?"

"I come home one day, Tuesday, and she's gone. Took most of her clothes and all the jewelry I give her. Except for the ring. The wedding ring. She left that. She put everything else in a suitcase. Left me a note and all, sayin' don't try to find her."

"You've got no idea where she might be?"

"I sure don't. That's the God's honest truth. I called the place she worked and they told me she give 'em notice two weeks before she run out. She knew the whole time she was gonna do it, and she never let on a thing. Not to me."

"Where did she work?"

"Newman's. It's a construction company over on Ringling. She was a secretary."

"She didn't tell them where she was going?"

"Unh-unh." He frowned. "How come you're looking for Michelle?"

"A case we're working on."

"And she's like, what, a suspect?"

"No. Would any of her friends know where she is?"

"I dunno. Maybe. Probably Susie does. She says she doesn't, but she was Michelle's best friend, they were always hangin' together. I bet you money Susie knows."

"Susie who?"

"Susie Harper. She works over at the Dillard's, at Southgate. A whattaya call it. A cosmetician."

"Dillard's will be closed now, Mr. Spurgeon. There's a hurricane coming."

"Oh, right. Yeah."

It was amazing that Michelle would walk out on a prize like this.

"Do you know her phone number?" Sophia asked.

"Unh-unh. She's in the phone book, though. Want me to get it?"

"Please."

He turned, walked over to an inexpensive end table by the sofa, picked up the Sarasota phone book, carried it back, handed it to her. She opened it, held it in her left hand while she riffled through it with her right. *H.* Harper. Too many S. Harpers.

She looked up at Spurgeon. "You know her address?"

"Um. Cooper Street, I think. Over off Beneva. It's under her husband's name. Stan."

Harper, Stan, 1556A Cooper Street.

She handed the book back to Spurgeon, took her cell phone from the purse, flipped it open, dialed the number.

"Hello?" A woman's voice.

"Mrs. Harper, this is Sophia Tregaskis. I'm a police officer from St. Anselm. I'm trying to locate Michelle Spurgeon."

"Yeah, right." Scornful.

"Mrs. Harper, it's very important. It's about a case we're working on."

"Listen, you tell that jerk Neil he's gonna have to do better than this, okay?"

"Mrs. Harper, I'm a police officer. I—"

Harper hung up.

Shit. Shit, shit, *shit.*

Everyone in the world was hanging up on her.

She looked at Spurgeon. "How do I get to Cooper Street?"

Chapter Forty-five

It was eight fifteen when Sophia got to Cooper Street. There was almost no traffic on the roads, but the rain was falling harder now, drumming steadily against the windshield, smearing the image of the streets. The wipers could barely keep up.

No. 1556 was a small, two-story brick duplex. Lights were lit on both floors, behind curtains—dark curtains on the upper floor, light curtains on the lower. She parked in front of the building, buttoned the top button of her raincoat, tucked the purse under her left arm, snatched up the umbrella, opened the door.

It was like walking into a waterfall. The umbrella was useless—the rain was coming from every direction. Her head lowered, her hair whipping at her eyes, she ran up the sidewalk to the front door of the lower unit.

Beside the doorbell buzzer was a number—1556A. The right apartment.

She got out her badge, held it up, pressed the buzzer.

After a moment the door was opened, no more than six inches, and a young man's head appeared between the door and the jamb. He winced as a scatter of spray hit him. "Yes?"

"Detective Sophia Tregaskis. I need to talk to Susie Harper."

"Right now?"

"Yes, right now. Would you let me in, please?"

He backed away from the door and Sophia stepped in. She wiped water from her face and stood there for a moment, dripping.

The young man—jeans, running shoes, a red Old Navy sweatshirt—was staring at her.

"I'm sorry to bother you, but it's very important. I need to talk to Mrs. Harper."

"Honey?" called a woman's voice from the next room. "Who is it?" The voice was closer now, and then the owner of the voice came into the small foyer. Thin, mid-twenties, brown-haired, she would have been beautiful if she hadn't been wearing quite so much makeup. Like the young man, she wore jeans and a sweatshirt. Her sweatshirt was gray.

"She's a detective, Susie," said the young man.

"Oh my God," said the woman, her eyes widening. "You called on the phone?"

"Yes. Sophia Tregaskis."

"You're really a cop?"

"Yes."

"Look, I'm really sorry. That creep Neil—Michelle's husband?— he's been bugging me every way he can, trying to find her. I thought maybe he got someone to call for him. Um, this is my husband, Stan. Stan Harper."

Stan nodded. He didn't look too happy about having a dripping detective in his foyer.

Well, the detective wasn't all that thrilled about it either.

Susie Harper frowned. "How did you get my name?"

"From Neil. I just left him."

"But how come you're looking for Michelle? She hasn't done anything."

"I need—"

The young man said, "Do you want—should I take your coat?"

"Thanks, but I won't be staying." Sophia turned back to Susie Harper. "You know about the killings in St. Anselm? The women?"

"The ones who're getting cut up? That Diet Doctor guy?"

Screw that reporter.

"Yes. Michelle doesn't know it, but she may have information that'll help us. All I want to do is talk to her."

"How could Michelle know anything about him? She doesn't live anywhere *near* St. Anselm."

"It's something that happened a long time ago. Before her mother died. Mrs. Harper, it's very important."

The young woman looked at her husband, looked back at Sophia. "I promised her I wouldn't tell anyone, ever. Neil is a such a *total*

290

loser. She deserves a chance at happiness, and she'd never get it with that jerk. Not in a million years."

"Could you call her? Let me talk to her?"

Harper looked at her husband. He nodded, and she turned again to Sophia. "I'll call her. Hold on."

She walked back into what was presumably the living room.

Sophia glanced down. Her ruined shoes were standing in a puddle that was slowly expanding across the carpet.

"You sure you don't want me to take your coat?" Stan asked.

"Yes. But thanks."

"Bad night to be out."

"Yes."

She looked at her watch. Nearly eight thirty.

Stan said, "They say the winds tomorrow are going to be something fierce."

"That's what I understand." Where the hell was Susie Harper?

"We've got some coffee we just made. Want some?"

"No thank you."

Susie Harper returned, holding a white cordless phone out to Sophia. "She wants to talk to you."

Sophia took the phone. "Michelle?"

The voice was firm: "I don't know anything about those women who got killed."

"Michelle, do you remember Marla Weston, a woman who taught at Morgan Prep with your mother? Do you remember her son, Robert?"

No answer for a moment. Then, with a curious flatness: "I remember them."

"Robert is Robert Ambrose. He's the man we think killed the women."

Another silence.

"Listen to me, Michelle. If you have any information at all, anything that might help us, I've got to talk to you."

More silence. Finally: "I guess you better get up here."

"Where are you?"

"Kenneth City. You know where it is?"

In Pinellas County, directly on the route that would take her back to St. Anselm and the station.

Sometimes God was good.

"On Sixty-sixth Street? Above Tyrone?"

"Off Sixty-sixth." Michelle gave the address.

"Alright. I'm leaving now. It'll take me a while. I've got to go the long way, through Tampa. The Skyway's closed."

"I'll be here," said Michelle. She sounded resigned.

Chapter Forty-six

Once again, Robert drove down Bank Street.

The storm was *wonderful*!

Rain pounded against the roof of the car and streamed along his windshield. On either side of him, trees writhed and twisted. Leaves shot through the air like frantic bats.

It was *so* exciting!

He had always loved wild weather. The sheer mindless power of it—the wind, the rain, the sense that the whole world might get completely swept away, trees ripped from the earth like tufts of weed, buildings leveled, bricks and timber flying, human bodies hurled through the air and smashed against the rubble.

And tonight, of course, there were *many* other reasons for excitement.

And here we are. Palmetto Court.

He turned the car into the parking lot, took a quick look at Fallon's apartment.

Still no car in front of it.

Fine.

We'll just wait then, shall we?

He circled and returned to Bank Street, turned right, and pulled over to the side of the road.

He knew that, parked here, he wasn't likely to be spotted by any passing patrol car. Most of the local gendarmes would be prowling around near the beaches.

He could just sit here, snug as a bug in a rug, and wait.

Chapter Forty-seven

Sophia had planned to call Courtney when she got out of Sarasota and reached the Interstate. But, as it turned out, she called her a bit sooner than that.

She was heading east on Fruitville Road, the street nearly deserted now. Except for a slowly cruising Sarasota PD marked unit, she hadn't seen another car for two miles.

The rain slashed at her windshield. Despite its heavy-duty shocks, the big police Ford occasionally rocked from side to side as gusts of wind slammed into it.

Suddenly, out of the corner of her eye, she saw something hurtle out of the light of a streetlamp and come racing across the roadway, directly toward her. It was moving so quickly that for a split second she thought it was alive, and then she realized what it was—a big galvanized garbage can, tumbling and bouncing as it came. She swerved to the right, but the can careened into the rear of the car with a sickening metallic crunch.

She pulled over to the side of the road, beneath another streetlamp. No point using the umbrella now—too much wind. She climbed out of the car, into the slashing rain. At the rear of the car, she saw that the can had scored a deep, irregular gouge across the entire top of the trunk.

Worse, in the center of the trunk, where the radio antenna had been, there was now only a useless stump of metal.

Shit!

She stomped back to the driver's door and got inside. She pulled out the phone and speed-dialed Courtney.

"Lieutenant Courtney."

"Hi. It's Sophia. I just lost my radio."

"Lost it?"

"The wind. A garbage can snapped the antenna." With the back of her hand, she wiped rainwater away from her forehead. "It's pretty bad down here. But the cell phone's still working."

"If the landlines go, the network will overload and the cell phone'll be useless. Where are you?"

"Just leaving Sarasota."

"Fallon told me about the daughter. You find her?"

"I talked to her. She lives in Kenneth City. I'll be stopping there on my way to the station."

"She know anything?"

"She knows *something*. I don't know what."

"Once you get on the north side of the bay, you'll be coming south on 19?"

"Yes. I'll get off at Sixty-sixth, where 19 crosses Ulmerton."

"It'll take you two or three hours to get there."

"Two, if the rain lets up."

"It's died down a bit up here. Maybe you'll get lucky. Okay, look. After you talk to the daughter, give me a call."

"Should I come to station afterward?"

"No. Go to your apartment, rest up for a couple of hours."

"If the apartment's still there."

"It's there now. But the whole island may be gone by tomorrow night."

"Is Fallon at the station?"

"I sent him home for a while. He'll be back here later."

"When do you want me?"

"No later than two in the morning. One would be better."

"I'll be there."

THE RAIN HELD STEADY FOR TWENTY MINUTES or so on I-75. With the windshield distorted by water, Sophia had to keep the Ford below sixty miles an hour. Even so, she passed car after car, people slowly heading away from the coast and toward the relative safety of inland Florida.

After she passed the exit for Gillette, the rain began to ease up, and she let her foot become a little heavier on the gas pedal. Seventy,

seventy-five. The winds were still buffeting the car, but the stiff suspension kept it on track.

At a quarter after ten she was approaching Tampa. She was just about halfway to Kenneth City.

Chapter Forty-eight

Up ahead, standing in the road beneath the streetlight, was a St. Anselm cop wearing an orange plastic slicker, the hood upraised to cover his cap. He was swinging his flashlight, the beam sweeping back and forth across the wet asphalt.

Fallon slowed the car.

The cop walked around to the window, aiming the beam at Fallon. When he saw who it was, he turned off the light. Fallon pressed the button and the window rolled down, cold spray blowing in immediately.

The cop was Del Morton. Squinting against the rain, he said, "Hey, Sergeant. Didn't recognize the car. Can't see a damn thing in this rain."

"It's a mess. How's the causeway?"

"Got some water along the road, but not much. You should be okay. You're coming back later, right?"

"Around one thirty."

"Can't guarantee anything for then. The wind shifts, the causeway could be underwater."

Fallon hesitated. He could go back to the station, rest for a while on one of the cots that had been set up on the second floor.

But he wanted an hour or two to himself. He wanted a shower and a change of clothes. He wanted a drink.

"I'll make it back," he said. "Thanks."

Morton nodded, tapped the hood of his slicker with the flashlight. Fallon put the car into gear and moved forward.

It had been a long day. The beer down in Sarasota had given him only a brief lift, quickly fading away and making him feel drained and worn. The return trip to St. Anselm through the rain, with poor visibility and slick streets, hadn't helped any.

And as soon as he'd returned to the station, he'd had to tramp out into the storm again, climb back into the car, and start patrolling the streets along the beach. As Courtney had said, it would take a fairly determined looter to brave that wind and rain, but the job had to be done.

He'd been pleased to hear from Courtney, finally, that he could take some time off for a while. And he'd been pleased—and a bit surprised—to hear that Tregaskis had located the daughter of Weston's friend. Or lover, or whatever she'd been.

He didn't think anything would come of it—no matter what Tregaskis said, he couldn't believe that the girl would know anything that would help them locate Robert Ambrose. But he admired Tregaskis's determination. She'd said that she would find the kid, and she had.

He peered through the windshield. Morton had been right—there was water on the road. The wind was kicking up fat ragged waves in the Intercoastal and heaving them at the boulders planted along the side of the causeway. Spurts of spray shot through the air and slapped against the pavement.

He was halfway across when a big one hit. He didn't see it coming. One moment he was squinting out the windshield, trying to see through the tracer bullets of rain in his headlight beams, and then suddenly a rush of water surged across the glass and he was driving blind.

He slowed down, pulled over to the narrow shoulder.

Maybe he should head back. It wasn't really a great idea, driving around in a storm like this.

No.

He wanted clean clothes. Dry clothes. And he wanted that drink.

Chapter Forty-nine

When Fallon returned to Palmetto Court, Robert almost missed him. He was busy going through his bag, setting his tools out on the passenger seat, making sure he'd packed everything he needed—which was really silly, because he'd checked and rechecked it something like a million times before he'd left home.

But this little episode would be a tad different from the others, and he wanted to be absolutely certain that everything went perfectly.

He would never have heard Fallon's car, what with all that splendid racket the rain and the wind were making. It was just another marvelous piece of luck—at the exact moment that Fallon's car turned into the driveway, Robert happened to glance up into the rearview mirror.

Ah. Welcome back, Jimbo. Good to see you.

He smiled.

There was no real hurry. He had plenty of time.

And this last check had confirmed that his satchel held all the tools. He had everything he needed.

Chapter Fifty

Fallon turned on the shower, walked back into the bedroom, lifted his glass of bourbon from the dresser, took a drink, felt the welcome chill of the bourbon roll down his throat and turn into that familiar expanding warmth in his stomach. He put the glass back on the dresser and sat down on the bed. His shoelaces were so wet that he had a hard time getting them untied. The shoes were soaked through, and so were his socks. He tossed the socks to the side.

He stood, stripped off his sodden pants, kicked them toward the socks. He tugged down his boxers and flipped them onto the pile. He unbuttoned his shirt and tossed it. He grabbed the drink, carried it into the bathroom, set it on the sink, and stepped into the shower.

As he soaped himself up, he wondered what Eva Swanson would think about Marla Weston and her relationship, whatever it was, with Charlotte.

Eva didn't know yet about Weston.

What kind of woman "adopted" an eighteen-year-old student? What kind of relationship would the two of them have?

Why don't you just call old Eva up and ask her, Jimmy?

After the shower, he slipped into his bathrobe, padded back into the kitchen, and made himself another drink. He took it into the living room, sat down on the recliner, sipped at the bourbon. He put the glass down on the end table, beside the things he'd dumped from his pockets when he'd reached the house—wallet, comb, change, the cell phone. He picked up the wallet, opened it, took out Eva's business card.

He looked at his watch. Quarter to eleven. A little late.

But her input could be useful.

What the hell.

He lifted the cell phone, flipped it open, dialed her number. At her end, the phone rang once, twice, three times, once more.

He was about to hang up when he heard, "Hello?"

"Eva?"

"Jim! What a nice surprise. Hold on, I'm just getting into my car. One second." He heard a muffled slam. "Okay. What a mess!"

"Where are you?"

"At the Walgreens on Pasadena. I just realized that I didn't have any candles in the house. They're saying on the news that the power's already gone out in Tampa."

The Walgreens on Pasadena was less than two miles from Fallon's apartment.

"How *are* you?" she said.

"Fine, thanks. You?"

"A bit damp at the moment, but otherwise fine. Can I help you with something?"

"No, forget it. It's not important. You go home and get out of the storm. I'll call you tomorrow."

"I've got time now. Really. What is it?"

"Or . . ."

"Or?"

"Well," he said, "there are a couple of things I'd like to ask you. About the case, I mean. I'm not very far from the Walgreens. If you wanted to cash in that rain check, come over for a drink or something . . . coffee, whatever . . ."

You're one suave son of a gun, Jimmy.

She said, "I think that would be very nice. I'd love to. Where are you?"

"Bank Street. Two fifty. It's the lower apartment on the right."

"How do I get there?"

He told her.

"All right, I'll be there as soon as I can. Oh—do you need anything? Any emergency supplies? Candles, batteries?"

"No. Thanks."

"All right, Jim. See you soon."

He flipped the phone shut, put it back on the end table. For a moment he simply sat there.

What the hell are you doing?

You're the last thing Eva Swanson needs.

Too late now, he realized. She'd be here in a few minutes.

Maybe you'd better lose the bathrobe before she shows up, Jimmy.

He got up and took a step toward the bedroom. His cell phone rang. He reached for it.

Chapter Fifty-one

Showtime!

Robert screwed the cap back on his flask, leaned forward, unzipped the satchel, slipped the flask inside.

He raised the satchel and opened the driver's-side door.

The wind nearly ripped the door from his hand.

He stepped out into the rain, closed the door.

It was *marvelous*! It was *fantastic*!

All around him, the storm raged at the world. It sounded like the roar of an animal—some huge, elemental, demonic beast.

Rain pounded at his face, the wind clutched and pawed and whacked at his body.

Walking around the car, he tucked the satchel under his arm. Bent slightly forward, he started up the driveway.

RAIN STREAMING DOWN HIS FACE, he edged along the back wall of Fallon's apartment. Up ahead, at the patio's glass doors, a light was coming from the edge of the curtain.

He eased up to the gap in the curtain, cautiously peered around the edge of the cedar-shingled wall.

The living room. A tacky plastic recliner. A cheap veneered end table. Just about what we'd expect from Fallon.

Where are you, Jimbo?

The rain hammered at him.

Fallon, in a ratty old bathrobe, walked across the living room floor and disappeared to the right.

Love the bathrobe, Jim.

Fallon reappeared, a drink in his hand. He set the glass down and picked up his cell phone.

Whatever you do, Jimbo, don't invite anyone over for a little late-night snack.

You and I, we don't want to be interrupted.

Chapter Fifty-two

It was almost eleven o'clock, but Sophia had made good time from Tampa. The rain had held off and the streets had been nearly empty of traffic. She was on Route 19 now, almost at the exit for Sixty-sixth, and only seven or eight miles from Kenneth City and Michelle Lorimar.

It had been an eerie trip. Some of the neighborhoods she'd passed had looked like ghost towns—the streets deserted, the windows of the houses boarded up. Twice, the main power had failed, the streetlights flickering briefly before they snapped back on.

The rain was back again, blurring her vision, but there was no wind behind it, and she was able to keep the Ford at a steady sixty miles an hour.

Her left hand on the wheel, she pried open her purse with her right, found the cell phone. She flipped it open and speed-dialed Fallon's number.

"Fallon."

"Hey," she said.

"Hey. What's up?"

"Did Courtney tell you about the daughter?"

"Yeah. Good work. You talk to her yet?"

"I'm almost there now. I just wanted to check in, see how you're doing. How's the cold?"

"Better. Look, I've got to run. Eva Swanson's coming over."

"Now?"

"I want to talk to her about—" The line crackled.

"What was that?" she said. "You're breaking up."

The line crackled again.

"What did you say?" she asked.

Crackle. "—Weston."

"Fallon, I can't hear you. I'll call back later."

She closed the phone, slid it into her purse.

Don't go getting all hot and bothered, *koritsi mou*.

Just because Eva Swanson was going to that little apartment in Pasadena. At eleven o'clock at night. In the middle of a hurricane.

He'd said something about Weston. Probably he just wanted Swanson's help with the case.

And what difference did it make anyway?

THE ADDRESS MICHELLE HAD GIVEN her was a small frame cottage beneath a gigantic live oak tree. Looking up from inside the car at the huge swaying branches of the tree, Sophia thought that if she lived in that house, underneath that tree, she'd make a point of not being home during a hurricane.

She opened the door, got walloped immediately by the rain, shut the door, and ran to the front door. No doorbell. She knocked, digging herself down deeper into her coat as the wind pummeled her back, tugged at her hair.

The door opened. Another young woman, waving her forward. "Come in, come in."

Sophia stepped inside and the woman shut the door. The wind stopped howling.

The woman was slender and petite, maybe five foot three, and she wore black leggings, open-toed leather sandals, and an oversize man's white shirt that fell to her thighs. "You're the detective?" she asked gravely.

"Sophia Tregaskis. You're Michelle?"

The woman nodded, a solemn nod, almost melancholy, as though she were admitting some sad truth that there was no point in denying.

She was blond, the hair cut close to her scalp. She was about the same age as Susie Harper—if Michelle had been fifteen in 1991, she'd be twenty-eight now, but the stillness, the gravity, of her face made it seem older.

After all the running around tonight, all the frantic driving, a part of Sophia wanted to grab her by the shoulders, right there in the entryway, and shake loose from her everything she knew about Robert Ambrose.

But another part, probably wiser, counseled patience. Be nice.

"Can I take your coat?" Michelle asked.

"Thank you." Sophia unbuttoned it.

"It's a terrible night to be out." Even this she said with that slow solemnity, as though she meant every word of it.

"It is. But I don't really have any choice." Sophia handed over the coat.

Michelle hung the coat on a peg jutting from the wall, beside two other coats, one of them obviously a man's.

Sophia looked down. Another puddle at her feet. She looked at Michelle. "I'm sorry about tracking in all the water."

"Don't worry. Come on into the living room."

Sitting on the couch was a man who was almost certainly the owner of the raincoat in the entryway, and probably of the shirt that Michelle was wearing. He was a big, broad-shouldered, good-looking man, a couple of inches taller than six feet and about the same age as Michelle. His curly black hair was closely cropped and he was clean-shaven. He moved with the slow assurance of someone who'd always been bigger than the people around him.

He held out his hand. "Jeff Carson."

Sophia took it. "Detective Sophia Tregaskis."

He nodded. "Good to meet you."

"Would you like some coffee?" Michelle asked her.

People kept offering her coffee. She didn't want coffee.

Be nice.

"Yes, please. Thank you."

"Milk? Sugar?"

"Both, please. One spoon?"

Another grave nod. "I'll be right back." She turned and walked into the small kitchen.

"Have a seat." Carson gestured toward the chair opposite the couch.

He waited to sit until Sophia was seated, then said, "Have you been a policewoman for long?"

Usually that was the sort of question people asked when they were trying to make small talk, but Carson seemed genuinely interested.

"Two years now."

"You like it?"

Sophia suddenly flashed on Deputy Conners, up in Elfers. He had asked her the same question.

"Most of the time." She looked around the room. "You have a nice house."

It was, in fact, a pleasant house. Not as luxurious as the Hatfield place, down in Sarasota, but cozy and warm, neat and clean. Maybe because of the storm raging outside, it had the feeling of a haven, a place of safety.

If you forgot about that big tree swaying overhead.

Carson smiled, and his pleasure, too, seemed genuine. "We like it," he said.

"Jeff went to Morgan," said Michelle as she returned to the room, carrying a big mug of coffee. "Morgan Prep. We were high school sweethearts." She said it, as she had said everything else, without a trace of irony.

"I went away to college," Carson said, "and we lost track of each other for a while."

Michelle sat down on the couch, next to Carson, and put her hand on his thigh. He placed his on top of hers. There was nothing possessive, nothing demonstrative, in either gesture. It seemed simply a sign of the easy comfort they took in each other.

She turned to Sophia. "You wanted to know about Marla Weston."

"Yes." And Robert Ambrose.

Just then the lights in the house flickered. They came back on again, flickered again, and then died.

In the darkness, the wind seemed suddenly louder.

"Don't worry." Carson's voice. "We've got candles."

A small flame appeared, hovering in the air across the room. By its light Sophia saw Carson moving toward the end table, one hand cupping the flame. He lit a candle there, and then another. He moved around the room, and one by one he lit another five or six candles, one of them on the small table to Sophia's right. The room became cozy again. Became maybe even cozier than it had been—the trembling candlelight made the room feel like the warm interior of a tent during a rainy camping trip.

Carson returned to the couch. Michelle took his hand.

Outside, the wind howled.

"Marla Weston," Sophia prompted.

"She was a wicked woman," Michelle said. "She killed my mother."

Spoken in Michelle's small, grave voice, in that candlelit room with the wind screeching outside, the phrase was chilling.

"Killed her," repeated Sophia.

"She didn't shoot her," Michelle said. "She didn't have to. They were lovers. Did you know that?"

"I knew it was a possibility."

"My mother was a very lonely woman. My father died when I was only three and she was alone for years. Then she met Marla Weston. After Robert Weston went away to college—well, you say his name wasn't really Weston."

"It wasn't. He wasn't Marla's son."

"Why was she saying he was?"

"We don't know. After Robert went away?"

"After he went away, my mother got involved with Marla Weston. I don't really think that my mother was a lesbian. Not that it matters. I certainly don't care. But I think she just needed someone to be in her life. Someone intelligent. Someone she could talk to."

"I understand."

"And then Weston deserted her. She moved away one summer. Just disappeared. She never said good-bye, she never explained why she was leaving. My mother never really got over it. She said the world had turned black. I used to come home at night and find her crying."

Michelle looked down for a minute, then looked back up. Her small shoulders moved in a shrug. "She just didn't want to live anymore. After a while, she got cancer. Have you ever watched anyone die of cancer, bit by bit? For a year?"

"Yes," said Sophia.

Michelle nodded. "Then you know. I dropped out of college to stay with her. She wouldn't go into the hospital, and we didn't have anyone to help us."

That was the source of Michelle's gravity. A deathwatch. Like the deathwatch that Sophia and her family had undertaken when Uncle Niko got sick.

It would have been harder for Michelle. She'd been on her own.

"That's when I met Neil," said Michelle. "He helped. Susie said you saw him. Is he okay?"

"He's fine."

"He's not a bad person. It's just that I couldn't be with him anymore."

Sophia nodded. "Michelle, I don't think that Marla Weston disappeared. I think that Robert Ambrose killed her."

In the candlelight, Michelle's face was unreadable. "Killed her?"

"You said he went away to college. Do you know where?"

"Michigan somewhere."

Michigan. Someone had mentioned Michigan recently.

Michelle said, "You don't know about Robert, do you? You don't know how wicked Marla Weston really was. I didn't know myself, until after."

"Know what about Robert?"

Michelle stood. "My mother kept a diary. While she was sick. Wait here." She walked from the room and beyond the entryway.

Carson said, "Can I get you some more coffee?"

Sophia glanced down at the coffee in her mug. She'd barely touched it. "No. Thanks. Did you know about this? Weston and Michelle's mother?"

"She told me. A couple of months ago. It was part of the catching-up we were doing. But she never mentioned this Robert. Is he really the guy who's killing those women?"

"We think so."

"How—"

"Here," said Michelle. She was carrying a leatherbound volume. "I found the right page." She opened the book, handed it to Sophia. Then she stood there, as though reluctant to move away from the diary while it was in someone else's hands.

Sophia shifted closer to the candle on her right.

Michelle leaned toward her. "Here." She pointed to a passage.

The handwriting, done with what must have been a fountain pen, was thin and feathery, but it was legible. Nothing scratched out, no notes in the margins.

Sophia read the passage, and then, disbelieving, she read it again.

Oh, Jesus!

She grabbed at her purse, snatched her phone from inside it. She flipped it open.

Nothing. Not even static.

She sprang from the chair. "Your phone," she said to Michelle. "Where is it?"

Michelle was frowning. Puzzled, alarmed. "The kitchen."

"Show me."

The phone hung on the wall next to the side door. Sophia ripped the receiver from the cradle.

The phone was dead.

Chapter Fifty-three

When Fallon came to, he was sick.

Overhead, thunder clapped, the sound of it barreling across the sky.

In the darkness he couldn't see anything at all, but he knew he'd been gagged—he could feel the cloth taut against his tongue and digging at the sides of his mouth. He knew, too, that he couldn't afford to be sick. He would choke to death on his own vomit.

His head felt as though someone had kicked it—a huge dull, overpowering ache that, at its center, along the back of his head, had a core of excruciating pain.

His hands had been tied behind his hips, his feet tied at the ankles, and he was naked, lying on his side. Beneath his skin he could feel a cold sheet of plastic.

He knew, immediately, that the plastic was a tarpaulin, and that it was blue.

He tugged at the rope at his wrist. No give at all.

None at the ankles either.

How the hell had it happened?

Eva had arrived—

Eva! Where was Eva?

Desperately he swung his head left and right.

Useless. In that pitch-blackness, she could have been lying two feet away, and he wouldn't be able to see her.

But he knew she wasn't lying there.

He knew the scumbag had her.

Ambrose had her.

How the *hell* had it happened?

She had arrived, bringing along a bottle of wine. He'd poured each of them a glass. They had talked about Weston. And then, yeah, right, and then Eva had said she thought she saw something at the window. "But that's not possible, is it?" she said. "In this storm?"

He'd gotten up, walked to the curtain, looked outside. Nothing but the wind and the rain. He'd walked toward the front door, opened it—

And that was all he could remember. After that, everything was a blank.

A head wound. Concussion.

Retrograde amnesia.

He remembered the textbook definition—caused by a blow to the head, wiping out any memory of the time that preceded the blow.

How long had he been out?

Just then, lightning flashed outside, so brightly that its glare penetrated the curtains. For an instant he could see where he was.

In the center of the living room, facing the curtains and, beyond them, the sliding glass door that led to the patio.

A huge burst of thunder cracked. Fallon could feel its vibrations through the carpeting, through the plastic sheet. It rumbled, growled, slowly diminished. The wind roared.

The kitchen, he thought.

Knives.

Awkwardly—his arms and wrists were in the way—he rolled onto his back. He dug his heels into the tarp. They slipped against the plastic. He tried again.

"Jim?"

A voice—Eva's?—coming from the bedroom, muffled and faint.

He turned in that direction and he bellowed as loudly as he could, bellowed from deep down in his throat.

He had to let her know where he was. Let her know she wasn't alone.

He raised his legs, slammed them down against the tarp. He bellowed again.

Far off, it seemed, the darkness began to lighten. A dull glow wavered along the hallway wall. Someone carrying a candle down the corridor. The light grew closer, grew brighter.

And then Eva Swanson walked into the living room, wearing a

clinging black silk dress, strapless, slit up the right thigh. Her long blond hair trailed along her bare shoulders. She wore plastic gloves on each hand. In her left, she held one of Fallon's candleholders, the flame of the candle fluttering as she moved. In her right, she held a long kitchen knife.

"The power went down." Her voice wasn't right. It was lower, deeper, uncannily *not* Eva's voice. "But I think candlelight is much more romantic, don't you?"

Fallon stared at her. This was impossible.

But of course it wasn't. There she was.

There *he* was.

Ambrose.

A chill went through him.

"Like the dress, Jim?"

She walked to the sofa, placed the candle on the end table, and then sat down, leaning back and demurely crossing her long legs. She rested the knife on her lap.

He closed his eyes.

Eva. It had been Eva all along.

Volunteering her help, staying as close to the case as they were, learning everything they learned.

And she had virtually confessed to them, during the briefing.

They practice walking, they practice talking. They learn how to behave and how to sound exactly like a woman.

Jesus. She had been talking about *herself*.

"Hey. Jimbo." That strange male voice.

He opened his eyes.

In the voice of Eva, she said, "Pay attention when I'm talking."

Smiling, she leaned toward him, over the knife. "See, Jim? I told you. All it takes is practice. Practice makes perfect."

She sat back. "I'm really very glad you called." The male voice now. "I was standing out there in the rain, getting myself ready for my big surprise appearance. Reconnoitering. And I saw you pick up the phone, and I thought, oh no, he's going to invite over some company."

She smiled. "And then my very own little cell phone started to vibrate! I had to run back to the car to answer it, of course. Splash splash splash, through the dark and stormy night. Otherwise you might have heard me out there. And that wouldn't have been good, would it?"

Fallon closed his eyes. *Fuck you.*

A sudden sharp ribbon of fire shot down his leg. He snapped open his eyes. Eva was crouching on the carpet, only a few feet away, left hand braced against the floor, right hand pointing the knife at him. "I told you. Pay attention."

He craned his neck to look at his leg. He could barely make out the cut she'd made, a long thin line along his skin, black blood bubbling out. But he didn't have to see it. He knew it ran from his knee to his ankle.

She stood up, swiftly, gracefully, then moved back and demurely sat back down. "Do you know why I was pleased? Go ahead. Say no. Shake your head, Jim."

He didn't move.

More heavy, rumbling thunder.

She raised the knife. "Another love scratch?"

He shook his head.

"Because there'll be a record of your cell phone call, won't there? And that gives me an excuse for having been here, doesn't it? And *that* means I don't have to worry about leaving any evidence. Tomorrow I can always say"—she shifted to Eva's voice—" 'But of course I was there. Good old Jim called me over for a drink. It's just *awful* what happened to him, but he was perfectly fine when I left.' "

She leaned toward him. In the male voice she said, "It means I don't have to wear my Magic Suit. The coveralls. The ones the Cow figured out. Tregaskis. They're useful, of course, but they're terribly confining."

Resting the knife on her lap, she leaned back and put both arms along the back of the sofa. "You've been looking for me, Jim. And now I'm right in front of you."

She set the knife on the sofa, stood up, extended her arms, her hands limp, and then turned slowly around. She made a complete circle.

Facing him again, she smiled. "It's perfect, isn't it? Isn't it just absolute perfection?"

She put her hands on her hips. "A lot better than Tregaskis, wouldn't you say? Did you ever think of me while you were sticking it in her, Jim?"

Years ago, Fallon had faced a big hulking kid who'd flipped out on angel dust. He had looked into the kid's eyes and he had seen nothing in them, nothing beyond them but a huge, empty galaxy of madness. He had felt a fear then as strong as anything he'd ever felt in his life. He felt the same fear now.

"What does the cow sound like when you're poking at her? Does she moan and groan? I'll bet she does. I'll bet she just *loves* that big old thing of yours."

Fallon was sweating again.

"You know what I think would be perfect, Jim?" She smiled, turned around, picked up the knife from the couch. She faced him again. "I think it would be just perfect if Tregaskis could have your thing with her *all* the time."

Smiling, she moved toward him, the knife held out. The light from the candle wavered along the sleek silk of her dress.

With no warning, the electric lights snapped back on.

It made no difference to Eva. She kept coming.

Frantically, Fallon tried to squirm away, his heels thumping uselessly on the tarpaulin.

Eva smiled.

Chapter Fifty-four

The Smith & Wesson in her right hand, her unlit flashlight in her left, her shoulder against the cedar that shingled the house, Sophia staggered closer to the glass door. Rain swirled madly around her. The wind was so fierce that she could barely move forward.

It had taken her half an hour to get here, dashing frantically through the storm. She had driven faster than she could see, outrunning her blurry forward vision, going so quickly that the tires couldn't properly grip the road. Twice the big Ford had gone into a skid and she thought she'd lost it. But each time she'd been able to countersteer, sweat it out, bring the car back into line.

And then the lights had gone out. Everything around her—houses, streetlamps, the neon signs on shop fronts—had suddenly winked away.

She had kept racing through the black, blurry night, thunder crashing overhead.

There hadn't been any other choice. She had tried, every few minutes, to get through to the station, but the cell phone was shot. Going to the Pasadena police would just waste time.

She'd kept telling herself that Fallon wasn't necessarily in any danger. Swanson—or Ambrose, or whoever she was—whoever *it* was—had no idea that anyone knew about the operation, about the change of identity. According to Charlotte Lorimar's diary, the young Robert Ambrose had never known about the relationship between Lorimar and Marla Weston.

But Weston had told Lorimar about Ambrose. About the year living as "Eva" in Michigan, before the operation. About attending college afterward.

According to Lorimar, Weston had seen all of it—Robert's change to Eva, Eva's long-term adoration of Weston—as a kind of personal, and well-deserved, tribute.

Lorimar had written, *I truly believe now that Marla Weston was insane. To be connected in that way to that disturbed young man. And today, God have mercy on me, I believe that I must have been insane myself to have been connected, in any way, to that woman.*

Ambrose—Swanson—had to know that Fallon and Sophia had gone down to Sarasota. Courtney would've told her everything.

And maybe Swanson was running scared. Maybe she was worried that Fallon and Sophia *had* learned something down there.

It didn't matter. Whatever Swanson might be thinking, whatever her motives for visiting Fallon tonight—that was all irrelevant.

The fact was, Sophia's partner was alone in his apartment with a psychotic who had already killed at least three people, and probably four.

They had all wondered how the killer had gotten into those women's homes. Eva Swanson could've done it easily. Marcy had known her. Cyndi Purdenelle wouldn't have suspected a thing, not with a beautiful, elegant woman on her doorstep. She would have simply invited Swanson in.

Now, as Sophia approached the glass door, she saw a small gap between the curtain and the edge of the wall. Putting her left hand on the wall, bracing herself against the wind, she leaned closer.

Above her, around her, a peal of thunder shattered the air, crackling, booming, rumbling away into the wail of the wind.

It was dark inside the apartment. No, not completely dark. A candle was burning. She could make out . . .

Christ!

Swanson was in there, standing by the couch, wrapped in a tight black dress. As Sophia watched, Swanson held out her arms and turned in a slow, graceful pirouette. She was talking—Sophia couldn't hear what she was saying—and she was smiling down at something on the floor. A long, dark form.

Fallon.

Naked. His hands behind his back. Tied.

Get in there! she told herself. *Shoot through the glass!*

No. The glass might deflect the bullet, and Swanson was too close to Fallon.

As Sophia watched, Swanson turned to the couch, picked up something, and turned back to face Fallon.

A long blade glimmered in the candlelight.

Do something! Move!

Just then, the lights in the apartment flashed on. Swanson stood suddenly sharp and detailed—the knife, the beautiful slender body in its sheath of silk. She was still moving toward Fallon. She was still smiling.

Sophia stepped back, aimed the Smith at the center of the door, away from Swanson and Fallon, and fired twice. The door exploded.

Before the glass had finished falling, Sophia was through the opening, sweeping aside the curtain with the Smith.

But Swanson had already danced across the floor, and now she was hiking up her dress with her left hand and she was spinning, her right leg coming up as Sophia brought the pistol to bear, and then Swanson's foot slammed into Sophia's hand and the pistol went flying. In a single continuous move, Swanson followed through on her spin and twirled swiftly around, her right arm swinging, and she slashed the knife at Sophia.

Sophia ducked beneath it and hurled herself at Swanson.

But Swanson wasn't there, she had loped away, and Sophia hit the floor and went into a roll and lurched up onto her feet again, but by then Swanson had the Smith in her hand and she was laughing, a clear, musical laugh.

"Both of them!" she said, and laughed again. *"Perfection!"*

Sophia glanced quickly around the room. Where was the knife?

There, on the floor by the door.

She took a step forward.

Smiling, Swanson leveled the gun at her. "Naughty, naughty."

On the floor, Fallon said something, grunting behind the gag at his mouth.

Swanson said, "Oh, shut up, Jim," and she shot him twice.

Looking back at it, afterward, Sophia realized that at that moment she was suddenly as insane as Swanson was. She rushed at Swanson, heard the sound of a shot, saw the muzzle glare, felt something punch against her side. She slapped the pistol away with the back of her left hand. Putting all her weight behind it, the way Uncle Niko had shown

319

her, she drove her right fist as hard as she could into the exact center of Swanson's face.

She felt something crunch and she didn't know if it was Swanson's nose or her own hand, but Swanson squealed and dropped the gun and lowered her head and clutched at her face with both her hands. Blood was spurting between them. Sophia grabbed at the blond hair with both hands, and then, stepping back as though she were at the batter's plate and about to hit a long slow softball, she swung the woman out away from her, across the room.

Swanson smashed against the wall, her arms flailing. Sophia took a step toward her and felt her legs begin to go. She took another step.

Her eyes wide, looking for a way out, Swanson jerked her head from side to side. Blood flew off her face.

Sophia took another step and her leg buckled. But as she fell, she reached out for Swanson. Swanson slammed Sophia's arm aside and darted around her.

On one knee, Sophia turned and saw Swanson disappear through the curtain.

She put her hand to her side. Warm and wet.

Got to take care of that.

Fallon.

He lay on the blue tarpaulin, unmoving. There was a small neat hole in his chest, and his face was streaked with blood.

Chapter Fifty-five

Sophia stopped just outside the door and, lightly, touched the fingertips of her left hand to her side. She was using a thinner bandage now, one that wasn't visible beneath her blouse. The wound had stopped hurting, and so had the wound at her back, where the bullet had exited. Both had settled down to a dull ache, quiet and well behaved unless she moved too suddenly. But the edges of each, where the sutures ran, sometimes itched so badly they drove her crazy.

According to the doctors, this was a Good Thing. It meant that the wounds were healing nicely. She wished that the doctors, for just five minutes, could itch the way she did.

The sutures would be coming out in another two days. Thank God.

She held out her right hand, looked down at it. Yesterday they'd put a new splint on her broken middle finger. Aluminum, very stylish.

Okay, *koritsi mou,* so you're a bit battered. But you're still here.

That's more than you can say for Marcy and the others. Cyndi Purdenelle. Millicent Ambrose.

With her left hand, she touched her hair.

The hair is fine. You're stalling.

She knocked on the door.

A familiar voice from inside: "Come in."

She opened the door and stepped in.

Even knowing what she knew, she was shocked by Fallon's appearance. He looked as though he'd lost twenty pounds—and a man as thin as Fallon couldn't afford to lose twenty pounds. Beneath the bandage that covered the top of his head, his face was haggard and drawn. There were deep hollows at his cheeks, dark shadows at his eyes.

From the bed, he smiled at her. "Thanks for the vote of confidence." His voice was frail.

"I didn't say anything," she protested.

"You look like you just saw your dog die."

She nodded. "So I guess the coma didn't improve your disposition."

He made a sound that was almost a snort. "Only while I was in it. Stop standing there. Grab a seat."

She sat down in the visitor's chair.

He turned his head toward her. "I talked to Courtney. She said you were the one who got me here."

She shrugged. "There wasn't really anyone else around at the time."

"Couldn't have been easy."

"I've had better nights."

She'd been afraid to move him, but she knew he needed medical treatment. And she knew that the only way to get it was for her to bring him to the hospital. She'd used the kitchen knife to cut away the ropes, and then, despite her own wound, despite her fractured finger, she'd somehow lugged him across the floor of the apartment to the front door. Somehow, half-carrying him, half-dragging him, she'd gotten him out into the wind and rain, and into the passenger seat of the big Ford. She didn't remember most of it clearly now.

She remembered that she'd been woozy and light-headed as she drove. She remembered thinking how odd she must've looked to passersby—if there had been any passersby, out in the middle of that wild rainstorm—how odd she must've looked as she drove along, sitting beside a naked and bleeding and unconscious Fallon. But the hospital—thank God—was less than a mile away. She'd parked at the emergency entrance and staggered into the building, wet with rain and with blood, her own and Fallon's. She'd told someone he was out in the car, shown her badge, and then she had collapsed.

Her own wound, it turned out, hadn't been serious, a simple in-and-out, some blood loss but no major organs damaged. She'd been released from the hospital after three days.

But Fallon had gone into a coma. He'd been shot twice, once in the chest and once in the head. Because the head wound had been a graze, with no fracture of the skull, the doctors had concentrated on the chest wound.

Only later, when he failed to regain consciousness after the chest surgery, did they discover that the graze to the head had caused a trauma to the left side of his brain. Unknown to them, pressure had been building up inside Fallon's skull.

The surgeons had dealt with that, but it had taken Fallon four more days to come back.

"Courtney tells me," he said, "that you're getting a commendation."

"So they say."

"And Agent Messing wanted to recruit you."

"He talked about it."

"You turned him down."

She nodded.

"And Courtney said she's still loose. Swanson. Ambrose."

"She went back to her house, grabbed what she needed, and took off. By the time we got there, she was gone."

"She have money?"

"Not in her bank account, and she made a good living. We think she kept cash at the house, probably a lot of it."

He nodded. "She could be anywhere."

"We'll find her."

But it had been five days, and no one had seen her.

"How did she pull it off?" Fallon asked.

"The switch from Ambrose to Swanson?"

"Yeah."

She told him.

About Ambrose's taking the Eva Swanson name from a classmate who had died shortly after graduation from Elfers High School. Using the girl's birth certificate to accumulate ID. Moving to Michigan, living for a year, as the law required, as a woman before she had the operation. Then using the real Eva's transcripts to get into college. When she graduated, more surgery—the face, the breasts. By the time she entered medical school, she was a young version of the woman they had known.

"College, medical school," said Fallon. "No one ever guessed who she was? What she was?"

"Who knows? Maybe someone did. But she'd had the operation at the minimum legal age. As a man, physically, she was probably undeveloped. Not much musculature. That's what one of the shrinks says, anyway—Dr. Landers. And then afterward, she had years and years to practice. You saw her, Fallon. She was good."

"Who was paying for all that education?"

"Marla Weston."

"Jesus. You were right. Weston *was* a bucket of worms. They were *both* crazy."

"Crazier than I thought. When Swanson had her face done, she had it done to look *exactly* like Weston. Weston either went along with that, or she actively encouraged it. Landers thinks she encouraged it. She was creating a mirror image of herself in Eva."

"Wait a second. How do we know that Swanson looked *exactly* like Weston? Did we find Weston?"

She nodded. "We found her body. At Swanson's house."

It had made all the papers, all the newscasts. But for those four days, Fallon hadn't been reading newspapers or watching television.

"In a deep freeze," she said. "Wrapped in a blue tarpaulin."

"He killed her?"

"The ME says natural causes. Heart. What we think happened was, after Swanson moved to St. Anselm, she went down to Sarasota from time to time, to visit Weston. We know the two of them spent their summers together in Mexico. A Mrs. Weston and her niece Eva stayed at the same hotel in Puerto Escondido, the Hotel Inez, every year from 1984 to 1990."

"And Weston didn't go in '91. She was dead."

She nodded. "We figure that in June, when Swanson went down to visit, she found Weston's body. She carted it back to her house, here in St. Anselm."

"Why?"

"According to Landers, she had an 'idolatrous' relationship with Weston. In a sense, Weston had created her. Eva couldn't let her go."

"Was the relationship sexual?"

"Landers thinks it was."

"With Ambrose or with Swanson?"

"With both. There are a lot of transsexuals, Landers says, who get married as men, and who keep up a sexual relationship with their wives after the operation."

"So Weston took someone who was already pretty well screwed up, and then she screwed him up a whole lot more."

"Yes. But now we come to the part you're really going to like."

"Be a nice change," he said.

"Dr. Landers thinks that Weston's death is what caused Swanson—Ambrose—to kill his real mother. Landers is convinced that Swanson had Dissociative Identity Disorder."

Fallon frowned. "Multiple personalities."

Sophia nodded. "He thinks that before the operation, the Eva personality and the Robert personality probably alternated. After the operation, Eva was dominant. When Weston died, Robert re-emerged. He brought Weston's body up here, and then drove up to Elfers and killed his real mother."

"Why?"

"Maybe, for some reason, he blamed her for Weston's death. Or maybe he'd always hated her, and now that Weston was gone and he was dominant again, he could do something about it. After she was dead, Robert went dormant and Eva became dominant."

"And then later, when Marcy Fleming showed up, she was a dead ringer for the mother."

Sophia nodded. "She was the 'precipitating stressor.' Robert re-emerged again."

"Okay, that's why Swanson killed Fleming. Why'd she kill Purdenelle?"

"Landers has a theory."

"I'll bet."

"The surgery had given her a beautiful body, and she improved it. She went to the spa every day. She swam laps, she lifted weights. She made herself as close to perfect as she could. According to Landers, she despised women of size."

"Despising them is one thing. Killing them is something else."

"They reminded the Robert personality of his mother. And maybe, after the first time, after she killed Marcy, she decided she liked it."

Fallon closed his eyes again. "That I can buy. But I can't buy the multiple personalities. When Swanson was talking to me that night, she was switching voices, going from male to female. She knew what she was doing." He opened his eyes, looked at her. "How could she *not* know about Robert? She *was* Robert."

"Landers says she could've created an entire false history for herself, including childhood memories, and never realized that none of it was true."

"I don't believe it."

"Swanson *was* helping us. She was giving us good advice."

Slowly, he shook his head. "All part of the game."

"Maybe, without knowing it, she was trying to explain herself."

Shaking his head, he closed his eyes. "No."

She waited for him to reopen his eyes. When he didn't, she leaned slightly forward.

"I'm still here," he said. The eyes opened.

"They told me I shouldn't take too long."

"I'm okay."

"One thing more?"

"I'm okay," he repeated. "What?"

"You told Courtney it wasn't really you that Swanson wanted. It was me."

He nodded. "You scared her."

"But why?"

"She knew how smart you were. She was afraid that you were going to find her. And she was right. You did."

"Luck."

"No." He closed his eyes.

She stood up. "You should get some rest. I'll come back tomorrow. If you want."

He nodded slowly. "Yeah. I'd like that. What about your friend? Bondwell?" She could hear the exhaustion in his voice.

"He decided he didn't want a cop girlfriend."

It had been more complicated; but that, in the end, had been how it had gone down.

He smiled faintly, his eyes still shut. "You can't really blame him."

"Get some rest."

"Oh? Sophia?"

He had never called her that before. "What?"

He opened his eyes, turned to her. "I didn't go out right away." His voice was getting weaker. "After Swanson shot me. I was conscious for a while. I saw what you did. You looked damned good there."

She blushed. Like an idiot.

"Anyway," he said. "I owe you."

She stepped over to the bed and put her hand on the sheet that covered his thin shoulder. She saw, with surprise, that his eyes were shiny.

She felt a sting at the corners of her own eyes. She smiled. "Maybe there's hope for you yet, Fallon."